INDIGO LAKE

**Also available from
Jodi Thomas
and HQN Books**

Ransom Canyon
Rustler's Moon
Lone Heart Pass
Sunrise Crossing
Wild Horse Springs
Winter's Camp (ebook novella)

JODI
THOMAS

INDIGO LAKE

HQN™

HQN™

ISBN-13: 978-0-373-80404-7

Indigo Lake

Copyright © 2017 by Jodi Koumalats

The publisher acknowledges the copyright holder of the individual work as follows:

Winter's Camp
Copyright © 2015 by Jodi Koumalats

This edition published by arrangement with Harlequin Books S.A.

For questions and comments about the quality of this book, please contact us at CustomerService@Harlequin.com.

www.HQNBooks.com

Printed in U.S.A.

CONTENTS

Sometimes people come into my life who leave me with
a greater understanding of this life we all live, and two of them are:

Ernestine Wakefield—Born in 1926 in her grandparents' home
five miles east of Jayton, Texas, Ernestine was one of those rare people
you meet for a moment and know if you talked longer, you would become
best friends. I'll always remember one line she wrote: "Bury me
in boots and jeans because I'll be heading into heaven two-stepping."
I smiled June 5, 2016, because I knew she was dancing.

Police officer Gerald E. "Jerry" Cline—My character Jerry Cline
is named after this policeman who died EOW (End of Watch)
February 24, 1983, in the line of duty in Albuquerque, New Mexico.
I never met Jerry, but I saw the love in his wife's eyes when she spoke of
him one afternoon when we had lunch in Albuquerque. To all the men and
women in blue, thank you for standing in harm's way to keep us all safe.

INDIGO LAKE

prologue

The Ides of March, 2016

Deep in the backcountry, where no paved roads cross and legends whisper through the tall buffalo grass, lies a lake fed by cold underground springs.

Indigo-colored water, dark and silent, moves over the pond where secrets hide just below the surface and an old curse lingers in silent ripples.

Two ranches border the shores. Two families who haven't spoken for a hundred years.

A few of the old-timers claim the water is darker on Indigo Lake because of the blood washed away there.

Only tonight, one man stands listening, debating, wondering if breaking tradition will save him or kill him.

one

―――

Last day of February, 2016

Blade Hamilton walked to the dark water's edge and stared into Indigo Lake. He didn't belong here. He didn't belong anywhere. He'd wasted his time coming to this nothing of a place.

By birth, the land was his. *You're the last of your branch of the Hamilton line,* the judge in Crossroads had said an hour ago when he'd handed over the deed to Hamilton Acres. Only, Blade had never heard of this old homestead before a week ago. He'd known nothing about his father or a dilapidated ranch that carried his last name.

He'd picked up the keys and a map from the sheriff in town and ridden out before dark on his vintage 1948 Harley-Davidson. He'd paid sixty thousand for the Harley, and Blade would bet it was worth more than his inherited land and house put together.

The last quarter mile had been dirt road, ending in an old bridge that groaned as he crossed onto what the judge had called the old Hamilton place.

A weathered two-story house stood a hundred yards off the road, like a sentinel blocking his entrance. Fifty or so years ago someone must have painted the homestead bright red, but the wood had weathered to a sangria color that almost matched the mud along the lake. Huge cottonwoods waded into the water with their bony-kneed roots and haunting skeleton forms still naked from winter.

Thanks to a stream with a wide-yet-shallow waterfall flooding the open land, small trees and bushes grew to his left like a wild miniature forest. The house sat on high ground where vines, now brown with winter, seemed to be crawling across the ground and almost covering the porch. Another few years and the vines would probably pull the place down.

Leaving the bike on dry ground beside a small barn, he moved slowly toward the house, his mind already mapping out the route back to Denver. He'd grown up in cities and the silence of the country made him uneasy.

Blade dropped his saddlebags on the porch and unlocked the door. He slowly walked into a museum of hard times.

Most of the windows downstairs were boarded, so he used a flashlight to navigate. Guns were racked on the walls and animal hides served as rugs. The place must have been furnished about the turn of the twentieth century and left to age. The smell of neglect hung in the moist air, and a thick layer of dirt rested over draped furniture.

Pictures showing four or maybe five generations hung in the stairwell. Faces stared back, resembling him so closely Blade had to take a second look. Ranchers on horseback, soldiers in uniforms, an oil field worker leaning from a rig, a fisherman next to an old Jeep, a man in a suit with a string tie. All were identified by tiny plates at the bottom of the frames.

Hamilton men, many of whom carried Blade as their first or middle name. His father, Henry Blade Hamilton, stared back from an army photo. Vietnam, Blade guessed. It must have been taken when he was Blade's age, early thirties.

Until a week ago, he hadn't known he'd been named after the man his mother left before he was born.

When he stopped by his mother's place last week she'd simply handed him a huge envelope and announced, "Looks like it's from your father's side of the family."

"I have a father's side?" Blade grumbled, thinking this was a hell of a way to start his monthly visit with her.

She gave him that you're-dumber-than-rocks look she'd perfected during his teen years and walked away.

Blade swore, claiming in a loud voice that he never should have bothered to stop by. She never wanted to talk to him, anyway. Or maybe he simply didn't want to hear what she had to say. From childhood he'd convinced himself he'd been adopted from another planet, and his mother was the only female who'd take him in.

She also took in stray dogs and cats along with an occasional out-of-work drunk, so being adopted wouldn't have made him feel special.

His mother's answer to any questions about his other parent was simply the slamming of a door, so Blade had learned early not to ask. He swore his dear old mom hadn't liked him since birth, and once he left home, she'd never asked where he lived or what he did. A few times when he'd dropped by to check on her, she'd even had the nerve to look like she'd forgotten him completely. He'd thought of introducing himself.

His mother might be surprised if she had kept up with him. He wasn't the loser she'd always predicted he'd be. He'd finished college after the army and was doing quite well. Turned out he was good at solving puzzles, and as an agent for the Bureau of Alcohol, Tobacco, Firearms and Explosives (the ATF), he got plenty of practice. He might be based out of Denver but as a special investigator, he traveled often.

Blade pushed thoughts of his mother aside as he climbed the stairs and looked out the old Hamilton house's one unboarded window. The huge second-story window faced the open land of Hamilton Acres, its heavy leaded glass pieced together in almost a spiderweb shape. The image it showed seemed fractured. A broken world, pieced back together.

"Creepy," he whispered aloud as he remembered how the sheriff of Crossroads had followed him out of the county offices, warning him to be careful.

Blade had taken the time to formally introduce himself, even shown the sheriff his federal badge. But Sheriff Brigman still had that worried look lawmen get when they think someone might be stepping into trouble over his head.

Blade grinned. He knew *the look* well by now. He saw it every time he parachuted behind the fire line or suited up with the bomb squad. He'd learned a long time ago that if you want answers, you have to go where the trouble started.

It wasn't the adrenaline rush that made him step into danger or the belief that his skills would always save him. Blade was good at his job but it was the absence of fear that kept his hand steady. He didn't think about tomorrow. He didn't believe in it.

Living for today was all he thought about.

From this crow's nest vantage point of the second-story window, he could see a brilliant sunset spreading across the western sky. One lonely windmill was all that marked any kind of civilization in that direction. From here he could almost believe that he could catch a glimpse of the future, or maybe the past.

For once, he'd found a land as alone as he felt. In an odd way, he sensed he could bond with this untamed landscape. Maybe it was because generations of his family had been buried here. Or maybe Blade just wanted, for once in his life, to feel like he belonged.

Hamilton land. His land. Roots Blade wouldn't know how to handle after a life of drifting.

When he called to tell his mother he'd inherited a ranch in Texas, she'd laughed and said, "Sure you did. Better be heading out to buy some cowboy boots. I hear they don't like biker boots in cattle country."

"Don't you want to go have a look with me? After all, you were married to Henry Blade Hamilton." When she hadn't answered, Blade added, "You do remember the name of the man who fathered me?"

"I called him Hank and I've been trying to forget him for thirty years." She swore in her usual jumble of words that didn't fit together. "It hasn't been easy to block him from my mind when you turned out to look just like him."

"Then go with me. He's dead, so you're not likely to have to face him. We'll visit his grave and maybe you can bury the memory."

"Not a chance. He'd said the place was worthless when we married. Nothing but tumbleweeds and wild plum bushes. Good for nothing. Turned out, so was he."

"Was he a cowboy?" Blade asked.

"I don't remember." She ended the call without saying good-bye.

He didn't call back or try to see her again. He packed a change of clothes, climbed on his Harley and rode down from Denver to explore a side of the family he never knew existed.

So far nothing about the place impressed him besides the sunset. The lake was dark, the land rocky, and the house looked like it belonged next to the Bates Motel. Obviously there was nothing worth stealing or someone would have dragged it off years ago. The lawyer told him over the phone that his father had died in New Orleans six months ago, and apparently old Hank hadn't stepped foot on the ranch since he'd walked off the place at sixteen.

However, Henry Hamilton had paid the taxes every year and filed his will both with the lawyer in New Orleans and the county offices in Crossroads, Texas. Henry might never have contacted Blade, but for some reason he wanted his son to have the land.

As he walked back down the stairs, Blade noticed that not one woman's picture hung on the wall. There had to have been wives, mothers to these guys, a grandmother or great-grand-mother to him. Maybe none had stayed around long enough to do more than birth the next generation. From the dates and names on the frames, Blade traced his family tree.

He had his father's and his grandfather's dark hair, their gray eyes, their skin that never burned but always tanned. Their tall height and wide-at-the-shoulder build.

But nothing more. They were strangers.

All the other pictures were black-and-white, but if they'd been in color, he'd bet the traits would be the same.

Slowly, Blade moved from room to room. It looked like some-one had just walked away from the place one day. Moth-eaten clothes hung in the closets, dishes were in the sink, rotting com-forters and pillows were still on beds.

No electricity on, no water.

When he opened the back door, wild rosebushes barred his exit. Vines twisted and crawled up the house almost to the sec-ond floor. They were thorny and bare. When he twisted one branch to see if it was alive, a thorn sliced into his finger. It was indeed alive, and he felt like the plant was drinking his blood. Dropping the branch, he closed the door, thinking the roses could have the house for all he cared but would get no more of his blood.

As nightfall crept in, he moved out onto the old porch of the house. Boards creaked beneath his boots, but the place must have solid bones to still be standing.

He was tired and bothered that he had no memories of the man who'd fathered him. He should have pushed his mother for answers, but when he'd asked about the past, she always said that the time would come for talking.

Only, he had a feeling it never would. She'd married three times since he'd been born and each time, like a chameleon, she shifted and changed into someone he barely knew. She'd been a preacher's wife in Kansas, married to an oil field worker who moved all over Oklahoma, and, for a few months, the wife of an out-of-work actor in California. Between marriages she'd waitressed some, sold cars once in Houston, and finally settled into selling homes in Denver. He doubted she even remembered what she was like thirty years ago when she'd given birth to him at eighteen.

Blade told himself he didn't care. She had her life and it hadn't included him for years. It hadn't mattered to her if he dropped by once a month or once a year.

He moved out to the lake. It was time to get out of here. This wasn't where he wanted to be after dark. Maybe he'd go back to town and find a hotel. Tomorrow, he'd take another look around, not searching for a thing to take away, but maybe he'd get a feeling about the man he'd been named after. Henry must have grown up here.

Blade could feel change in the air like he had a dozen times before in his life. His mother had wanted no roots and she'd raised a son without any until now.

Roots he didn't want, he reminded himself again. He didn't know anything about this land, these relatives. He wasn't sure he wanted to. He had a feeling whatever stories this house held were sad ones.

Lightning flashed to the east and he saw another house across the lake. It was built low to the ground, almost blending into the landscape. Probably another abandoned home. More land that the next generation didn't want.

He zipped up his leather jacket and walked to his bike. Let the coyotes and hawks have this place. Maybe one more circling of the land tomorrow and then he was leaving. When he got to Denver, he'd call the lawyer who contacted him about this inheritance and ask for a Realtor who'd sell the place. Land, house, and heritage. They could buy it all.

two

―――

Dakota Davis turned off the county road, driving way faster than the speed limit. In five minutes the dirt road would be a river of mud. If she wanted to get home without all her supplies soaked, she'd better make the farm pickup fly.

A few minutes later, as she passed the old Hamilton place, she thought she was hallucinating. A man dressed in black was standing knee-deep in the muddy lake, looking like he was swearing at heaven.

For just a moment he reminded her of something her *shichu*, her grandmother, had said about a legend of the lake. Shichu said the last man to die in a battle over this land was a strong warrior, but he'd simply walked out to the middle of Indigo Lake until the water was over his head because he'd lost his will to live. Apache legends, tales of her people who fought and died over this land, were common, but this story was about the Hamiltons.

Shichu knew them all. Ancient tales and stories of battles fought near this quiet lake between neighbors who'd settled here over a hundred years ago. The Davis family and the Hamilton

clan. Curses once screamed across the water now simply whispered in the trees lining its banks.

Grandmother said the land was damned and all who fought
to keep it would die in water. Maybe that was why the last one,
Henry Hamilton, stayed away, Dakota thought as she stared at
the vision before her.

When the man in black turned to stare at her pickup, she had
to remind herself she didn't believe in ghosts. But the stranger
looked exactly like the Hamilton men she'd seen in pictures
at the museum near Crossroads. Tall, broad-shouldered, slim.

Only, all the Hamilton men were dead, even Henry, who
she'd never seen. Folks in town said he was killed six months ago
in a car crash somewhere in Louisiana. As far as anyone knew
he hadn't been back to the place for forty years, but the Franklin sisters whispered that the crash had pushed both his car and
him off the highway into water.

The man standing in the lake looked very much alive and
was waving for help. Curiosity got the better of her, and Dakota turned away from her farm and toward Hamilton Acres.

A heartbeat later she slammed on her brakes.

The bridge that usually stretched across a stream that fed the
lake was now halfway in the water. There must have been an
accident: what looked like the back wheel of a motorcycle spun
in the lake as if trying to tread water.

Jumping from the truck, she yelled to the man, "You need
help?"

"No," he yelled back. "I'm fine. My bike just wanted to go
for a swim."

Dakota frowned, then turned around. "Oh, all right. Sorry
to bother you." She climbed back into the truck.

"Wait." The man stormed out of the water. "I'm sorry. The
bridge gave way as I was leaving. I just watched a classic 1948
Harley drown."

"I can see that." She thought of asking what he was doing on

Hamilton Acres in the first place, but she had a feeling he belonged here. Black hair. Angry. Too noisy to be a ghost. "Why don't you pull it out and dry it off?"

"It doesn't work that way. I'd have to take it apart and rebuild. It will no longer be original, and parts cost more than the bike, if I can find them."

Too much information. She didn't have time to visit or cry over the loss of a motorcycle.

Her grandmother had told her once that the men of this ranch only had two possible traits: stubborn or crazy.

This one had both, plus he had the look of a Hamilton. She'd bet his eyes were that funny color gray of a wolf. "Anything else you want to educate me about motorcycles? I need to get these supplies home."

"You wouldn't want to help me pull my bike out?" he asked in a calmer tone.

"Nope. I don't go on Hamilton land. There's a curse. Anyone named Davis who steps foot on that land dies a violent death." She didn't add *by a Hamilton bullet*. Never give ideas to the insane.

"We all die sometime, lady."

She stepped into her truck. "I'll have to test the curse later. Good luck with your bike." Thunder rolled over the land as if pushing her away. "I'm in a hurry."

"Wait. I'm sorry. Let me try again. I'm Blade Hamilton and I've just lost a sixty-thousand-dollar bike in the mud. Forgive me for not caring about an old curse or your groceries."

"You're forgiven, Hamilton, but I'm not stepping on your land. The good news is that bike isn't going anywhere. It will still be right there in the mud tomorrow, but if I get these supplies wet, we'll lose a week's income."

Lightning flashed as if on cue. The blink of light showed off the skeleton trees dancing in the wind near the water. Dakota fought the urge to gun the engine. For as long as she could remember she'd always feared this land. It felt like Halloween night without a light.

The man didn't seem to notice the weather or the creepiness of the place. Who knew—maybe Hamiltons were used to scary nights.

"Fine," he said. "Any chance you'd rent me your truck? I just need it for ten minutes and I'll pay you fifty."

"Nope," she said. "But I'll loan it to you if you'll help me get these supplies under cover before it rains."

"Deal," he said, and walked toward the passenger side of her old Ford.

"In the back, Hamilton," she ordered. "I don't want mud all over my seats." She fought the urge to add *or you near enough to strangle me.* Her grandmother told her once that there was an old cemetery, way back on Davis land, where all the deaths were recorded on headstones. Died in childbirth. Death from cholera. Died in accident. Death by Hamilton.

Besides, she didn't have time to clean all the property listings off her passenger seat. Her mobile office was always a mess. Four mornings a week, the farm truck was her business vehicle.

He swung up into the bed of the truck with the ease of a man who'd done it many times and she started backing up before he was seated. The sooner she was home safe, the better. She'd loan him the pickup and tell him to just leave the keys in it. He could cross the pasture and walk back to his place easily enough.

The road was bumpy between her land and his, but she flew toward home, not much caring if the man bounced out or not. Her people had always hated Hamiltons. They told stories about how mean they were and even though she'd been told they were all dead, she felt it her ancestral duty to hate this new one.

So, why was she loaning him her truck?

Dakota shook her head. It was the neighborly thing to do. Having a grandmother with Apache blood and an Irish grandfather had messed her up for life.

A guy she'd dated a few years back broke up with her because he said she had Apache skills with a knife and an Irish temper. She almost hit him for insulting both sides of her family, but then she would have proved his point. She'd told him this was the twenty-first century and she was a skilled chef like her sister, which wasn't true, but it sounded good. He left before she cooked him anything and proved herself a liar, as well. She heard him mumbling something about being afraid to sleep beside her for fear he'd be carved and thin sliced if he snored. He'd called her hotheaded just before he gunned the engine and shot out of her life.

Dakota gripped the steering wheel, realizing the old boyfriend had been right. She did have a temper, but with a Hamilton riding in the back of her truck, now didn't seem the time for self-analysis.

She could be nice. She'd loan Hamilton the truck, and when he brought it back she'd tell him to never step foot on Davis land again. Simple enough.

When she slid to a stop a few feet from the kitchen door of her place, she glanced back. He was still there and raindrops were spatting against her windshield.

She jumped out and ran to haul the boxes of supplies to the cover of the porch.

To his credit, he did his share to help. More than his share, actually, because he carried a double load with each trip.

The guy was strong and obviously well built. And a biker. Black leather jacket. Leather pants hugging his legs. Boots to his knees. His cowboy ancestors were probably rolling over in their graves.

In a few minutes they had the boxes on the covered porch and the rain started pouring down in sheets.

"We made it." She laughed. "Thanks. No supplies got wet."

"I'm glad I could help. I'm already soaked so the rain won't bother me."

She decided he didn't sound like he meant it about how glad
he was to help. Maybe it was the tone in his voice—it didn't
sound right without a Texas twang. She frowned at him, wondering what northern state he'd come from.

He looked down at her with his gray wolf eyes and added, "If
you got wet, you might shrink and then you'd be about elf size."

Dakota studied him a moment. No obvious signs of insanity.
"You don't have many friends, do you, Hamilton?" She tossed
him her key. "Park the truck at the turnoff on my land. You
won't have as far to walk. Leave the keys in the glove box."

"Aren't you afraid someone will steal it?"

"Nope. Nobody but you."

He nodded and disappeared into the downpour.

Dakota straightened to her five-foot-two height and frowned.
"Sounds just like what a Hamilton would say," she mumbled,
thinking it was obvious the Hamiltons had been the ones to
start the feud.

Elf size. No one had ever called her that.

three

———

Lauren Brigman stood in the shadows of hundred-year-old cottonwoods planted to slow the wind off the open plains. The lights of town were nothing more than a glow of tea candles in the distance.

The night's breath rattled the dried leaves in the trees as it had a dozen years ago. She felt a hint of old fear creep over her as a memory circled in her mind.

Strange how you live thousands of days, thousands of nights but only a few live in your mind, in your heart, as clear as the moment they happened.

She stared at the home her high school friends had called the Gypsy House. An old woman who'd died there decades ago was almost a skeleton before anyone had come to check on her. After her passing, the house was left to rot and became the setting for ghost stories told around campfires.

Finally, the grandson of the old woman, Yancy Gray, moved to Crossroads and found himself drawn to the place. He'd discovered he owned the house and had completely remodeled it. Yancy had painted the outside a cream color with shutters the burnt orange of sunset's last glow. He'd enlarged the second floor and landscaped beautifully.

Yet in Lauren's mind, the house was still abandoned and rotting, as it looked when she was fifteen. She'd danced with death that night twelve years ago; they all had. Tim O'Grady, Reid Collins, Lucas Reyes, and her. Just four kids walking home, looking for something to do, hoping for an adventure they could brag about at school.

Three boys and her, the youngest, the only girl, all in their teens. Sometimes she felt as if they'd been bound together by fear and the lie they all kept after that night. She'd never be free of the memory. One day she'd be bent over with age, but she'd still come to this spot every year and remember what had happened.

Footsteps played a rapid tap on the wet pavement behind her as thunder rumbled above.

Lauren stepped farther into the shadows and watched. There was no mistaking Reid Collins's quick, confident step. He might be twenty-eight now and rich, thanks to a trust fund from grandparents and a ranch a few miles from town, but there was still a bit of the little boy in him. Spoiled, arrogant, and handsome. Word was that he'd be running for mayor of Crossroads in the fall with his eye on the Texas State Senate in ten years, but Reid would never have her vote.

As far as she knew, he never finished college or anything else he'd started. Her father, the town's sheriff, told Lauren a few months ago that the only way to kill an improvement project in the county was to put Reid in charge. He'd never get around to the planning meeting, much less completion.

The tapping of his boots stopped a few feet in front of the cottonwoods. "I know you're in there, Lauren. That long, blond hair of yours glows in the dark. You might as well come out." His laugh wasn't quite real. Too polished, too practiced.

She slowly stepped onto the road. "I didn't think you'd be in town, Reid. Did they run out of parties in the big city?" He didn't look entirely sober, but she didn't mention it. "Pop said they canceled the city council meeting because you had to be in Austin today."

"I just got back. The Governors Balls are not what they used to be." He smiled as if really looking at her for a change. "You know, Lauren, I miss our once-a-year dates from college. You were the only girl I took out now and then that I didn't sleep with." His gaze traveled down her long, slim body.

She didn't miss him. Those dates had been torture. Putting up with his loud, self-centered fraternity brothers, trying to act like she was having a good time watching them brag. He'd said once that he liked having a tall blonde on his arm, like she was an accessory.

She and Reid were from the same town; their dads had been friends, so she'd gone out with Reid Collins a few times. She felt sure half the people in town wanted them to marry, but she'd never match with him. She loved learning almost as dearly as he loved partying.

"I was a perfect gentleman." He bragged as he moved closer, almost nose to nose with her. "Never even made a pass."

"You're right, but I'm surprised you remembered I was there. Weren't you engaged two or three times while you were at Tech?"

"Two. The third one was all in her head. Once I came home to run the ranch, I was so bored I almost married the first girl who came along. Big mistake. She's still spreading trash about me." He tried to loop his arm over her shoulder but she stepped away. "You're looking good, Lauren. Aging well."

"I'm twenty-seven, Reid, not exactly a centenarian."

"I know, but you wouldn't believe how some women change after college. I went to the planning meeting for my ten-year high school reunion and some of the kids I graduated with had slipped into middle age. I thought one girl must have sent her mother to the meeting." He slurred a few of his words.

Lauren didn't want to talk to Reid Collins, not ever, much less on the anniversary of the accident at the old Gypsy House. "I just came out to remember what happened twelve years ago. How about you?"

Collins looked around, as if he had no idea what she was talking about. As far as she knew, he'd never mentioned the night of the accident to any of the three who were with him. He'd simply taken credit for saving everyone that night. An account none of the others shared.

She smiled, wondering why they'd silently watched him play the hero. The school even had a pep rally for him, and the mayor had given him a key to the city. Lauren, Lucas and Tim remained silent and let the lie about that night stand, even though the truth wouldn't hurt anyone now.

"I spotted your car at the truck stop and decided to walk off the long drive. Thought you might have wandered down this direction," Reid said, a bit too loudly, almost as though he thought someone might be eavesdropping and he wanted them to hear him. "Strange we meet here at almost midnight. The people in this town are like ants. They disappear as soon as it gets dark."

"Maybe they don't disappear. Maybe you just don't notice them."

"You want to go for a drink?" he asked suddenly, as if the timer in his brain went off and it was time for another.

"No." She didn't bother with a reason.

He rocked on his heels and went back to their conversation. "I doubt anyone except you, Lauren, remembers that night we got trapped in the old Gypsy House. Ancient history. Four kids almost died when they ventured into an abandoned house. Why don't you do an article in that little online paper of yours about it?"

"You really think no one remembers? Twelve years ago tonight was when Tim was crippled. He still limps a bit, so he's not likely to forget."

"Oh, yeah, that's right. I was hurt too, you know." Reid backed away a few feet, as though not wanting her to see him so clearly. "My ankle still gives me trouble when I play tennis." He rushed on as if needing to change the subject. "My last stepmother put in a court and a pool at the ranch headquarters to make sure I exercise it regularly."

"How are your father and his *new* bride?" Lauren had no idea if this was number five or six.

Reid shrugged. "I don't know. They mostly travel. She hates the ranch so Dad bought her a town house in Dallas and she owns a vineyard outside of Paris, thanks to her last husband. Dad lucked out marrying this one. He plays golf and she shops while they're in the States, and who knows what they do in Paris? I run the ranch, you know, have for years. It's a real headache. Dad and I would both like to be rid of the place. He sold several pastures before he left town two years ago."

She started walking and he fell into step. Neither mentioned the light rain.

"Why don't you drive out some weekend? It's only a few miles, but it might feel like a retreat after living in this town. We could talk about our college days, maybe watch a Tech game. I've got the whole fall season recorded. Man, I miss those days at Tech. The games, the parties, the carefree life."

She smiled. He hadn't mentioned the classes. "You could invite Tim O'Grady and Lucas Reyes to come too. Maybe we could talk about the night the old house almost swallowed us."

"Sure." He dragged the one word out. "Only, come to think of it, I'm snowed under with work right now. We've got problems with some of the old cowhands on the spread that should have been fired years ago. My father always let them run the place, but I'm changing things, modernizing. Land's good for more than running cattle."

Lauren stopped listening to Reid's excuses as she spotted a lean shadow of a man moving toward them. His head was down, his collar turned up to the wind as he limped along. There was no mistaking the shaggy red hair always in need of a cut or the dark auburn beard.

"Tim!" Lauren bolted toward him. "You're home."

The shadow man looked up and straightened. A moment later she was in his arms and he was swinging her around.

"I figured you'd be out here, L." Tim held her tightly as only a lifelong friend can. "Did you have to return to the scene, like me? I figure once a year it's okay to let the memory roll over me."

She pulled away. "Reid came out too."

"With you?" Tim whispered.

Lauren shook her head and Tim faced Reid. "Hello, Collins. Haven't seen you in a while. Word is you don't spend much more time on the ranch than your dad did. A Collins ranch without any Collinses. Maybe you should think of another name for the place."

Reid offered his hand but his words were colder than the night air. "Good to see you, Tim. Still writing those little invisible books? Ebooks, right? Any money in fiction made of air?"

Tim turned back to Lauren as if he hadn't seen Reid's hand, but she could feel the tension between the two. They'd been best friends once, before the accident. High school football players, sixteen and invincible. She remembered they'd both had their football jackets on that night. Tim never played or wore the jacket again that she knew about.

"My books make more money than his invisible cattle, I'm guessing," Tim whispered to Lauren.

Forcing down a laugh, she linked her arm around each man's elbow and marched on toward town. The less time these two had to talk, the better.

It had been twelve years since they'd walked this road together. They'd grown up, they'd grown apart, but in many ways nothing had changed. Tim was still the dreamer, Reid was still full of himself, and she was still waiting to start her life.

As they neared town, she noticed all their cars were scattered around the parking lot of the fancy new truck stop with lights so bright Lauren was sure it could be seen from space. Years ago, the corner where two highways crossed had been only a little gas station/convenience store with a trailer park in back. Now the truck stop took over the block and never closed.

Tim's old Jeep, the one he refused to trade off, was by the gas pumps. Reid's Mercedes was parked on the side. Lauren's old blue Explorer was near the front door. Next to Reid's car was a rusty junker of a pickup with a man leaning against it, his boots propped up on Reid's Mercedes's fender.

"Lucas!" Reid jerked away from Lauren and stormed toward the lights of the truck stop. "I knew this was coming. Damn it, Reyes, get your boots off my car!" His order sounded hollow in the still air, with no one around to notice but the tall figure with his boots still on the Mercedes.

Lauren and Tim slowed, staying in the shadows between light circles. "What's going on?" she whispered.

Tim laughed. "I'm not sure, but I think Lucas Reyes is about to finally beat the hell out of Reid Collins."

"That's impossible. Lucas is always reasonable." She watched Reid running toward Lucas, his swearing firing in time to his footsteps. Reid was already out of control, but Lucas looked calm, driven, deadly. Something was wrong.

"You've got to stop this." She tried to pull Tim along. With no one else at the station, Tim was her only hope.

"Stop it? Hell, I plan on watching the fight, then swear I didn't see a thing. It's about time someone straightened out a lie Reid's been telling for twelve years. Maybe Lucas just got tired of him building on more lies. We all know he wasn't the hero that night, L, but Reid keeps bragging like he saved us all. He even did an interview with *Texas Monthly* about it a few months ago."

Lauren pulled Tim along. "No. This isn't about the lie he told at the Gypsy House. This is something more." Just from his stance she knew Lucas Reyes hadn't come to talk.

Before her words died in the air, Reid stormed toward Lucas and ordered him again to get his boots off the Mercedes.

When Lucas didn't move, Reid yelled names at him as if they were in high school and not in their late twenties.

Lucas, dressed in Western clothes and not the suit he wore into court, slowly stood and widened his stance as Reid reached him.

Reid pointed his finger at Lucas as cusswords flew in rapid fire.

Lucas raised a fist and swung.

Lauren and Tim froze, watching. The lawyer's fist connected with the part-time rancher's face. The sound echoed off the cloudy night as sharp as gunfire, then silence as Reid crumbled.

"Did you see that?" she whispered.

"Yep. He flattened the guy with one blow. I'm tempted to go over there and kick Reid for not putting up more of a fight."

They were still ten feet away when Lucas pulled out, leaving one of the richest men in Crossroads—a city councilman, a playboy, a liar—spread out on the oil-spotted concrete.

Tim reached him first and shook Reid's shoulder. "You all right, slugger?" Tim teased.

Reid groaned and rolled onto his side in the blood and dirt of the parking lot.

Tim finally offered his hand and pulled Reid to his feet.

"You two saw what that bastard just did?" Reid spit blood. "Damn it, I knocked my tooth loose when I hit the ground. I swear I'm filing charges. He may be a big-city lawyer, but he can't assault me just because I fired his old man."

Tim let go of him and Reid fell against his car, bloodying his nose again. Tim didn't seem to care. "Reyes has been fore-man at your ranch for years. The place would have never been a working ranch if he hadn't been there while you and your dad were traveling all over the country." Tim made a fist. "You fired him? That's the dumbest thing you've ever done, Reid."

Lauren gripped Tim's arm, fearing Reid was about to get hit again.

Reid didn't notice. He was still spitting blood. "That's why we're so far behind the times. I had to get rid of all the dead-wood around the place. I've got plans."

He wiped his nose on his suit jacket. "Lucas is going to be so sorry he did this to me. I'll file charges. He'll lose his license to practice law. I've got you two as witnesses."

Tim shook his head. "Sorry, Reid, I didn't see a thing. I was trying to kiss Lauren. I think I might have heard a popping sound but I'm not sure."

"What?" Reid swore. "I should have known I couldn't de-pend on you." He looked at Lauren. "At least Lauren is honest."

Lauren straightened and did something she never did. She lied. "I was fighting off Tim. He's been trying to kiss me since we were six. I'm sorry, I didn't see anything but you lying by your car. I figured you were drunk again. I could swear to that if you want me to. I've seen you drunk enough times to know."

Reid opened his car door, ignoring the blood dripping all over his white upholstery. "You two will be sorry. I can't be-lieve I ever thought of you as friends. The sooner I get out of this town, the better."

They watched him drive away, and then Tim whispered, "You sorry, L?"

"Nope. How about you?"

"I'm sorry I didn't see a thing. I would have really liked to help Reid out," Tim said in mock-seriousness. "He's been such a good friend of mine." Lies dripped out of Tim's mouth faster than blood dripped out of Reid's.

"Yeah, me too." She laughed as she tugged him toward her car. "How about we go check on Lucas."

"You have any idea where he is?"

"I have an idea."

Lauren approached the grassland of the Double K Ranch by the watery light of the midnight sky. She was on Kirkland land now. This was the first ranch established in this part of the country and still the biggest spread for a hundred miles around.

Staten Kirkland knew that years ago she and Lucas used to come out here to watch the stars. He probably wouldn't be surprised that they still did. The Collins ranch, where Lucas's dad had been foreman, bordered Kirkland's. Lucas had grown up near here and he'd spent his college years cowboying for the Double K on weekends. He'd ridden both spreads when he'd been growing up and knew them well.

Lauren knew that if she had a chance of finding Lucas anywhere, it would be at this lonely spot where no lights from any town or ranch house could reach.

Parking her car on the county road, she pulled on her raincoat and climbed through the fence. As she neared the windmill, she didn't see his car but she saw the outline of the old pickup he'd been driving in town.

She smiled. He might have been dumb enough to hit Reid Collins, but Lucas had enough sense not to drive his low BMW over dirt trails that didn't even qualify to be called roads.

Slowly she walked toward the silhouette. She knew the moment he spotted her. He straightened and faced her. Lucas Reyes might be a lawyer now, but he fit here. He was a man who came from the land. He was as much a part of it as it was of him.

"Where's that new BMW your mother told me you bought last month?"

"I traded it for the pickup. Told my dad to take it out for a spin." Lucas's voice was clear but his face was lost in the night. "Mom suggested a vacation might be nice. My father hasn't taken more than a long weekend off in years.

"Where's Tim?" the shadow asked when she was ten feet away.

"He didn't believe you'd be out here. Tim said he'd bet you were at one of the bars. There's only two but he said it would take until closing time for him to make a complete sweep of the places."

Lucas huffed but didn't comment.

She moved closer, not knowing what to say to a man she hadn't seen in over a year but had been in her thoughts almost every day. They'd been close once, but now she felt she barely knew him. Maybe she never had. His dark good looks were still there, but the favoring of his Hispanic heritage was almost gone from his voice.

"Reid will probably sue me for hitting him, but I'm not sorry."

"He might, if he had a witness."

Lucas raised his head. "You two were standing right there. You must have seen it."

"I wasn't looking," she answered. "Tim didn't see anything, either."

Lucas relaxed. "If I'm asked in court, I won't lie. I did hit him."

There it was, she thought, that bone-deep kind of honesty that she loved about Lucas. Since she'd known him, Lucas had always done the right thing for his family, his career, his parents. The only one he'd left out had been her. There wasn't room for her in his life, not in high school or college or now.

"Reid wouldn't ask. He'd figure you would just lie as he would."

"You're right. Gambling on people to be honest is a fool's bet most of the time. I learned that in court."

She pushed away thoughts of a love that had long ago died of starvation and tried to keep her mind on Lucas's problem. "You didn't tell anyone that Reid ran and didn't save us that night at the Gypsy House. He convinced the whole town that he was a hero. Remember, they even had an assembly to honor him? I'd been too shy to speak up and Tim was home recovering, but you could have said something."

"No one asked me what happened." Lucas put his hands on her waist and lifted her onto the pickup's open tailgate. "Everyone was listening to him. I didn't lie. I just didn't say anything." He moved a foot away and leaned on the side of the truck.

Lauren smiled, liking being at eye level to him and sensing they were still as comfortable around each other as ever. In the darkness it almost seemed like they were teenagers again and not a big-city lawyer and a small-town newspaper editor. "Never argue with a lawyer, right?"

"And never believe a storyteller, right?" he added. "I've been reading your 'Legends of the Plains' articles online. I doubt all our ancestors were as brave as you painted them."

They both laughed.

He raised his hand and brushed her cheek. "I've missed you, Lauren. I think of you often."

When he leaned in to kiss her, she backed away. "We're friends, Lucas, nothing more. That's all it can be between us." She almost added that her heart wouldn't take another disappointment. They'd almost connected a dozen times over the years and it always ended with him walking away.

"Then why are you here?" His words came fast and cold. "I thought you came out to see me, but you're looking for a story?"

Maybe she'd hurt his pride or maybe she'd simply reminded him that nothing more than friendship ever worked between them. The easy way they'd had with one another a moment ago was gone. She wanted it back, but she wasn't brave enough to deal with him stepping closer again.

"I'm worried about you, that's all," she answered. "Did Reid really fire your father? He's the best ranch foreman around."

Lucas hesitated and she feared that he wouldn't talk about it. Ranch folks usually kept their business close to the vest. Finally, his words came low. "Yes. Fired him yesterday morning and told him to be moved out before dawn tomorrow. After thirty years, my parents had forty-eight hours to load up." His voice was dull, all emotion spent. "He also fired most of the hands. Told them to have their belongings out of the bunkhouse by dark. My folks had everything crammed in one of the cattle trucks by the time I drove in from Houston. They're sleeping in town tonight with friends."

"What about your brothers and sisters?"

"The youngest two are away at college. I don't think Dad's even told them yet. My two sisters are married and farm down by Brownfield. One brother joined the army last year. The girls drove in to help yesterday. All the cowhands on the place pitched in to help, but it was chaos. I heard Mom cried all day. I finally got them settled after dark and went looking for Reid." He laughed without humor in his tone. "To tell the truth I didn't think I'd find him. When I saw his car at the truck stop I didn't have a plan."

"Why did he do this all at once? What was the hurry?"

"They've been selling off pieces of the ranch for years. My dad wasn't surprised. I think he saw it coming." Lucas plowed his fingers through dark straight hair. "He said last Christmas that if they sold any more land there wouldn't be enough pasture to switch cattle into."

"I don't think the people in town were aware of it shrinking." Ranch folks might not talk, but town people did.

"One of the hands told me today that Reid hired a manager out of Fort Worth to come in and close the ranch down while he rushed over to Austin to go to a party. The manager brought in a crew, men who look like hired thugs, not cowhands. He's selling off the cattle left on the place, and word is the horses are going tomorrow."

"Do you think Reid's father knows what he's doing?"

"I don't think he cares. Most of the good pastureland is already gone and who will want a big house in the middle of nowhere? But once the land's gone, it's gone. If I had the money, I'd be tempted to buy it and show Reid what a ranch like that could be. If profits were poured back into the operation it would really be something, but they've been bleeding it dry for years."

This Lucas, Lauren understood. The planner. The kid who was born on a horse and loved the land. If he ever got the chance, he'd build a ranch just like he built a career in law.

Only ranches like the big ones in Texas were inherited, not bought.

She brushed Lucas's hand. "You're losing the place where you grew up."

"Yeah, but it was never mine. My folks moved into the foreman's house not long after they married, but it wasn't theirs. The place where they raised their kids vanished in forty-eight hours."

Lauren understood but didn't know how to help. "The memories will be with you, Lucas. The love in that house lives on."

"Right," he answered quickly. "But I swear before I ever bring a child into this world, I'll have a place that's mine."

Another hurdle, she thought. Lucas had to have everything right, everything in place before he'd allow himself to think about living his life. There would never be enough time for all his dreams…enough time for her in his life.

A light began to glow from the north, almost like the sun had decided to come up early in a new location.

They turned and watched it for a few heartbeats, then Lucas whispered, "Fire!" as if saying the word too loud would make it real. "It's on the Bar W. Dad and the cowhands aren't there to deal with it."

Lauren stood watching in disbelief. The Bar W, Collins land. She knew little about ranches, but she knew fire in this open country could be deadly.

He grabbed her hand and they started running toward the front of the pickup.

"I'll call 9-1-1," she shouted as she climbed in the passenger side of his truck.

Lucas nodded and headed across the open pasture. "Where's your car?"

"About half a mile back on the road."

He was there before she could finish her call.

As she climbed out of the truck, Lucas yelled over the incoming storm, "Get out of here as fast as you can. I don't think it will spread on this wet grass, but you don't want to be caught in the middle of a grass fire."

She watched the flames shooting high in the air. "It's not a grass fire." It was too big. Grass fires crawl along the ground. This was shooting thirty feet straight up.

He followed her gaze as another flame shot into the black sky a mile to the left of them. "You're right," he said. "Something or someone is burning the barn. If it catches grass, it might spread to Kirkland land. I'll call him."

A half mile away, another flame shot up.

"Another barn," Lucas shouted. "This is no accident."

She reached for her car door, but just before she stepped in she heard him say, "I'll find you when this is over. It's time you and I had a talk, Lauren. Until then, stay away from the fires."

four

———

"Hello, darlin'," Sheriff Dan Brigman said into his cell phone as he drove toward the Collins ranch. "I know I'm calling early, but I'm headed out to a barn fire and might not get a chance to call before you go to sleep."

"Anything bad?" Brandi's voice came through, making him miss her ten times more than he had a minute ago.

"No. You know nothing ever happens around here. How was your flight to Nashville?"

"I started missing you before I got off the plane. I slept part of the way and had this great dream about you."

Dan smiled. He loved his wife's sexy low voice. "Tell me about it tomorrow night. I don't want to be driving and accidently miss a word." He couldn't stop thinking how beautiful she'd looked when she left this morning. "I miss you. Wish I could have gone with you this time. I know it's only a few weeks, but it'll seem like an eternity here without you."

"I know. I feel the same, but I'll be working most of the time. The band is already here. They'll watch out for me. We'll start rehearsals tomorrow. I'll be home before you know it."

"I'll be waiting. Better say good-night. I'm almost to the ranch. I can see the barn burning even before I pull off."

"Night," she whispered, then added, "Be careful."

He drove the last mile thinking of his wife and not some fire in a barn on a ranch no one cared about. The owner had been gone for years, and his son ran the place like it was his own ATM. Dan had heard that the foreman, along with a few dozen cowboys, had all been fired yesterday.

Brandi, his wife, was three states away trying to get some sleep. How could he miss a woman so much who'd only been gone a few hours? When this duty was over Dan knew he'd be tempted to go home and call her again. Just to say good-night one more time.

He'd married her late into his forties. They might never make it to dance at their fiftieth anniversary party. He'd just have to love her in double time for the rest of his life to catch up.

five

One by one, Dakota turned on the lights in the beautiful old stucco home on Indigo Lake that her grandparents had built in the twenties. The day had exhausted her. She'd spent most of her time talking to people who didn't know what they wanted in a house. Window-shoppers were just part of the job; they didn't seem to realize that she didn't make money if they didn't buy.

Once in a while, when everything went wrong, she wanted to scream all the way to heaven. "I can't take it anymore. Not one more step. Not one more ounce of worry. Not one more day of people wasting my time. I'm not strong enough to carry the load."

But she had to be. There was no one else.

Just as she reached for the light in the kitchen, a gentle voice whispered from the shadows. "About time you got home, little sister."

Dakota forced a smile as she flipped on the light. "Sorry I'm late." Being home before dark was a rule she'd agreed to years ago. Not that Maria would ever complain.

"Did you get all the canning supplies?" Maria moved toward

her, gliding one hand slowly over the counter. "I thought I heard someone else on the porch."

"Yes to both." Dakota tried to sound lighthearted but today seemed stormy everywhere. "I got everything you ordered. Even picked up extra jars while they're on sale. Wes, at the store, helped me load them. If that man gets any quieter he'll be a mute." She followed her sister toward the porch. "And, you're not going to believe it, Maria, but there's another Hamilton alive."

"You saw one?" Her sister turned back so quickly her dark, curly hair floated like a cape around her shoulders.

"Not only saw, I loaned him our pickup." Dakota had already concluded that that decision probably hadn't been a bright move. First, he was a Hamilton. Second, he was a stranger. Third, he was a biker. Maybe she should have thought twice about being neighborly. The only thing the guy lacked was a prison shirt hand-painted with Looking for My Next Victim.

"Let's go kill him now and save some time." Maria laughed as she slapped her hand over her mouth. "Sorry. That just came out. Killing Hamiltons must be deeply buried in my DNA."

Dakota didn't want to admit she'd already thought of that. "It's been a hundred years since the Hamilton-Davis feud began. Maybe we should do some research to see if anyone remembers what started it. Maybe Grandmother's stories might just be that—stories."

"But he might remember the curse," Maria whispered. "He could be across the lake plotting our deaths right now. Grandmother swore Hamiltons are trained from birth to kill any Davis that sets foot on their land."

"I don't think he knows about that oath. He would have mentioned it if he had." Dakota wasn't sure Blade would care either way. He seemed more like the type who hated all folks in general, so why pick on Davises. "We're probably safe."

When Maria's sweet face wrinkled into a frown, Dakota added, "I did try to bounce him out of the pickup, but he hung on. Which was lucky, I guess, because he was still alive to help me get the supplies to the porch before it started raining."

Maria carried in boxes of canning jars. In the home she never tested her steps. She knew the pattern of the floor by heart. "Tell me all about him. Then we murder the guy just so we know the curse is broken." She almost managed to sound serious. "Oh, and before we pay him a visit, tell me, was he good-looking? Tall? Old or young? Ugly with wolf eyes?"

Dakota joined her sister in the work of organizing everything exactly as Maria needed: flour in the left bin, sugar in the tin on the counter, cinnamon on the right side of the first shelf. Everything had its exact place for Maria. "Wolf eyes, definitely. And tall, but mean looking. Not ugly. Young, I think; he was too muddy to tell. He was standing in the lake, covered in pond scum, when I met him. It didn't really go with his skin."

Maria giggled, sounding much younger than her thirty-three years. "I have an idea. If he's just homely, one of us should marry him before we murder him. Then we'll get the land. Someone said there are plums growing all over that land. I could double or triple my plum jelly production."

"What good is a place we can't step foot on? Remember what Grandmother said, Davises die when they walk over Hamilton land."

"I don't believe Shichu. The older she gets the more stories rattle out of her brain." Maria moved her fingers lightly over the jars, counting them. "How old is he? I'll marry him. It wouldn't matter to me if he's ugly."

Dakota watched her beautiful sister, wondering how she could speak so lightly about being blind. Forcing all emotion from her voice, she answered, "Couldn't tell much about looks, but he had a nice build. I have a feeling he's meaner than a rattler though. He told me if I got wet I might shrink to elf size."

Maria, an inch taller than Dakota, reached in the kitchen

drawer and drew her butcher knife. "That does it. We kill him tonight. No one insults my little sister."

Dakota laughed as the vision of them tromping down the muddy road with their only weapons, a big knife and baseball bat, flashed through her mind. "We can't go tonight. It's raining. We'll both be elf size before we get to him and he'll probably stomp on us with his biker boots."

"He's a biker? Like Hells Angels or the Bandidos? Does he have those biker tattoos? You know, the kind that frighten any woman when she rips off his shirt in wild passion."

"I didn't look but next time I'll ask him to strip, then I'll come home and describe them to you." Dakota grinned, thinking she might like seeing Hamilton nude. Only for reference so she could report back to Maria, of course.

Maria seemed lost in her own dream. "I'll bet he has a wicked tattoo running across his chest. I listened to this romance novel last month where the hero was a biker. He had a skull and crossbones on his chest and said he was a pirate who stole hearts. The story was so hot it burned my ears."

Dakota shook her head. "We've got to cut down your subscription to audiobooks. How many books did you listen to this week?"

"One nonfiction, one biography and only four or five romances." Maria shrugged. "Sometimes I listen to the romances twice. I have a feeling if I could see, I'd be an untamed spirit rushing out to midnight affairs and romantic afternoons with men whose names I wouldn't even bother to learn. I'd call them all 'lover.'"

"You've never done anything wild in your life, Maria." Dakota couldn't imagine her shy sister ever being brave enough to talk to a man, much less draw him into an afternoon of passion.

"I know I haven't gone crazy yet, but I'm making mental notes from the books. Once I find the right man, I've got a list of things to try. He'd better have stamina."

They both laughed and began preparing dinner.

As Dakota worked on the wide, wood-block countertop that her grandmother had cooked meals on, the stress of the day slipped away. This house made of stucco and logs had withstood every storm that had come along for years, and it would withstand this one tonight.

"So," Maria said as she made the salad, "tell me about your day."

Dakota made a face but kept the worry out of her voice. "I swear being the only Realtor in a rapidly growing small town is like chasing bees in a tornado. One retired couple from Amarillo just wanted to move to Crossroads because it was so tiny. They said they were tired of the big city and fighting traffic on a street called Soncy. They claimed they'd love the quiet of a little community and the fact they could get so much house for their money here. But then he complained that there was no golf course or gym. She asked twice how far the nearest mall was."

"What did you show them?"

"Not much. They hated the row of new garden homes going up by the museum—too small. The houses over by the school were bigger but too old, too many stairs, too plain. I showed them one three miles from town and he said it was 'too far out.' In the end, I think they were just daydreaming."

Maria smiled as she worked. "I know, it's not fair," she said. "You try so hard, but not everyone is serious."

"Right. I told them to think about building. Good news is they said they'd consider it. Bad news is I won't make much money off the sale of a lot."

"Anyone else?"

Dakota felt a little of the day's tension leave her shoulders. "The mothers of a bride and groom were trying to pick out their newly married children's home while the kids were on their honeymoon. I showed them everything in town and the mothers couldn't agree. My guess is I'll be showing the newly-weds the same houses next week."

They talked as they ate: Dakota about her work in town and what needed to be done on the farm every weekend before spring, and Maria about what fruit she planned to can tomorrow. Her business was growing, but another ten jars of jam sold next week wouldn't be enough to pay the bills this month.

As they finished supper, the rain finally stopped. Maria cleaned up and began setting her ingredients out for tomorrow. Dakota knew if the rain started again during the night, her sister would get up and create her delicious jams and jellies without the light. Since the accident that took her sight five years ago, Maria couldn't sleep if it rained or stormed, so she worked at what she loved: cooking.

Collecting her laptop, Dakota headed for the barn. Her day job might be over, but her studies were just beginning. If she ever planned to do what *she* loved, she had to work—rain or shine.

six

Blade Hamilton worked half the night trying to pull his bike out of the Texas mud. Indigo Lake seemed determined to keep it. Finally, with the help of an old rusty winch from the shack of a barn on his land, he managed to drag the Harley out of the lake and get it on solid ground.

The night seemed to fight him as well, first with a chilling mist against his already wet clothes, and finally with shadows from the low clouds moving over the midnight land like creatures crawling toward him. Once, he looked up and swore he saw a figure, round as he was tall, glaring at him from behind a bare elm as if the intruder thought invisible leaves might hide him.

Blade thought he could make out white teeth smiling. Then the wind whipped up and the stout body turned, as if rolling into the night. Blade kept glancing toward the lone elm, but the figure didn't appear again. After cussing and yelling at it a few times, Blade calmed down and examined the damage to his bike.

Forget the round figure. If he didn't get this bike fixed he'd be here forever, and tonight it was far too dark to even predict how many hours or days it would take him. The way his luck was running, he'd probably have plenty of time to visit with the ghost.

Exhausted, he climbed into the pickup he'd borrowed and drove back to Dakota's place. Her house wasn't far; he'd seen the lights there go out hours ago. But, thanks to the lake, the road circled around, making it seem miles away.

When he crossed onto her property, he noticed a few buildings besides the main house scattered over the rocky, uneven land. Barns, sheds, a short house that looked like it might have been the original dugout when the place was homesteaded.

Like she told him to, he parked the pickup at the beginning of the drive. Maybe she didn't want it getting stuck in the mud, or maybe she'd planned to park it in one of the little barns scattered around the house. Only, he'd kept it so long she must have gone on to bed. He was too tired to care as he cut the engine and climbed out.

If he had a pen, he would have left a thank-you note. He'd probably run her battery down using the headlights as his only light source, and the driver's seat was muddy, not to mention the bed where he'd climbed in and out of the truck several times.

Half the papers she had scattered across her front seat were now floating on the lake. He'd tried to collect them, but his efforts looked more like a first-grade art project than anything she might want to read.

He'd apologize for that also, he decided.

He was too tired to even bother trying to scrape off the mud tonight. He'd say he was sorry, or better yet offer to pay for a wash tomorrow, but tonight he'd promised to bring the old piece of junk back and he had. The ten minutes he'd said he wanted to borrow it had turned into three or four hours. She probably needed it in the morning to do whatever she did for a living.

From the way she was dressed he'd guess it wasn't farming. Wool skirt six inches too long to be fashionable, navy blazer a bit too big for her tiny frame, and shoes practical but so ugly he wouldn't suggest even giving them away. No clue what her job was, but one thing was obvious, she was making herself look older.

He grinned, thinking of how she'd ordered him to ride in the back. She could be the role model for the kind of woman he hated being around. Bossy, quick-tempered, superstitious, and short. But, he had to admit, she was kind of cute for an elf.

He decided to walk up to the house and leave the keys. No lights were on at her place or in the yard, but his eyes had adjusted to the darkness.

He'd just put the keys on the porch where she'd stacked the boxes.

Bad luck found him about the time he was within twenty feet of her house. The rain started again. The slow steady plopping around him sounded like a thousand tiny drummers. He'd been soaked for so long, Blade barely noticed he was dripping as he walked. Maybe this slow drizzle would wash the pickup off a little. If it didn't, his only neighbor probably wouldn't be speaking to him come dawn.

Ten feet from the house he saw the shadow of a woman appear on the porch. The watery moon didn't show her clearly at first and he thought it was Dakota. Small build, hair tied back away from her face, a crochet shawl wrapped around her shoulders. He almost yelled a greeting, but something wasn't right.

The woman let the shawl slip. She wore a white nightgown that gave the impression that she was floating.

Blade frowned. No wonder people around here believed in curses and spirits. He'd only been here one night and he'd already seen two.

He moved a few feet closer and the woman took shape. She was taller than he remembered Dakota being, and so thin she reminded him of a willow swaying in the night breeze. Only she was flesh and blood.

He studied her. She wasn't Dakota. He could see that now, but the resemblance was there. A sister, maybe. This woman was a few years older and beautiful in a no-makeup, freshly scrubbed kind of way.

Six feet away. Five. The wet grass silenced his steps. She was looking right at him. Even in the night he couldn't understand why he didn't startle her.

Blade stopped. He wasn't sure what to do. He didn't want to frighten her, but if she hadn't seen him yet, one word would surely do just that.

She closed her eyes and leaned her face out so the gentle rain could tap against her skin. Then she smiled and he knew…she was blind. She might not have seen him, but he had the feeling she observed more than most. She saw the night, the softness of the rain, the caress of the damp wind, the silent world after a storm. Tapping her fingers along the porch railing, she moved inside and disappeared as though she'd been nothing more than a vision, a will-o'-the-wisp, impossible to catch.

Blade couldn't move. He felt like he'd seen a ghost, though his life had always been ordered by reason and logic. This whole part of the country made him feel like he'd stepped into another world, or maybe another dimension. He was the outsider here, and yet he didn't feel as out of place as he thought he would. Somehow, deep down, a part of him belonged here. Blade dropped the pickup keys on the porch.

There was a kind of magic in the air. Dakota had spoken of a curse. In an isolated place like this, he could almost feel the past whispering as he walked around the house that looked like its walls were a foot thick. Before he reached the open field between his land and Dakota's house, he passed a small place built low, almost into the earth. Smoke circled from the chimney, but no light shone from the windows. An old, white rocker on the porch moved gently in time to the wind.

He slowed his steps, not wanting to wake whoever lived in

the little cabin. Twenty feet later he passed a huge winter garden now sleeping. Further on he spotted a shed made of roughly
cut boards near a stand of low trees.

When he turned the corner to the barn's side door, he caught
a flicker of light.

Slowly, drawn like a moth, he moved toward the light and
slipped through the opening into silent, warm air.

From the looks of it, most of the barn was used for storage.
Farm tools, an old wagon, a tractor, all looked abandoned. Leftovers, too valuable to toss, too worthless to sell.

One corner near the back reminded him of a mad scientist's
study. Drawings of houses and floor plans were nailed to the
wall—some old and curling at the edges, some new and more
detailed than the originals.

Blade was so interested in the plans, he almost didn't notice a
woman sleeping in a multicolored blanket between the sides of
an old wingback chair. She looked tiny, with only her face left
uncovered and the rope of a dark braid spilling over the blanket. The old leather office chair seemed to be holding her, cuddling her in its arms.

Obviously, she'd been working at the bench of a desk. These
were her plans, her drawings on the wall. He'd studied enough
blueprints in his investigations to know what he was looking
at. Not office buildings or compounds, but homes. Big beautiful homes where every inch of space was put to use, every detail refined.

He clicked Save on the laptop and powered her computer
down. He'd bet Dakota had to be at work in a few hours and
guessed she'd sleep better somewhere else.

Another brightly colored blanket was spread out on a mound
of hay near the door. He was too tired to worry about what
might be wrong with picking up a sleeping woman he barely
knew. For once, Blade didn't weigh his actions. He simply lifted
her in his arms and carried her to the makeshift bed.

A big yellow cat complained when Blade shoved him off the blanket and knelt as he carefully laid her down. Dakota wiggled slightly, settling back into sleep.

He knew he should leave, but he didn't have the energy to stand. He'd been up for two days and had spent most of the night digging in the mud. Exhausted, he almost didn't notice that he was also wet and muddy. He wasn't sure he had enough energy left to walk the mile back to his place. Not in the dark. Not in the rain.

Blade leaned back. He'd just rest a few minutes. It was warm and dry in here. He'd be long gone by dawn.

His head gently bumped her shoulder as he closed his eyes and breathed in. Before he exhaled, he was sound asleep.

seven

—————

Lauren watched the sun coming up over the small lake community a few miles from Crossroads where she'd grown up. The light seemed to fight its way between the clouds in no more hurry to start the day than she was.

Rain had charged in waves during the night, making staying out at the fire site or sleeping impossible. The fact there had been a fire on the Collins ranch bothered her, but the possibility that Lucas would get involved worried her more. Reid and Lucas had never been friends and after Reid fired Lucas's father, she was afraid they might be well on their way to becoming enemies.

Maybe that was why she'd come here to her father's house last night. She needed to feel safe. Here, just as she had in childhood, all seemed right and fair with the world.

She had her own place above the small office she rented in town, but this house on the lake, Pop's house, would always feel more like home. Sometimes she just needed to be here, if only for one night.

Since her father had remarried a few years ago, laughter and music always seemed to echo in the small rooms where she'd grown up. It had always been a safe place, but now it was a happy place, as well.

Last night she needed to feel as if she belonged somewhere. Her father had gone to the fire, and his bride was in Nashville for a few weeks recording songs she'd written in the lake house. Lauren could come home and no one would notice.

She admired her stepmother, Brandi. She'd followed her dream to be a singer, but she'd been smart enough to find Lauren's father to marry. She'd proved to Lauren that a woman could have both.

Memories circled round, reminding Lauren of dreams she'd lost or given up without ever seeing how far they might take her. She hadn't been brave like Brandi. She'd always been afraid to try.

The trouble with burying dreams is it leaves you hollow, she decided. But sometimes hollow is better than broken. She'd never been brave enough to risk losing. A brave sheriff's daughter afraid to try.

Walking out onto the deck Pop had painted blue when they moved in over twenty years ago and never remembered to repaint, Lauren stared into the pale light, wishing she could feel its warmth. The whole world seemed cold and silent as darkness still held to the shadows of the empty house.

Brandi had hated leaving Pop, but he'd insisted she go. He had no doubt she loved him, but she loved music too.

They couldn't seem to get enough of each other. Lauren had the feeling, thanks to Brandi's income from songwriting and performing, that they could afford the biggest place in town, but they were happy here. The little lake house. The home Lauren's mother had always called "the tiny house" and often complained about, even though she'd never lived in it. When Lauren's mother left her dad and Crossroads, she'd left Lauren too.

Footsteps sounded on the boat dock just beyond the deck.

Lauren turned and watched Tim stumbling up to the steps. His bad leg never seemed to take steps without a struggle.

Tim O'Grady had kept his parents' old cabin on the lake as a vacation home, but he rarely dropped by. Tim had become a drifter in many ways. He traveled, lectured some, said he was doing research in cities all over the world. He told her about all the places he'd visited in long blogs he kept online, but she sensed he made up the people he said he met. Never any pictures of people, only places.

In her online newspaper, Lauren did a weekly post of Tim's travels and book deals. He didn't know or care that hundreds followed his career.

He smiled as he stepped into the yellow light of the one deck lamp. "I figured you'd be over here at your dad's place, L."

"You heard about the fires at Reid's ranch?" She wrapped her sweater around herself and moved closer. "Fire department probably woke up half the town heading out a few hours ago."

"I knew before then. When the volunteer firemen started getting calls on their cells, half the bar cleared out. Fire at the Bar W is big news. I dropped by the sheriff's office to see what was going on, but Pearly didn't know much and didn't seem to appreciate me calling 9-1-1 to ask questions."

He grinned. "Wish your pop's wife would have been there taking calls like she sometimes does. She is one beautiful woman, but she barely talks to me, either. Mind telling me how a guy like your dad landed someone as classy as her?"

"I have the feeling Pop asks himself that every day. She's grand. She makes him take a vacation twice a year and insists they eat right. When they married, I stopped worrying about him and passed the job to her."

They sat down on a bench that faced the lake. Tim took her hand as if he wanted to hold on to something familiar, something real. "I feel out of the loop. There was a time I knew everyone in town. I knew about every call that came into the county offices. Hanging out at the sheriff's office gave me ideas for my first three books. I thought I was in the center of the world back then."

"Pop will be home soon. He'll fill me in, then I'll tell you everything." Lauren patted his shoulder, knowing how he loved details. Tim saw life, his and everyone else's, as simply an ongoing story. "Pearly told me two hay storage barns on the Collinses' place went up. Both total losses. Since it was stormy last night, lightning could have set one but not likely two."

"Agreed. Something's going on out there." Tim finished her thought.

"Something?" Lauren echoed.

"Anyone could have set them out of anger." Tim thought out loud. "Plenty of people hate the Collins family. I know I do. Reid has a lot of good-time buddies, but he's made his share of enemies too."

"I know. Besides you hating him, there's about thirty cowboys who lost their jobs yesterday. Lucas's dad might even be suspected. He was the Bar W foreman forever. I can't believe he was just kicked off land he'd worked for thirty years."

Tim shook his head. "Don't seem much like the cowboy way to set a fire. I wouldn't put it past Reid to set them himself. Maybe collecting insurance money is faster than selling hay. Or maybe Lucas went a step further than taking a swing at Reid. I've never seen him so angry. He may be a lawyer, but that swing last night was personal. Reid hurt his family. I wouldn't be surprised…"

"It wasn't Lucas." She interrupted Tim's rant.

"Oh, yeah? You haven't seen the guy in years and you think you know him?"

Tim's words came fast, almost angry. "L, you always put him on a pedestal. Lucas the Great."

"I know he didn't set the fires because I was with him. We

were on Kirkland land only a mile away. We saw the first one flame up and before we could call it in, another one went up."

Tim stood up so fast she jumped. "Of course you were, L. Lying about seeing Lucas hit Reid is one thing, but giving him an alibi is another. One lie too many, maybe. How many times do you have to pay the guy back for saving you that night at the Gypsy House? He caught you. Kept you from falling. It was instinct. You don't owe him anything."

"No. I *was* with him. I found him out looking at the stars like I said I would. I'm not covering for him. I'm just telling the truth."

Tim offered his hand and pulled her to her feet. "I'm sorry. I'm not sober enough to be reasonable or drunk enough not to care." He wrapped his arms around her shoulders. "It's good to be home. You're the one person I miss when I wander." He hugged harder. "You're the last person I should yell at."

She hugged him back. "I miss my best friend also," she whispered.

He rubbed his chin against her hair. "No one's hair feels or smells like yours. It smells like it looks, like sunshine on a spring day."

She laughed. "That's what you miss, my hair?"

"No. That's not all. I miss laughing with you and talking like we used to. I think I've told you every secret I've ever had. How about we both get some sleep? It's almost daylight. I'll pick you up for dinner tonight. We'll catch up."

"It's a date. I'd love to talk to you about my next book. I'm thinking of doing nonfiction. *The Ghosts of West Texas.* A friend of mine tells me there are places around here where spirits walk the land on moonless nights."

He smiled. "I can't wait to hear about it." He kissed her forehead. "Get some sleep. I'll be back.

"Or," he laughed, letting her know he was joking, "we could sleep together and order takeout from bed."

"Crossroads doesn't have takeout."

He nodded. "And we're not sleeping together."

"Right." She almost added, *been there, done that*, but she didn't want to bring up the past. She'd almost lost her best friend when she'd ended their short affair, if she could even call it that. Lauren wished they could both erase those few times when they were more than friends, less than lovers.

He turned and walked back the way he'd come, mumbling something to himself. At the dock, he waved and called, "See you later, alligator," the same way he had all those years ago when they were kids.

"After a while, crocodile," she said so low she doubted he heard her. Lauren watched him, thinking her life would be so simple if she loved Tim as more than a friend.

Only she didn't.

Deciding it was too cold to stay out any longer, she walked toward the door that opened into her father's study. She'd finish the night in her father's recliner so she'd be there when he came home.

Just before she stepped inside, a lone truck turned off the highway and rattled down the steep incline to the lake.

For a moment she watched, hoping it was Pop, knowing the headlights were too close together for it to be his cruiser.

Without moving, she watched Lucas park and climb out of the old pickup. The new sports car his mother said he'd bought didn't seem like it would fit him. The Lucas she knew was always more like a cowboy. He'd ridden full-out through college and law school, as if running across open land. He was determined, headstrong, driven, but he wasn't the type who drove a sports car.

Or set a fire, she thought.

Lauren stepped into the light as he stormed up the steps.

When he was a few feet away, she could smell the scent of fire on his clothes. "What happened?"

He stopped suddenly and coughed as if clearing his lungs so he could breathe in clean air. "Both hay barns on the Collinses' place are gone. By the time I got there the firemen were just watching them go up and making sure the fire didn't spread. There was nothing anyone could do."

"Lightning?"

He shook his head. "No one thinks so. The few cowboys packing up their gear didn't help, and the guys Reid's new manager brought in didn't know where anything was. Someone might have saved them from a full burn when the fires first sparked, but no one stepped up. By the time the fire trucks got there, it was too late."

He dug his fingers through hair that had looked styled earlier but now was windblown and wild. "It was like going to a midnight funeral. All the cowhands who'd worked on the Bar W for years just stood and watched. Memories were burning and we all knew the ranch would never be the same. A final bonfire to the death of what had once been a great ranch."

She brushed his arm in comfort. "Pop says if ranches aren't careful they follow the rule of three. The first generation builds it, the second enjoys it and the third destroys it. A hundred years from birth to death."

Lucas's rough hand covered hers. "Maybe so, but the owners don't seem to realize how many lives are built around a ranch. I grew up there. The ranch was more than just where my dad worked, it was our home too."

"Where was Reid tonight?" She hated to think he'd be dumb enough to set his own land on fire, but he might. Reid and his dad had been slicing off pieces of pastureland for a few years. Lucas might love the land, but Reid only cared about how much income it brought in.

"Someone said they found him at his house, passed out drunk. He must have gone there right after I hit him. The housekeeper said he came in cussing and trashing his office. She said he guzzled down all the liquor he could find, yelling about how he hated the ranch. She claimed he'd been in the headquarters all night."

"Did you tell my pop you had a fight with Reid earlier?"

"I told him I took a swing at Reid, but it wasn't much of a fight.

"The sheriff was at the first barn five minutes after I pulled up. The firemen had called him. Knowing your dad, he followed the first truck out." Lucas paced in front of her, pent-up energy still building from the excitement. "He's over at the main house talking, or trying to talk, to Reid now. I guess Reid had a right to set fire to his own property if the fire was set. It's not illegal unless you claim it on insurance. But if he does file a claim on something he did, or if someone else set the fire, your dad will be dealing with a crime. He'll know more after sunup."

Lauren relaxed. No one would probably ever know what or who started the fires, but in a few hours everyone in town would be guessing. "Thanks for letting me know. I was about to put some coffee on. You want some?"

"No. I didn't come here to post a report. I came here for this." He closed the distance between them. His lips brushed her cheek before she had time to react.

"Am I still welcome this close?" he whispered. "If not, you'd better say so because I really need to kiss you."

She thought of saying "always," but couldn't open her heart that far. She nodded slightly. One kiss for old time's sake wouldn't matter. He was the lover she never had but would miss forever. The *almost was* was sometimes far more painful than the *had been* that died.

His kiss was hard, almost painful, but she made no effort to pull away. Lauren couldn't tell if this was a goodbye kiss or a hello kiss. Whatever it was, it was borne from need.

Slowly, like a man dying of thirst swallowing his first gulp,

Lucas relaxed and the kiss softened, but his hold on her arms did not.

"I'm sorry," he whispered when he finally broke the kiss. "I didn't mean to come on so strong." He wasn't letting go, not this time. His grip on her arms would probably leave bruises. "I just had to do that."

For once in her life, Lauren's logical mind stopped thinking and she simply reacted. She'd wanted a kiss like this…full-out passion, no hesitation, nothing held back…and she'd wanted it from Lucas. "Do it again," she ordered.

If her mind and body would have to endure withdrawal from him later, she might as well take a full hit now. "Kiss me like it matters, Lucas."

And he did. Softer but with no less need.

She met his hunger. They were no longer children. Both knew what they wanted even if now wasn't the time or place. She felt it then, a need they shared. A longing that would always bind them and one kiss, a hundred kisses wouldn't quench the fire building between them.

He finally loosened his grip and let his hands slide down her arms until his fingers laced with hers. She leaned into him, absorbing his warmth. Feeling their bodies move against each other. Feeling his heart pound against hers.

When he broke the kiss, he smiled, kissed the top of her head and walked away.

Anger exploded in Lauren. She wasn't the shy little sixteen-year-old he'd kissed once on her birthday or the freshman in college he'd lost control with for a brief moment under a midnight sky.

"Lucas." His name came out as almost a curse. "You said you wanted to talk to me."

He was off the steps heading to his truck. "I just wanted to hold you tonight. For a quiet woman you sure do say a lot with a kiss. We'll have time for that later." His words carried on the predawn wind, a promise whispered.

"Stay." She'd learned that later never came for Lucas.

"I can't. I have to get to my dad and tell him what's going on." He grinned at her. "We'll get together later."

"Don't bet on it." She stepped inside and slammed the door so hard everyone at the lake probably heard it. He'd walked away again. Just when she trusted him. Just when she wanted him. He'd put her last again. Never first. Never important.

In the silence of her father's study she fought to keep from allowing a single tear to fall. "I don't love you, Lucas Reyes. I never have and I never will. You can't walk back into my life and mix me up again." She'd been on this merry-go-round before and she wasn't getting on it again.

Without another word or a single tear, she stormed into her old room and slammed the door. The whole lake house seemed to rattle in protest.

The room looked the same as it had when she'd left for college nine years ago. Organized. Plain. Solid. But she'd changed. She'd shifted and morphed into a stranger, even to herself. "I don't love him," she said to her reflection. "I never have."

Tonight, lying apparently had become a habit.

eight

The sun sliced through the cracks in the boards along the east wall of the barn, waking Dakota.

She groaned. She'd fallen asleep without making it back to the house and her bed, again. What an idiot. Last night Dakota told herself she'd only work an hour. Just until the neighbor brought back her pickup.

But he hadn't returned in an hour and the gentle rain must have lulled her to sleep. She'd dreamed of houses. The kind she would design one day. Beautiful homes that blended in with the canyons scattered about this part of the country. Her father died young, trying to farm rocky, uneven terrain, but her goal for the land was different.

She dreamed of someday building a secluded community near Indigo Lake. A place for people who worked from their homes or were retired. She could almost picture the winding streets and trails for walking and horseback riding, crossing through large parks and natural landscape. A place where people could see the sun rise and set over nature.

Her mind was working, memorizing last night's plans like an

artist tucks away sketches that would someday blend into a mural. She knew it was time to stop dreaming and get up, but her eyes refused to open. Just once she wished she could sleep a whole night or wake at dawn, then roll over and go back to dreaming.

But there was too much to do. If she planned to design homes instead of just trying to sell them, she had to study, and the only time she could study was at the end of the day—when her job was over, when Maria had her supplies, when all was right on the farm, when Grandmother had been checked on.

At least, for once, she hadn't awakened cold. The wool blanket she'd spread out just in case she needed a short nap had kept her warm. She didn't even remember climbing out of the chair and lying down, but she'd slept soundly for once.

Something moved along her back. Sam, the fattest cat in Texas, must be keeping her warm. He thought he had to come out with her to the barn every night, as if he considered himself a guard cat.

Her eyes flew open. Sam might be long, but he didn't run the length of her body.

Dakota slowly rolled over and stared at her new neighbor, who was sleeping an inch away.

The Hamilton was back.

She sat up carefully. He was muddy from the top of his dark brown, curly hair to his leather boots laced with buckles. He had what must be a week's worth of stubble along his square jaw and a bruise under his left eye. Probably given to him by the last stranger he'd curled up with.

It occurred to her that he might be some kind of pervert. Sneaking up on people and curling beside them when they were dreaming. She wasn't sure that was a criminal offense, but it would definitely be a dangerous one.

She felt her clothes. All still buttoned. He hadn't come to rape her apparently, just sleep beside her. Which wasn't near as frightening she decided, so she'd consider letting him live.

She smiled, thinking that he was downright cute in a baby dragon kind of way. Big, well built and younger than she'd thought he might be last night when he'd been standing in water and growling like a bear.

Maybe he was like a cold-blooded snake who only crawled into the barn for warmth.

Grandmother's stories about how mean the Hamiltons were came to mind. She said no one in the county crossed them for fear of being shot on a dark night. Wolf-gray eyes can see in the dark and they were all crack shots.

Grandmother would whisper that if you stole from their ranch, they'd find out and take back double. She even claimed she heard a rumor that the Hamilton men branded their women so they could never run off. That might explain why there were no pictures of Hamilton wives at the museum.

Dakota stared at the man beside her. His being cold-blooded and mean didn't seem out of the question, but he hadn't killed her, so she might give him the benefit of the doubt. Her mother told her once that Grandmother's stories grew darker every year, and longer than bindweed on a fence post.

As carefully as she could, Dakota moved away, covering him with the blanket she'd been wrapped in all night. Picking up Sam, she silently left the barn. Maybe it would be better to let sleeping dogs lie. There was no telling what kind of mood he'd wake up in.

"Some guard cat you are," she whispered as she scratched Sam's head.

The old cat didn't even have the sense to look guilty.

When she stepped in the shadowy kitchen, she wasn't surprised to hear Maria making breakfast. Routine was Maria's clock. She lived by it and so did Dakota. The reason she always had to be home before dark was Maria's clock. The same time to do meals, to deliver her products to the grocery, to go to church, were her sister's way of keeping in balance in her world of forever midnight.

"Morning," Dakota managed as she walked past the kitchen on her way to the bathroom. "I fell asleep in the barn again."

Maria held out a cup of coffee. "I figured that. I'll have breakfast ready by the time you finish showering."

Dakota stopped as she took the cup. "Better cook extra. That Hamilton who borrowed my truck is asleep in the barn."

"Shichu will not like that." Maria giggled as if she were three and not thirty-three. "Lucky she didn't show up last night. The rain must have kept her from her normal wandering around the place."

"We're not telling Grandmother. I swear, she gets more Apache every year. She may have been born mixed, but the Irish seems to be bleeding out. The other day she came over wrapped in a blanket and wearing Grandpa's old floppy hat. She's starting to look like the short, squatty ghost of Sitting Bull. She's also going back in time as she ages. I don't think she knows what decade it is."

"Probably not, but her senses are keen. She found a bushel of wild plums last week." Maria raised her flour-covered palm as if swearing an oath. "And the old girl can probably smell a Hamilton. So tell me, did he just drop by to kill us in our sleep and decide to nap first?" Maria's tone told Dakota that her sister thought the whole thing was a joke.

Dakota gulped down one swallow of hot coffee and came full awake. "I think he brought the truck back and decided to wait out the rain. He probably just fell asleep. Don't let him frighten you when he comes to the door. I have a feeling when he wakes he'll drop by to tell us he's leaving." She shrugged. "If he smells breakfast, we'll probably have to feed him."

"He won't startle me. I'm sure I'll hear him coming." Maria lifted her butcher knife. "I'll meet him at the door armed and ready. Or—" she set the knife down "—I'll do the neighborly thing and invite him in for breakfast. Killing someone with a full stomach seems the right thing to do, and no man could possibly turn down my blueberry pancakes."

Dakota shook her head. Maria's life might be dull and ordinary, but in her mind she lived the great adventures she listened to in her books.

When they'd been kids, Maria often elaborated on Grandmother's stories. She made the Hamiltons monsters with the smell of death on their breath. Or zombies who never stopped coming, no matter how many bullets hit their chests. Or aliens with nine long fingers on each hand, perfect for choking someone.

Now they laughed about the nightmares they'd had as children because of Maria's imagination. Dakota smiled as she grabbed her robe and stepped into the tiny bathroom. She doubted any of the stories Grandmother or Maria told were based on an ounce of truth, but she'd count Blade Hamilton's fingers the next time she saw him, just to be safe.

Twenty minutes later when Dakota walked back into the kitchen, tying a towel around her head, she could smell cinnamon bread in the oven and hear Maria's laughter.

Maria wasn't alone.

Blade, looking like a mud truck had run over him, was sitting at the counter drinking coffee and smiling at Maria.

"Have a seat, little sister. Breakfast is about to be served." Maria waved her spatula toward Blade. "Mr. Hamilton will be joining us. I decided to let him live after he told me that he slept with you last night."

Blade silently raised his hands in surrender, but Dakota didn't miss the way his gray eyes moved down the thin robe now clinging to her wet skin.

"I was just planning on resting a few minutes before walking back to my land." He held up two fingers. "Scout's honor."

"You were a Boy Scout?" she snapped. "You're probably lying."

"Elf, I've been a Boy Scout all my life."

"Don't call me Elf." She could feel deep anger climbing up her entire body.

"Don't call me a liar, Dakota." He said her name slowly.

Dakota frowned at him, fighting the urge to yell *Go away*. He must have hypnotized Maria, because she barely talked to the mailman, much less a stranger.

Maria carefully served her pancakes. "So, did you sleep with him, little sister?"

"I woke up and he was there." Dakota knew Maria was already thinking up something romantic in her mind. Biker guy falls in love with pickup girl at first sight, in the dark, in the rain, covered in mud.

Dakota figured she'd be teased about this for months. She might as well play along. "I guess I'm guilty. I did sleep with him."

"Well, we'll keep him alive until we find out if you're pregnant." Maria reached for the coffeepot. "Do you have a job, Hamilton? We'll need the child support."

Dakota gave Blade her best go-to-hell look. He'd started this and he didn't even try to look innocent.

He grinned as if she were teasing him. "I've got a job. After the army, I was hired as a special agent for the Bureau of Alcohol, Tobacco, Firearms and Explosives."

"Which one are you?" Maria asked, as if she thought he'd given her a multiple-choice question.

"Forest fires mostly. Occasionally explosives. We're federal, so we go where needed. I parachuted in the army, so now and then, while the burn is still hot, I'll go in and try to find where it started."

"But about the kid you might be carrying, Miss Maria—" he winked at Dakota as he changed the subject back to sleeping in the barn "—if I'm going to have to pay child support, I want to name the baby. If it's a boy, of course. I don't much care what you name her if it's a girl. Girls don't seem to stay around the Hamilton place."

Both sisters let out a yelp, then laughed a moment later when they realized he was kidding.

Maria smiled and Dakota saw that her sister wasn't afraid or shy around this man. Maybe she was comfortable in her own kitchen, or maybe she was simply playing a game from one of her romance novels. It really didn't matter. Maria was happy and not just pretending to be.

"Tell me," Maria said. "Are you tolerably handsome, Hamilton?"

Blade laughed. "I'm afraid not. My own mother couldn't love me." He shoveled food into his mouth as if he'd been starving.

"Then you're not married?" Maria finally asked when his plate was almost empty.

"Nope." Blade had the gall to wink at Dakota again, letting her know that he was enjoying the game as much as Maria was. "Women tend to run in the opposite direction. Men wearing badges don't make that much money unless they carry life insurance, and until a few days ago I didn't think I owned enough land to bury me on. I wouldn't wish a husband who darts out the door every time there's trouble in the air on any woman."

Maria leaned on the counter and said, "Then you wouldn't have any objection to marrying my sister since you've already slept with her and probably got her pregnant. In the interest of full disclosure, I might as well mention the fact that you've got plums on your land that might work for my business. I have to be thinking about what I'm getting out of this mating, you understand."

Dakota fought down a scream. Maria and Mudman laughed as if they were old friends. Somehow, these two people who seemed to have nothing in common had become allies, and she felt a little left out. If Maria could see how close he looked to the villains Grandmother described, she might not talk to him, much less feed the guy.

"Now, Hamilton," Maria said, pointing her spatula in his general direction. "I don't want to be rude, but I can smell you from here. You're welcome to use our shower if you like. I doubt the water works at your place, and from the odor about you, I'm guessing you've already tried bathing in the lake."

"I'd like that very much. I'm afraid any hotel would take one look at me and put up the no-vacancy sign. But first, I'd like to borrow Dakota's truck and go back to my place to get my only pair of clean clothes." He stood. "I'll finish this fine breakfast when I get back and help with the dishes."

"We'd appreciate it, Hamilton," Maria said. "You finish eating, but stay out of my kitchen. It's off-limits. Understood?"

"Understood, General," he answered.

Then without a word, he walked out the door.

Dakota gave up eating and decided she'd best finish dressing before Mudman returned. Hopefully, he'd get back before she had to be at work, but the last time he borrowed her truck for ten minutes he was gone half the night.

She thought of yelling at Maria for being so neighborly, but then again, Dakota had started it last night. Now she'd just have to put up with him for a few more minutes, and then hopefully they could go back to their quiet lives and forget a Hamilton lived across the lake.

Dakota quickly dressed in one of her three work outfits: milk-white blouse, dark blazer, modest A-line skirt made of the tartan plaid her grandfather wore to church every Sunday. He'd always said he wanted the Lord to know what clan he came from when he got to heaven.

She glanced in the mirror, realizing the outfit did little to flatter her. But for selling homes, she needed to look older than twenty-five. The clothes seemed to age her. She no longer felt like the baby of the Davis family. She'd had to take charge almost five years ago when her mother died and Maria was so badly hurt. At twenty she'd planned her mother's funeral, watched over Grandmother, managed the farm, and slept each night beside Maria's hospital bed. In a matter of days Dakota had aged into the head of the family.

As she combed her dark hair back and began to tie it up for the day, she listed everything she had to do. Sometimes when she felt like she was sleepwalking through her whole life, the list was all that kept her on the road. Pay the bills, fix the pickup, get Maria's supplies, work at a job she hated, clean house, check on Grandmother, pay the bills, get Maria's supplies. The list circled back around to the beginning, never ending in her mind.

Between Maria's sale of jams and jellies and her occasional sale of a house or lot, they were getting by. Living on dreams and hopes. Having no idea what "someday" would look like.

Maybe if she ran fast enough, hard enough, long enough, maybe one day she would simply fly away. For an hour. For a day. Just one day of being free and then she'd come back to duty.

Only, as the years passed, she realized that might not happen. She'd simply age into the clothes if she didn't keep fighting and learning and hoping.

As she stared into her bedroom mirror, she felt like she barely knew herself. She'd gone from being a kid just testing the world of college to being weighed down with responsibilities. She'd grow old and wrinkled without ever having lived if she wasn't careful. She'd seen people who had done that and she understood them, but she swore she'd never be one. She had dreams and they'd come true even if she had to give up sleep every night.

When she walked back down the hallway from her room, the bathroom door was closed and she could hear the shower.

He was back. One more thing to worry about. Add that to her list.

She tried not to let thoughts of a nude man in their house

concern her, but as soon as Dakota reached the kitchen, Maria whispered, "Did you open the door to see if he has tattoos?"

"No." Dakota sat down at her now cold, still untouched, breakfast. "And before you start, nothing happened last night."

Maria was busy wrapping tiny loaves of cinnamon bread. "I know that. I know you. But I can always hope. You haven't had many dates lately. Maybe even a Hamilton would look good."

Dakota almost said, *Since the accident five years ago. Since the night Mom died and Maria lost her sight.*

She'd never forget stepping out of Maria's hospital room and looking around for her mother, needing her hug, even if she was twenty. That moment, reality hit her like a sledgehammer to the heart: she was alone. There would be no more hugs from Mom. Dakota had walked out of the hospital and sat in the dark parking lot, crying, for hours. Until no more tears came.

She'd never cried again. She worked to take care of Maria and keep things together. There was no time, no thought of dating.

Now, watching Maria, she remained silent. They talked about everything else, but not the accident. Not that day. Mom had flown over to Dallas to ride home with Maria for Christmas. The roads were bad. Maria had worked the late shift at her café and crawled into the back of the car to sleep. Mom was never good driving on snow.

Dakota should have been the one to go, but she'd wanted to relax at home after she got back from college. She'd fallen asleep before dark, before the ice storm moved across the plains.

The phone woke her hours later. The sheriff's call. He'd been kind and honest, but she knew his call had changed her life forever.

She should have been in the car that day. She would have been the one driving. Maybe somehow she could have avoided the wreck on the icy highway. Then Mom would be alive, Maria would still be running her restaurant in Dallas, and she'd be…

Dakota closed her eyes and let out a breath before she let her *might have been* settle in her thoughts.

She might be graduating from architecture school about now.

Maria broke into Dakota's dark thoughts. "You need to get out on a date, little sister. Have some fun. Have an adventure. I'm fine here. I've got my work and my books. I'm happy."

Dakota forced her tone to be light. "I'm happy too. And I'm doing fine. I slept with a biker last night, didn't I? How much more excitement can I take?"

They both laughed as the bathroom door creaked open and steam filled the hallway. The man who stepped out was bare chested, with jeans riding low on his hips. He had a towel wrapped around his neck but his tanned chest and back sparkled with moisture. His hair was slicked back, reminding Dakota of a handsome pirate in one of Maria's books.

"You mind if I finish dressing in the hallway?" he asked, staring straight at Dakota. "It's so foggy in there I can't see a thing."

She couldn't turn away, but managed to swallow a few times and whisper, "No tattoos."

"Darn." Maria looked disappointed. "I already had that picture in my mind. Since he hangs out around fires, do you see any scars?"

Dakota stared, not really knowing what to expect. She couldn't have imagined a man who looked as good as the man standing before her. "Yes," she whispered back, knowing that Blade could hear them. "No tattoos, but a few interesting scars."

He didn't react as he scrubbed his hair with the towel, then finger-combed it back into place with one deep plow. He pulled on a white T-shirt and then a collarless sweater of army green. "I left my boots on your porch. Got them covered in another layer of mud when I parked your pickup and jumped the stream to where my bike was. Luckily, last night I'd dropped my saddlebags on the porch when I looked at the house. My clothes and camera survived the night."

When he looked up at her, Dakota forced her gaze down at her food.

He ignored her as he walked past her stool and took his place at the bar. "All right if I finish breakfast, Chef Maria? Then, if Dakota is still speaking to me, I thought I'd catch a ride into town."

Another favor?

She nodded, trying to decide what she was so mad about. That he'd spent the night? That he'd hit it off with Maria and not her? That he was good-looking and obviously knew it?

Maybe Maria's first suggestion was right. They should have killed him the minute they found out a Hamilton was alive. He might not look dangerous, but he looked good enough to drive her crazy.

"Sure, she'll take you in." Maria smiled. "I'll put a few loaves of cinnamon bread in a bag for you. If you want any more breakfast, eat up quick because she'll be flying out of here any minute. She may be the only one in her office, but she thinks she has to open on time."

As Maria poured his coffee, he glanced at Dakota and asked, "How does she do that?"

"She's holding the cup. She feels the weight and the warmth as the cup fills," Dakota said. "And she's blind, not deaf. If you want to know something, ask her." Her words came out hard, cold.

"Sorry," he said to Maria, ignoring Dakota again. "I've never been around anyone blind. You're a great cook."

"For a blind person?" Maria added.

"No. For anyone." Blade might not have experience, but he was a quick learner. "This is the best breakfast I've had in years. Most of the time I'm traveling and it's fast food at an airport or continental breakfast at the hotel."

"You travel lots?" Dakota asked.

"So much so I feel like I don't have a home, just a place where I change clothes. When I found out about the place across the lake, I took some time off to investigate. I've never owned a square inch of land in my life."

"Are you planning to stay?" Maria asked as she handed Dakota her bag with a tiny loaf of bread.

"No. I'll sell it. I wouldn't have any idea how to make a farm work."

Dakota suddenly saw a light at the end of her dark tunnel. "I could list it and sell it for you. That's what I do for a living." All she had to do was put up with him for a few days, sell his place, and she just might make twice the commission she usually did.

"Sounds exciting, Hamilton," Maria said. "Your job, I mean."

He turned back to Maria. "It can be, but mostly it's just paperwork or standing around waiting for something to happen. Not near as exciting as I thought it might be when I signed on."

They were ignoring her again, Dakota thought. He hadn't even answered her offer to sell his place.

Dakota thought of asking questions, but right now all she could think of was getting him out of their kitchen. The last thing Maria needed was a friend who'd be around for only a few days. After the accident, all of the friends her sister had had in Dallas melted away like ice cream left on a summer porch.

Maybe she didn't believe in curses, but still, avoiding any Hamilton seemed to be a rational precaution.

The sheriff's cruiser pulled up in her yard before she had time to push Blade out the door.

"Morning, ladies," Sheriff Brigman shouted through the screen door without stepping foot on the porch. "Any chance a guy named Hamilton is here? He couldn't have gone far. I saw his bike parked on his land."

Blade hurried outside with the bag of bread in his hand. "I'm just finishing breakfast, Sheriff. What do you need?"

Dakota watched the two men talking but couldn't make out what they were saying. If Hamilton already knew the sheriff, that could mean bad news. He could have lied about his job.

He probably got that killer body in the prison gym. Maybe he had to check in with every sheriff in every county he passed through? He probably said he was ATF because that was who arrested him.

Maria had just joined her at the door when Blade picked up his boots and saddlebags off the corner of the porch and waved.

"Thanks," was all he said before the sheriff backed the car away from the porch with Blade riding shotgun.

"Probably off to fight a forest fire," Maria reasoned. "What a hero."

"There's not five trees standing together for a hundred miles," Dakota said, pointing out the obvious.

Maria looked surprised. "Now you tell me."

Both girls laughed.

"I have to go to work." Dakota grabbed the old briefcase she'd bought at the secondhand store three years ago.

"Me too," Maria added. "See you before dark, little sister."

"See you before dark," Dakota answered.

Halfway to town Dakota was still thinking of how Blade had looked in the hallway with nothing on but his jeans. Surely he could have pulled his shirt on before he stepped out. Then she realized something: he'd been showing off.

And not for Maria, but for her.

He'd probably deny it to his dying breath, but she'd grown up on a farm. She'd seen roosters. Maybe he came not just to look at his place but to con them. He'd said he wasn't a liar, but probably every liar said that. It would be a waste of time to ask him if he was a serial killer.

She might as well go with believing he was telling the truth for now, but she planned to watch him. Maybe check out his funny biker saddlebags for weapons.

She smiled, planning to hold her cards close to her chest until she figured him out. If he was playing some kind of flirting game, maybe she should warn him that she didn't know the rules.

He'd winked at her twice. That must mean something.

Maybe he had a twitch?

He'd kept her warm last night, but never touched her.

Or at least she didn't think he had. Did she want him to? Just the thought made her warm.

Suddenly Dakota felt like she was just out of high school again and trying to figure out how guys think. She glanced in the rearview mirror. Cheeks flushed, eyes wide.

She wasn't growing older. Not today.

nine

Blade Hamilton didn't know a thing about farming or ranching or barn fires. All the way out to the Collins ranch, the sheriff talked about how he needed an expert fire investigator to have a look at it and it would be a week, maybe more, before he could get a fire marshal to this part of Texas.

Blade hated to bust the sheriff's bubble, but Sheriff Brigman still didn't have an expert on the kind of fire he was dealing with. He had studied arson fires and even worked a few bomb sites in the army. So, Blade kept quiet while the sheriff drove and hoped he had enough experience to fake it.

For the past five years he had worked fires set in wooded areas. That was different from this, and the only tool of his trade he had with him was his camera. But he'd known his enemy in the woods of northern Washington and the hills of California. The opponent hadn't changed, just the location had. Blade began to collect facts about the land, and mentally started a list of questions.

When they turned off under a ten-foot gate with a Bar W brand, Blade had stopped listening to the sheriff and started trying to remember what he'd learned over the past five years. The same rules should apply—well a few of them, anyway. He could help. If the sheriff wanted a special agent helping out, he had one.

The soaked ground had probably kept the whole ranch from being a disaster. Winter grass, if it had been dry, would burn fast and hot. There wouldn't be much chance of stopping it except at roads or creeks. Barbed wire wouldn't slow it down. And there probably weren't enough men in the county to fight it on a dry night.

Last night the rain had given him hell, but it had stopped the fire on the Bar W from spreading.

"Who am I kidding?" Sheriff Brigman asked, pulling Blade back into the conversation. "No one will come out this far because a few barns burned down. I'd never get a fire marshal or the ATF agent here. Not unless we find a body in the ashes. If I hadn't remembered meeting you, I'd be on my own. It's lucky you're here, Hamilton."

"You might want to ask the Davis women about that." Blade wished he'd been awake enough last night to remember one thing, but he was dead on his feet when he got to the barn and found Dakota sleeping in that old chair. "They mentioned Hamiltons tend to kill Davises, so they weren't too happy when I showed up. Every now and then the youngest one looks at me like she's checking to see if there's a weapon in my hand."

The sheriff laughed. "From what I heard, bullets flew in both directions back during the feud. Like most good Western stories, it started with stolen cattle and ended with a woman. Legend goes that the last man to die in the bloody battle that night killed himself. Walked right straight into Indigo Lake until the water covered his head. Only I've heard whispers of an even darker ending. No one really knows. There was not one man named Davis or Hamilton left alive to tell the story, and the women told them more to frighten the next generation than to be passing along history."

Blade swore he felt his blood chill. What could be darker? One of his relatives, maybe even one on the staircase wall, had committed suicide? Blade decided he didn't want to know the darker ending if suicide was the good choice.

He took a deep breath and thought of Dakota. She was the other half of the feud. Maybe, if she was still speaking to him later, he'd ask her about her family stories. Even in her very proper, very boring clothes, he saw the flash of a fighter in those dark eyes of hers and in the crimson glints in her hair. Maria had mentioned they'd come from strong warriors on both their Irish and Apache sides. Stubborn. Independent. Deadly.

Her hair, he almost said aloud. He remembered the smell of her hair when her head had rolled against his jaw as he carried her. It smelled of soap and rain and something else. She must have braided it as she studied. A loose braid, thick and dark with no clip or string tying off the end. The opposite of the tight bun she was wearing at breakfast.

Blade forced his mind back to the problem at hand. "You're right. A fire marshal is not likely to come out, but I'm happy to help if I can. Why not? A good mystery while I'm on vacation will hold my interest."

The sheriff was silent for a moment. "Thanks. I've got a few of the volunteer fire department standing guard at each barn. I told them to keep an eye out for any embers starting up again, but what I wanted them there for, in truth, was to make sure no one steps near. Maybe we'll get lucky and find a clue."

"I'll help if I can, but not as an official. Just doing you a favor."

"That mean you're not charging and I don't have to fill out paperwork?"

"Right."

"Good. The county doesn't have any money to pay you, anyway."

They drove a few miles before the sheriff asked, "You sleep last night in that old house on your land?"

"Nope." Blade smiled, thinking of adding that he'd slept with Dakota, but in a small town, that might not go over well. "I slept in the Davis barn. They loaned me their pickup so I could get my bike out of the mud. After I take a look at the burn site, I thought I'd ask you for a favor. You know where I can rent a truck? If you'd give me a ride there, I'd have wheels again."

"You're staying around?" The sheriff sounded surprised.

"Yeah." He shrugged. "For a few weeks, anyway."

"I would have guessed you'd be out of here as fast as possible. The only way you'll make money on that haunted house is to charge for tours on Halloween."

Blade didn't argue. "If I run now, the locals will think I'm afraid of an old curse on that land."

"Some folks think ghosts haunt your land. You might want to keep an eye out. A few people around here think the accident that caused Maria's blindness and killed her mother was linked to the curse. It happened where cars turn off the highway toward your place. Her car rolled to within a few feet of where your land starts. Indigo Lake holds the bones of many a story." The sheriff pulled up to the first barn and the conversation turned to fire.

Blade was surprised how informed the sheriff was about burn sites, and within a few minutes they were agreeing on possibilities as they approached the first barn. The frame was still standing against the cloudy sky like a smoldering border around a disaster.

"We're lucky both barns that burned were hay barns. The other ones on the property have expensive equipment in them."

After they'd circled several times, Blade said, "If I was guessing, I'd say, from the burn patterns, that the fire started in the dead center of the barn and spread out."

Brigman didn't argue. He simply nodded.

Finding the cause would be a process of elimination like any crime scene. They'd rule out one reason after another for the burn until only one scenario made sense. Lightning might be a possibility, but lightning hitting two barns on a ranch that hadn't had a lightning strike do damage in ten years was not likely.

Blade walked the perimeter of both barns, reading the story of how the fire happened. He talked with the tired firemen standing guard. What did they see? Any people around when they arrived? Any cars or trucks leaving the place that might have passed them when they were heading to the fire? What did the fire look like, smell like? What color was the smoke? How did the blaze react to water?

He asked the same questions of each man at the scene while he took pictures of tire tracks in the mud. There were too many footprints to tell which had come first. Plus whoever set the fires probably did so before the heavy rain started. Their tracks would have been washed away.

Over and over the cowboys mentioned that he should talk to Lucas Reyes. The owner and the ranch foreman might not have been at the fire, but Lucas was there. He'd be able to answer more questions.

The few hands from the ranch spoke of Lucas more with respect than accusation.

Blade moved to the edge of each burn, taking pictures, making educated guesses.

The sheriff left the second site to go get the owner. The guy claimed to be too drunk to remember hearing anything last night and, according to one of the firemen, Reid Collins hadn't even been out at the sites this morning.

What kind of rancher doesn't check his own ranch? Blade wondered as he continued his investigation alone. Looking for something different. Something new. Something that didn't belong. Law enforcement often says that the average person committing a crime makes a dozen mistakes in a matter of seconds. Blade only had to find one.

At the back of the second burn site, he stopped to pull off his sweater and noticed a lone man on horseback, watching him from about thirty yards away. He was on open land and making no effort to hide.

Blade lowered his sunglasses and walked directly toward the rider. If the man had something to hide, he'd ride away, and Blade wanted to collect every detail to report. He snapped a few shots as he moved.

The stranger was tall, lean, and so thin his shirt flapped in the wind like a sail. He wore a tan shirt and trousers that were tucked into muddy boots. Conchos ran a dark line down the outside of his pants and a few others were shining off his saddle. His wide hat was worn low so that his entire face was shaded.

"Morning," Blade said in greeting.

"Afternoon, kid," the old man said. "You missed lunch an hour ago so it ain't morning."

Blade never remembered being called kid, even when he was one. He'd reached six feet in the sixth grade. He was close enough to the stranger to see a smile behind a tobacco-stained, gray mustache. "I ate a big breakfast at the Davis place. That Maria is a great cook. I may not be hungry till tomorrow."

If he had any chance of getting this old guy to talk, Blade at least had to sound like a local. As a stranger, he doubted he'd have a chance, but as a friend of one of the farm families, he might learn something.

The old guy leaned on his saddle horn and looked down at Blade. "You sweet on one of them girls?"

This had nothing to do with the fire, but Blade played along. "I'm crazy about them both."

The stranger laughed. "You sound like your daddy. He never could turn down a pretty girl. I cowboyed with your grandpa, boy, and he said your dad had a steady girlfriend from the first grade on."

Blade forced himself not to react. "How could you know who I am or who my father was?"

"You look just like him, boy."

"I'm not a boy or a kid."

The cowboy spit a line of tobacco off to his left. "That you ain't, but I am long past old and into being ancient. Name's Fuller. Dice Fuller. Don't mean no harm, Hamilton. Anyone under sixty is young to me. I may be thin, but like a tree, cut me open and you'll find more than seventy rings."

"None taken, old man, and the name's Blade. I'm here investigating the burn site."

"I think I could have figured that out." He leaned down and lowered his voice. "I've been watching you. You're here with the sheriff so I'm guessing you're not just a sightseer."

"Right. I've got a badge that says special agent for the ATF, but I'm here unofficially. Just trying to help out." Blade moved closer. "You wouldn't happen to know anything about the fires, would you?"

His answer came too slow to be true. "I'm just looking for my friend. He's in trouble, I reckon. We was both rounding up the last of the cattle yesterday and got separated. I stayed around the bunkhouse until long after dark talking to the cook while she packed up. LeRoy never came in. His pickup and trailer are still parked at headquarters so I'm thinking he got thrown in the dark. There's canyons around here a man could tumble into and not even the coyotes would find him."

"Maybe he worked all night, or left with a friend."

"He's been known to drink all night, but if LeRoy worked he would have come in by dark and switched mounts. We're used to pushing ourselves, but he wouldn't push a horse. Something's wrong. I can feel it in the wind. Might have nothing to do with the fires. Or maybe it does."

Blade knew Fuller had to be the first cowboy he questioned when they got down to paperwork. If anybody saw anything, it would be this old guy. Only, Blade knew Fuller's type. He wouldn't be in any hurry to give up more than the facts.

"I'm walking around looking for what happened here. You wouldn't want to walk with me?" Blade began developing that rapport he'd need. "If you've worked this spread, Mr. Fuller, you'll spot something wrong or out of place before I do."

The stranger thought about it a minute, then slowly climbed down from his horse. "I'm happy to talk to you about the ranch, Hamilton. I don't know what happened here, but we all know there's trouble on this spread. Something is going on. How's a cattle ranch going to run without cattle? And—" he lowered his voice "—how do two barns half a mile apart catch fire within minutes of each other?"

Blade nodded. "You said 'we'? Who else?"

"The cowhands. Those of us left, anyway. All the single hands headed up north last night. They heard an outfit near Denver is hiring. Those married will try to hold out until spring. Then they'll hire on as day workers till they find another steady job."

"You know who might have had a reason to set these barns on fire?" Blade asked, before the old guy told him everyone's work history. "Because we both know it wasn't an accident."

"I know it weren't no accident, Agent Hamilton." Fuller smiled as he addressed Blade with respect. "But what I don't know is if it was a crime." The cowboy pulled off his hat and scratched his head. "If it was breaking the law, I've got a duty to report it. If it's not, it ain't none of my business. One thing you learn working big spreads. There's some things you see and some things you forget to see."

Blade knew he'd be wasting his time pushing. He offered his hand. "I'm glad to meet you, Dice Fuller. Hoping we have some time while I'm here to talk about my grandfather. I'd love to learn what he and my dad were like. Until last week I didn't know much more than my father's name." He paused, then added, "But first, we've got a fire to figure out."

Dice's grip was strong. "You can count on me, son. I'll help if I can."

They walked toward what had once been a thirty-foot-high barn, still smoking in places. The old man seemed to respect the fact that Blade didn't push him with questions. As they moved around the still-hot barn, Blade did most of the talking.

He told Dice that he'd worked a few arson fires, most in national forests, and handled several bomb alerts, but this was unknown territory for him. An isolated barn on private property. No witnesses. No reason.

"We all specialize at the bureau, but we're federal so we go where needed. I guess that's what I love about the job. Like this fire. If it was a crime, I think the *why* may be as important as the *how*."

Dice seemed interested and even offered bits about how the hay was stacked and how most of it was probably a few years old. "Not worth much," he said.

He also told how little was used last year or even the year before. Most of the supply in the barns was old because Collins sold off more and more cattle every year.

Half an hour later when the sheriff returned without the owner, Dice seemed to think he was part of the investigation team. They began listing all the scenarios: frustrated employee of the ranch, angry at being fired, rode through the rain, setting the two fires to make a point. With the rain there was a good chance the grass wouldn't catch. Maybe once he saw the fire he got scared and bolted.

Next possibility: Collins set the fires or ordered someone to. No crime unless he claims insurance.

There was always the possibility of kids playing around, looking for excitement, maybe smoking pot. They could have decided to start a fire for warmth and it got out of hand. But that only explained one fire.

About the time Dice ran out of ideas, a four-wheeler pulled up. The man who climbed out didn't look like he belonged on a ranch, but the sheriff introduced him as the owner, Reid Collins.

Collins must have crossed someone last night. His left eye was almost swollen closed and was several shades of blue. His right eye was bloodshot.

When Blade looked over at Dice he thought he could see anger building up behind the old guy's watery blue eyes. Collins might have been his boss, but there was hatred in Dice's stare. If all the hands felt that way about Collins, no amount of questioning would probably help find who set the fires.

Blade watched Reid Collins closely. His movements were slow for a man still in his twenties. He wore deck shoes and stepped carefully through the tall grass. Blade had no idea what Reid was on, or if he was simply hungover, but one thing was obvious: the landowner didn't care about the damage to his barns. Half the time he showed no hint of even keeping up with the conversation.

They moved to the other site. Reid followed the sheriff's cruiser in his four-wheeler, then reluctantly walked with the others, obviously thinking this outing was an entire waste of his time. As the embers cooled, they circled the skeleton of the barn, looking again for any clues.

When Blade turned toward the back left corner of the barn at a spot where he suspected the last fire had been set, he almost gagged. Earlier he hadn't been able to get within ten feet, but now it had cooled some and a terrible odor drifted around him.

The air had turned putrid with a smell so bad that once you smelled it, you never forgot. It drifted into your mouth and seemed to decay there, leaving a taste almost as bad as the smell.

Dice was a few feet behind him and froze in midstep. He tugged his bandanna up over his nose. "Double damn," he whispered. "There ain't but one thing that smells like that."

It was a smell like no other in the world. So terrible Blade felt his throat close up trying to keep the odor from his lungs. He'd encountered it in the army a few times and at several burn sites.

Human flesh burning. The odor of burned hair. Blood boiling to the point that it gives off a heavy, acrid odor so thick you swear you can taste it all the way to your gut.

The sheriff was several feet behind, busy writing notes. He looked up suddenly and Blade knew Brigman recognized the odor.

Reid Collins bumped into the sheriff, then yelled, "Damn! What is that smell?"

No one answered him. Brigman stepped forward and knelt in the pile of ashes spilling out of what had been the barn.

He brushed away ashes with his pencil and a hand rolled out of the rubble, its flesh burned away, its boney fingers stretching out as if for help. A gust of wind circled ashes exposing more bone.

Blade clicked a picture. The skeletal hand was curled up, with bits of charred muscle still attached to the bone.

Brigman stood. "Looks like he must have been trapped."

"The smoke probably got to him before he could fight his way out the back." Blade hated the smell, but he did his job. He clicked shots.

"No!" Reid yelled. "No! This isn't happening. Maybe it's an animal or an old skeleton buried in the barn years ago. Someone did not die in this fire last night." The owner seemed to think yelling would make his words true.

Brigman shook his head. "Look closer, Reid. Someone did die. Looks like the fire caught him just before he reached the back door." He noticed a padlock on burned wood that could have been the rear door to the barn. "Maybe he ran for the back door and found it locked. He was trapped by the fire."

Reid glanced over the sheriff's shoulder, gagged, and stumbled backward.

Blade and the sheriff moved in closer, trying to see something, anything, that might give them a clue.

"We're dealing with a crime scene now," Blade whispered.

"Shut the ranch down." The sheriff's voice bore no hesitation. They both knew what had to be done. Blade offered, "I'll help stand guard until the state troopers get here, Sheriff. We don't want anyone trying to cover this up."

Both men walked toward the sheriff's car. "I'll call it in." Dan's voice hinted at how tired he was already, and his day wasn't close to over. "We may have a murder here. Unless he was the one setting the fires and got caught in the last one."

"Not likely. I want to go back to the other site with equipment as soon as it cools. This was the only lock on any door that I saw," Blade said. "He might have been sleeping it off in the barn, or maybe riding the land and spotted the arsonist setting the fire."

Blade turned to Dice. "What do you think? How many cowhands were out riding last night?"

"Half a dozen, maybe more, but all the hands knew this barn had locks on it, front and back. Collins put them on six months ago. I figured it was to keep drifters out, but he said it was because as soon as the hay was gone he planned to store cars in there."

"Did he store cars?"

Dice shook his head. "Not that I ever saw, but he did keep this one barn locked."

Blade pushed. "You didn't think that was strange?"

Dice grinned. "I'm a cowboy. I'm not paid to think beyond cow level."

He pointed with his thumb. "We got a new problem."

"What's that?" Brigman said as he opened his car door and tugged out his radio.

Dice pointed back in the direction he'd come. "Boss man fainted."

All three looked back at Reid lying spread-eagle in the mud halfway between the rubble of the barn and the cars.

"What do I do, Sheriff?" Dice tugged off his hat and started worrying the brim. "Officially, I don't work for him since the night of the fire, and if he ain't breathing I'm sure not giving him mouth-to-mouth with all that throw-up on his face."

Brigman looked like a man who had his hands full. "Check to see if he's breathing. If he is, leave him. He looks like he could use some sun."

When Dice walked off, Brigman moved to the trunk of his car and pulled out a box. "You got a weapon, Hamilton?"

"I do. I carry a Glock 17 and my badge in my saddlebags. They're in the back seat of your cruiser."

"Then strap on a weapon." He pulled another badge from the box. "I'm also deputizing you." The sheriff glanced at his watch. "I don't know what we're facing but as of 1:45 p.m., I want you working for the county. We'll finish up here and by four I'll have men coming in to question. I'm going to need your help."

Blade slipped the badge in his pocket and reached for his saddlebags. "This mean I'm getting paid?"

"Nope, but if you don't want the job my next recruit is Dice."

They both looked back at Dice slowly walking around Reid Collins like the ranch owner was a half-dead snake.

Blade knew he was cornered. "I'll take the job."

ten

Lauren sat in her tiny office in what everyone called the strip mall. Three ten-by-twelve offices with small loft apartments above and a parking lot out front for eight cars. She'd opened a site for online news called *ChatAroundCrossroads* after she moved back from Dallas. She planned to sell ads on her webpage for income in the morning and work on her writing in the afternoon.

Only, everyone read the news, but no one bought ads, so she was forced to take editing jobs to pay the bills. Still, broke in her hometown among friends and family was better than being broke in Dallas alone.

Lauren had always thought her real money would come from writing. Short stories, poems, articles. After all, every English teacher she had in college told her she could write.

But they hadn't told her what to write.

So far everything she tried only dribbled in small change. But last month she'd had a new idea. Dakota Davis, in the office next door, had told her scary tales about her neighbor's place and she'd pitched the idea to *Texas Monthly*. They said they'd consider it.

Lauren didn't believe any of the stories, but that might be

something people would read. A feud over cattle. A gunfight over love. And a ghost who walked the land by Indigo Lake.

From there she could write other stories. Ransom Canyon was full of legends and stories.

She stared out the glass door, thinking she'd managed to get nowhere with her writing career in her five years since college, so she might as well try this road. There was good money in magazine writing if she could just make herself write. At the rate she was going she'd die of old age with her obituary only half-written.

But if she wrote about legends and curses people passed down, she might build a name for herself. She could do a series of shorts and eventually put them together in a book. The people around here knew her, trusted her. They'd open up to her.

Tapping her pencil against her forehead, she decided if she stepped into nonfiction, she'd check her facts, make it almost like a historical account. Somewhere back in the history of this area must be a real event that started the stories.

"Write, write, write," she mumbled to herself as her fingers danced across the keyboard too lightly to produce words. She had to work, or go back to wondering why Lucas had kissed her last night like he was leaving for the front lines.

Lucas reminded her of a recurring dream that never ended. Part love story, part nightmare. She sometimes told herself he was the reason she never made up her mind about anything.

Maybe this was just puppy love that hung around ten years too long. But the truth was, she hadn't met anyone she wanted to move on with.

Sometimes hanging on to a maybe was enough to last awhile. She'd let go of the dream of her and Lucas so slowly it had drifted out of sight before she realized it was gone. Even when he'd kissed her last night, she hadn't allowed hope to crawl into her heart again.

She glared through the glass door at the antiques store across the street, which usually looked abandoned except on Saturdays. Maybe the town had evacuated and had forgotten to tell her. Zombies were probably roaming the streets looking for fresh brains, and here she was worrying about an almost-love she couldn't get over.

She'd die of boredom here in her ten-by-twelve office. Passing tourists visiting the ghost town years from now would find her skeleton at her keyboard. Her fingers typed her thoughts almost as if she were really working.

Lauren hit Delete. Even when jotting down her thoughts she was overwriting. Overthinking everything.

Back to the legend of Hamilton Acres.

"Ring," she whispered to the phone. If something didn't happen soon, she'd fall asleep at her desk...again.

A rapping on the wall made Lauren jump. Three knocks. Dakota's code for "ready for lunch." It must be after one o'clock.

Lauren rapped back once and reached for her purse. The soup special at Dorothy's Café would do today. She'd be going out with Tim tonight and he had the money to buy steak.

Lauren stepped out just as Dakota came out her door. "Have a good morning?"

"No. Not enough sleep."

Lauren grinned. "The Hamilton ghost haunting your dreams again?"

Dakota laughed. "It's more than that. This Hamilton is very much alive." She giggled as if she were sixteen and not twenty-five. "I'll tell you about it over lunch, but first, I have a surprise. I got a call off the website you set up for me."

The conversation turned to the real estate business as they walked to the café. Lauren wanted to talk about her idea for her series, "Legends of the Plains," but it could wait. If one of the Hamilton clan was still alive, she planned to interview him as soon as possible. If she could include pictures, *Texas Monthly* might be impressed.

Just as they reached their destination, Lauren's phone rang. She waved Dakota in and answered, noticing the call was coming in from the county sheriff's office.

"Hi, Pop, I thought you'd be sleeping by now. Brandi called to check in and said you were out at the Collins place all night."

"It's Pearly," a high-pitched woman's voice said. "Your dad doesn't know I'm calling. He's still out at the ranch."

Lauren waited. As the county clerk, Pearly was one of her best sources of info on the happenings around town. Lost dogs. Wrecks on the highway. Bobcat sightings near Ransom Canyon. "What's new?" Lauren asked, already digging in her purse for a pen.

"Your father's been calling in orders all morning. He's finishing up at the ranch and heading back in soon. Wanted me to know he hired a new deputy on the spot." Pearly hesitated.

New deputy, Lauren wrote down, then waited for the name. "Fill me in on details, Pearly. Was he already in law enforcement? Where'd he find the guy? What's his name? Old? Young?"

"That's not why I called." Pearly ignored all the questions. "They found a body in one of the barns that burned."

"What!" Lauren's mind was already running through a list of possibilities.

A homeless person bedding down—the barn was not too far from the road. He could have been trapped.

A drunk cowboy—not likely; everyone was moving out, but one might have decided to get drunk first, then leave.

A thief caught at the crime scene—went into the barn to steal something and was caught when lightning struck.

A murder—someone thought they'd cover the evidence with a fire. No, not in Crossroads.

Pearly ended her guessing game. "The body was burned too badly to tell who it was. The sheriff's made all the right calls and secured the crime scene. I just called to give you the heads-up. Sheriff says he's got a real special agent on scene investigating. Only, where he'd find one of them this far from nowhere, I haven't got a clue."

"Thanks, Pearly." Lauren hung up, thinking of how she'd put the news together so everyone in town would check in on her site. Then she'd email the stations in Amarillo, Lubbock, and Abilene. They might run the story and give her credit, or even send out a crew.

Suddenly she felt guilty. Someone had died. Maybe he had been dead a long time, years even, buried in the back of a hay barn. Whatever the facts were, she needed to get them to the press first. She couldn't change what had happened, but like they say, *If it bleeds, it leads.* A burned body might not bleed, but it was a violent death in a small town. Unless some old cowboy just died of old age and accidently got cremated when lightning struck the barn.

That didn't make sense. There wasn't much lightning last night, and she was out there when the barn fired up.

She rushed into Dorothy's Café, ordering her soup as she passed the waitress, and sat down across from Dakota. "I've got a crime scene. A burned body. A real mystery."

Dakota, like Lauren, would probably feel guilty later, but she said, "It's not in a house that's for sale? I'd hate to have to put up a this-house-is-not-haunted sign on one of my listings."

"No. It's at the Collins ranch, you know that big spread they call the Bar W," Lauren said as she began jotting down questions.

"Reid Collins's place?"

"Yeah. You know him?" Lauren was writing, only half listening.

Dakota nodded. "He's older than me by a few years. I know he's a town hero, but the guy always struck me as a little on the creepy side. His only topic of conversation is himself."

Lauren grinned. "You know him, all right. He was a year ahead of me in school and we had a few dates in college. Our fathers were friends years ago, so he invited me to a few football games at Tech. I was bored to death on those dates."

Dakota added sugar to her tea. "He asked me out last year. I hadn't been on a date in months but I said no. I told him to ask again in ten years. I'm not that desperate yet."

Both women laughed as they downed their cup of soup and hurried back to their little offices. Lauren had news to report and Dakota always feared she'd miss a call. Of course, since she was the only housing agent in Crossroads, whoever called once would probably call back or try her cell.

As if on cue, Lauren's cell started ringing as she unlocked the door.

She stepped inside as she waved at Dakota.

"More news, Pearly?" Lauren said as she tugged off her jacket. Two calls in a row from the sheriff's office.

There was a long pause, and then her Pop said, "No, this is your father."

Lauren cringed. He never used that tone unless he was angry.

"I'm guessing Pearly has already called you." At least Pop was quick enough to recognize the facts, even if he hadn't had any sleep. "I fear the leak in this office is more like a waterfall."

"Yes. She's just keeping the press informed, Pop. Don't yell at her." Lauren was already typing out the few facts she knew on her website.

His voice was scary calm now. "I never yell at Pearly. She'd probably yell back."

Lauren laughed. For twenty years she'd always suspected her brave father was a bit afraid of the county secretary. "What's new with the investigation that I can put out? I know you found a body in one of the barns that burned. That's all the facts. Give me more."

Another long pause. Lauren typed in all caps, BODY FOUND AT LOCAL RANCH. This was big. Everyone in town would be reading her news site today. She'd feed them one fact at a time.

"Nothing to report beside the facts you already have, Lauren, but I thought you should know that we're bringing Lucas Reyes, along with pretty much everyone from the Bar W, in for questioning."

Lauren's fingers froze on the keyboard.

Her father's voice sounded more worried than official. "Several people have reported seeing him on the county road that runs between the Collinses' spread and Kirkland's land. And he did have a reason to be mad at Reid. After all, Collins fired his father yesterday. Everyone I've talked to this morning thinks Reid Collins handled the closing of his ranch badly. He didn't even give the notices himself. He hired a ranch manager to do it. I don't blame Lucas for being angry."

"Oh, no." Part of her wanted to tell her father that she'd been with Lucas when the first fire flamed. "You don't think he did it, Pop? Not Lucas."

"No, I don't. But if he was on that road, he may have seen something out of the ordinary. Right now I'm following any lead I have." He hesitated. "You can report that Reid was fighting to keep the sale of the ranch quiet until it was completed. As of this morning that sale has been put on hold until we find out more about both the body and the fires."

Before she could say anything, he said he had to run and then hung up. Her father's way of never answering questions.

Lauren sat back in her chair. The sale of one of the big ranches would be front-page news. Her father wouldn't have told her about it unless he wanted it out. The sale of land owned for generations and the body found must be somehow linked. What a mystery!

She'd heard rumors that Reid and his dad had been selling off small sections the last few years, but not the whole ranch. She also knew Reid hated ranching, but didn't he realize that if he sold, the income stream would stop? The older Collins probably had plenty of money for his lifetime, but Reid lived big. He'd run through whatever he made from the sell in a few years.

Lauren hesitated, her fingers over the keys. Another problem. If she told Pop she was with Lucas last night, she'd have to tell him that Lucas had punched Reid. That would only make Lucas look more guilty. But if she didn't tell her father, the sheriff, she might be somehow withholding evidence.

She typed more details to follow and posted the few lines under Breaking News. There would be no mention of Lucas.

Lauren snapped her laptop closed. More news on the story could wait twenty minutes. Right now, she had to talk to Tim, her best friend. Maybe they could think of a way to help Lucas without making him look guilty.

If Lucas needed her testimony, she'd gladly tell the world he was with her, but if he didn't, Lauren promised herself she wouldn't say a word. If her dad knew about the fight earlier, he'd know there was bad blood between the two men.

"Be home, Tim," she whispered as she headed for her car.

eleven

After lunch Dakota walked the few feet to her office, catching only bits of Lauren's phone conversation, but what she did hear hinted that something must be happening. Lauren would be off doing her investigative reporting, and she, Dakota, was heading in to wait for emails. At least she'd had one call about a house, and it sounded promising.

A couple from Plainview, Reta and Howard Wilson, had called this morning and wanted to come down and look at everything Crossroads had under a hundred-fifty thousand. Something with trees, he'd said. Something away from any railroad tracks or grade schools, she'd insisted. Something with a sunset view, they both claimed, was a must.

Dakota had emailed them the two listings that kind of fit. One had huge pecan trees in the big yard, but it needed work— one branch of the tree nearest the house had crashed into the front window. The sellers were a thousand miles away and in no hurry to do repairs. The second listing fit all their *musts* but it was small—very small.

As Dakota always did, she also sent houses that cost more, but fit their musts otherwise. She'd been told people often said they were looking for less than they could actually afford.

She'd included a map of the town and a list of this month's activities at the library before she pushed Send and tapped on the wall to go to lunch.

Now all she had to do this afternoon was wait until the Wilsons got back to her. If they did?

Open time. She smiled as the sun reflected off her office door. Rainy nights always made the next day seem so much brighter. She just wished it were that way in real life too.

Afternoons, her favorite time each day, when she allowed herself a slice of freedom. She'd pull out her notebook and draw up plans for a house that had been drifting in her mind all morning. A big house with the family rooms in the center and wings for bedrooms spread out like spokes on a wagon wheel in every direction.

She smiled, thinking she'd spend an hour designing a house for generations to live in, but where everyone would still have their privacy. A house with more than one bathroom.

As she reached to unlock her office door, it gave to her touch and her daydream was shoved aside by reality.

Dakota fought down a few swear words. Forgetting to lock the door was something that often happened. After all, there was nothing to steal but paper and a ten-year-old computer. The worst thing that could happen was someone would break in and buy a house while she was gone. She had the same philosophy about the old farm pickup. If someone stole it, let them pay the repair bills.

She bumped her way into the office, purse in one hand, the refill on her tea from the café in the other.

The afternoon sun came into the tiny office with her and spotlighted her desk. Nothing amiss. Stacks of flyers, notepads, two phone books, and three siphoned cups from past days.

Dakota glanced over the mess and froze. Someone was sitting in her chair. A big broad-shouldered shadow.

Correction. A Hamilton.

"About time you got back," he said. "I've been talking to the Wilsons and they want to drive over to look at the houses you emailed them."

"You answered my phone?" Dakota glared at him in disbelief.

"Sure. It rang." He didn't look the least bit sorry. "Took me a minute to find it on this desk."

She set down her take-out cup of tea, looped her purse strap on the one wall hook and pulled off her jacket. "How'd you get in? What are you doing here? Get out of my chair." She might as well spill everything out at once before he killed her. Murder was the only reason she could think of that he'd drop by.

And if he didn't murder her, she'd be surprised. After all, he'd simply walked into her office, answered her phone, and took over her desk. Murder was the only crime left.

She fought down the urge to swear again. She wasn't mad, she was furious. It wasn't that she could pinpoint why. It was more like her anger was coming from too many reasons to settle on just one. Fury swirled like a tornado in her mind and sitting in the middle of it, all calm and comfortable, was her new neighbor.

He stood, making the office seem even smaller. "You left your computer on. I looked at the Wilsons' potential homes. If I were you, I wouldn't even bother showing them the one with a tree in it. Howard Wilson said he uses a walker so he'd have trouble moving around in a living room full of branches."

Dakota was starting to shake with anger. She'd spent the past five years hiding all her emotions and now they were exploding inside her.

Blade Hamilton walked around to the front of her desk and sat down on a stack of flyers. "While I was waiting, I ordered a few things online since it looks like I'm going to need more than one change of clothes. I had them overnighted here because I probably won't be home during the day and they can't deliver them to my house because the bridge is out."

When she just glared at him, he added, "Oh, I forgot to tell you. I have to stay around this area for a while. I got a job."

"I thought you had a job."

"I did. Correction, I do. This is just helping out the sheriff. It's kind of my vacation job."

He folded his arms and leaned his head sideways as he studied her. "Is something wrong with you?"

She thought of yelling, *You. You are the thing that is wrong.* But she just looked into those gray eyes and said, "No, I'm just tired and have a great deal of work to do. If you'll excuse me, I need to get back to my desk." When he didn't move, she added, "I work best alone in my office."

He slowly stood. "Oh, sure. I didn't mean to interrupt. I've just had a busy day and thought it would be nice to see a friendly face."

She grinned a no-teeth smiley-face grin. If he thought of her as a friendly face, the man must have no survival skills.

"Oh, a Dodge Ram I rented is being delivered to the sheriff's office this afternoon, so you don't need to worry about taking me home."

"I wasn't worried," she answered. She hadn't planned on taking him home. After all, the sheriff had driven off with him, so Blade was no longer her problem.

"Unless it rains again, that truck will have no problem crossing the stream or hauling my bike. I borrowed your internet to get a carpenter to go out to give me an estimate on the bridge. Sounds like a nice guy and said he'd start today. He seemed excited about the job. Said he just got laid off yesterday and appreciated any work he could get."

Blade was walking too close to her life. Dakota didn't have that much time or space to call her own. She didn't want this stranger so near, but if he used her computer to make calls and her office as a drop for his clothes, maybe that would help get him gone sooner.

"Fine. The house will be easier to sell if we can get to it. So build the bridge. As soon as you get the place cleaned out, I'll post the property. That should keep you very busy while you're not working your vacation job." She wondered if posting a sign near the highway that said Not Haunted would hurt or help. His place wasn't big, but the land rolled nicely with fruit trees in the low spots out of the wind and wild plum trees so thick a horse couldn't walk through them.

He didn't respond to her last comment. He seemed more interested in staring at her than putting Hamilton Acres up for sale.

"What?" she snapped.

"You ever think of wearing your hair down?"

"No."

He shrugged and added, "I'm glad you finally ditched the jacket. You look professional enough without it."

She noticed his leather jacket on her chair. "I see you're back to being a biker."

He smiled. "Leather is the only thing to wear when you ride. Maybe you'll understand that one day if you decide to take a ride with me."

"Not a chance. I'm one of those practical women who keeps both feet on the ground." Even if she'd wanted to, Dakota couldn't risk it.

She began checking her mail. He seemed to have finally run out of anything to say now they'd discussed her business, his truck, and both their wardrobes.

The air stilled in the room as they both waited. Finally, he broke the silence. "If you'll loan me your keys one more time, I'll go have your pickup washed."

"It's not necessary. I'll do it later."

He leaned closer. "I want to. You've been real nice to me. I'd like to pay you back a little, and I've got a few hours before I'm scheduled to be at the sheriff's office."

She looked up, wondering if people always kept him at a distance. If he traveled all the time, stayed in hotels, worked in unfamiliar cities, he might not have many friends who'd loan him a pickup or offer to let him use their shower. He'd hinted he had no family. Maybe the man really didn't have anyone even to be neighborly to him.

Standing up, she walked back around her desk and opened the glass door for him. "All right. The keys are in the truck. But don't be gone long. The Wilsons might be on their way."

"How are you going to get them in the truck if he's on a walker?"

"I always have buyers follow me. It's a small town. They won't get lost." She raised her hand to wave goodbye but he caught her fingers in a gentle hold that surprised her.

It reminded her of the first time she'd held a boy's hand in middle school. Casual, but silently saying so much.

"Anything else I can do?" His voice lowered a bit. "I got time to kill."

The urge to hit him came to her mind. He must be up to something. His words sounded practiced, like when a salesperson says, "Let me know if there is anything else I can do," even though you both know you'll never see them again.

What was wrong with her? He was being nice. Too nice, maybe? Confusing her. Maybe he was a con man or something? Serial killers are often thought to be nice guys at first.

"Sure," she said very politely. "Remove that tree branch from the Platt home on Rainy Day Lane. Without the tree in the living room it's just the right size for the Wilsons."

To her shock, he leaned over and kissed her fingertips as if she'd just given him a quest, and then walked out of the office.

Dakota sat at the desk, trying to fit all the pieces of her nerves back together. She'd been polite, even helpful to him, but she hadn't been friendly. Yet when his lips brushed her hand she'd felt his slight touch all the way to her toes.

They barely knew each other. How could she react to his touch? She didn't even like him.

Well, she had slept next to him, but that didn't give him the right to kiss her. However, a kiss on the fingertips wasn't exactly an assault. Probably nothing more than a handshake to him.

Only Blade Hamilton didn't seem like a man who went around kissing women, or even being nice to them. Or even talking to them. Yep, no doubt about it, this stranger was up to something.

She remembered how he looked standing knee-deep in Indigo Lake. He hadn't looked nice then. In his black leather, he could have been the devil himself come to call.

She scrubbed her fingers against the wool of her skirt. He was messing with her mind.

They should have killed him at first sight.

An hour later he was back, her truck clean and full of gas. She thought of asking him why he took so long. He'd had time to drive every street in town twice, maybe three times. The station that had a drive-through car wash was five minutes away, but Dakota didn't really care. She had too much to do this afternoon to visit with him.

"Thanks," she said half-heartedly as she grabbed her purse. "I have to run. The Wilsons are heading this way. They want to see everything so I told them to meet me at the house on Rainy Day Lane. Once they see the worst, the others will look better."

Blade just frowned at her and followed her out. "Better remember to lock the office door."

She turned back. "No one has ever broken in but you, Hamilton." She turned the key and flipped her sign to the out-showing-homes side. "You're not planning to hang around and break in again, are you?"

He followed her to the truck. "No. I was thinking of coming along with you. I've got time. Fire's out. From here on it's mostly paperwork."

"So, you are helping with the sheriff's investigation?"

He raised an eyebrow. "How'd you know?"

"Small town. Word is, you and the sheriff are waiting until the ashes cool enough to pull a body from the barn, or what's left of it. Who do you think set the fires? Did the arsonist kill someone and start the fire to cover it up? Or maybe the guy committed suicide. Or maybe he was just caught in the back of the barn when someone else set the fire."

"We could have used you this morning," he said, not looking at all comfortable discussing a case with someone who was guessing at the facts. He opened the passenger side door of her pickup and climbed in without being invited.

To keep from screaming at him to get lost, Dakota opted to continue guessing. "Or maybe he was killed a while back. Maybe whoever set the fires was simply covering up for an old murder. He might have figured someone would find the body once the ranch was sold." She grinned. "Oh, by the way, as of today everyone is convinced Reid is selling out, not just downsizing."

"Who is 'everyone'?" Blade asked.

"You know, everyone. I went to eat at the café and by the time we left every table was having the same conversation."

She started the pickup and backed out, noticing he'd taken the time to vacuum the seats, which had never been so clean before. "You and the sheriff have got a lot of questions to answer. This case won't be easy to figure out, Hamilton."

"That's what I do for a living. The answer is usually there. All I have to do is work backward." He leaned back as if settling into not only her truck, but her life.

"What makes you think that I wanted you to come with me?"

"I read it in your face, Dakota. You're an open book. You're bored, maybe lonely, definitely looking for something new. I'm guessing you rarely even talk to anyone about anything other than houses. Except maybe Lauren Brigman, the sheriff's daughter. Who, by the way, is way overqualified for the job she's doing."

"How do you know?"

Blade shrugged. "Maybe I looked her up or maybe I visited with two old ladies at a gift store who told me all about everyone in town."

"Everyone?"

He looked her way. "Well, you and Maria. How you work together taking care of your grandmother who lives out back in her own place because you understand that she'd die if she couldn't walk her land. And about Lauren, who you eat lunch with most days. According to the Franklin sisters, both of you spend your lonely lunches wishing you were living another life."

"You're wrong about me and about Lauren. She loves her job as an online newspaper editor and she loves living here. And we go out with friends sometimes, so neither of us is lonely."

He shrugged. "Let me guess. She's a shy, studious type, and if you two do go out more than once a year it's probably for a quick dinner because you have to be home before dark. She lives alone, just as you would if you didn't feel you had to take care of Maria. Lauren probably sleeps with her cat like you do and the main topic of conversation between the two of you is the town."

"What makes you say that?" He'd described Lauren exactly. They'd been friends for two years but rarely mentioned anything but the happenings in Crossroads.

They drove in silence for a few blocks. He didn't answer her and she wasn't sure she wanted him to.

"You don't know me, Hamilton," she whispered. "I don't feel like I have to take care of Maria. When we were growing up she always took care of me. In a lot of ways she still does."

"Why don't you call me Blade?" he said, keeping his voice as low as hers.

"I haven't decided if I even like you enough to call you a friend."

"Maybe you don't, Dakota. We don't have to be friends, but I know you want me to kiss you. I can see it in those beautiful brown eyes. Anyone ever tell you that you have the kind of eyes a man could get lost in?"

"No. And I don't want to kiss you." In truth, she hadn't really thought about it, but she had thought about touching him. All morning she'd wondered how it would feel to let her fingers slide down his wet chest.

"Look, Dakota, I'm a traveler and will be all my life. It's who I am. Roots aren't for men like me. In a few weeks I'll be gone, out of your life. I don't have time to play games or try to become friends, but I do make it a point to never lie. Why don't we skip all the dancing around? I'm attracted to you and would enjoy spending some time with you." He looked out the window as if remembering all the times he'd said this line before. "I can't promise love or even hanging around for a season, but I can promise when we walk away we'll both be smiling."

She fought the urge to stop the pickup and slug him. Or, better yet, shove him out of the cab, then run over him a few times.

He must have some kind of learning block. Love dyslexia. She didn't want to hook up or have an affair or try a slam-bam-thank-you-ma'am thing. Deep down she believed love wasn't something you did, it was something you felt. This traveler would never understand that.

"That must be them," he said in a normal voice.

"Who?"

"Reta and Howard Wilson. He's getting his walker out of that van."

Dakota had forgotten all about where she was going. The house! When she slammed on the brakes she almost rammed the pickup parked beside the house. Two men were loading up logs while two more hammered a window into place.

Hamilton jumped out of the pickup and hurried to help Mr. Wilson.

Dakota ignored both the workmen and Mr. Wilson as she sat, clenching the wheel in a death grip, and trying to stop her mind from whirling.

No one had ever suggested an affair to her like it was nothing more than a business deal. He made no promise except that they'd walk away smiling. He wasn't promising anything. Not love or forever or even tomorrow. He would so *not* make it into one of Maria's romance novels.

Leaning her head on her knuckles she tried to think. He was right about one thing: she was attracted to him. And she didn't want to go into middle age without ever having a lover. The few guys she'd dated in high school didn't count. They didn't know any more than she did about making love. And college hadn't taken her much further.

She was twenty-five and didn't know firsthand what he was offering, exactly. Even her sex dreams were only rated PG-13.

She had a feeling Blade Hamilton had a great deal of this kind of experience. He probably had no trouble connecting with a woman in every town. He probably used the same line on them. It was too simple, too honest not to work. He probably changed women like people change number settings on a bed.

But it wouldn't work on her. The thought crossed her mind that maybe the way Hamilton planned to kill her was to simply break her heart.

She wouldn't allow that. She couldn't. She had responsibilities.

As she stepped out of her truck, she noticed two things were missing. One, the tree branch that had crashed through the front window was now driving away in pieces in the bed of a pickup.

And two, Hamilton and the Wilsons seemed to have vanished.

Dakota snapped her mind back to reality and tried to focus. No wonder she had trouble making it in the real estate world.

She couldn't keep up with her clients and one of them was on a walker.

Since the front door was open she decided to try there first. The living room was empty, but the guys putting in the window had made an effort to clean up. With the tree branch out of the way, the picture window would have a great view of the sunset.

"I know it's small," Hamilton's voice came from the back of the house, "but so will be your taxes and bills. This place will cost almost nothing to heat and cool, plus it wouldn't take much to build a patio off the back and on nice days it'll be like having another whole room."

Dakota followed his voice.

"The house has a great flow, and with just the two of you it seems to be about the right size." Hamilton turned and caught her stare. "Oh, I'm sorry, folks, I didn't know my girl was back. She was delayed. Probably tied up thinking about another offer."

Reta Wilson grinned at Dakota. "We love this place, dear. It's just what we were looking for."

"Any chance there's a golf course around?" Howard asked.

Mrs. Wilson glared at him. "No more golf, Howard, and that's final."

He glanced at Dakota and blinked a smile. "I fell out of the golf cart three months ago. Broke two bones in my left leg. The wild times are over. Reta says my new retirement hobby is building birdhouses."

Dakota reminded herself to be an agent. She pointed out all the highlights of the house and how, with an addition of one wall, the extra bedroom that ran the entire back wall of the house could be transformed. A workshop for him and a quilting space for her.

"What with the hospital bills, we can't afford much of a remodel," Howard offered, "and birdhouses are pretty much the limit of my skills."

"I'll be happy to get a few estimates." Blade jumped into the conversation as if he belonged. "I know a few guys who can do the work. In fact they dropped what they were doing and came over to put the window in."

Mentally she made a note to advise the Wilsons to offer a little lower to cover the cost of the wall. The owner would jump at any offer since the house had sat empty for months. She'd also pay for the window repair out of her commission. It would only cost a few hundred and she stood to make thousands.

Dakota also named a few things they might want to ask to be updated before the sale and promised to ask for a price break if the owner didn't want to bother doing them himself.

Fifteen minutes later, she and Blade walked out with the Wilsons, who were already planning how they'd arrange their furniture in the small house.

Hamilton smiled at her and she couldn't help but smile back. A sale! She'd finally broken the dry spell.

Hamilton shook hands with Howard. "I'm sorry, folks, but I have to get back to work. Dakota will take care of you. I'm a deputy sheriff here in town so don't speed on your way back to Plainview."

When she raised an eyebrow, he leaned over and kissed her cheek, but his words were for the Wilsons. "If you two don't mind giving Dakota a ride back to her office, I'll catch up with her later."

Dakota thought of arguing, but Reta and Howard were already leading her to their van. When Hamilton started her pickup she realized she'd left the keys in the ignition. The new town deputy was stealing her truck.

"Your man's nice," Reta giggled. "And not bad looking."

Dakota thought of saying he wasn't her man, but she just smiled, thinking of how she'd kill him later.

twelve

Lauren hurried up the long circular steps to Tim's place. When they'd been kids, the home was a colorful mixtures of shapes, like the lake house had been built of Lego blocks with each one a different primary color. Now the outside was painted the sandstone colors of the rocky ribbons that striped the canyon walls down toward the lake. The home blended into its surroundings, almost disappearing to anyone above looking down.

Tim took his time coming to the door. Not surprising. He often wrote at night and slept during the day. Lauren knocked again.

When the door swung open, Tim was fully dressed and fully alert. He also didn't look surprised to see her. He simply stepped back, held the door wide and waved her in.

"Lucas is in the den."

Lauren walked slowly, trying to decide if she was here as a friend, or a reporter. But, the moment she saw Lucas, she knew she had to be a friend. He looked terrible. He still wore the clothes that had smelled of smoke last night when he'd talked to her on her father's deck.

Only now, his eyes were bloodshot and worry wrinkled his forehead.

"You may need a lawyer," she said as she stood in front of him. "Pop wants to question you."

"I am a lawyer and I've already heard I'm on his list to question."

Lauren sat down next to him. "It's probably only routine."

Tim sat on the other side of Lucas. "No, it's not, L. One of the cowhands called Lucas an hour ago to say that the sheriff has clues indicating that Lucas set the first fire. And whoever set the first fire probably set the other one."

"What clues?"

"I was the first one there. That's the clue."

Tim shook his head. "If you had set the fire, you wouldn't have rushed over to look at your work."

"What are you going to do?" She laced her fingers with Lucas's. "Do you want me to go with you?"

"That won't be necessary, but thanks." His words came fast and cold.

"But I know you weren't there when the fire went up. All I'd have to say was that I was with you and then you wouldn't be a person of interest to them."

"Or," Tim tried again since no one seemed to be listening to him, "the sheriff might think you both set the fires. A kind of Bonnie and Clyde thing."

Neither looked at him.

Lucas stood and stared down at her as if he were memorizing her face. His tired gaze told her he had the weight of the world on his shoulders. "Don't say a word, Lauren. If you do, I'll deny it. I don't want you involved in this mess."

"But what else can we do? You and I both know you didn't set the fires."

"I can go down to the county office and see what evidence

they have. I'll simply say I was driving by. That's why I was the first one there."

Lauren couldn't move. Couldn't breathe. Her gut told her there was more that Lucas wasn't telling her. He knew something else…about the fires, or maybe about the body.

Before she could think of anything to say, Tim joined Lucas in the center of the room. "I'll drive you to the sheriff's office," he said as he put his hand on Lucas's shoulder. "I don't know what's going on, buddy, but I want you to understand I'm on your side."

"No. Not this time, Tim. I have to do this alone." Lucas pulled away. "I'll go clean up, tell my parents not to worry, then I'll walk into the sheriff's office alone. I don't want either of you involved."

Lucas kept his hands at his side as he glared at her as if he'd just lost something dear to him and there would be no going back at this point. "Stay away from me, Lauren. Goodbye."

Lauren stared as Tim walked Lucas to the door. She could hear his footsteps on the winding walk outside the door. Then nothing. No farewell kiss. No simple "I love you." Nothing.

She moved to where Tim still stood by the open door. "I don't understand. Lucas didn't do this. Why would he cut us out of his life?"

Tim pulled her against his side. "I know that he wouldn't set the fires and so do you, but I wouldn't be surprised if he confesses to something he didn't do to protect another."

She could hear Lucas's old pickup pulling away but she couldn't move. Lucas might confess to a crime he didn't commit. It made no sense. Lucas never lied. He was the one totally honorable person she'd ever known.

She'd been with him on Kirkland land when the first fire started. She was the only one who could swear he didn't do it and he'd told her to stay out of it.

All the world went silent as she curled into Tim's arms. Tears silently dripped down her face, but she didn't cry out. She felt like she'd just witnessed all her might-have-beens die.

Reporting the news didn't matter. Nothing mattered. Lucas, who'd worked so hard all his life to make something of himself, might just toss it away, and she had no idea why.

As the tears slowed and her breath finally stopped coming in gulps, she realized something. Guilty or innocent, Tim O'Grady had stood beside Lucas no matter what he planned to do.

But she wouldn't. She planned to fight, even if she had to fight Lucas for the answer. She pulled a few inches away and looked up at Tim. "I don't know about you, but I'm not staying away."

Tim grinned. "That thought never crossed my mind. Maybe the best way to help Lucas is to find out what happened." He raised his hand.

She placed her hand, palm to palm, against his. A silent oath they'd done since they were kids. "We do this."

He nodded. "We do this, all we can, for as long as it takes, till we find the truth."

"Agreed."

This time, somehow, she'd save him, even if she had to break Lucas Reyes out of her father's jail.

thirteen

———

By the time Dakota finished the paperwork on the Platt house on Rainy Day Lane, she felt like she'd known the Wilsons for years.

Reta seemed to think she needed to carry the conversation while Dakota worked.

"Howard was in the army when we married. Best-looking sergeant I'd ever seen. Then, when he got out, he drove a bread truck most of our married life. I worked off and on at part-time jobs until our daughters grew up." She patted Howard on the knee. "We had some grand times with the girls. I thought I'd babysit the grandkids, but the two girls fell for army men just like their mother. One is in Germany and the other's in DC."

Howard finally added, "I told Reta if we downsized, we could swing a visit to each daughter's family for a month every year. Since they move with each new assignment, there is a good chance we'll finally get to see the world." He looked at his bride of forty years. "She don't care about the travel. She just wants to see the grands."

"Oh, you know you're just as crazy about them as I am,"

Reta added. "He swears every new one is the prettiest baby he's ever seen."

These two might be old and round as two matching salt and pepper shakers, but Dakota envied them. They had something special. Something that would take a lot longer than two weeks to build.

She handed them the offer for the Platt house to sign and waited, thinking how grand it would be to travel with some-one so close to you that you could read each other's thoughts.

But that dream wasn't for her. Who would take care of Maria and Grandmother if she left? Grandmother had gone wild in her old age, or *free* as she called it. Maria spent her days daydream-ing about Tall, Dark and Handsome stepping out of the pages of one of her romance books and into her life.

Grandmother! Dakota hadn't heard from her since Hamilton had appeared. She often spent days without checking in, but Da-kota didn't want her frightened when she discovered he'd been on their property. As soon as possible, she needed to find the old lady and tell her about him. Only, finding Grandmother was never easy. After her only child, Dakota's mother, died, she'd begun to roam the canyons around their place.

Most people her age wanted to knit or quilt. Grandmother wanted to become one with the land. Her *shichu* had a mule named Patience and two dogs that looked just alike named Pete and Repeat. The dozen chickens who nested in her barn every night provided them with more eggs than they could eat, but Grandmother refused to call them hers. She claimed they were wild birds who simply liked to live with her.

Grandmother's two dogs were too lazy to bark or follow her, but Patience walked behind her carrying the baskets as she col-lected wild plums.

Dakota figured Grandmother believed if she ever slowed down, death would catch up with her. The old girl might be wrinkled, but she was still healthy and fiercely independent in her little cabin a hundred yards behind their main house.

She came in to visit with Maria sometimes while Dakota was at work, and she'd eat a meal with them now and then. For her, the day of the week wasn't important, only the season.

Once, a doctor asked Dakota if she worried that Grandmother, well into her eighties, might be losing her mind. Dakota answered that she doubted it. Grandmother was no more or less crazy than she'd always been.

Growing up, Maria sometimes told Dakota stories about grandmothers who played with their grandchildren or took them for ice cream. Their *shichu* taught them how to make traps and howl at the full moon. Her stories were never bedtime stories, but more stay-awake-all-night stories. When Dakota had needed her all those months when Maria was in the hospital, Grandmother never left the land to offer help.

When Maria came home, Grandmother began leaving food on the porch. Homemade rabbit stew. Bushels of apples, apricots, and wild plums. Maria couldn't stand for the fruit from the trees her ancestors had planted to go to waste, so she taught herself to can without the light.

Cooking had always been her passion, and losing her sight hadn't taken that away.

Somehow, as the Wilsons told Dakota their life story, she began to look at her own. By the time they left and she'd faxed the offer, she was deep into thinking about where her life was headed. Maybe she was more like her grandmother than she thought. They were both wandering in their own way.

She thought about Blade's offer. A two-week lover would be something different. A path she'd never gone down before, but she feared it would be a trail to nowhere.

About four o'clock Hamilton brought back her truck. He simply walked in and handed her the keys without saying a word. He looked bone tired.

At the door, she caught up to him. "You okay?"

His smile didn't reach his eyes. "I'm fine. Just dealing with a mess at the sheriff's office. I'm used to working fires or bomb threats but this is different. This time we may be working a murder investigation and everyone wants to point the finger at someone else."

Her phone rang.

"Wait." She pointed at him. "Let me take this call and I'll drive you back."

"I can walk," he said as she answered her phone.

Three minutes later she tracked him down a block away. He was walking slow, his head down, so deep in thought that he didn't glance at her when she pulled up beside him.

She had to put the truck in Park and scoot across the old bench seat to roll the window down. "Get in!" she yelled as she tried to pull her bunched up skirt down over her knees.

He didn't argue. He just climbed in. "I said I could walk. It's only…"

Hamilton stopped in midsentence, obviously noticing her wool skirt that had just become a mini.

"Nice legs." His grin was wickedly crooked.

"Shut up." She slid back and the show ended.

He shrugged. "Did you pick me up just to yell at me, Elf?"

"I told you not to call me Elf."

He grinned. "You did pick me up just to yell at me. Things must be really dead in this town. I guess the one stoplight doesn't cause much road rage so the locals just pick on—"

She broke in. "I sold the Platt house. The owners accepted the offer. All they have to do is fax the paper back and it's a done deal. They agreed to everything, even the small things you suggested the Wilsons put in. New oven and countertop. New handicap toilet. They don't want to fix or paint anything, but they said they'd pay for whatever minor repairs needed to be done."

This time his smile was real. "That's great. We sold a house and you got them a super deal. I'm proud of you."

She drove right past the sheriff's office and noticed a huge blue Dodge Ram parked out front. "I called and left the Wilsons a message to contact me, but we've got to celebrate right now. You really did help with the sale and I owe you a bonus. Ten minutes and I'll bring you back to the sheriff, but right now I'm buying you a chocolate-dipped cone."

He didn't say anything but she thought she saw his shoulders relax a little. "You should just show me those legs again and I'd call us even."

She frowned at him but before she could open her mouth, he added, "I know, shut up."

He looked out the window. "I guess we're back to square one."

They drove through the take-out window and picked up the ice cream, then parked at the back of the lot. One wooden light pole and a barbed wire fence were all that stood between them and open land for as far as they could see.

"You parking at the edge of town, Elf, so you can take advantage of me?" he asked.

She rolled her eyes, telling him without words that he'd never get that lucky.

He gave up talking as he watched how she ate her chocolate-coated ice cream.

She finally paused long enough to rejoin the conversation. "Pretty much every parking lot that doesn't face one of the two highways in town faces the edge of town. We're not a very dense settlement." She pulled a bite of the chocolate off with two fingers. "I loved these things when I was a kid. My dad used to call them Brown Derbys."

"I love watching you eating that thing but I'm not really an ice cream kind of guy."

She looked up from her dessert into gray eyes staring at her as if she would be his next course. She found the look a bit frightening in its intensity, but sexy as hell. If those wolf eyes got any hotter, he'd probably melt her ice cream.

"Try it, Hamilton, you might like it."

He'd just been holding his Brown Derby and the tiny crack where the chocolate almost met the cone was beginning to drip melted ice cream on his fingers.

She fought the urge to lick the tip of his finger just to see what he tasted like.

He took a bite and chocolate exploded, sending a waterfall of ice cream onto his hand.

Suddenly, they were both laughing and trying to clean up the melting mess off his clothes with the tiny napkins that came with the treat.

"This is great." He licked some of the chocolate off his hand.

She looked at him with chocolate on his cheek. "You've never had a dipped cone?"

"Nope." He took another lick. "I've seen them on signs but I never thought they looked worth trying."

She leaned over and wiped the chocolate from his cheek. "Hamilton, you're a puzzling man. First, you say you're only staying two weeks and then you hire half a dozen cowboys to build you a bridge to a house you don't even want."

"I just called the same carpenter who got rid of the tree at the Platt house. He said he could finish the bridge in three days with the help of a few friends, and I got the feeling they could use the work."

Blade's wolf-gray eyes studied her and for a second she felt like the prey in the sight of a predator.

He leaned a few inches closer, making the cab of the pickup seem smaller. "You keeping up with me, Elf? I know I didn't mention the extra help when I brought back your keys."

"No. That carpenter's sister just called me to see if you also need a plumber. Her husband was one of the hands who got laid off at the Bar W. Cowboys do ranch work because they love it, but most take on other jobs. That carpenter is named Jerry Cline. He married my best friend right out of high school."

"More information than I need to know," he said as he tossed his empty cone into the trash can five feet beyond his window. "But, since you're friends, tell her to have her husband go to work. The whole place will probably need replumbing."

"You can eat the cone, you know," she said as she took a bite of hers.

"You can?" He leaned over and closed his fingers around her wrist, then slowly pulled the hand holding her cone to his mouth and took a bite.

She forgot what they were talking about. If his hand hadn't been holding hers steady, she would have dropped the last of her ice cream.

Dakota just stared as he moved closer.

"Mind if I taste yours?" His eyes seemed to be sending a completely different request.

"I don't mind, but I usually don't share…"

His mouth touched hers and the tip of his tongue brushed the bottom of her lip, and then he whispered, "You taste like chocolate. I could learn to like this bonus."

Dakota closed her eyes and gave in to the kiss. His lips were cold at first and his gentle kiss sent a shiver down her spine. She opened her mouth slightly and he began to taste her. The world slowed and her senses came alive. She could feel the warmth of him as his arm circled just below her breasts and his kiss melted into passion.

His hand slid beneath her jacket and tugged her tighter against him. "Let me warm you up, honey."

Maybe it was the fact that she didn't know him well enough to call him by his first name or maybe it was the way he said "honey," like he'd called a hundred other girls that, but Dakota woke up from her trance.

"Get out."

Confusion flashed in his gray eyes for a second as he moved away, then anger flared. "You're the one who told me to get in. Make up your mind. I don't deal with crazy and, Elf, you're the definition of it."

He was gone before she could think of an answer. She gunned the engine and took off, having no idea where she was going.

Of course he was right. She was crazy. She was always kind, always nice, ask anyone. He seemed to be the lottery winner for every mean thing she would say this year.

Maybe it was the curse. Or she might be allergic to him. Or maybe the way she felt about him scared her to death. Passion all mixed up with need and longing. Attraction drew her to him and logic pushed her away.

She didn't have time for complicated. Her life was overloaded now with dreams and a job and responsibilities.

She couldn't handle more. Not even for a two-week affair.

But what-ifs were already taking root in her mind—not to mention a few other parts of her body.

fourteen

Blade jogged the few blocks back to the sheriff's office. He couldn't believe a short elf of a woman had him off his game. It wasn't like him. He could usually read the signals.

Since his college days, he'd always considered himself easygoing where women were concerned. He'd never chased one, or run from one, for that matter. In fact, they'd usually been the ones to suggest hooking up. He liked to keep it casual and easy. Always tall girls, usually blondes. Then, after college, he seemed into strong women with high-powered careers. No long-term plans, no getting too involved in each other's lives. No lovers with baggage. No fights when it was over. No cats!

He was honest. Straightforward. Dakota didn't seem to appreciate that. The ground under him when she was near was about as solid as the chocolate on that ice cream. It would settle after they made love a few times. *If* they made love. Hell, he didn't even think she liked him.

"Forget her," he mumbled to himself. "I don't need complicated right now." He had a house to get rid of and a life to get back to. He'd fix the place up good enough to sell while helping a competent sheriff collect evidence, and then leave.

Blade walked into the sheriff's office, fighting down a grin. Man, she tasted great with chocolate on her lip. It would take a long time to forget Dakota Davis.

Sheriff Dan Brigman glanced up from his desk and handed Blade a stack of papers. "You ready to get to work? Not near as exciting as being a special agent, but I could really use the help."

"I'm ready, but until we solve this crime, how about you call me deputy. I'm working for the county while I'm on vacation."

The sheriff nodded. "Glad to have you around. We need to start asking questions. I've had three people from the ranch who didn't know the second barn door had a lock."

The sheriff stood and began to pace. "I know it's a little point. One lock on one barn, but it doesn't fit. The Bar W has six barns total. The two with hay burn. The four with expensive equipment don't burn. Dice said Reid Collins planned to put cars in the barn that was locked but who buys the locks six months before he buys even one car."

Blade moved into the puzzle. He loved puzzles. "What did Reid say when you woke him up and told him about the barn fires?"

Dan stopped pacing and said slowly. "He had a hangover, a bad one. He didn't look surprised when I told him. It was more anger, like he was losing control of something or someone."

Lowering his voice, Dan added, "After he threw a bottle of brandy across the room, his shoulders relaxed and he turned to face me again. For a moment I saw fear in his eyes. He backed away, looking around as if he thought someone else might be behind me, watching, listening. If I was guessing, I'd say he was far more afraid of who set the fires than he was about the barns burning."

"Our one clue," Blade said. "If we find the answer to that

question, it might solve both the question of who set the fires and why one body was trapped inside."

"Not much of a lead to go on so far." The sheriff rubbed his forehead. "With your help we might find another during the interviews. I'm glad you're here, Blade. I've got folks lining up to talk about Reid Collins, but I want to start with people who were on the ranch when the fires flared."

At least that made one person in Crossroads who wanted him here, Blade thought. "I'll start with the guys out front on the bench waiting, unless you think the cowboys will open up more to you?"

Brigman shook his head. "I don't think they'll open up to either of us. It's not their way. But they will give us the facts if we ask the right questions, and then maybe we can piece everything together."

"What's your gut feeling, Sheriff?"

"A man was killed in that second fire, and the lock on that back door to the barn suggests it might not have been an accident. Maybe he was put in there already dead, or trapped in the back. Either way, we're dealing with murder. Right now I'm thinking our most likely suspect is one of three men, and I wouldn't want to arrest any of them."

Blade waited. He might not know this sheriff, but he knew lawmen. If Dan was going to talk to anyone it would be him. They might wear different badges, but they were brothers in this fight.

The sheriff lowered his voice. "First, there is Dice, the old cowboy you met, who admitted he was out in the area last night. And he'd just been let go from a job he probably had for fifty years. Then, there's Lucas Reyes, who doesn't have an alibi, and he grew up on the ranch. And he was the first one there after the firemen arrived. Then there is the owner, Reid Collins. The housekeeper said he was drunk, but was he sober enough to light a match? All three men know the land well enough to stay out of sight."

"Add the dozen other cowboys who were on the ranch packing up gear when the barns went up in smoke." Blade had a list of names he'd asked to stop by the station. He'd question every one of them. "Also, it was late, so pretty well anyone could have driven onto the land and started the fires just for the fun of it. I've seen men who will light up a forest just to watch the burn."

The sheriff shook his head. "Whoever did this wanted to make a point."

"Was there anyone on the land who didn't belong?"

Brigman nodded. "The new ranch manager Reid hired. Simon Rarrie. A few of the men he brought in to close the ranch have records. I had Pearly run their names. From their employment records I'd guess they are not used to working cattle, either. One of the day workers said they planned to use four-wheelers to round up the last few strays, but from the looks of them, I'd say they were there to make sure everyone left without any trouble."

Blade nodded once. "I asked the new ranch manager to come in for a talk and he said he didn't have time."

"What's the big hurry on closing? I'd think closing a ranch would take at least a few weeks." Dan frowned. "Dice said up until two days ago the closing was mostly rumor. Then, he said, something happened and it was in full swing. You think the barns burning was the turning point?"

"Maybe, but I doubt it. There were still half a dozen cowhands around the place."

"When we find out why the ranch has to be closed so quickly, maybe we'll find out who wanted to do so much damage to kick it off." Sheriff Brigman smiled. "I'll tell the new manager he can drive in today or I'll come out to get him tomorrow morning and he'll be riding in the back seat with cuffs on. He'll be spitting nails to keep from cussing me out."

The front doors of the county offices opened and Blade heard several men's voices. "Sounds like the stampede is here."

Blade gave a quick salute with the corner of his stack of papers. "It's time to go to work."

Pearly showed Blade the way to an empty courtroom on the second floor and he sat up at one of the long mahogany tables. One by one she sent in every hired hand who'd been on the ranch last night. Cowboys, cooks and the new men sent in to close the ranch.

The cowboys were tanned and polite. The new men acted bothered that they had to answer questions. None of them wanted to talk to Blade, but that didn't stop the questions from coming.

He jotted down their answers, detail after detail, but it was their body language he studied.

Despite their politeness, Blade could tell that the cowboys were angry and tired. None seemed to know much. The fires had started. There was no way of saving the two barns. The fire department did a great job keeping them from spreading. Yes, they'd miss the job. No, they didn't care much for the boss.

The new men were not as friendly. Less interested in talking. They all seemed in a hurry. Not one met Blade's eyes. Most didn't seem too bright. Two claimed they were hired for security and none could name the directions of the barns from the headquarters.

Three hours later he'd taken statements from a dozen people, and as near as he could guess, half of them were lying.

Only why? And which half?

Pearly opened the door as formally as if she were the butler at the White House. "Deputy Hamilton," she whispered in a voice anyone on the second floor could have heard. "You've got one more person who was there last night. He's been waiting to talk to you."

"Who?" No one was left on his list.

Pearly straightened. "Lucas Reyes."

"Great." Blade was tired. It had been a long day and he still didn't know where he'd sleep tonight. Dakota wouldn't welcome him back and, unless he wanted to relive a horror film, he didn't plan on sleeping at Hamilton Acres. He might as well work late.

"Send him in. It's already dark, I'll take one more statement." The thought of sleeping in his rented truck or staying in a cheap hotel didn't really appeal to him. Maybe he'd just spread out on one of the court benches.

The man who stepped through the door wasn't a cowboy but a polished professional in a thousand-dollar suit. He walked straight to Blade and offered his hand. "A pleasure to meet you, Agent Hamilton. I admire your service to our country, both in the army and in your current position with the federal government."

Blade stood. Finally, someone who didn't look like he wanted to start a fight. "You were at the Collins ranch last night, Mr. Reyes?" Somehow this guy didn't fit with either group.

"I was. I grew up on that ranch. My father was the foreman until two days ago."

Blade decided this guy must be running for office. Lucas Reyes looked so open and honest Blade would vote for him, and he wasn't even registered in this county.

"You are aware that you are considered a suspect?" Blade couldn't believe he was saying the words to the man before him. Everything about his body language said the guy was honest, even the way he looked directly at Blade.

"I'm aware that Reid Collins said I was probably the one who set the fires. I was one of the first people on the scene of the first fire. I have no alibi."

Blade felt like he was playing chess with an opponent who just moved his king into checkmate position. "I think I should read you your rights and tell you to find a lawyer, Mr. Reyes."

"I am a lawyer. Read me my rights and lock me up. I'm prepared to stay in jail tonight."

"Are you confessing to setting the fires last night?"

"I'm not saying another word." Lucas didn't move. Didn't blink. If they were playing poker, Blade had no idea who was bluffing.

The sheriff broke the silence in the room when he entered. "I'll lock him up, Deputy Hamilton. It might just be the safest place for him tonight." Dan didn't glance at Lucas. His stare remained on Blade. "Why don't you go across the street and order both of you the special for supper? Then, if you're willing, I'd like you to take the first shift watching our new prisoner. I've got to get a few hours' sleep, then I'll relieve you about two."

When Blade turned to Lucas, the lawyer was smiling as if he'd just been invited to stay over.

Blade followed Lucas and the sheriff up the third flight of stairs. The entire third floor consisted of two rooms. The first ten-by-ten room was empty, looking like it served as only a pass-through for a small two-celled jail behind the next door. A wide aisle in the middle separated the two cells. Two old desks formed a table in the center.

Brigman used the table in the aisle space to ask Lucas to empty his pockets. While he patted down the lawyer, Dan said to Blade, "You'll be more comfortable in the empty cell than sitting outside the door at the top of the stairs. There are only two sets of keys for the cells and the two doors leading to the stairs. I'll take one set and you take the other. No one will come inside the building, much less step in here unless either you or I open the doors. Once you throw the dead bolts on both room doors, no one enters until you unlock those doors."

Glancing at the thin mattress in the open cell, Blade shrugged. It looked clean, as did the pillow and white blanket. The rest of the cell was empty except for a metal chair and a toilet with a sink on top. The bare quarters right now looked far more inviting than the truck. "Reminds me of a few hotels I've slept in." Blade nodded once. "I'll be fine here. And, Sheriff, don't worry about coming back until morning. I've got no bed waiting for me at Hamilton Acres and no bridge to get across the stream even if I did. I'll be fine here till morning."

"Fair enough. I'll be back to relieve you at seven. After you get back from the café, I'll say good-night. You'll have my number. If you need me, I can be back here in less than five minutes."

Blade followed orders. Collected two specials from the café across the street and his leather jacket from his rented Dodge. He took the time to swing by the truck stop for twenty dollars' worth of snacks and a six-pack of root beer. On a whim he also bought a cheap travel chess set.

An hour later when the sheriff finally left the building, Blade stood at the top of the stairs and listened for any sounds or movements.

None. The place was silent.

Stepping into the first room he locked the first door, and turned the heavy-duty dead bolt. Then he did the same to the second door, to the room with the two cells. No one, not even the sheriff with his key, would pass through the doors until Blade flipped the dead bolts.

Someone at some time had thought out this system to not only keep the prisoner in jail, but to protect the area from anyone trying to break in. Which seemed strange. Why would people break into jail? He made a mental note to ask the sheriff about it.

Lucas Reyes hadn't said a word while the sheriff had talked. He'd handed over everything in his pockets—his college ring, his tie and his suit jacket, as if he were settling in for a long stay. He now stood tall as he stared out the one barred window in his cell. His take-out tray had barely been touched.

Blade studied him. They must live very different lives, but Lucas was the same size, almost the same build as Blade. Maybe storming through a courtroom wasn't all that much different from being dropped in the middle of a forest fire. Both of them had been tested and the steel in their backbones showed it.

"You didn't do it, did you?" Blade said his thoughts aloud. "But there is some other reason you're here, isn't there?" He stared into Lucas's dark eyes and guessed he'd just spoken the truth.

"I'm not talking to you or anyone else. As a lawyer, I'd advise you to keep me in jail for as long as legally possible."

"I don't know what's legal or illegal, Mr. Reyes. I only know about fires, and right now I don't have a clue about the one on that ranch where you grew up. You must know the place. You could be a great help."

Lucas's dark brown gaze stared at Blade, reminding him of frozen chocolate sauce. Hell, everything, even in the jail, reminded him of Dakota. The dark night, as black as her hair. She was crawling into his brain even when he didn't have time to think about her.

Maybe she really was trying to kill the last Hamilton, but first she wanted to drive him mad.

He'd offered her a good time and she'd acted like he'd insulted her.

He didn't like short women. He liked tall blondes. She was going to pay for making him feel half-nuts. When he did make love to her, he'd do it so completely that she'd miss him, think of him, ache for him, for the rest of her life.

"You all right, Officer Hamilton?" Lucas asked. "I'm the one in jail, but you're the one who doesn't seem to be taking it too well."

Blade pulled out the chess set. "How about a game? I don't feel any more like talking than you do."

Lucas smiled for the first time. "I'm good at chess."

"I have no doubt." Blade shoved the center table up against the bars of Lucas's cell.

Lucas pulled his one chair to the bars. "When I win the first game, I get the bag of Cracker Jack." He glanced over at the snack pile Blade had accumulated.

"Fair enough. You can have your pick, but I get the M&M'S. I've grown fond of chocolate lately."

Lucas straddled his chair. "I deduced that already, Hamilton. You've got chocolate spotted all over your shirt. I thought maybe your last bar fight was with a Snickers."

"No. With an ice cream cone, but I don't want to talk about that, either."

Lucas laughed. "I can see why. You obviously lost."

They began to play. Two strangers learning each other by the way each moved in a game so old that King Arthur's knights might have played.

fifteen

———

Wind blew her midnight hair skyward like thin tree branches as Dakota walked the edge of Indigo Lake. Moisture whispered in the breeze, promising another storm, but she didn't turn homeward. From this one point, she could look across the water to Hamilton's place.

No truck. No lights. No one home. Hamilton hadn't come back to his place.

Yet she felt, more than saw, something moving low over his land. Maybe a coyote hunting or a bobcat heading back to one of the caves a mile away along the canyon edges. The landscape seemed alive in the cloudy night.

"You see it too." A voice whispered from behind her.

She didn't bother turning around. "Grandmother, stop sneaking up on me."

The old woman laughed. "If you had more than an eighth of Apache blood, I would never be able to sneak up on you. The Irish mix weakened you, child. Then when your mother married a soldier, who said he didn't know where his people came from, you added water into your veins. How can your father's soul rest if he does not know his land?"

"My father is not dead. At least not that I know of. He just left us the month after I was born, remember?"

Dakota thought of mentioning that her grandmother's father was Irish and she herself had married a short Irishman everyone called Hap.

If Grandmother took the time to look, she'd see that her granddaughters were far more Irish than Apache. But arguing with Grandmother was like spitting into the wind. Grandmother would either call her Apache names or put an Irish curse on her.

"What do you see, Grandmother, with your Apache eyes?" Dakota whispered.

"He who moves in the trees near the old house is not an animal, but he is more wild than human I think." She closed her eyes. "He will battle with the ghosts tonight if he does not leave soon. Perhaps the spirits will take him underground, never to be seen again."

Dakota glared at the outline of the short old woman wrapped in an army-green blanket. Grandmother might be three feet away, but sometimes it felt like she was a hundred years in the past. She never talked in facts, but always danced around every question. "You heard the son of Henry Hamilton come to the house. Henry is dead. His son owns the land now."

"I smelled the new Hamilton before I saw him. Knew he was from the line long thought dead even though he'd never stepped foot on their land before yesterday. He has the build of his father and grandfather. I fear he's wild and reckless."

"Maria told you he was here, didn't she? Plus, you probably saw his bike." Grandmother always acted like she had a crystal ball tucked away somewhere beneath her layers of clothes. "I knew she would. Maria always tells you everything."

Grandmother puffed up as if insulted. She crossed her arms

over her chest and stood perfectly still as if waiting for someone to take her picture.

Dakota added, "Did she also tell you that he's only here to sell the place? He's not staying. He told me he was a traveler who wanted no roots."

Grandmother spit on the ground. The old woman's voice was as cold as icicles on tin. "That's the only reason he's alive. He wasn't born here. He's leaving. A man who has no roots cannot hear his own heart beating."

"Stop talking like we live in the 1880s, Grandmother, or the sheriff will come lock you up." Dakota decided that might not be too bad an idea. Her grandmother got five degrees crazier every year, but then again, sanity wasn't a strong family trait.

Her mother used to say that she grew up with two uncles who came home from the Second World War with their brains scrambled. One thought he was dating the moon. He'd go out every bright night and talk to it. The other liked to sleep on the warm county road after dark like a rattlesnake might. One night he got pancaked by a bread truck that took a wrong turn. According to Grandmother, no one wanted to write "Killed by a bread truck" on his headstone, so they wrote, "Died in his sleep."

Dakota turned back to the lake. "Maybe it's just Hamilton moving around over there. It's safer to sleep in the shadow of the trees than in that old house. He may have lost his flashlight, or maybe the batteries are dead."

The old woman shook her head. "What moves there carries death in his pocket. I've watched him for a week now. He hides in the light and only works his evil at night. Some nights, long after midnight, he walks to the road and a black car picks him up. The same car brings him back to hunt in darkness again."

"That makes no sense."

"Not to us, but to evil it might."

Dakota put her arm around her grandmother. "I love you,

Shichu. How about we forget about evil and go inside for some cobbler? Maria made her best ever tonight."

The old woman nodded. "Does it come with beer and bananas on top?"

"That it does. Why not?"

They ate their late-night dessert, and then, when the tiny old woman fell asleep on the couch, Dakota covered her grandmother with a colorful blanket. When she kissed her wrinkled forehead, Dakota decided most people live in their own reality—Grandmother's was just more imaginative than most.

The hours of night seemed endless. Thoughts drifted through Dakota's mind like the shadow that had moved across Hamilton land. She told herself she didn't care where Blade was, but still she worried about him. Maybe someone truly didn't want him on his own land. The Davis women might joke about killing him, but what if his land was being used for something illegal? She'd heard of abandoned farmhouses being turned into meth labs or used as stopover points for human trafficking.

As the night aged, darker thoughts circled in her mind. What if Blade was on the land and he wasn't alone? Drug dealers or men hiding out from the law could have already killed him. Or what if he'd been moving in the house after dark and fallen over something? He could be slowly bleeding out across the lake while she cuddled into her warm bed.

Finally, she drifted into dreams. In the point between dreams and reality, she thought she felt Blade take her hand, and she slowed her breathing and relaxed into sleep.

As sunlight crawled across the tile floor of her bedroom, she awoke to full daylight.

Eight o'clock! She never slept so late and today was the day she had to take Maria into town to put up her jams and jellies at the grocery store. Today, of all days, she needed an early start. She had to load the truck, then drop Maria off at the grocery, walk to her office, work, then wait for a call to go back and get her sister.

Dakota bolted from the bed and ran for the shower, tugging at her tight T-shirt as she ran.

A moment before she reached the bathroom door, she heard Maria say something from the kitchen, but Dakota's mind was still too sleepy to understand.

Opening the door to a warm, foggy world, she blinded herself with the T-shirt that refused to slip over her shoulders.

Her angry words were barely out before she slammed into a very warm, very hard body.

The impact shocked her fully awake and she tugged the shirt down enough to see Hamilton staring at her. He had a towel wrapped around his waist, spots of shaving cream on his face and a slow smile spreading over his lips.

The fog made it seem he'd stepped out of a dream and was not in the real world, in her bathroom, almost in the buff.

"Morning," he said in a low voice. Then, as if he'd done it every morning for years, he leaned down and kissed her soundly.

She tugged the now damp shirt down over her breasts, praying he hadn't noticed her body. Fat chance.

She felt herself melting against his warmth and gave in to the kiss. This was better than any dream she could have imagined.

His hands circled her waist and lifted her up on the counter so they were at eye level. Then, his fingers moved to her back, pulling her so close against him she could feel him breathe.

She could taste the mint from his toothpaste and the hint of soap on his lip. Drops of water from his wet hair dripped onto her cheek as his hands moved over her body. She spread her fingers along his chest, but she couldn't bring herself to push away. The feel of his warm skin was heaven to touch.

Just a moment more, she told herself. Just for a memory.

Maria's voice came from the other side of the bathroom door. "Breakfast is about ready. Grandmother is joining us."

Blade broke the kiss as he dug his hands into Dakota's hair. "I'm looking at what I want for breakfast," he whispered. His gray eyes were dark now, fiery with need.

Dakota couldn't speak. She couldn't even breathe.

He closed his fingers into the tangle of her mane. "I knew your hair would be wild like this." He kissed the corner of her mouth. "I love seeing sleep still in those beautiful eyes instead of daggers usually aimed right at me." He drew her closer, letting her feel each word on her lips. "You fascinate me. It's like you crawled into my brain when I wasn't looking and now every other thought is wondering about you."

With his fists still full of her hair, he kissed her again and she realized all the other kisses she'd had before were nothing compared to this one. Her breath came faster as his chest pressed against hers and the warmth of his body set her on fire. Steam from the shower filled the room, making it seem for a moment that there was no world outside his arms.

Maria's call came again. "Breakfast!"

Dakota closed her eyes, mentally pushing away the best moment she'd ever had as she whispered, "Grandmother is here."

"So?" he said, nibbling on her throat.

She leaned away, stumbled off the counter, and headed toward the door, feeling like she was fighting her needs and him at the same time. "Get dressed." Her voice shook slightly. "Fully dressed before you step out of this room. She's going to explode when she sees you, so try to get mentally prepared."

He caught her hand before she reached for the knob. "First, tell me you're okay with what just happened between us, because you blew my mind."

She met his eyes. "I liked it, but don't look at me that way when you meet Grandmother. In fact, don't look at me at all. Don't even speak to me."

He stared at her a moment as if trying to figure out if this was all a game. "All right, I'll play along, but you have to kiss me goodbye first."

She didn't have time to argue. She leaned in and kissed him on the cheek.

He didn't move but his words reached her. "I'll play whatever game you Davis women are playing, but tonight we play my game."

"Not a chance," she said, as she opened the door and disappeared before he could answer.

Dakota glanced toward the kitchen. Thankfully, Grandmother wasn't on the bar stool. She must be loading the jars.

Dakota ran down the hallway and jerked on some clothes, not caring if they matched. What did it matter? She'd just ordered the only man who'd ever really looked at her not to look at her at all.

She smiled as she combed her wild hair into a knot at the base of her skull. Blade had said he loved her hair. Closing her eyes, she remembered how his gray eyes seemed to drink her in. The moment they'd shared had affected him as deeply as it had her.

She stared into the mirror, trying to see if she'd changed. She'd always thought of herself as passably pretty, but never a woman a man would really desire. Not the way Blade had. Like he couldn't keep his hands, or mouth, off her.

Somehow knowing that one man, even if he was a Hamilton, looked at her that way made her feel different inside.

Of course what was between them wouldn't go any further, but it had been exciting for a moment.

When Dakota walked into the kitchen, Maria was the only one there. She was filling four plates and humming to herself.

"What happened to Grandmother and Hamilton?" An answer of "a fight to the death" wouldn't have surprised her.

"He's helping her load the truck. I made more jams than I usually do this week. Hope Wes will be able to take the extra."

"Wes is so nice he'll buy whatever you bring, Maria."

"He's a good businessman. Stocks my jars close to the front for every person passing through to take home as a souvenir."

Dakota took the middle bar stool. "Then the next time they pass through, they stop and buy double. But, it's not his business sense, it's your product that keeps them coming back."

"Wouldn't they be surprised to know that the top graduate from the best culinary arts school in Dallas makes their jams?" Maria grinned.

Dakota agreed. Maria didn't know that the store owner always stood guard when she was stocking the shelves he'd built to fit her jars exactly. He'd also ordered all his employees to stay out of the way and keep the walk between the side door and her shelves clean. Maria had a guardian angel and she didn't even know it.

"Lately it seems longer and longer before you call me to come get you," Dakota teased.

Maria blushed. "Wes and I have kind of got into a habit of having a cup of coffee after I finish stocking."

Dakota thought of asking what two shy people talk about, but she could guess. Probably the weather.

Grandmother stomped her way into the kitchen and sat down on the first stool she came to. She wore the same men's trousers and flannel shirt she'd had on last night. Her philosophy of dress was simple: unless you had a bad spill or an unfortunate accident, anything you put on should last at least three days and nights. Why bother with changing into pajamas that you'll just change out of at dawn?

Shichu rattled her coffee cup like she thought she was at a café. "I'm so hungry I could eat backward and still get full," she announced.

Maria and Dakota had long ago given up hope on understanding most of the old woman's sayings. Maria just slid her a plate of eggs while Dakota filled up her coffee mug.

"Thought I'd have that Hamilton finish loading. He might

as well make himself useful if he's only going to be here two weeks."

Both girls let out a long-held breath. Blade wasn't lying spread-eagle in the red ant bed.

Maria whispered, "You're not going to kill him, Grandmother?"

"I told him I'd give serious thought to letting him live. If I change my mind, he'll be the first to know."

Hamilton came in, dusting hay off his leather jacket.

He didn't belong here, she thought. Leather jacket, biker boots, collarless shirt, and an ugly green sweater.

He took the stool on the other side of Dakota but didn't even look at her. "Thanks, Maria, for letting me use your shower and for the offer for breakfast. I spent last night in jail."

"Figures," Grandmother grumbled. "Out thieving and murdering, were you, Hamilton?"

"No," Maria laughed, as if she didn't think the comment was serious. "He's watching over a prisoner, Grandmother."

"So he says." Grandmother shoveled a helping of eggs into her almost toothless mouth. "Comes on our land asking favors and the next thing you know he'll be stealing cattle."

"We don't have any cattle, Shichu," both girls said at once. "And Patience would never go with him."

Grandmother shrugged. "If you two hadn't told him we didn't have a herd, he might have spent a few days looking. Keep the man occupied."

Everyone but the old woman laughed. Blade kept his eyes on Maria as she moved her plate to exactly the right place and ate her meal so gracefully no one would ever know she was blind.

He also played with Dakota's knee under the table, which she intended to object to later.

As they finished, Blade fell into the routine of the Davis house. He scraped his scraps into the chicken feed bucket and put his plate in the sink. Grandmother gathered up the bucket for her chickens and a half loaf of bread Maria had wrapped for her. With no goodbye, she walked out the back door, mumbling something about needing to sharpen her knives.

Maria grabbed her coat. "I'm ready, Mr. Hamilton."

"I'll get my briefcase." Dakota jumped into action. She'd forgotten how late they were.

Maria moved toward the door, barely brushing the bar for direction. "Don't hurry, Dakota. We loaded my jars in his truck. Blade is off this morning and said he'd take me in."

"But he doesn't know—"

"I'll tell him. I know the way."

Dakota knew better than to question Maria's judgment. From the time she was able to walk after the accident, she insisted on managing for herself. She would not be handicapped. She set rules and everyone followed them. Nothing in her usual paths. Nothing out of place in her kitchen. No one tried to help her unless she asked for it.

"Great. I could use the extra time." Dakota looked at Hamilton for the first time.

He gave a slight nod as if to say he had this, but his words were casual, "I'll see you in town later."

"No need. When Maria calls for a ride back, I might just come home. I could use a nap. Haven't been sleeping well lately."

"I might have a few deliveries to pick up at your office. Any objection to me dropping by?"

"No. If I'm not there, just break in and make yourself at home."

He brushed her slightly as he passed and walked onto the porch.

Dakota stood at the door and watched as Maria moved down the porch steps.

"Three feet straight ahead," Hamilton said. "Raise your left hand and you're at the truck bed."

Maria followed his directions then moved her hand gently

along the open truck bed, her fingers barely brushing the straw between the boxes. She opened the passenger door and climbed in with a jump.

Hamilton looked back at Dakota. "She's amazing, isn't she?"

Dakota smiled. "She is."

Maria Davis might be blind, but Dakota had no doubt that she knew her way through life far better than her little sister ever would.

sixteen

The sun was high over the town, sparkling off the tin roof of the hardware store and the windshields of passing cars, as if teasing everyone that spring had arrived in February.

But it felt like dark winter in Lauren Brigman's heart as she walked over to her father's office.

When she'd been little, she used to sit on the steps of the county offices and count the cars. Crossroads, Texas, sat on a big X of two highways. East-west. North-south. All those years ago she'd sworn she'd travel every road when she grew up. But she hadn't. She seemed to be one of those people who never learned to pack.

As she walked into the sheriff's office, Lauren realized there was nowhere she'd rather be than this town. She was right on the X, the crossroads, the center of the world.

Pop looked up from his cluttered desk. To her, he'd always be handsome in his pressed uniform. He was one of the true heroes in life. There might be a touch of gray at his temples now and wrinkles in the corners of his eyes, but neither tarnished him. She'd often wondered, when she was a kid, how her mother could have left such a man. Correction, how she could have left *them*. Margaret Brigman had abandoned both husband and daughter for her career goals in Dallas.

Lauren had been five then and thought everything had to make sense. Her pop might not have been able to explain what was happening, but he was there to go through it with her.

Life still didn't make sense, but two things were constant. Her father loved her, and he never stopped asking her questions. "Morning, darlin'," he said with a smile. "You have breakfast yet? If you're here as the press, turn around and walk right back out. If you're hungry, there are doughnuts in the box."

Lauren sat on the only clean corner of his desk. "Pop. The press has a right to know what's going on."

"I don't have any more facts than I did last night."

"You arrested Lucas Reyes."

"I'm only detaining him for questioning. In fact, Lucas told me to lock him up."

"So, he's not your prisoner?"

"Not exactly…" Her pop, the best sheriff in the world, frowned as if he could feel a trick question coming on.

"Then you won't mind me visiting him, as a friend." She held up the cup she'd carried in. "I just brought him coffee."

The sheriff's frown didn't go away. "You're the third friend this morning bringing coffee. I'm beginning to suspect a plot. He's probably upstairs braiding the cups together for a rope now."

Lauren stood. "Let me in to see him before this coffee gets cold. No questions, I promise."

Dan Brigman stood. "All right, but I'm locking you in the jail room with him. I don't have time to keep running up and down two flights of stairs. I've got too much work to do and Pearly's late this morning."

As they climbed the steps, she noticed how tired her father seemed. "You need help, Pop? Hire another deputy. When is the last time you had eight hours' sleep? Or ate a real meal?"

"You're starting to sound like Brandi. And what happened to the no-questions clause to this agreement?"

"That only applies to the guest of the county you have locked up, Pop. About that deputy you need? First, it has to be a real one, not the two-week substitute you hired yesterday. He looks like a biker and doesn't even have an accent. None. Like the guy is from nowhere."

"I'll get around to hiring another. Hamilton is only filling in, and as he's a federal agent, I'm sure he's more than qualified. Deputies are impossible to find or keep around. About the time I advertise for one, interview and get him trained, he moves on to the big cities like Lubbock or Amarillo. They pay better and the work is far more exciting."

"You just miss Fifth Weathers, Pop. It's not likely you'll find another who will fill his shoes."

Pop laughed. "Literally. I think his shoe size was fifteen. Best deputy ever and what did he do? Move one county over to become sheriff." His last sentence came out as if Fifth had committed a crime.

"And he's a great lawman because he trained with you." She bumped her shoulder against his. "What about hiring someone local this time?" she asked as the sheriff unlocked the first door on the third floor.

"I've tried, but haven't had much luck even getting anyone to talk to me about the job. The last local I picked up for smoking pot asked if he could fill out an application while I was booking him. Said he'd be a perfect deputy. He knew every drug dealer for a hundred miles around." Pop grinned at her. "I'm so desperate I considered his offer for a few seconds."

Lauren made a note to put a few lines in *ChatAroundCrossroads* about a job opening. Who knew, maybe other businesses needed help also. Crossroads was getting too big to just ask around when looking for new employees.

They passed through the empty room that had probably been

built for interviews or client-lawyer talks but no one had ever bothered to furnish it.

When Pop opened the second door, he whispered, "I'll be back in ten minutes." He held the door for her, then locked it as soon as she passed into the jail area.

She stepped through the door into a room with a ten-foot square cell on either side of her.

Lucas was standing at the window with his back to her. Tall, dark, lean. She'd always thought of him as good-looking, but in his late twenties he was maturing into a man who seemed cut from a cloth meant for greatness.

Since high school he'd always been in a hurry to make something of himself, and he had. In another ten or twenty years he'd be a judge maybe, or governor.

If he didn't get mixed up in the mess at the Collins ranch.

The bars framed him now as he turned. She couldn't miss the dark stubble along his jaw or the anger in his eyes.

"You shouldn't have come, Lauren."

"I just..." *What?* she thought. Why had she rushed up here this morning? To ask him questions? To make sure he was okay? To demand he say what he'd almost said a minute before they'd seen the glow from the barn fire.

She didn't even know why she'd come. How could she tell Lucas that he mattered so much to her, when she knew he wouldn't return the feelings?

He'd told her not to come. He didn't want her help. He didn't want the alibi she could easily give him. If she told the world that she was with him the night the barns were burned, she'd also have to tell about how she'd seen Lucas knock Reid Collins flat on the ground in anger. Some people might believe that if he was mad enough to hit Reid, he'd probably be mad enough to burn two barns.

Lauren took a step backward. He was right, she shouldn't have come. He must have changed his mind about whatever he'd planned to say to her. The talk he'd promised would never come. This was just her dreaming and him hesitating, as always.

The locked door stopped her steps. For the next ten minutes she was as much a prisoner as he was.

"Leave," he said more calmly.

"I can't," she whispered. "Pop locked me in. Like it or not, you're stuck with me."

He turned his back and continued staring out into the town. "I don't want the coffee, if that's what you brought."

She moved the few feet to a table sitting between the two cells. "I do." Her hand shook a little as she pulled off the lid. "Are you ever going to talk to me, Lucas? Or just spend the next ten minutes mad at me?"

"I'm not mad at you. This just isn't the right time to talk about the future. I don't want you involved in what's going on. You have no idea what a mess this is. I tried to help once and only made it worse."

Studying him, she said. "Oh, right. I see it now. You were trying to knock some sense into Reid when you hit him."

"Something like that." He finally looked her direction. "I thought I'd get him to think twice about destroying the Bar W. I didn't realize it was already too late."

She leaned against the wall a few feet from where Lucas stood, but they still seemed miles apart. She drank the coffee she'd brought for him, and he stared out the window.

Lauren didn't know if they were even friends anymore. In high school she'd had a crush on him. In college she'd spend most of her time waiting for him to notice her, to start something between them.

But it never happened. A few wild kisses. A thousand daydreams. Whispered promises spoken in the night that never saw the day. If they couldn't find the time to talk, she'd never find her way to him.

Maybe everybody has that *almost* kind of love. As you grow

up and grow older, it shifts and changes like some kind of parallel universe, no more than a thin shadow walking in your mind beside your real life.

But it's there. A could-have-been. A love you could have had, if only there had been a time or place for it in the real world.

Lauren studied him now, wondering why she blamed him for them not becoming lovers. Wasn't she half the equation? Half the reason? Half the problem?

Setting the coffee on the table, she walked to the bars. "Look at me, Lucas."

He turned as if he'd almost forgotten she was there.

Lauren took a stand. This might be her own personal Alamo, and what she'd thought they had might die right now, but for once in her life she was going to fight. This might not be the time or the place, but they needed to talk.

"Come over here."

He hesitated, then moved to stand in front of her. Only five inches separated them. Five inches and a line of steel bars.

"I came because I care about you. I've always cared about you."

"You don't owe me anything, Lauren."

She gripped the bars, fisting her hands so hard her knuckles whitened. "I care about you." She said it again; she couldn't bring herself to say the word *love*. "Whatever this fight is about, I'm on your side. You pushing me away won't change that. I know you, Lucas, and I want to help."

Lucas's hands covered hers. "This is too dangerous. Too risky. I don't know who we're dealing with, but they don't play by any rules. You'll be safer if you don't know anything. The only way I'll know you're out of any danger is for you to ignore me. Walk away. No one needs to connect the two of us. It wouldn't be safe for you."

For the first time, she thought she saw fear in him. This wasn't about him being mad and hitting Reid Collins. This was far more. She could see it in his eyes. Lucas was fighting, struggling to hide something from her.

"I can't." Lauren pressed her forehead against the cold bars. "I don't want to be safe. If something happened to you and I didn't help I'd never forgive myself. Like it or not, you're a part of me, a piece that would leave me hollow forever if you were gone." A single tear rolled down her cheek.

His hand slid between the bars as he brushed her tear away with two fingers. "All right, *mi cielo*. Don't cry. You're right. We're linked. I think we have been since that night in the old Gypsy House." His hand moved along the side of her face in a caress. "You're so beautiful. Sometimes just remembering your face gives me hope that the world is a good place. Sky blue eyes and sunbeam hair."

For a moment they just stared at each other. His dark eyes looking so deep into her soul she swore he could read all her secrets.

"There are words that need to be said between us, but not now."

She nodded. It was enough just to be that honest. He was right, this wasn't the time.

"Can I trust you?" He was so close to the bars she could feel the warmth of him.

"Always."

He slid his fingers over hers again and pulled her hand into his cage. His skin was warm, the bars cold.

She stared as he unfolded her hand and moved his fingers along her palm. Then, in a blink, he laid a key in her palm and rolled her fingers into a fist. "Don't say anything to anyone. Just keep this key with you. It holds my future."

"I promise." She pulled her hand back through the bars and slipped the key into her pocket.

He seemed to relax, even smiled at her. "You know, I almost married a woman in Houston once. I thought she had every-

thing—beauty, money, ambition, a daddy with political con-
nections."

"Why didn't you marry her, Lucas?"

He covered her hand still resting on the bars. "She wasn't you.
I would have never trusted her with my life."

"And are you trusting me that much?"

His voice was so low it seemed to be more a thought than
words passing between them. "I am. If something happens to
me, that key will let you know how I feel about you."

The rattle of the far door clanked and their time was ending.

"Don't come back," he whispered. "I'll find you when this
is over."

She nodded.

As her father opened the second door, she said in as cold a
voice as she could manage, "Well, if you're not going to talk
to me I might as well leave." Her hand shivered as she pulled it
from beneath his.

Pop simply held the door open as he watched her storm out.
For once he didn't ask a single question as they walked down the
two flights of stairs. When they reached the lobby, she darted
around a dozen people waiting to see the sheriff and was gone
before she had to say another word.

Shoving her hand into her pocket, she gripped the key Lucas
had passed her. A secret she couldn't tell anyone, not even her
pop.

Marching down the street, Lauren felt different. More alert.
Watching. Aware of everyone around her. If Lucas was worried,
mixed up in something dangerous, not all was what it seemed.
What if Crossroads wasn't safe for him? If he had to keep a secret or hide something? Then it wasn't safe for her, either.

Once back at her office, she pulled the key from her pocket.
It didn't look very important. Just a key that unlocked a door.
But somehow it held a secret that could change lives.

She pulled off her necklace and put the key on the chain.

When she put the chain back, she looped it only once and the key dropped down between her breasts. She'd keep it there, next to her heart, until he asked for it back.

seventeen

———

Blade had planned to drop Maria off at the grocery store, make sure she had all she needed, and then go looking for Dakota. He could still feel her skin on his fingers. After the way she'd kissed him this morning just after he'd stepped out of the shower, there was no way she would walk away from his offer for a short affair. He'd tasted passion, real passion. It had been a long time since a woman had affected him like Dakota did. She stirred up something inside of him, a deep longing he didn't even know how to define.

He smiled. If she was having trouble sleeping now, wait until tonight. She might as well give up sleep for the next dozen days or so. He planned to. She was worth it.

He couldn't stop making plans as he unloaded the crates of jams and jellies in exactly the spot the store owner insisted. Wes Whitman reminded him of a hawk as he hovered over Maria. She wasn't even five foot three, and he had to be six-four. They might both be in their thirties, but he seemed older. You'd have thought she was delivering precious cargo and not just jars of jelly.

"Go, Blade," Maria said, shooing him away with her hand. "This will take over an hour and I'll call Dakota when I'm finished." She smiled. "I might even have coffee with Mr. Whitman before I call for a ride. We like to talk business after the shelves are stocked."

Whitman nodded, but didn't smile. "I'll watch over her." He straightened, as if he considered himself the palace guard.

Blade backed away, knowing he was leaving her in good hands. With plans of continuing what they'd started in the shower this morning, he climbed into his truck and backed away from the side door of the grocery store. Before he could swing around to leave the parking lot, the sheriff pulled up beside him.

"Park that truck and jump in," Brigman yelled. "We got trouble."

A minute later Blade swallowed his swear words and rolled into the cruiser. "What's up? Don't tell me it's time to go back to work. I've only been off long enough to take a shower and eat breakfast." Blade had the feeling being a deputy was one of those jobs where you punch the time clock in and never punch out.

The sheriff flipped on his lights but didn't bother with the siren. "We've got another dead body."

"Hell." Blade let the word slip as he felt his daydream of Dakota vanish. "This is way over my head, Sheriff. I investigate fires, remember?"

Brigman shrugged. "I need another set of eyes. You're trained to observe. So observe these guys you're about to meet and tell me which ones are telling the truth. I've got a feeling one of the men in the crowd we're heading toward is a killer or knows who is."

"Fine. Anything else?" The deputy job description seemed to be growing by the minute.

"Yeah, you are carrying, aren't you?"

"Hell," Blade said again as he shifted, feeling the shoulder holster tighten against his arm. "This isn't going to be that easy, is it?"

Brigman laughed. "I'm expecting nothing, but I want to be prepared if I'm wrong. I need to know you'll have my six."

Blade nodded. "I've got your back." He could do that. He'd spent two years in combat zones doing just that with a partner. They'd both made it stateside alive.

"We're going in to ask questions, but to be honest, bodies aren't something I have to deal with often. Bar fights, speeding, and drunks are more my expertise."

"Where was the body found?" Blade asked.

"At the site of the first barn fire, but it wasn't burned. Blunt force trauma to the head was probably the cause of death."

"How do you know?"

"Dice found him at the Collins ranch. Said the left side of his skull was caved in. He said it looked like someone just dumped him on top of the ashes. Didn't even try to cover the body."

"You think the two deaths are linked?"

Brigman nodded. "What are the odds two men die within two days of one another on the same square of land? Before this morning I was hoping the body in the fire at the barn was somehow an accident. You know, like whoever set the fires didn't know someone was sleeping in the back. But now I have little hope of that being the case."

"Any ID on the second body?"

"Looks like it's a cowhand who'd worked on the ranch for ten years. His initials were engraved in his boots. Coffer Coldman, C.C. Dice said he'd moved out with all the others two days ago. Several men saw him drive away. Shouldn't have even been on the ranch." Dan pushed his Stetson back. "I'm thinking he came back for something and ended up dead."

"What's Dice still doing on the place?" Blade thought about the old guy who'd walked with them around the burn sites. He'd been on a horse so long his long thin legs still took the shape of it even when he walked. Staying around the Collins ranch didn't seem like a very healthy thing to do.

The sheriff pulled into the ranch. "I tried to tell him that the burned body we found that first morning may be his friend, but Dice won't believe it. He claims he'll ride the ranch until he finds either his friend or the horse he was riding."

The road turned rough but the sheriff didn't slow the car or his lecture. "LeRoy, Dice's friend, is the only man missing that I've heard about. But the way the ranch hands scattered, who knows? LeRoy's old beat-up Ford and trailer are still parked behind the bunkhouse. It doesn't make sense that he'd leave without them. For most of these men, their rig is about all they own."

They pulled up to the blackened frame of the first barn that had caught fire. Several men were standing around. Only two looked like they belonged on the land. The others, including the owner, were dressed more for the streets of downtown Dallas than the open country.

The sheriff climbed out and handed Blade the rifle. "Carry it easy, but keep it at ready. I have no idea what we're getting into here, but one of the men standing around looking at the latest body may be our killer."

"Just a hunch?"

"Yep." Brigman shrugged.

Blade fell into step with the sheriff. He was starting to feel like Doc Holliday at the OK Corral. "I guess we know one man who is not a suspect," he whispered.

"Who, besides me and you?" Brigman glanced his direction. "And I'm not positive about you."

"Lucas Reyes. I know he was in his cell all night because he kept pacing, keeping me awake."

The sheriff shrugged again. "I tried to let him out this morning after you left, but he refused to go. Said he'd deck me if I tried to make him leave."

"Isn't there something wrong with the idea of fighting your way into jail?"

The sheriff lowered his voice. "Sometimes small towns can be a little quirky."

They moved into the small crowd of men. Reid Collins was there, wanting to do all the talking. He was nervous to the point of panic. The first body had frightened him, but this one seemed to be driving him over the edge.

Blade took his time looking around, and noting the men who refused to turn toward the body, even when the sheriff pointed something out.

Dice Fuller was standing across from Reid, but he didn't say a word. Neither did the men Reid had behind him. Yesterday there had been two. This morning there were half a dozen.

Blade studied each man. Most, if not all, of the thugs Reid hired to help close the ranch were armed. One had all the knuckles on his right hand scraped clean of skin. Another was limping.

The sheriff was right. Far more was going on here than just barn fires. The thugs, as the cowboys called Reid's new crew, didn't fit on a ranch, but it was obvious they were moving in, taking over.

Reid ended his account to the sheriff by adding, "Not one man here has any idea how this body got on my property. I swear, I may have to put a no-dumping sign on the fence to keep people from dropping off bodies."

Dice finally stepped forward. "Coffer worked for you for ten years. He might not have always been sober at dawn, but he put in his day." The old man looked straight at Reid. "You may act like Coffer up and died just to ruin your party, but I doubt it went down that way. He didn't kill himself or walk over here dead to tumble into the ashes, so maybe we need to start looking for who killed him."

Reid turned away as if he hadn't heard a word the old man

said. The owner looked straight at the sheriff as if this whole mess was his problem.

"Was he your friend?" Blade stepped in front of Dice.

"I can't say that, but he always pulled his share of the load around here. It was his job to keep the tack room clean. Most nights, when everyone else was filling their dinner plates, Coffer was making sure the gear was all put up right."

Reid rubbed his forehead. "I don't have time for this. Sheriff, do whatever it is that needs to be done. When you finish, call the funeral home in Lubbock. I'll pay for the burial. I've already checked his employment records and Coffer listed his dog as his next of kin."

Dice ignored the boss as he continued to talk to Blade. "We found his pickup out by the old west entrance. Nobody uses that gate except cattle trucks now and then. His truck was pointed toward the county road, like he'd stopped to open the gate before pulling out."

"Find his dog?" Brigman asked.

"Nope, he's missing along with my friend and his horse."

The sheriff nodded once, thanking the old man, then turned to Blade. "Collect all names here. They'll each have to give statements. I'll talk to anyone left at the headquarters who might have seen Coffer yesterday."

Brigman turned back to the crowd. "No one leaves the county until I get their statement. That includes you, Reid."

A groan went up from the crowd. The thugs settled into silence, but two cowhands swore, not at the sheriff, but at their bad luck. Blade began collecting names and setting times for them to come into the office. He paused long enough to watch Reid Collins storm off. Apparently, he didn't think the summons should apply to him.

When Blade circled back to Brigman, the sheriff paused his official phone calls long enough to tell him to go back to town. He'd handle everything here and call in any findings. "I need

you to start the interviews before these men have time to com-
pare their stories, or in some cases, rewrite what they saw. Also,
draw up a timeline. I want to know where everyone was from
the night of the first fire to when Dice notified us of the second body."

Blade looked around at the crowd. "I doubt most of these
guys will be able to remember back twenty-four hours, much
less forty-eight."

"Give it a shot." Brigman smiled. "You know what the deputy's main job is in a two-man office?"

"What's that?"

"Doing what the sheriff doesn't want to do."

Blade grinned. "We need to do one thing to make this job
perfect."

"What would that be?"

"Hire a deputy in training."

The sheriff frowned. "You find me one, Hamilton, and I'll
consider it."

"Me?" Blade sure didn't want another duty on top of a job he
didn't want in the first place. At the rate duties were piling up,
he'd never get back to Dakota and her soft skin. He'd be rewind-
ing the memory of holding her so many times he'd wear it out.

Dice stepped nearer. "How about I take you back to town,
Hamilton? I could use a break, and if the coffee's still free in
the sheriff's office, I might stop in to visit with Pearly. Always
did fancy that woman. She still wearing those sexy earrings that
hang down almost to her shoulder?"

"Yep," the sheriff answered as he nodded for Blade to take
the offer for a ride.

He had a feeling he and the sheriff were thinking the same
thing. Dice's idea of sexy was more Halloween decoration to
them. But, when you're nearing eighty, a woman in her late
sixties might still be wild and sexy.

"Thanks for the offer. I'll stop by and pick up a few dozen

doughnuts to go with the coffee. If you have time, Dice, maybe you could even help me with the timeline."

"Sounds like a plan, kid." Dice patted Blade on the shoulder.

"Glad to have your help, old man," Blade answered.

They both laughed as they walked to his rusty truck.

eighteen

A weak sun tried to fight its way through the clouds as Dan Brigman stopped his cruiser halfway back to town. Another body and still no answers. Worry made his mood as gloomy as the day.

He pulled into a forgotten roadside park and dialed his bride. They'd been married two years and he still thought of them as newlyweds. Funny how a man doesn't know how lonely his life is until he finds the right person.

"Morning, sunshine," he said when she answered with a sleepy hello. "Did you close the bar down last night?"

He heard what sounded like covers being pulled up. His Brandi loved to sleep in. He could imagine her cuddling into bed with the phone close by.

"I did. We played the final set at the Blue Bird last night, then went out for pancakes. Harry, our new drummer, ate so many we had to roll him to his car."

"And did they love your new songs?" He closed his eyes, wishing she was close enough to touch.

"They did. I've got some work to do with the new label execs, then a few more days in the studio and I'll be home. You wouldn't want to fly up for a long weekend before I leave Nash-ville? I booked the condo for another two weeks. We could sleep days and check out all the new artists at night."

"I wish I could," he said, already thinking of how they'd spend their time. "But I got another dead body here to deal with."

She laughed. "You got a body here to deal with, Sheriff, and I'm very much alive. This body is warm and willing."

He leaned back. "I miss you every hour of every day you're gone." He wished he had the words to tell Brandi how much she meant to him. Half of him seemed missing when she wasn't close. He didn't sleep well, didn't eat right.

Her low whiskey-smooth voice came back to him. "I know. I miss you the same. I also know, thanks to Pearly's latest call, that you've been working night and day. When I get home you're going to spend some time in bed. So stock up on ice cream and frozen pizza because I'm not cooking and you won't be dressed enough to go out for food."

He laughed. "Promise?"

"Promise." She made the little sound she always made when she needed his touch. "Now tell me about your case."

He knew what she was doing. Pulling him back to the day, even though they'd both be thinking of the night after she made it home. "All right. Not much to tell. Two hay barns burned on the Bar W. No owners there except Reid, and if crimes were solved by votes, he'd win the rap. His cowhands hate him, and the men he brought in to basically kick everyone off the land don't seem to like him much, either."

"What else?"

"We found a body in one of the burned barns. Could have been someone sleeping it off, but the back barn door was locked from the outside. If the guy was alive when the fire started, he may have been trapped. If he was dead, we're dealing with a murder, and whoever set the fires might have been trying to cover up his crime."

"Have you heard from Reid's father? You know, the one you claim collects women like some people do stamps. One wife from every country."

"Reid said he's in Europe and doesn't want to get involved with anything going on back in Texas. Handed over the ranch to him a few years ago. Said whatever happens to the place is Reid's problem. The father is making so much money off the oil rights, he doesn't much care about the land."

"Doesn't Collins have another son?" Brandi sounded like she was fighting a yawn.

"He does. Charley Collins. The old man disowned him years ago. Cut him off with nothing but the clothes he walked out of the headquarters wearing."

"Could he be causing the problem?" She was starting to sound sleepy. Police work always had that effect on Brandi. If she was having trouble sleeping, all he had to do was talk shop to her and she'd cuddle into his arms, sound asleep.

"I don't think Charley is involved. He's happily married and owns Lone Heart Pass. It's not a big spread, but they raise horses there. Sells them all over the world, I hear."

Brandi didn't answer. He could hear her breathing. "Good night, Sleeping Beauty," he whispered into the phone. "I'll talk to you tonight."

He clicked off his phone and pulled back onto the highway.

nineteen

It was late afternoon when Blade Hamilton finally got a break from taking statements and could check on the county's only prisoner. He felt like he was trapped in that movie *Groundhog Day*. He'd spent hours interviewing the same men he'd interviewed yesterday. Same men, same ranch, same burn sites, different body. Only difference was, they knew who this body belonged to. Coffer Coldman.

When he'd asked each man he interviewed to describe Coffer, two of the cowboys said he was on the dumb side. One of the thugs said he was nosy, always asking questions.

As Blade closed the notes and headed upstairs, he thought the repeat day would continue into night. It looked like he'd be sleeping in the same bed, in the same jail, with the same man, who shouldn't even be there, pacing in the cell across from him.

As he walked up the second flight, he thought about how he liked the county's one prisoner, Lucas Reyes. Blade was a few years older, but they were about the same size. They might come from different backgrounds, but they'd talked enough last night that they'd each developed a respect for the other.

Reyes had said he admired Blade for being brave enough to fight fires and Blade had decided that Lucas was one of the good lawyers who really tried to make a difference.

In all the hours they'd talked, Reyes had only made one comment about the barn fires. He'd told Blade that the fires might have been some kind of warning, or maybe a nudge to get Reid moving. Someone wanted the ranch closed, fast.

When Blade unlocked the second door to the jail cells, he almost didn't recognize the place. The table in the middle was full of food and clothes were hanging from the bars.

"What's up?" Blade asked. "You moving in?" Both cells now had several blankets and pillows. There was a stack of magazines higher than at any doctor's office and books lying on the floor.

Lucas shrugged. "What can I say? I'm from a big family. Plus, I know most of the folks in town. Everyone, including two of my old teachers, has dropped by. A few even demanded Pearly let me out." Lucas laughed. "She said that duty was not in her job description."

Before Blade could ask, Lucas added, "Pearly let them all in and every time she climbed the stairs, she threatened to murder me if I had one more guest."

"You could leave, you know."

"I'm not leaving." Lucas's strong tone left no room for argument.

A tap sounded from the open door into the jail cells, and Dice slipped in.

Blade had enjoyed hours of the old guy's tales between interviews, but was ready for a break. "What are you doing up here, Dice?" he asked. "I thought I left you to man the office in case someone else comes in to tell me what they didn't see at the Bar W."

Dice shook his head as if he had a few loose vertebrae. "You left me down there alone with Pearly. I wasn't sure I could trust myself to be that much of a gentleman. I was tempted to steal a kiss every time she walked by in those two-inch heels."

Both Blade and Lucas grinned.

Dice wiggled his tumbleweed eyebrows. "You wouldn't believe the women who want a chance to take a roll of the Dice. By the time I was you boys' age, I was looking twenty years older. Had to stop coming to town so I'd have enough energy to last the day at work."

Blade, who rarely laughed aloud, roared, and so did Lucas.

The old man chuckled, proud of his one joke. He moved close to Lucas's cell. "You want me to bust you out of this place, Lucas? I'm sure it's hell behind those bars. I've known you all your life and you don't belong in here, son." He looked over at the table of food and saw a seven-layer orange cake. "Is that your momma's cake? And are those Lupe's tamales? I haven't had them since the New Year's party."

He helped himself to one, eating it in two bites. "On second thought, how about I break into this place and keep you company? I've been living on day-old doughnuts downstairs."

Dice nudged Blade out of the way and ate his way around the table. "You got to try these peanut butter patties. I can guess who made them but I might have to eat another one to be sure. They got enough sugar in them that your breath will sweeten your tea for a month."

"How about I leave you to guard the prisoner, Dice?" Blade ignored Lucas's frown.

"Sure," Dice said with his mouth full. "Tell Pearly to bring a few coffees up. Man her phones while she's up here taking a break. She needs to get off her feet for a while and I got the lap that'll take her weight."

"Of course. Why not?" Blade said as he tapped an imaginary brim of a hat. "You're the chaperone, Mr. Reyes."

Blade was out the door, but he could hear Lucas yelling something about being tortured in prison.

By the time Pearly climbed the stairs for her third break of the afternoon, the sheriff was back. He told Blade to take a few hours off and be back by seven. No need to bring meals.

"I'm guessing I'm spending the night upstairs?" Blade tried to keep his voice even, like it didn't matter, but Dakota had moved from a memory to an ache deep inside him. He felt like he was going through withdrawal as the hours piled up away from her.

"You're guessing right," the sheriff said. "I could relieve you at two."

"No. I don't have anywhere to sleep, anyway. I'll drive out and check how the repairs at my place are going and then be back for the night. One of us should get a good night's sleep."

Brigman didn't try to talk him out of the night shift. The sheriff was already working twelve-hour days.

Blade drove over to Dakota's office in the tiny strip mall. She wasn't there and neither were any of the boxes he'd ordered. If he had time, he'd drive back to Denver just to pick up clothes, but it didn't look like deputies got more than a few hours off in a row.

He tried to call Dakota to see if she'd collected any deliveries, but her cell went to voice mail. He wanted to hear her voice. He'd try again later.

Next he stopped by his land. Jerry Cline and his crew were working hard on the bridge, and Jerry's brother-in-law said he had the plumbing in the house operating fine in the kitchen and one bathroom. He also commented that they were counting dead squirrels in the house.

Blade bumped his way across pasture, then the shallow creek that fed Indigo Lake and found enough boards to roll his bike into the bed of the rented truck. He tied the hog down, hating to see his beautiful bike so damaged. It would take thousands to fix it up.

"What about the house?" Jerry called from the bridge. "I could find guys to clean it out. Gut it if you like?"

"Do that. Everything gone but the pictures on the staircase wall."

"It'll cost you."

Blade smiled. "But you know someone who knows someone who can do it."

"Right."

Blade thought about how Dakota would be more likely to sell the place if it looked better. "Got someone who can do the porch repair, replace any rotting boards on windows and string new wiring?"

"It'll cost you."

Blade shrugged. He hadn't spent much money over the years. He could afford to build a new place on Hamilton Acres, but he liked the idea of fixing the old home up. "And paint it outside and in?"

"What color?" Jerry was writing down the list.

"I don't care. White, I guess." He thought of calling Dakota to ask her opinion, but decided to wait and ask her in person.

"I can do that. I'll have this bridge finished tomorrow if it stops raining and we'll start on the house." Jerry looked happy to have the work.

Blade pulled out five one-hundred-dollar bills. "This won't pay for the supplies, but it will get you started. I'll set up an account for you at the hardware store. If you need to find me..."

Jerry grinned. "I know where you are, Deputy Hamilton. You're helping the sheriff out. Working there is far more interesting than painting, but I'm happy to find this job. It'll be another month before ranches are hiring for spring, and all of us here have bills to pay."

Blade nodded his thanks and turned to his truck. A slow rain dripped from low clouds just often enough to be bothersome. And probably slow down their progress.

Jerry called after him. "If you wanna get that bike fixed, take it over to Theodor's Salvage a few miles north of town. He's got a guy named Lou over there who might fix it up but..."

"I know, it will cost me."

"Tell Theodor that I sent you. He'll give you a good price. He still owes me money on a welding job I did for him two years ago."

"Do you think he's going to pay?"

"Oh, sure. He will eventually. Until then he's happy to do me a favor now and again."

Blade waved and climbed back into his truck. Small towns. He'd never lived in one and would probably never understand them, but it was interesting. He'd never heard of passing on favors.

By the time he delivered his bike to Theodor, it was almost dark and his only change of clothes was soaked through to his skin. His boots were covered in mud.

Lou at the salvage yard, or boneyard as he called it, was a wannabe biker. He almost cried when he saw what a state the Harley was in, and he asked Blade if he'd been an 81er. Translation: the eighth and the first letters of the alphabet, respectively, standing for Hell's Angels.

In truth, Blade wasn't into the biker culture. He just loved the freedom of the ride, but he played along with Lou, knowing that his bike would be handled with loving hands.

Blade laughed, thinking the guy who looked like he not only worked but slept at the salvage yard had ridden *donor*—that is, without a helmet—once too often.

Blade set his helmet on the seat. "I'll check back with you. If you do a test run, wear this."

"Don't bother to call," the mechanic said. "I'll call the sheriff's office when I know anything. It'll take a few days to get parts."

"Good luck getting anything shipped."

Lou walked off, talking to the bike, not Blade.

He tried Dakota's cell as he drove back toward town. No an-

swer. So, he parked in the county's back lot and walked into the
sheriff's office, trying to shake off enough dirt to look present-
able, but it was hopeless.

The sheriff and Lucas were playing chess when he climbed
up to the jail.

Brigman frowned. "Don't you have any clean clothes, Hamilton? You look like someone would arrest you for littering just
for stepping outside."

"Nope," Blade answered. "I only thought I was driving down
for a night or two. When I found out I was staying, I ordered
a few changes of clothes online, but FedEx can't seem to find
this town. I don't have enough time off from my vacation job
to drive anywhere to buy clothes."

Brigman shrugged. "Doesn't sound like a problem for law
enforcement. My uniforms wouldn't fit you."

Lucas raised his gaze from the board. "Sheriff is right. You
look like Crossroads' first homeless man. Pick one of those jogging suits over there. My mother gets me a brown one every
Christmas. I always leave them in a closet at their house. You'd
think she'd get the hint that I'm not wearing them. If they fit
me, they'll probably fit you."

"Do you run?" Blade asked as he pulled one hanger down. It
looked like something he wouldn't wear even around the apartment, but at this point he felt too dirty and wet to be picky.

"No. I swim when I have time to work out. It's something
I rarely got to do as a kid." Lucas smiled. "Take the running
shoes too. Your boots would look terrible with running pants."

Brigman stood. "If you guys are going to talk about fashion,
I think I'll head on home. I think *Project Runway* reruns might
be on."

Blade stripped off his wet clothes, used one of the fluffy towels
in his open cell to dry off and pulled on the clean pants. "These

feel great. Not my style, either, but they'll do. They're dry and clean. That's all I need."

Lucas leaned against the bars. "You got some pretty mean scars there, Hamilton."

Blade never thought much about his scars. One, as wide as a tire track, ran across his back, and the other slid along his shoulder, a tiny river of twisted skin. He'd been burned a few times. Once from a falling tree and another time when he'd carried a firefighter out who'd been caught in a reburn. It was just part of the job, and he'd learned a long time ago to handle pain.

"Just scars." Blade wanted to change the subject. "What happened to Dice?" he asked as he tugged on the sweatshirt. Then he carefully hung his shoulder holster next to the cot he'd be sleeping in. His weapon likely wouldn't be needed, but as a federal agent, he'd been trained to keep it near.

"The old guy left on a date with Pearly, I think. Should be interesting." Lucas smiled. "He said he's heading back to the Bar W at dawn to continue searching for his friend, but I got the feeling he's given up hope."

"You think LeRoy is out there somewhere on the land?"

Lucas shook his head. "I've known those two old guys all my life. Dice is a real cowboy. Lives on a horse, loves the life, but LeRoy just found a place where he had a roof and food. I never got the feeling he even liked his job much. Every weekend he got drunk, and Dice was usually the one to haul him back to the ranch. My father probably would have fired him years ago, but Dice might have gone with him."

"So where is LeRoy?"

Lucas shrugged. "He might have fallen off his horse and died out on the land, I guess. More likely he sold his horse to one of the cowhands leaving, caught a ride into town with someone, and he's spending his last paycheck on whiskey. When his money runs out he'll be looking for Dice to help him."

"Could he be the burned body we found?"

Lucas shook his head. "Maybe. LeRoy had his hiding places to avoid work, but I remember hearing the cook say once that he was the last to leave the bunkhouse and the first to return. He'd hide out in his room, and with Dad gone there was no one to bother him if he slept in or drank too much. So, it doesn't make sense that he'd be getting drunk in a barn."

"Dice seems to be the only one searching for him. I don't think Collins cares one way or the other about his employees or the ranch."

"I think you're right. My dad's hinted at pretty dark rumors about what has been going on around the ranch. He told me that if it didn't involve the cattle, it was best if he just didn't see it. If any of the hands knew about the rumors besides my father, it'd be LeRoy and Dice."

Blade laced his new shoes, thinking that he had a lot in common with both old guys. He loved his job, but he had no one to report to other than a secretary at the main office. If he disappeared no one would probably bother to come looking for him, either. "I'll pay you for the clothes or replace them."

"Don't bother. I'll get the same thing next Christmas. My mother must search for weeks to find the same ugly brown jogging suit. She decided I looked best in brown and I don't think she's ever bought me another color. Once I got out on my own, I never bought anything but blue or black."

Blade stood and pulled the hood over his still-damp hair. "I left my cell in my jacket. I'll lock you in and run down to get it before it starts raining again."

"I'm not going anywhere." Lucas laughed. "Grab my cell too if you don't mind. I left it in my old pickup out back. The door won't lock and the phone is in the ashtray. If I had my cell, I could call my folks and tell them to stop calling everyone to keep coming up to check on me. They took off before they unpacked. Dad said it was about time for a vacation since he had no job and no home."

"You worried about them?"

"No. I'm more worried about my BMW they borrowed. They said they planned to see how fast they could make it to the coast. They're probably in Mexico City by now, reliving their honeymoon."

"What color is your pickup?"

"Mud-colored rust."

Waving, Blade headed out, locking doors behind him.

He thought cell phone access might not be standard procedure for inmates, but neither were home-cooked meals and a wardrobe. Lucas was no more a prisoner than he was, but for some reason he wanted to be here. He was either protecting someone or waiting out his time.

Blade carefully locked both doors to the jail and then the front door to keep any visitors out. He jogged his way back to his rented Dodge Ram, which was parked behind the county offices.

Rain hung in the air and the low clouds made the night seem darker than usual. The lot had a snaggletooth fence on two sides and barbed wire along the back. A collection of trash as tall as the fence had blown up in one corner, reminding him of a Christmas tree made of plastic bags and twisted cups.

He was used to bright lights and city noises. The small town after dark suggested a great setting for a ghost town from a B-rated movie. Silent except for the slicing sound of cars flying past on the highway. Nothing moved behind the wire fence, where the landscape looked like it was no more than a silhouette portrait. Black on gray.

His cell was in the left pocket of his leather jacket that had finally gotten too dirty to wear. He grabbed it, then climbed out of the rental and locked the Ram door. Blade looked around at the lot, a graveyard of wrecked or abandoned cars.

Three old cars. A horse trailer and one old muddy pickup. It wasn't locked. No need. A thief wouldn't even bother to think there would be anything worth stealing inside.

He grabbed the cell phone from the ashtray and walked slowly down the middle of the back lot. Twenty parking spaces. Four vehicles other than his. Only the sounds of the night, nothing more, but Blade felt the hair on the back of his neck stand up. For a moment he sensed he wasn't alone.

He reached for his weapon and realized he'd left it upstairs.

Another sound, no louder than a click of a twig.

Just as he turned, he heard a crisp *pop* ring out and saw a flicker of light blink in the night.

The sound had barely registered when fire plowed into his arm. Blade lurched, as if he could push away from the bullet that had hit him, and felt another blaze along his side.

Movement shifted at the edge of the lot, and Blade thought he saw a shadow disappear behind a fence. Then silence. Only silence.

As he inhaled one long breath, he studied his surroundings and weighed his chances. The back door was ten feet away, but it would be locked, and there was no one inside to answer his knock. The front door was maybe fifty or sixty feet away, and he'd be in light twice. Once at the corner of the building and once on the steps. If the shooter was watching, waiting, he would have two chances at a clear shot.

Blade knew he had to be fast. He could feel blood dripping down his arm, and his side burned like liquid fire. He had no way of knowing how fast he was losing blood. There was no time to treat the wounds.

His mother's words echoed from his childhood. *Ignore the pain. Shut up about it.* She'd never offered comfort, no matter how bad the scrape. Caring wasn't her thing and he'd learned young not to expect it.

So he ignored all pain now. As he had in the army, he concentrated on one command. Focus!

With his lungs full of air, he took off running, veering first right, then left, leaning low, keeping his head down.

All he could hear was his running shoes crunching against the gravel. *Run, run, run*, his heart seemed to be pounding.

In seconds he hit the front door of the county building and it opened. Blade swung around and locked the door, just as he thought he'd locked it when he'd left five minutes ago.

That meant that someone, maybe even the shooter, could be in the building. Or, maybe Pearly or the sheriff was back?

No lights on at her desk.

No light from the sheriff's office.

What if the front lock had been picked in the few minutes between the time he had left, then returned? Someone could be inside, in the dark, waiting for another chance to shoot him.

There was only one reason someone with a gun would want into the county office. Lucas! The almost-prisoner was in danger.

Blade took the stairs three at a time as he pushed redial on his phone.

When Dakota picked up on the first ring she said, "I got…"

"Listen," he shouted into the phone. "Call the sheriff and tell him to get back to his office as fast as possible. Tell him we've got a man down."

There was a pause and for a heartbeat he thought she'd hung up on him. "Now, Dakota."

"Will do," she said, and the call went dead.

He dropped the phone in his pocket, unlocked the first door on the third floor and stepped into the passageway room. With the door closed and locked behind him, he took a moment to breathe. If someone was in the building, they hadn't made it this far.

Before he opened the second door, he yelled, "Lucas, you all right?"

"I thought I heard shots," Lucas yelled back. "You hear them?"

"I felt them," he said between clenched teeth as he unlocked the next door. Blade took one step, then pitched Lucas the keys to the cells as he tumbled to the floor. "No!" was all he said as he fell.

He could feel his heart pounding, but the room was drawing darker and darker around him. Lucas was yelling at him. Then the cell door clanked open. Lucas was above him, ordering him to stay awake, but the night was closing in and it didn't matter if his eyes were open or shut. All was black.

Blade's last thought was that he'd heard men call for their mother when they were dying, but all he saw was Dakota's face. "Come get me, Elf," he whispered. But the words didn't come out, they simply circled in his mind.

twenty

Four minutes later Dan Brigman hit the front door of the county office with what felt like half the town behind him. He'd called 9-1-1 as he'd run to his car. Pearly answered on the third ring. He barely gave her time to say hello, yelling, "Get the fire department and an ambulance headed toward my office. Now!"

He'd dropped the phone in his shirt pocket and shot out of his drive. Sirens blaring, he'd hit ninety by the time he pulled onto the main road and didn't slow down until he saw his office. As he ran up the steps, the fire truck that had only three blocks to travel was pulling up.

"Stay here," he yelled at the firemen. "Don't let anyone in until I give the order. We may be dealing with an active shooter." Dan had no idea what he would face. Dakota had said "man down," and Blade was the only man he had working.

"Will do, Sheriff," Cap, a retired fire chief, who must have come from his home across the street, yelled from the crowd. "I'll take care of things here."

Dan stepped inside. The lobby was dark and still, as if holding its breath. Dan was relieved when he found nothing waiting for him in the entryway. Still, not a single one of his muscles relaxed.

He moved up the stairs, listening, alert.

On the third landing, Dan turned and unlocked the first door to the jail cells. The key turned. Good sign. The jail was locked up tight.

"Blade? Lucas?" No answer. "Blade!" Again, no answer.

Weapon in hand, he slowly unlocked the second door. One inch. Two inches.

The scene came into sight, into his comprehension, one slice at a time. Dan found exactly what he prayed he wouldn't see.

Trouble.

His deputy was on the floor with blood everywhere. Lucas's white shirt was also bloody, but from the way he was working on Blade, the prisoner wasn't hurt. Blade's shoulder holster was on the cell floor where the deputy slept, but his gun lay beside Lucas, within ready reach.

For a second Dan thought Lucas Reyes had shot Blade Hamilton, but that didn't make sense. Why would he be fighting so hard to save him? How could a man behind bars shoot an armed federal agent?

There was no time to analyze. Dan went with his gut. He rushed to the landing and saw the two EMTs trying to fight their way around Cap. The retired fire chief was holding them back, waiting for Dan's orders.

"Let them up, Cap, but no one else."

"Will do." Cap shoved them inside, yelling for them to pick up their feet and hurry.

As they stormed up the stairs, carrying what looked like about a hundred pounds of gear, Dan ordered Cap to clear a path. "We got a man down. Call in a bird."

"Already have," Cap shouted. "Just in case you needed it."

Dan rushed back to the jail and knelt beside Lucas. "Is he breathing?"

"He is," Lucas answered. "He's been shot twice. I tied off the arm, but I can't stop the bleeding on his side."

Dan took a breath and tried to reason. Two men locked in a room. One gun. One man shot. This might be the dumbest question he'd ever asked but Dan looked directly at Lucas and said, "Who shot him?"

"I don't know. He went to get his phone. I asked him to stop by my truck and pick up mine. I thought I heard two shots. A few minutes later when he ran back in, he'd been shot." Lucas leaned back as the medics moved in.

Lucas stared at Dan with tears in his eyes. "They must have thought he was me. He had my clothes on. We're about the same size. He'd pulled the hood up because of the rain. I... I..." Lucas pulled himself together as if testifying. "The bullets were meant for me."

"We don't know that," Dan said, unsure if he was trying to convince himself or Lucas.

The medics laid their hands over Lucas's and replaced pressure on Blade's wounds as Lucas slid his bloody fingers away.

Dan linked his arm under Lucas's shoulder and helped him up. The lawyer was badly shaken. They moved to the cot that would have been Blade's bed for the night. Lucas took a few deep breaths, as if there weren't enough air in the room to fill his lungs.

"It's my fault, Sheriff. This is all my fault. If I hadn't been so close when the barns burned. If I hadn't been one of the first there. They wouldn't have thought I saw something. Knew something."

"Who is 'they,' Lucas?"

"Reid's new men. They saw me there. In the firelight I saw worry in their eyes and I looked back silently shaking my head like I knew they'd set the fires. Like I might have some evidence. That's why I encouraged my dad and mom to leave. I knew there would be trouble, but not this. I thought one of the thugs would just break and come forward when they couldn't get to me."

Dan knew Lucas was rattling. Somehow, Lucas felt this shooting was his fault.

He thought he was doing the right thing.

"I loaned him my clothes. I didn't think." Lucas's eyes turned liquid with pain. "Don't you see? It's my fault. Whoever shot Blade thought he was me. I was bluffing that I had information on the chance of breaking their line. I thought if they could get to me they might try to frighten me off."

Dan patted Lucas on the shoulder, knowing that he didn't feel any comfort. "This is not on you, son. It's not. You didn't fire the shot."

Lucas nodded and dropped his head into his bloody hands.

Dan rose and walked back to Blade. Lucas needed time to calm down.

A fireman was cutting the ugly brown jogging suit off as two men treated Blade.

Dan reached for the gun that was lying beside the special agent in a stream of blood. The barrel was cold. It hadn't been fired. Dan carried the Glock back to the cot where Lucas sat. "Why'd you have the gun, Lucas?"

"I was afraid whoever shot him would come after us both. Finish him off and kill me. If you hadn't yelled our names, if I hadn't heard the sirens, I might have shot you."

"But you didn't. You did the right thing, Lucas. You protected him until you knew I was on the other side of that door."

One of the EMTs looked up. "Steady vital signs. We'll make sure he's stable and then get him ready to transport."

Dan hadn't noticed that two more men had come in, carrying a board to move Blade. They all worked like a well-oiled machine, each with his own job, as if they were professionals and not volunteers who trained on their own time.

In what seemed like seconds, they were lifting him, tied to the board, into the air.

"How is he?" Dan asked.

Only one man glanced back as they began to move their patient. "Stable. He'll be up and riding that hog by the time I get it rebuilt."

"Take care of him, Lou," Dan ordered.

"I will, Sheriff." The mechanic smiled. "Like he was a vintage Harley."

Slowly, the men carried Blade down the two flights. The helicopter was landing in the middle of the highway, stopping traffic in both directions.

Dan walked down beside Lucas and they watched from the shadows as the firemen handed Blade off to men and women in scrubs.

As the crowd observed the helicopter, Dan leaned next to Lucas and said, "How about we go somewhere and talk because we both know we're not going back to that jail cell."

"Where?" Lucas finally seemed to relax a bit.

"Somewhere safe."

Lucas let out a sharp laugh. "I thought I was somewhere safe."

"See that rust bucket of a Jeep? You can slip off the side of the porch and be in it before anyone sees you."

"Tim's Jeep?"

"You got a better idea?"

"No."

"Good. I'll round him up and tell him to go home. Stay at his place. I can walk from my house to his after I get back from Lubbock. I need to talk to you, but I have to make sure Blade is okay first."

"I don't want to get Tim mixed up in this. It's just a rumor that I know something and they're after me." He shook his head. "I even egged them on at the fire. Thought I was being smart." Lucas looked up. "I'm an idiot, Sheriff."

Dan patted his hand. "Never heard a lawyer admit that. You got a chance of being brilliant and don't worry about getting Tim involved."

"It's dangerous. I see that now. I don't want him hurt."

"Are you kidding? Tim will love this kind of thing. He's been hanging around this office for years, wanting to get involved. He'll jump at the chance to help you and maybe fuel his own imagination. Who knows, we might make it into one of his books. Reid's men will never guess you're with him. I doubt anyone will even remember you two guys were once friends."

"We still are," Lucas said. "Or at least I hope we are."

"If anyone is looking for you, they will try your three cousins and their families first. That's your closest kin in the county after they learn your parents are gone."

Lucas nodded. "All three live on farms so far from town they'll see trouble coming and meet it armed. You'll let them know I'm safe?

"I'll call my brothers and sisters. Half the time I can't find them, but I'll leave a message for them to report anything strange."

"I plan to tell everyone in town I transported you to a safe house. No one, and I mean *no one*, is to know where you are. Not until I figure out why someone wants you dead. They must be holding some kind of secret to be willing to shoot someone they think might know something. I got enough bodies showing up in my county. I don't want another one."

"Got it," Lucas said as the engines of the helicopter roared and dust whirled in the air, blowing trash and tumbleweeds around like brown snow.

When the dust settled, Lucas had vanished, and Dan walked through the crowd, knowing that somewhere among the curious was one man who'd meant to be a killer tonight.

twenty-one

Dakota stood among the crowd, watching with her sister on her left and Grandmother on her right. They'd heard Dakota talking to Blade when he'd called and a moment later when she'd relayed the message to the sheriff. There was no way either would have stayed home.

Yet even with them by her, Dakota felt alone. She'd searched the crowd for Blade. He had to be there; he'd called.

"What's happening?" Maria whispered.

"They loaded a man into the helicopter," Dakota answered. "He looks hurt bad. I can see blood on the blanket and more on two of the firemen."

"Is it our Hamilton?" Grandmother said, not caring who overheard. "I couldn't see the bloody man's face."

"I think so. I heard one of the firemen say that the deputy was shot." She looked for one detail, one thing to prove it wasn't Blade. "I see dark hair. The guy on the stretcher is about his size."

Grandmother grumbled. "He's our Hamilton. If anyone is

going to shoot him it should be us. This makes me fighting mad."

"What should we do?" Maria asked.

"I vote one of us goes to the hospital." Dakota saw the fear on her big sister's face. "I'll take you and Grandmother home first. But, I have to go, Maria. I have to know if it's him."

Maria nodded. "He'll understand why I can't go. Tell him I wanted to, but I can't go back there. The smells. The noise."

Dakota gripped her sister's hand and held on tightly like she had years ago when Maria was so afraid of the dark that she couldn't find her way out of. "I'll tell him. He'll understand."

"If he's got any sense left," Grandmother added. "A bullet in the brain could scramble him good. I wouldn't want that, not even for a Hamilton."

"He told me to call the sheriff. All he said was 'man down.' He didn't tell me it was him."

Maria gripped Dakota's arm. "Maybe he didn't want to worry you. Maybe he knew he was dying."

An old man slapped the side of the helicopter and yelled, "Get Deputy Hamilton there fast, boys!" The engines roared.

Dakota felt tears on her cheeks. "It's him. I have to go."

They started back to the pickup with Grandmother talking to no one in particular. "I'd go with you, girl, but I've got to get back to watching that ghost crawling around near Indigo Lake. I need to be on guard, or he might just float over the water and step foot on our land."

Dakota didn't want to fall into one of Grandmother's stories. Not tonight. Not with Blade on his way to the big Lubbock hospital.

They rode home in silence. Once inside, Maria made her a basket of food while Dakota packed a few things in a bag. Hospital things she might need. Water, a toothbrush, aspirin, change, a notebook, a small pillow.

"Call me and let me know how he is." Maria hugged her. "He's a good man. Don't let him be there all alone."

Both women knew the other's world. When time was measured in shift changes. Dakota couldn't leave Blade there, hurt and by himself.

"I will," she promised. She was in a hurry.

"He doesn't have any family, Dakota. Stay close. Someone tried to kill him." Maria had come to the same conclusion she had.

"You mean besides Grandmother?" Dakota smiled.

Maria shook her head. "I think Grandmother likes him too. She asked me if we had enough in the Mason jar to buy his land. She said it wouldn't be Hamilton land anymore if we bought it. It would be Davis land."

"I'll suggest that if no one looks at his property. Maybe he'd let us pay him in jelly because the Mason jar only has ones in it." She picked up her bag and the basket. "I'll call in with reports. I promise."

They hugged as if Dakota were leaving on a long journey and not simply driving two hours to Lubbock. Maria remained on the porch, worry on her beautiful face as Dakota got into the pickup and headed out.

Dakota drove the two hours to the hospital, playing the radio as loud as it would go, but she didn't remember a single song she heard. Once parked and in the hospital she spent half an hour talking her way up to Blade's room. The guard just outside the door searched her bag and the basket, then frowned when he finally let her in. "I was told he wouldn't have visitors."

"I'm family," she answered. After all, her family had killed most of his family, so that had to make her near to being next of kin.

She bumped her way in and was surprised to see Blade sitting up in bed. Bandaged, plugged into machines and looking very sleepy.

"Hi, Elf. About time you got here."

"How'd you know I'd come at all, Hamilton?"

He was drugged up enough on painkillers to be honest. "Whether you want to admit it or not, we're attracted to each other and I don't mean in a let's-be-friends kind of way. I'd find you if you flew off in a bird and I figured you'd find me."

She moved closer, making sure one of those shots he took wasn't in the head. Absently, she combed his curly hair back. She needed to touch him.

He closed his eyes and smiled. "You could do that all night."

"I'm just checking that some of your brains aren't leaking out. I heard someone say you were shot in a dark parking lot wearing black. Were you trying to hide or just make it hard on the shooter?"

"Brown." His eyes slowly closed. "Get the facts right, sweetheart."

"Since when did I become your sweetheart?"

"When I passed out from losing a few quarts of blood in the third-floor jail, the last face I saw before all went black was you. I guess that makes it simple. You're my sweetheart. We need to sleep together to make it official, but not tonight. I've had a rough day." He was fighting sleep and losing the battle. "There's no privacy around here, anyway. They even cut my underwear off." He managed a weak smile. "Want to look?"

"No." She laughed.

She might as well be honest. "I'm not a one-night-stand kind of girl, Blade. I thought you understood that, so you might as well give up on the sweetheart label. We won't be sleeping together."

"And I'm not a stay-around kind of guy so you won't have much time to change your mind."

He closed his eyes and she wondered if he was asleep.

She moved along the bedside and took his big hand between hers. There were tubes attached to him, but she needed to feel

him, flesh on flesh. He was an interesting man. If she ever decided to sleep with a stranger, it would be a man like him. Someone who could make her laugh. Someone who could make her
feel.

She had dreams, goals, responsibilities. She didn't have time
for a few wild nights that would probably mix up her mind for
months. One-night stands were for wild people, free people, but
the what-if settled into the corners of her mind.

What if she risked one night of her life? One piece of her
heart. Would she live the rest of her life regretting it, or trea-
suring the memory?

He opened his now bloodshot gray eyes and mumbled,
"Couldn't we meet in the middle? You come away with me for
a few weeks. I could recover. We could talk and go out to eat,
and sleep together if it felt right and I was up for it. Think of it
as a vacation."

Shaking her head, she realized that wasn't what she wanted
at all. It would have to be far more, or nothing at all.

She thought of hitting him, but that didn't seem fair. His
left shoulder and arm were bandaged and his right side had a
long line of tape on it. "No, Hamilton. I can't leave for weeks,"
she answered politely, "but I will stay here and watch over you
while you sleep."

He closed his eyes again but his hand held on to hers.

"Now get some sleep, Hamilton," she whispered.

"You running my life, Elf?" he whispered with a smile.

"Someone needs to," she said, knowing he was probably too
far into sleep to answer. "The minute I wasn't watching over
you, you managed to get yourself shot."

She studied him as he rested. Cleaned up, he looked almost
handsome. His jaw was cut a little too hard. His hair a bit too
long. But his lips were perfect. She leaned over and kissed those
lips softly. "In another lifetime, maybe," she whispered. This
one was already packed.

He didn't open his eyes again as the night slipped away into morning. Dakota never left his side, not even when the sheriff came in to check on him. Brigman stayed awhile, then went out in the hallway to talk to the guard. The sheriff didn't leave until the nurse assured him they would watch over Hamilton.

Dakota snacked on the cookies and fruit in the basket Maria had sent and watched the nurses come and go, but she didn't talk to them.

Finally, a team of doctors came in. They didn't seem to notice her as they checked Blade.

As they were leaving, one doctor, a woman in her forties, smiled at her, so Dakota asked, "How is he?"

The doc raised an eyebrow, "You family?"

"I'm all he's got," Dakota lied.

"I figured that, or the guard outside wouldn't have let you stay." She moved closer to Dakota and lowered her voice.

"The federal agent has had many inquiries about his health. He is doing great. He was very lucky. The bullet in his arm didn't hit any bone, so it wasn't hard to extract. It'll heal quickly. The one at his side slid along, tearing up flesh and causing blood loss exacerbated by heightened activity after being shot."

Dakota finally relaxed. Blade wasn't going to die.

The doctor paused at the door. "You can go home if you like. We'll watch over him."

"If it's all right, I'll stay just a little longer."

She pushed the recliner close to his bedside to hold his hand as she slept. Just before she drifted off, she smiled. He might not know it, but they were finally sleeping together...again.

twenty-two

Dan pulled out a cot he kept in his office. There wasn't enough time to bother going home. He'd made the two-hour trip to Lubbock and back. He'd rest a few hours, and at sunup he'd start his investigation.

Someone had shot his deputy last night and Dan didn't have a single clue why.

He didn't call Brandi tonight. He couldn't. What could he say to a woman he missed so badly, even in all the insanity? It was a mess here. He hadn't solved one crime, and they were piling up. Two barns had been burned. Two bodies found. One burned. One with his head bashed in. Reyes was playing some kind of dangerous game, trying to figure out what was going on at the ranch where he grew up. And now, tonight, Blade had been shot while wearing Lucas's clothes.

If Dan called Brandi and told her, she'd hear how frustrated he was and say she'd come home on the next flight. It had taken him two months to talk her into going to Nashville to record the new songs. Like it or not, he was married to a woman that loved country music, and he had to share her now and then.

He told himself it was better that she wasn't in town right now. He needed to work every waking hour. But he missed her all the way down to his soul. She was the one love he'd never stop loving, never hold close enough, never ever let out of his heart.

Turning on his cell, he texted, Working late tonight. Miss you, sunshine. Will call tomorrow afternoon.

Before he could relax back on the cot, his daughter texted, Where are you, Pop? I'm at the lake house. After all the excitement I don't think I can sleep in my apartment, so crashing here.

He answered back, At office. If you sleep at home I'll see you at breakfast.

Will do. See you then, she answered. I want you to tell me what is going on. How is Blade? Where is Lucas?

He replied. Deputy out of danger. No clue why he was shot. Lucas is safe. We'll talk in the morning.

Ok, Pop. Night.

He stared at the phone, wondering if one day people would stop talking altogether and just text each other.

Sleep didn't find him for a while as he juggled the pieces of the puzzle in his mind. Somehow, Lucas and Reid, whether they knew it or not, were the center of all this trouble. They were both tied to the Bar W ranch. Both had been raised there. Both knew all the cowboys who worked there. Only, they were all gone, except Dice, who kept saying he was going back to look for his friend.

Reid had a right to sell off his land, or maybe just stop raising cattle, but why hire all the thugs? He'd downsized. Maybe he was switching to wind power or oil? Maybe he'd figured out how to claim the Bar W was really a reservation and he was planning to open a casino. No, that wasn't possible.

Dan swore. His brain was so tired he was beginning to ramble. Maybe he'd find a few answers if he could figure out why there was such bad blood between Lucas and Reid. Another why.

One more person kept circling in the sheriff's mind. Reid's older brother, Charley Collins. Everyone knew he got a girl pregnant just out of high school and she'd left him with the kid to raise. Everyone also heard, three years later, how Charley had slept with his dad's third wife, who happened to be about the same age as Charley, twenty-one at the time. Collins kicked his oldest son out with nothing but the clothes on his back. Charley had to quit school to make enough to keep food on the table for his daughter.

A few years later he met and married Jubilee, and they ran the Lone Heart ranch. In a small town, everything you've ever done weaves into the fabric of who you are. Some folks said that Jubilee was a little crazy, but all Dan knew was that she and Charley were crazy in love.

Funny thing about Charley, he'd screwed up his life a few times but folks liked him. Some even swore he was the best Collins who ever breathed. He was always willing to help anyone in need. Did a great job of raising his daughter and even took in a kid who might have headed in the wrong direction if it hadn't been for Charley.

He wasn't interested in his father's ranch, but Charley might know the same facts that Reid and Lucas did. If he'd be willing, he might help the sheriff put this puzzle together.

Now that Dan finally had a plan, he relaxed. The only thing that still worried him was why someone shot Blade.

Maybe Lucas was right. It was just a simple case of mistaken identity.

The thugs might think Lucas knew something that would be worth killing him for to keep a secret.

If the shots were meant for Lucas Reyes. The lawyer. The son of the Bar W foreman. The only man Dan had ever heard of who refused to leave a jail cell. Then Dan needed to know what the thugs feared.

But trying to figure out why anyone would want to shoot Lucas only seemed to lead to more questions.

twenty-three

The night had aged into silent sleep when Lauren pulled on her windbreaker and walked out onto the deck of Pop's lake house. This was the place she always went to think. It was quiet, peaceful. For a lonely, only child, this was her safe haven.

She watched the full moon dance along the water. Unlike Indigo Lake, out in the country, this hold of water was man-made. In the early years, a creek had been dammed up to act as the town's alternate water supply, but now it was simply a small lake community, where most residents fished the long days of summer away.

This time of year she always thought of the lake as hibernating until spring. People bought a lake house for the summer months, but Lauren loved the winter here. Most of the homes were empty now, resting, but come March there would be boats on the water.

She played with the key around her neck. Lucas had given it to her the last time she saw him in the jail. It felt cold on her skin, almost like it was branding her with ice. Somehow, he had said, the key held his future and she had to keep it safe. Lucas had said to tell no one she had it, and that was exactly what she'd do.

For the first time, she knew how much she meant to him. He'd trusted her. According to Pearly, people had been coming and going from the jail cell all day, but he'd trusted her. If her dad frisked him when he went into jail, then someone had to have brought him the key, hidden it in a pocket of something brought up to the jail. Pop would have checked each piece of clothing coming in, but Pearly might not have.

Keep it safe, he'd said, as if she was saving his life, his future.

She'd spent her day doing research about the Bar W, collecting information and thinking about the key.

First, she researched the history of the Collins ranch.

D.R. Collins, Reid's father, was the third generation to own the Bar W ranch. His grandfather—generation one—had built it up during the late years of the cattle drives. He hadn't married until his fifties, but his young bride gave him three children. Two girls and a boy. He'd left the entire ranch to his son.

The second Collins to have the ranch had two sons. But the will left it all to one, D.R. Collins, Reid's father. No one seemed to know what happened to the other son.

Reid's father always went by D.R. Some said it was because his mother's grandfathers had been Davis and Randell. She couldn't make up her mind which name to use, so she just gave her son the initials of both. Like most family trees in the area, there were a few Davises or Kirklands or Wagners or O'Gradys or Randells mixed into the branches.

But the Collinses didn't want any close relatives. Like the two generations before, D.R. Collins made it plain he was leaving the ranch to only one of his children. When Charley messed up, Reid became generation four. Like his father, Reid had never really run the ranch. Foremen like Lucas's father did.

Lauren had spent the day checking out every public record. She even found pictures of the last three weddings of D.R. Collins, now in his fifties. With each marriage, D.R. grew older and the brides grew younger. The last two nuptials had happened in Europe and to her knowledge, no one from Crossroads, including his sons, had been invited.

She had no idea how any of this could help her pop solve his case. There had to be trouble somewhere. Collins didn't get along with many of the locals. Reid Collins must have needed money fast or been sick of waking up every morning smelling cattle.

Lauren wasn't sure her father knew much about what had happened on the ranch for years. He'd once been invited out now and then, when Reid's father still owned the place, but D.R. was never home long enough to keep even a polite friendship going.

Walking out to the water's edge, Lauren saw a light on at Tim O'Grady's place. He was probably working late. He lived the glamorous life of a writer that she only dreamed about.

If it wasn't so late, she'd stop in and visit with him. They must have talked a thousand hours growing up. About nothing. About everything. They might not solve all the world's problems, but she'd always found it comforting to know one other person was as confused as she was.

She drifted toward the light, even though she knew she wouldn't interrupt him. Not tonight. There was too much on her mind.

Lauren had forgotten all about their dinner date last night and so had he, obviously. There was too much in the wind. Tim would call her in a few days and they'd laugh about it, and then they'd probably go to Dorothy's Café and talk.

As she circled the bend of the lake and looked up, she saw a man sitting on the rock Tim and she used to meet on when they were kids.

Only tonight it wasn't Tim's, but Lucas's outline she saw.

A dozen questions came to mind. She knew Pop had moved him away from the county jail, but it seemed odd the sheriff would come out and set him on a rock. Maybe he was hiding in the trees around the lake or staying in one of the cabins abandoned in winter. It was so late Lucas may have thought it would be safe to come outside.

She slowly moved toward him, her tennis shoes sinking an inch into the wet sand as she walked. Her father had said Lucas was safe and maybe he was. No one would think to look for him two miles from town.

If he'd tell her the details of what happened in the jail cell, everyone in Crossroads could read it in the morning. If they had a chance to talk, he might explain the key. It simply looked like an ordinary key. Maybe he'd tell her why he seemed to want people to believe he was involved in the fires on the Collins ranch. But he couldn't have been. He'd been with her when the first one lit the night. Nothing made sense right now.

She didn't say a word as she crawled up on the rock and took her seat beside him.

"I saw you coming," he whispered as he moved so his body circled behind her for warmth. "I thought of yelling for you to go back. I meant what I said about no one knowing we're even friends. Tim, you and me might be remembered for the Gypsy House incident years ago, but folks think we've all gone our separate ways. You should stay away from me."

"I'm not leaving. This is my rock."

"Oh, yeah, you own it?"

"Well, no, but I claimed it when I was five. I'll let you sit on it, but you need to know that it is mine."

"Then it's your rock. Thanks for sharing." He tugged an old blanket around them both, then hugged her tightly. "You know, every time I get near you it's like I have to absorb this pleasant blow to my gut before I can relax and simply enjoy you being close. No one's ever affected me like that but you."

She turned to face him and wrapped her arms around his neck. This was the Lucas she knew. Not the lawyer. Not the boy in a hurry to grow up. "You've never told me that." She smiled, wondering if he had any idea how good it felt to hear him talk of such things. He'd always been so serious. Even when they were in high school he was the grown-up, the voice of reason. There were times they talked that she thought he had to be far more than her.

"Remember when Kirkland gave us both cell phones?" She felt his laughter.

"Yeah, I wonder if he knew we'd just use them to call each other."

"I don't think so, but if he did guess, he never told Pop."

Lucas rubbed his jaw against her cheek, tickling her with his stubble. "I spent a thousand more hours thinking about what I'd say to you than ever talking to you. Looking back, I wish I'd been brave enough to make a few more of those midnight calls."

They were silent for a few minutes, both lost in what might have been.

Finally, she pulled away and faced him, wishing she could see his eyes, wishing he could read her thoughts. The words they never said hung heavy between them.

"Kiss me, Lucas. Like nothing exists in the world right now except me and you. Kiss me like you did once beneath a tree outside my dorm. Like it was something you had to do. Like it was more important than breathing."

"Bossy. That's a side I haven't seen." He touched her cheek.

"I just want to feel something tonight. For a few more seconds I'd like to believe a dream I once had isn't completely dead. Pearly said the other day that I'm in the spring of my life, but inside it feels like winter. It has for a long time."

He kissed her gently. As if it were a first kiss. A hesitant kiss. A hopeful kiss. When she didn't react, he pulled an inch away. "Aren't you going to kiss me back?"

"No." She stared at him, loving and hating this man all at the same time. "For once, I'd like just to feel you kissing me. I don't want to think about anything for a while except that you are here with me. Before everything in your life becomes more important, let me have your total attention, Lucas. Make me believe I'm the center of your world and not just some girl who lives on the fringes."

He kissed her again and when she didn't react he moved down to her throat and then kissed his way back up to the tip of her nose. Once, he stopped and looked at her. Even in the moonlight she could see confusion in his face. "You're in a strange place tonight, *mi cielo.*" Then he whispered very low in her ear. "My sky. My world."

She grinned. "I'm floating between planets, you know. I'm not even sure where I am but I'll let you know where I land."

"So, what do I do while you're floating, gentle beauty?"

"Make me feel. I've been sleepwalking through life, and I'd like to wake up."

He cradled her in the crook of his arm and kissed her again. Harder, longer, with less control. "You taste so good," he whispered. "Like home and Christmas and first love all mixed into one."

Pushing the windbreaker away, he moved his hand over her flannel shirt. "You feel so good this close. So often I think of you as a dream I can't quite reach."

Her only response was a low sigh of pleasure.

He grew bolder. One button tumbled open, then another as his lips slid along her skin. Maybe he needed to float awhile tonight also. Maybe they both needed to just feel for a change and not think.

"I've wanted to touch you like this since I first saw you." He laughed. "That night we were walking home when we were all in high school, I wouldn't have been there if you hadn't said you were going to walk home in the dark with Reid and Tim. I was there to be with you."

She closed her eyes, remembering how he'd walked beside

her, talked to her, while the boys talked football. Then, when the floor of the old house began to crumble, he'd held her safe. He'd been her knight, her hero, her dream lover. Someone not quite real. Someone she could never reach for.

Slowly, his hand pushed beneath the cotton of her T-shirt and covered her breast. He held it tightly and her breath came faster. "Tell me you want this, Lauren, because I'm finished waiting for the right time. If all we have is tonight, I want you to know how I feel about you."

"I want to be with you, but you should know, I don't think that I'm able to feel as deeply as other people. Something is wrong with me. I've tried intimacy and it didn't move me." Now wasn't the time to tell him that every time she'd tried sex, it was just an act, not a feeling. Maybe she wasn't built for passion. Her mother had told her once that it was something she could do without in her life. Maybe being frigid was inherited.

That might be the reason she hadn't dated much or run after Lucas. A tiny hope had always whispered in her heart that Lucas might be able to fix her, but now, if he couldn't, if he wouldn't, then she'd know she was broken.

"I find it impossible to believe that passion doesn't flow in your veins. I've thought of you like this in my arms even when I was more kid than man."

She lay back on the cold rock as he moved above her, slowly undressing her until his hand moved over her bare skin from throat to just below her waist. When she didn't say a word, he unbuttoned her jeans and slid them low on her hips so he could spread his hand out over her abdomen.

"You're deep-water beautiful. When the time is right passion will flow out of you like an endless ocean." He kissed her as he lowered his body over her. "I want to be the one with you when that happens."

Everywhere his fingers moved, her skin warmed, and wherever he wasn't touching felt cold, dead.

She couldn't help but move to his touch. He made her forget the entire world. There was nothing but him. *Feel*, she almost whispered. Now was the time to crack the shell that always surrounded her. This was Lucas. She could relax and just feel. She didn't have to be afraid.

"You're so beautiful in the moonlight," he said against her ear. "You really don't know how lovely you are or what it does to me inside just to be near to you. You've got a power over me."

When he kissed her with a hunger that surprised her, she didn't return his kiss. She wouldn't pretend with him, not Lucas. It had to be real or nothing at all.

A tear ran across her cheek. She could feel his passion, but not her own. She couldn't let go.

"Are you going to make love to me?" she asked, waiting for him to go further. Loving him would be perfect. Knowing that he loved her would make all the splintered parts of her life fit together.

He didn't answer for a few minutes as he learned the curves of her body. He was touching her with loving care, but passion seemed to be slipping away.

She floated between the world she wanted and reality.

"No," he finally said with a laugh that held no humor. "I want you to want me as much as I want you. Then we'll make love together. I feel like I'm about to lose control with you, and when I do I'd like you to make the jump with me."

Lauren closed her eyes so tightly tears dripped out. He might be talking about a time that would never come. Couldn't she just love him? Why did it have to be so complicated? Why couldn't she pretend and maybe it would come true?

But she couldn't. Not with him. No matter how much she wished for this, she would never lie to Lucas.

He pulled her into his hug and held her for a while, then whispered, "Passion starts in the blood, not just the brain, Lauren. You can't talk yourself into this. I'm not sure you really know who I am and, with all that's going on, it's probably not the best time for me to be thinking of anything but staying alive. When we get together, I want it to be just you and me. I may not be the hero you think I am. And maybe you're not the perfect sheriff's daughter you think you have to be."

She wanted to scream *No*. He was wrong. She needed to feel something *now*. She wanted to know that she was real inside, full, alive.

She lay still as he buttoned her pants, then her shirt, then the windbreaker. When she was fully dressed, he pulled her to her feet. "We'll try this again sometime. We'll go dancing. We'll drink wine. We'll take our time."

Anger built like a slow burn in her gut. "Lucas, we're not children. You can make love to me." She felt like she was offering him a gift that he didn't want.

He kissed the top of her head as he had ten years ago when she turned sixteen. "I don't want to just have sex, Lauren. I want to be in love with you so deeply that you're in my every thought." He caught the chain around her neck and pulled the key up. "But now is not the time or the place."

She pushed away, realizing he was stepping back from her again. She'd heard those words before. "It never is the right time with you, Lucas." All the other times he'd walk out avalanched through her mind. He'd even said they'd be together tonight and then he'd stopped when he'd heard her confession. She wasn't perfect, either. She couldn't feel.

He might say she wanted him to be perfect, more than he was, but he wanted the same.

She felt like they were mannequins, an aisle apart, always admiring one another but never moving a step closer. Perfection in wax and plastic.

"You don't understand, do you?" He sounded tired.

"You're right. I don't understand. I'm trying to love you when you're not ready to love me back. I'm sick of wanting you, or comparing every man to you and having none quite measure up. I'm through with waiting. Tonight was your one chance and you blew it." Being mad at him was easier than looking too deeply inside herself.

She was off the rock and running toward the one light along the shoreline before he could say a word. Part of her knew she was being unfair, but she'd waited so long to feel alive. All she'd wanted tonight was to feel, and Lucas was the only man who might have made that happen.

She veered off the shoreline and into the trees. She knew the path by heart even in the darkness, but she didn't know herself. She was drifting again, floating between planets.

A few minutes later she slid through the patio door of the O'Grady lake house and went straight to Tim's bedroom. She didn't know if she was shaking with cold or with anger. All she knew was that she hurt inside and couldn't be alone.

Tim was sitting in the middle of his bed with papers scattered around him and a laptop on his crossed knees. When she stepped in the doorway he didn't look surprised. "I guess you know Lucas is hiding out here. He sort of broke out of jail, with your Pop's help, and came here—can you believe it?"

She just stared at Tim. She had no idea what to say. For once she didn't want to talk.

Tim didn't seem to have the same problem. "He's probably sleeping. If you're here to see him, go down the hallway to the room that used to be my parents'."

She just kept standing in the doorway. The numbness she often felt was seeping back into her bones. She wouldn't allow her heart to break. "I didn't come to see Lucas. I came to ask if you'd hold me for a while. I'm cold."

Tim pushed the manuscript aside and opened the covers. "Want to sleep with me, L? You know you're always welcome."

She nodded, tugged off her jacket and wet shoes, then crawled into his bed.

He flipped off the light and drew her under his arm. "Want to have sex?" he asked. "I'm happy to put that on the menu too."

"No."

Tim laughed. "Of course not. How about we just cuddle?"

"Sounds good."

His hand moved along her arm, warming her. "You know, L, if I wrote this scene in a novel no one would believe it. I'm not sure it's normal for a grown man and woman to sleep together and not *sleep together*, if you know what I mean."

She rested her cheek against his sweatshirt and cried softly.

He pushed her damp hair off her cheek. "It's all right, L. You can come sleep with me for as long as you want to. If I get married someday, I'll just tell my wife to move over enough to make room for my best friend. I'm sure she won't mind."

Lauren laughed and pushed her tears away with her palm. "I love you, Tim."

"Yeah, I love you too. Go to sleep. We'll figure out the world over coffee in the morning."

twenty-four

———

Dan wasn't surprised to find his daughter having breakfast with Tim O'Grady when he came by to pick up Lucas. Tim had been his daughter's best friend since they were both five. He was a good enough guy, probably the perfect friend to make his shy Lauren laugh, but Dan's greatest fear was that she'd fall in love with the neighbor kid and he'd be stuck with a writer for a son-in-law. Then, with his luck, all his grandchildren would be red-headed beanpoles with no common sense, just like their father.

"Want me to go with you today, Sheriff?" Tim asked as he offered Dan a burned pancake. "I know you're short one deputy and I memorized all the lingo from watching *CSI*."

"No thanks." Dan caught Lauren's look. That don't-do-anything-to-hurt-my-friend's-feelings look all fathers recognize in their daughters by the age of five. "I was hoping you could man the office this morning, Tim. Lauren might have time to help you. I need someone I can depend on." The words even tasted bad as they came out, but Dan didn't want to disappoint his daughter, even if it meant putting up with O'Grady.

"Why?" Tim asked. "What's going on besides Blade Hamilton being in the hospital and not one crime around here has been solved in days?"

Dan just stared at Tim. He knew the writer would have more questions.

"Shouldn't I be issued a gun? Or does Pearly already have one hidden away somewhere in the office? She seems like the type. You know, little old lady who packs a .45 in her gym bag and doesn't even have a gym membership."

That was another tic he had, the sheriff decided. Tim always answered his own questions. Half the time he was too busy telling himself a story to listen to the facts.

"Pearly called in sick. Said she was still in bed." Dan rattled off facts while he had the chance. "My only deputy is in the hospital. Someone just needs to man the office phone."

Tim ate half his burned pancake in one bite. "I've never known her to miss a day of work. You think we should go by and check on her? At her age she could be dead from near anything."

Before Dan had to answer that question, Lucas walked into the kitchen. He was dressed in one of Tim's *The Aliens Have Landed* sweatshirts and his dark hair was still wet from the shower. Not the polished lawyer look today. He didn't bother to speak. He simply stared at the three eating breakfast.

"My house guest." Tim pointed with his fork at Lucas as if Lauren and the sheriff might not notice another person in the small kitchen.

As Lucas accepted a burned pancake, he took the seat next to Dan and seemed not to notice Lauren sitting at the end of the counter.

After drowning his pancake in syrup, Lucas muttered, "Morning, Sheriff."

Dan hadn't had enough sleep to figure out the three of them this morning. He decided to concentrate on Lucas. "I sent some of your clothes with Cap to the hospital for Blade. He may get to come home this afternoon. Since the jogging suit didn't work out, I thought we'd try Western clothes, including your boots."

Lucas finally gave a nod to Lauren, then turned back to the sheriff. "That's fine, but I get the feeling Western is not his style, either. Why send him home? He's probably safer in the hospital. Besides, I don't think he has a home."

"I talked to Dakota and she said she and her sister would take him in for a few days. After all, he is their neighbor, and that old house on his land will take weeks to make it livable. Once he's out of the hospital, he'll need somewhere to rest and someone to help change the bandages."

"Don't look at me." Tim tried to give Lauren a pancake but she wouldn't reach for it. "I'm running the hideout, not the recovery center."

The sheriff smiled. "I think he'll be in better hands at the Davis place. I'm told Maria is a great cook."

Lucas shoved his breakfast away after one bite.

Tim swallowed another half of a pancake and changed the conversation as if simply flipping channels on a TV no one was watching. "I hear they superglue bullet holes closed. What if the deputy springs a leak when he's recovering?" He lifted another pancake from the stack no one was eating. "I wonder if the superglue really works. I read it on the internet. Did they do that to you that time you got shot out on Highway 111, Sheriff?"

Dan motioned for Lucas to head toward the door. "Don't have time to talk. Thanks for the hideout, Tim."

He glanced at his daughter and felt like screaming *Don't marry Tim!* But maybe he shouldn't worry. They were just friends.

As he and Lucas walked out to the cruiser, Dan asked, "How long has Lauren been here?"

"I don't know. She was drinking coffee and talking to Tim when I woke up. You think there's something between them, Sheriff?"

"Yeah, me." Dan laughed. "Seriously, they've always been

friends but if I thought there was more going on, I'd either have to shoot him or myself. I couldn't live with his constant questions, and he tells the worst jokes I've ever heard."

Lucas climbed into the car and added, "You know, I think he's my best friend too. I know a lot of people in the city, but not one I'd trust to help me escape from jail. When he found me hiding in his Jeep, he didn't hesitate to help."

Dan started the car. "You're right. Tim's not so bad."

"Where we headed, Sheriff?"

"I want to talk to the one Collins we haven't talked to. Charley. We're driving out to Lone Heart ranch. One, maybe he can tell us something we don't know and two, you need to stay out of sight just in case your theory about the shooter thinking Blade was you is right. Our official comment on you is that you have been moved to a safe house."

"Do you have a safe house?"

"No, but no one has to know that."

Lucas leaned back and slept while Dan drove. The young lawyer seemed like a man with a great deal on his mind. Things he didn't plan to share with a lawman. Only, Dan hoped he might share a bit with Charley, and Dan planned to be listening to every word.

The sheriff played with the puzzle pieces in his mind. He had to figure this out before someone else got shot, or killed, or disappeared. At the rate things were going, Crossroads would be a ghost town before his term of office was up.

twenty-five

Blade stared at his reflection in the pop-up mirror on his hospital tray table. He'd been in Texas less than a week and he didn't even look like himself. Wild hair, the shadow of a beard, bruises everywhere and new wrinkles in the corner of his eyes. He was aging a year for every day he stayed around here.

The docs had done a great job of patching him up, but he still felt weak as a newborn calf trying to stand for the first time. "Hell," he said aloud. He was starting to think like a Texan. Next thing he knew he'd be wearing pointed-toe boots and chewing tobacco.

Right now he doubted he'd even be able to fight off the Elf or her grandmother.

Not that he'd ever try fighting off Dakota. If she ever came at him, Blade had a feeling it would be full-out, be it love or hate.

She'd been sleeping in the recliner in his room for hours. Her hair was a wild mess, half covering her face. She'd said she wouldn't sleep with him, but she'd offered to take care of him. He must matter to her. He couldn't think of anyone, including his own mother, who'd make that offer.

He thought of telling Dakota that sleeping with him would be a hell of a lot easier than having to take care of him, but he doubted she'd follow that logic.

The nurse came in about noon and said they were putting him through a few more tests; then, if all was fine, he could go home.

She'd added, "The University of Colorado Hospital sent over your records, Agent Hamilton. A few facts stood out. You're in great shape, have regular checkups, and always leave after an injury before the doctors tell you to. So the team has decided to get ahead of the game and release you early. Go home and rest." She handed him a folder and a sheet of *do-nots*.

Blade thought of telling her he didn't have a home. He'd never had a home. He barely remembered the houses they'd moved to during his childhood. His mother never put up pictures on a wall, or books on a shelf, or even a Christmas tree. He'd asked her once if she remembered his birthday and she'd said, *How could I forget? It was the most painful day of my life.*

But Blade just said thanks and tried his best to listen to the nurse's lecture. He knew the drill.

The elf in the corner woke up about the time a nurse was helping him on with the jeans and Western shirt Lucas had sent over. Dakota just rubbed her eyes and stared as if she'd fallen asleep at the drive-in theater and had woken up during the good part of the show.

Blade thought he looked like he should be trick-or-treating in the boots and pearl-snap shirt, but Dakota told him he looked fine.

The boots were a bit too big, but they would do. The jacket was leather, longer than his biker jacket, but it felt like it had been made for him.

When the nurse ordered him to sit in the wheelchair, he did so without a word. He'd fought this battle twice before and lost both times.

Dakota disappeared as he signed out and was waiting for him

at the hospital entrance in her old pickup. While she waited, she'd combed her hair, but her clothes were hopelessly wrinkled.

He let the nurses help him into the truck and even managed to wave goodbye. Another change from the last time he left the hospital. Maybe Dakota was a calming influence on him, or maybe it had something to do with all the drugs they'd given him.

"Mind if we stop at a clothing store on the way home?" He tried to sound like he was fine even though he was starting to hate that word. "I need to pick up a few things. Underwear, for one."

Dakota glanced at him as she drove. "You're going commando?"

"Yes. How about you?" He swore he saw her blush.

She didn't say a word until she pulled into the parking lot of a Western-wear store. "They've got everything in here."

"I don't dress Western."

"You look good in it. I'll pick a few things out for you."

"Only if I get to pick a few out for you." A blouse that wasn't two sizes too big and a pair of jeans that fit her like skin sounded good.

Elf didn't look happy, but she must have been in a hurry to get him home because she didn't argue. Fifteen minutes later he walked out with two bags. Hers held a sexy outfit with rhinestones. What she'd bought for him in the other bag was anyone's guess. He doubted he'd ever wear the clothes she'd picked out, but he couldn't wait to see her in what he'd selected.

He was exhausted, as if he'd run forty miles in mud, but for once she wanted to have a real conversation. Like nothing was going on in his world. Like he didn't have things he needed to think about. The top of the list being who shot him.

He had no idea.

Dakota talked as they drove the two hours back to Crossroads in an old truck that seemed to be trying to rock him to sleep.

About halfway between Crossroads and Lubbock, Blade felt like he was listening to the history of Texas on tape.

It took him a while, but he finally decided she was discussing history because she didn't want to talk about the two of them. And if she was afraid to even mention what might happen between them, then she was halfway there.

He fell asleep thinking about how she'd be as a lover. Hopefully she wouldn't talk through it.

Suddenly he laughed, waking himself completely, as he realized he didn't care. She could talk all night just as long as she was beside him.

Any hope that she'd help him undress once they got to her place vanished when Blade climbed out of the truck and noticed Dice Fuller propped on the porch railing like a buzzard dressed up in boots.

The old guy must have guessed what Blade was thinking because he was grinning the whole time he helped Blade. He even added that Dakota had to go to work so everything would look normal; after all, no one was to know that Blade was out of the hospital.

"But don't you worry about her being gone, Granny and I'll take care of you."

Nothing makes a man get well faster than having unwanted help. After Dice assisted him with the boots, Blade said he could handle the rest.

The only bright side to staying at the Davis place seemed to be that Maria had made gingersnap cookies. The whole house smelled like heaven. The dark side was, Grandmother delivered his milk and cookies along with a threat to cut him up for cat food if he stepped out of line.

From the size of the fat cat Sam, she'd probably carried out that threat a few times lately. No wonder the Davis girls weren't married.

When he was finally alone, Blade looked around the spacious

room, now his recovery home. Tiled floors, low ceilings, long windows facing east. The bedroom was neat and clean but had nothing personal in it except a picture of two little girls who had to be Maria and Dakota. Maria was obviously teaching Dakota to ride a bike, and both were smiling.

He knew without asking that this had been their mother's room. The third bedroom in a home where a mother had lived with her two children.

He sat on the bed and slowly cradled his injured arm, then stretched out atop the covers. This was what home should feel like, he thought, as he drifted off to sleep.

Someone covered him with a fuzzy blanket, but he didn't open his eyes. Hours later he was aware that the room had grown dark. When Grandmother came in to turn on a lamp, he asked if he could have a glass of water and a rope. If she thought the request strange, she didn't comment.

When she returned with Dice, they watched Blade drink the entire glass of water, and then he asked Dice to tie the rope to the center of the footboard while he looped the other end. Now he could pull himself up with his good arm without straining the muscles along his bandaged side.

"You've been knocked out of the saddle before, haven't you, kid."

"A few times, old man." After Dice left, with no one else in the room Blade asked, "What's new in the investigation?"

"Which one? We got several going on. I had to declare myself a temporary deputy just to help Pearly. Everyone in town thinks they know something, but most of them don't know nothing. Sheriff knows the second body found at the Bar W was Coffer Coldman, but the coroner still hasn't ID'd the first one who was burned."

Dice sat down on the room's only chair and continued, "Something is going on at the Bar W. Everyone hinted that Reid was selling the place when he loaded all the cattle and sold off back pastures, but I'm not so sure. I've seen some heavy equipment headed out that way. Town's got a wagonload of questions and not an answer in sight."

Blade's head began to pound. "How about starting with who shot me and we'll work backward? I'm interested in what the sheriff might have found out."

"Oh, we don't know nothing about that. Sheriff found a few shells, but it was so late when you were shot, nobody saw a thing. One neighbor heard the gunfire but he thought it was a car backfiring. A couple of guys from the firehouse said there are boys who hunt rabbits out in the field behind the office. Maybe they thought you were a jackrabbit." Dice grinned and put one finger up on either side of his head.

"Very funny." Blade rubbed his forehead. "No leads at all? Any hunches as to why? Surely the sheriff has learned something."

Dice shook his head. "Other than some random fellow who just hates strangers, I can't think of anyone. There's a group that meets now and then to practice shooting. Call themselves a midnight militia. They think it was terrorists. Said it was just a matter of time before they hit Crossroads."

Blade thought that the chances of ISIS even finding this town, when FedEx couldn't, probably ranked about even with a zombie attack, but he didn't say anything. Right now, Dice was ahead of him, even in guessing.

"What about the bodies at the burn sites? Any news there?"

"All I know is Coffer Coldman is still dead. Nothing else to report."

"Any leads on who did that crime?"

"Nope." Dice raised his voice. "Oh, we did find Coffer's dog. He showed up back at the bunkhouse. I told him he inherited two hundred and ninety dollars, but he didn't seem all that interested."

"What about your friend LeRoy?"

"Someone said they thought they saw him in one of the bars in Amarillo. Like I figured he would, he was spending his pay. I'd like to be out looking just to be sure, but since you've been shot I'd better volunteer to be your bodyguard."

Blade grinned. "You'd take a bullet for me, Dice?"

"Well, no. I'm smart enough to step out of the way, but once I knew someone was shooting at you, I'd return fire. You wouldn't have to worry. If someone killed you, they'd be DRT."

"DRT?"

"Dead right there."

"That's comforting. Downright considerate. You should put that on a greeting card, Dice."

"You're a strange one, Hamilton. Half the time you don't make a lick of sense. I'll go get your supper."

Blade wasn't hungry, but the food was too good to ignore. As soon as he thanked Maria, he lowered into bed using the rope and went back to sleep.

When someone touched his forehead an hour later, he awoke. "Dakota?"

"I'm just making sure you don't have a fever." She sounded concerned.

"I'm fine. Just sleepy. You didn't make it home by dark."

She sat on the edge of his bed. "I had a late showing. Also talked to the sheriff. He wants to know when you're coming back to work."

"Tomorrow, maybe. I could probably help out at the office for a while."

"Do you remember talking to Dan at the hospital? He asked you a dozen questions about the shooting."

"Did I make any sense?" He took her small hand in his. It felt good to be touching her. The woman was like an addiction. Every time he touched her, he wanted more.

"Not much. You said a shadow shot you. The sheriff told me

if you remember anything that will help, call him. Otherwise, he'll let you rest."

"I'd rest a lot better if you'd lie down next to me."

She laughed. "Don't tell me you're afraid of the dark."

"Maybe I am. Walking out in a dark parking lot behind the sheriff's office didn't work out too well for me last night."

To his surprise, she kicked off her shoes and stretched out on top of the covers. He didn't let go of her hand. He'd planned to say something to let her know he wasn't a jerk who just wanted to get her into bed. But, he didn't know how to talk to a woman about much else.

Just before he fell asleep again, he realized that he'd had sex with a lot of women, but he'd never truly known one. He knew funny things to say, sexy things, but most of the women he'd known were hollow in his mind. A few he couldn't recall their names, or what they did for a living, or where they were from.

He'd never wanted to really know, really understand a woman until now. Maybe it was the drawings on the barn wall she'd done, as if chasing a dream, or maybe it was the way she took care of her sister. A complicated woman. A woman worth knowing. A woman worth the effort.

Lifting her hand, he kissed her fingers. "Thanks for staying with me last night in the hospital."

"You didn't need me," she answered.

"You're wrong. I did." To his surprise, he meant it.

twenty-six

As Dan pulled onto the Lone Heart Pass, he still didn't know if putting Charley Collins and Lucas Reyes together was a good idea or not. After all, Lucas had decked the last Collins he'd come across. Not that half the people in town hadn't thought of punching Reid. He was destroying the ranching business that had made his family rich, and everyone was trying to figure out how he planned to make money. Some said he was smarter than he seemed and would be investing the profit. Others bet he'd gamble it all away within a year.

But Reid's big brother was a very different man. Charley practically raised himself on a ranch where his father had a second wife and another son. Dan had noticed one year that Charley wasn't even in the family Christmas picture. By the time Charley was old enough to help run the ranch, his father had married number three, a girl the same age as Charley.

The Collins boys were about the same height and looked like brothers, but all that money had twisted Reid inside. He was one of those people who could never pass astronomy because of his firm belief that the planets revolved around him.

But the sheriff had seen Lucas and Charley talking a few times in years past. They had a healthy respect for each other. Charley was a few years older. Lucas had still been a kid when Charley left home for college, so even though they had been on the same ranch, they might not have spent much time together.

The sheriff watched them closely as they shook hands. They were friendly enough. Charley asked about Lucas's father, and said he'd always thought Reyes was a fine foreman. "Him and a few of the cowhands taught me more about ranching than my father ever knew. Once my dad married number two, he didn't care if I was around or not. I think I grew up eating more meals at the bunkhouse than at home. Lucas, your dad raised me as much as anyone did. How's he taking the change?"

"Dad and Mom left on a long-overdue vacation." Lucas kept his voice even. "He's going to disappear for a while and rest. He told me he wants to be too far away to even hear what is happening at the Bar W."

The sheriff read between the lines. Lucas had made sure his parents were out of danger. Lucas hadn't said a word yesterday about his father leaving, he wanted to make sure they were miles away before anyone even knew they were gone.

It occurred to Dan that keeping his parents safe might have been why Lucas had insisted on being put in jail. He wanted the focus on him so they could slip away.

Charley, looking very much like the successful rancher, invited them in for coffee. He'd come a long way from the single father living over a bar he'd been a few years ago. His new wife had fixed up the old homestead beautifully, and he'd turned her run-down ranch into a profitable horse-breeding operation.

"Jubilee is in town buying more baby clothes. If our baby doesn't come soon, I'll have to sell the spring hay crop to pay the bills." Charley grinned, which told Dan that he didn't care about the money.

"How long till she's due?"

"Less than a month. She wants to move to town the last few weeks of the pregnancy. I tried to explain that I've delivered a dozen horses already this year. Surely I can handle one baby."

"What'd she say?" Lucas asked as he accepted a cup of coffee.

"She said if I even hinted at that idea again, I'd be sleeping in the barn with those horses. Turns out women don't take to that kind of humor."

Dan laughed. "I can see her side. You might as well start packing. Town would be an easier move than the barn."

The men sat at the kitchen table and finally got down to the problem at hand. There was something going on at the Bar W, and between the three of them they might just find a hint of what that would be.

The sheriff went first. "Charley, I'm sure you are aware of what's happening at your father's ranch. The fires. The two bodies found. One was Coffer Coldman and the other one, we fear, might be an old cowhand named LeRoy Smith."

"I've heard talk, but I'm not interested in getting involved. My family lives right here at Lone Heart Pass. I don't really care how my father or Reid want to live their lives."

"Would your father take a call from you?" Dan asked.

Charley shook his head. "I doubt it. We haven't spoken in years. When he kicked me out, he also cut off all my college funds. I was already working part-time to cover day care. Suddenly, I had to drop out in the middle of my senior year and work two jobs just to keep a roof over my daughter's head. He didn't care about me or her."

His voice bore no hint of anger or bitterness. "Reid is his only son now. I think he wanted it that way. My mother, his first wife, died on him and my dad hated that. Maybe that's why he's been the one to leave in all the other marriages."

Looking up at Dan, Charley added, "He might take your call, Sheriff. When I was growing up he always spoke of you as his friend."

The sheriff wasn't finished asking questions. "Have you been in contact with Reid lately?"

Charley took a drink of his coffee. "We meet for breakfast now and then when Reid's in town. The last few times he was too hungover to make much sense. He hates running the ranch, but loves spending the money. Last time I talked to him for a minute at the post office, he said he was tossing around another way to make money from the ranch other than ranching. Wouldn't tell me what it was.

"I think he spends as much time in Vegas as he can get away with." Charley shrugged. "Maybe he'll become a poker pro."

Dan set his cup down and leaned forward. "I got a theory, but it can't go any further than this table. I don't think Reid is running things out there. Not by himself. I'm guessing you both know more about what's going on at the ranch than I do, but if one of us doesn't start figuring it all out I'm afraid Reid may be the next body found."

The sheriff studied them both and neither man looked surprised. Lucas hadn't even spoken since they'd sat down, but he was taking in every word.

Dan had guessed right. Both men knew something they weren't talking about. He could see it in their eyes.

Charley looked at Lucas and Dan didn't miss the lawyer's slight nod. "You might be right, Sheriff. I'll step in to help my brother, but I want no part of the ranch or the trouble Reid has gotten himself into. I want that understood from the beginning. Tell my dad I don't want one handful of dirt or one dollar from him if you get hold of him."

"Fair enough. When we're finished talking, I'll call him. But first, I want to know what you two know, or even suspect." In a big city, Dan might have brought them in for questioning, but not here. Ranch folks don't talk about their troubles outside the boundaries of their own barbed wire. Big ranches, like the Bar W, were a world within their borders.

The lawyer and the rancher looked at each other. In an odd way they were brothers. Veterans of the same war.

The sheriff had their attention; now he had to get their help. "I have a feeling something illegal is happening and Reid is in over his head. I just don't know what."

Charley shrugged. "I've heard from the few friends I've kept up with that the new guy hired to help Reid close the ranch operation down is pushing everything along. He acts like he's in charge. They say the men the cowboys call 'the thugs' work for him, not Reid."

"Wish I could lock them up for a few days and find out what's going on there," the sheriff said more to himself than them. "When I was out investigating the fires, one of the new men was always within hearing distance. I felt like I was being watched."

"So what are they hiding?" Charley said what the other two were already thinking.

"I may have an answer to that." Lucas sighed. "I think it's some kind of smuggling operation. The ranch would be a perfect stopover, distributing whatever illegal product they sell in four directions on the highways that cross here. All we have to do is find what they're transporting and how they are hiding it."

"Sounds easy enough." Charley laughed, as if Lucas had just suggested they climb Mount Denali in cowboy boots. "Whatever they're doing has nothing to do with ranching."

The puzzle in Dan's mind finally began to fit together. Reid wasn't in charge of whatever operation was going on; he was just a pawn that someone else was moving around the board.

One thing about this case had been gnawing away in the back of his mind since the barn fire. Reid didn't care about the fire and he only seemed irritated about the first body found. He wasn't involved, but when the second body, Coffer Coldman, showed up, Reid went from irritated to afraid. He'd acted like a man who knew he'd already lost but was still holding his cards at the table.

Charley stared at Lucas. "You have the map of the ranch, Lucas?"

Lucas shook his head. "No, I only saw it once."

Dan hadn't been following the conversation. He was still thinking about what the bad guys were doing on the ranch. Some kind of smuggling operation made sense. "What map?"

Charley leaned back in his chair and stared at Lucas. The lawyer stared back. They seemed to be playing some kind of silent game. They both knew something and neither wanted to be the first to tell.

"This is not a standoff, boys. We've all got to share what we know if we have any chance at getting to the bottom of this." Dan felt like a referee.

Charley broke first. "When I was a kid I heard my father say once there was a box canyon way back on the ranch where the breaks for Ransom Canyon start. He claimed he'd seen it once and it could hold a dozen cattle trucks. He had a hand-drawn map to the place on the back of an old painting in his study. I studied it a few times when no one was around but I couldn't figure it out.

"I tried to get him to show me the little canyon tucked away, but he said he'd forgotten where it was. He claimed his father had walled the opening up with rocks so cattle wouldn't wander in. I didn't have any idea where to look. The map had no starting point but it was simple. I think I could draw it from memory, but that wouldn't help if we didn't know where to start."

Lucas nodded. "I heard the old cowboys talk about it a few times. Some say there was Confederate gold buried in there. Others said it was the bodies of the real owners of the ranch. The first Collins was rumored to have ridden in and killed the whole family, then taken over the ranch."

Dan had never heard this story. It wasn't something D.R. Collins would want out. The idea of a box canyon was possible. They'd made great hideouts for outlaws years ago.

Charley refilled Lucas's coffee. "Did your dad ever show it to you?"

"No. I'm not sure he believed the stories about the canyon but the day before he was fired, there were several cattle trucks moving down roads on the ranch as they rounded up cattle. He said LeRoy commented that he thought more went in than came out."

Dan picked up a clue in his mind. "And LeRoy disappeared."

Lucas's words came low, almost a thought. "And Coffer would have been the one to notice extra traffic. When I used to work the ranch in my teens I learned that Coffer Coldman counted everything. He might not talk much, but if you asked him how many chickens were in the coop, he could tell you without even looking that direction."

Lucas's low voice seemed to continue speaking his thoughts. "With my dad and every cowhand busy packing, Coffer might have been the last man to leave the headquarters. He'd want it all put up right, even if he'd been fired."

Charley grinned. "I could draw the map from memory and we could go looking. It's a long shot, but somehow the box canyon might be linked to the hurry to sell. Or maybe with a crime happening under Reid's nose." He frowned. "Only problem is, we don't know where to start. The first mark on the map is what looks like a conquistador's helmet. I swear I've covered every part of the ranch and I've never seen a helmet."

Lucas shook his head. "We got a few more problems than that, Charley. Neither of us is welcome out there."

"Lauren is," the sheriff added. "She told me Reid invited her. Maybe one of you could go in with her?"

"Not much help, Sheriff. Your daughter isn't speaking to me."

Dan frowned. "I knew it. Neither of you acted like the other was in the room this morning. What's the argument about?"

"I'm not telling. But believe me it has nothing to do with you, Sheriff, so stay out of it."

The sheriff stood. "If you tried…"

Charley slammed his cup on the table so hard coffee volcanoed out. "Look, Sheriff, you can threaten Lucas later. Right now we've got to solve this before my little brother gets killed. If Lucas got out of line with your daughter, I'll help you string him up later."

No fear showed in Lucas when he said, "She's twenty-seven, Sheriff. You should think about giving up on walking her across the street. She can take care of herself."

Dan backed down an inch. He knew Lucas. Whatever he did or said to Lauren hadn't been a crime. Brigman gave Lucas a murder-you-later look and turned back to Charley. The rancher might not care about his father's land, but he cared about his little brother. He'd help.

Charley nodded once and continued, "First we find out what's going on at the Bar W. The box canyon may have nothing to do with the trouble there but if it is smuggling, it makes sense they're using the canyon as a hideout."

Dan straightened. "But we do it legally. I'll get a search warrant."

Lucas added, "I'm not sure we have that much time. Even if we slipped in at night, the only ranch close to the Bar W near Ransom Canyon where a box canyon might be is Hamilton Acres."

Dan smiled. "That gives me an idea where you can hide out, Lucas, just in case those bullets fired last night were for you."

"In Indigo Lake?"

"No, in the house near it. No one has lived there for years and we both know the current owner." Dan now had a plan. "The ghosts around that place will keep you safe, Lucas. I'll just have to go over and tell the old woman who lives across the water not to shoot you. She's called me at least once a week for a month to tell me a shadow walks that land."

Jubilee, Charley's wife, waddled into the kitchen, ending their discussion. It took all three men two loads apiece to bring everything in from her car. She had to show them everything she bought, and they had to act interested.

Finally, when Charley walked them to the sheriff's car, Dan didn't miss that he mumbled something to Lucas. The two men were tighter than they'd let on.

Lucas nodded.

Dan frowned. "I want to make one thing clear. If we search for this canyon, we do this legally. We do it my way."

Neither man met his gaze.

twenty-seven

Dakota didn't like the idea, but Blade climbed into her old pickup with her when she left for work. She'd planned to leave him with Maria and Grandmother for at least two more days. The man had been shot twice—surely he should stay in bed.

"We are not arguing about this, Dakota," he said, without looking at her. "I'm needed. Besides, when I want you to take over my life, I'll let you know."

She turned onto the county road. "I don't want to be in charge of your life. I'm barely holding on to mine. But…"

But what, she thought. She didn't know him well enough. He was right. His life was not her problem. If he fell over dead, he'd figure out he should have listened to her.

Only she did know him. She knew his touch and the taste of his kiss. She knew the rhythm of his breathing in the dark of night and the gentle way he held her hand, even in his sleep.

They were both silent for a while, and then he said, "Can we change the subject?" As if they'd been arguing.

"Please," she answered.

He finally turned and grinned at her. "Thanks for sleeping

next to me. You know that's the third night we've slept together. Wouldn't mind making it a habit."

"Don't bet on it. And don't get too close to Maria and Grandmother. I don't want them missing you when you're gone."

"What about you? Will you miss me?"

"I'll miss you. But I'll get over it." He was the closest she'd been to a man near her age in months. He made her think of something else besides work and the farm and the bills.

"Not me. I'll never get over you." He studied her profile. "I'll never forget that chocolate ice cream kiss."

She laughed. "I'm sure you've had hundreds."

He didn't answer and they went back to silence. When she let him out at the sheriff's office, she saw how hard he tried to act like he wasn't in pain as he climbed out. "I can drive my rented truck back. If the offer is still open, I'd like to spend one more night at your place."

"Of course. Be home by dark. Maria will be planning on you for supper."

He walked slowly up the stairs without turning around to wave, but Dakota couldn't bring herself to drive away until he finally disappeared inside. He'd be all right, she told herself. The sheriff would watch out for him.

Blade seemed the type to always be alone, even when he was in a crowd. He'd managed his way through life without her. He didn't need her now.

When she made it to her office, she had to fight a dozen FedEx boxes to reach her door. All Blade's orders had finally arrived.

She thought of loading them up and taking them home. He could survive another day without them. He'd refused to wear the shirt and jeans she'd bought him at the Western store, saying he was saving them for a date.

She'd finally promised, if he was still around and healed enough to dance, that she'd go boot-scooting with him one night. Even though they wouldn't fit together. He was too tall, but the idea of being close, really close to him, did appeal to her.

There was a hardness in those gray eyes, but there was also a gentleness in his touch. He'd been right about them being attracted to one another. It seemed something so basic, almost primal. Even alone in her tiny office, she could almost feel him near.

Dakota checked her email. Nothing. Just a note from the couple who'd kept her out until after dark looking at houses. They didn't even thank her. They just said they wanted to look elsewhere. Hale Center sounded good, they said.

Dakota clicked Delete, wishing she could show them the beautiful little community she'd planned for someday. Houses that blended with the landscape. Canyon walls framing the community. Sunsets that stretched out for miles.

But those were only in her mind. No more than pencil sketches on a barn wall.

After pacing her office for an hour, she decided to drive over and give Blade his clothes. At least it was something to do.

A few minutes later she walked into the sheriff's office with her arms loaded down with boxes. "Where's Hamilton?" she asked the receptionist.

"You mean the walking target? Sheriff wasn't happy to see him so early. That guy isn't a man who takes orders easily."

"You're telling me," Dakota answered as she fought to keep from dropping the boxes. "Which direction?"

"Oh, sorry." Pearly pointed. "Sheriff told him to go lie down on the cot in the back office before he fell down." Pearly finally looked between the boxes at Dakota. "Why didn't you keep him at home? Any fool can see the man's not solid enough to fight off marshmallows."

"Me? I'm not his mother. Blade Hamilton is stubborn, bull-headed, irrational..."

Pearly waved her toward the sheriff's open office door. "I already get that picture, Dakota Davis. You don't have to tell me. Sheriff said not to wake the human target until he gets back, but you can check on him. If he's dead, don't call 9-1-1. I'm right here, just yell."

Dakota set the boxes on the first desk she passed and went back for another two loads. She took them to the back of an L-shaped sheriff's office, tripped on one of Blade's borrowed cowboy boots, and scattered the boxes all over the floor.

In the far corner, Blade was stretched out on a cot sound asleep. It was raining packages and he didn't even bother to wake up enough to yell at her.

She pulled up a chair, took out her cell phone, and waited for him to finish his nap.

Finally, an hour later, he moved his bandaged arm in his sleep and came awake all at once. For a second he looked at her as if he didn't know where he was. Maybe he was in pain. Maybe still a little foggy from the drugs they'd given him in the hospital.

"Morning, again." She smiled. "Have a nice rest while you're on the clock?"

He sat up very carefully. "Yeah, I did. But I've figured out that around here I'm always on the clock. By the way, I dreamed you were beside me and you kept patting on me like I was your pet."

Dakota was not about to analyze that dream or admit that she had patted on him a few times, just to see if he was still alive. "I brought you some new clothes. Looks like it's just in time. Your side appears to be leaking blood."

"Great." He looked at the red spot on his shirt. "You won't want to change my bandages and help me put another shirt on, would you? I'm not sure I can lift my arm enough to do it myself." He pointed over to a first aid kit as big as a briefcase.

"Sure. It's either me or Pearly."

"I'll take you," he said and pulled the shirt open with one jerk on the snaps.

She moved in closer and helped him get the shirt off his

shoulder and over his bandaged arm. Then she pulled off the lopsided dressing along his side. The blood was spotty, but not still coming out of him, thank goodness. "Who put this on?"

He shrugged. "Maria couldn't see it. Grandmother didn't want to look at it. And Dice said he was no good at bandages or diapers, so I did the best I could while you were showering. I wanted to be ready by the time you left. The sheriff may have other investigations going on, but my priority this morning is finding who shot at me."

Dakota used water from a bottle to clean off the dried blood and then covered the raw skin with antiseptic like she'd seen the nurse do in the hospital. Next, she made sure the bandage was big enough and thick enough to both protect him and catch any blood.

"You're good at this," he whispered as her fingers moved over his skin, making sure the tape held.

"Maria had some bad cuts from the accident that killed our mom. I learned."

"It must have been a hard time for you. Maria said you were only a sophomore in college. She said you didn't leave her side for weeks." He brushed a strand of her hair back behind her ear as she worked. "Did you ever go back to school?"

"No, but I'm taking one class a semester online. I should have my degree in another six years." She stepped back, hating to see the bandages on his perfect body. "Finished. Hope I didn't hurt you too much."

"No pain," he said, but his eyes gave away his lie. "Thanks."

They opened a few of the boxes. She'd already guessed his selections wouldn't be Western, or biker. The shirts were dress casual, but not sporty. The trousers were tailored. The moment she helped him put them on she thought he moved differently. Comfortable. Relaxed.

"Thanks," he said simply as he slid his Glock pistol into the folds of the sling that held his arm in place.

"Do you really need that?" she asked.

"I'd rather have it and not need it than not have it and need it. The sheriff wouldn't have cleaned it up and had it waiting for me today if he didn't want me to carry."

"I understand," she lied. She didn't even think he should be on the job—much less armed—today.

Only, like the clothes, the weapon seemed a part of this man. His look, his actions, had shifted and settled into a man now comfortable in his clothes. She had a feeling he was the kind of person who could fit in anywhere, but this was the real Blade. She, on the other hand, only belonged one place and had never found a style that fit her.

"You look good in those clothes," she admitted. "I think that's the first time I've been so close to you that you didn't try to kiss me or touch me."

"I'm afraid I'm a little handicapped in that department, with only one working arm. I doubt even you would have much trouble knocking me down today. But if you're missing the at-tention…"

"A man who doesn't have the energy to kiss a woman. In-teresting."

He took her words as a challenge. "Come over here and let me give it a try, just for a test."

She took one step closer. He raised his hand and held it palm up. She laid her fingers on his warm skin. When he took one small step closer, she did the same.

It didn't work. He couldn't bend down without crinkling the bandage at his side.

With a smile, he moved sideways and lifted her hand as she stepped onto one of the boxes they hadn't opened.

They were suddenly nose to nose.

"Perfect," he whispered as he pulled her hand behind her back and pressed it against her spine. "If I can only use one arm, so can you."

She sighed and rested her free hand against his heart. "Let's do this nice and easy. I'm not sure you can take any stress. I fear I may be far more woman than you can handle, Hamilton."

He brushed her mouth with his lips and she leaned a bit closer, loving the gentle kiss.

He couldn't pull her close. She couldn't press against him for fear of hurting him. The kiss should have been innocent, chaste.

But it wasn't. It was the best kiss she'd ever had. A caring touch between two people getting to know one another. She slowly pressed against him, loving that she could feel him breathing against her.

"I could do this all night," he whispered against her lips. "You given any thought to our wild affair? We can make the next few weeks magic. I can tell. There is something about you that feels so right when you're close to me."

She didn't pull away this time. It felt too good. "I thought about it when you were in the hospital. How I'd said no and how there might not be another chance." She kissed him slowly, melting even closer. "But it's not who I am. If I took the few weeks of heaven you're offering, I'd also have the hell of missing you when you're gone. Something tells me you wouldn't be an easy man to get over."

"We could still see..."

They heard voices in the foyer and pulled away as Lauren and Tim rushed into the sheriff's office.

They both stormed toward Blade, asking questions. How was he feeling? What did he see two nights ago? Did he know anything new in the investigations? Did anyone know where the sheriff took Lucas?

No one seemed to notice that Dakota was standing on a box.

Lauren set up her computer on the back desk and Tim took over the sheriff's office chair. He answered a call and started taking notes while Lauren dived into a search site.

Blade motioned for Dakota to follow him and they moved out of the office.

"It looks like you may have more help than you need," Dakota whispered.

"Right." He walked her to the front steps. It wasn't private, but at least they could talk. "I wish we could continue what we started in there. I feel so good when you're that close."

"Me too." She was surprised how truly she meant it. "It was nice."

The sheriff pulled up in front of them. He was alone in his car. "Deputy, you feel like a cup of coffee? We need to talk."

"I'll be right out. Let me grab my coat and camera," Blade said but when he glanced back at Dakota, she saw the truth in his eyes. He didn't want to leave her.

She followed him inside, where he'd hung the leather coat he'd borrowed from Lucas.

"You'll be home before dark?" she whispered, fully aware that Pearly could probably hear them.

"I promise." He pulled her close and whispered, "And tonight when you're lying beside me I plan to talk to you about a problem I'm having."

"Talk to me? I thought all you wanted to do was have a wild time and move on. What are we going to talk about, Hamilton?"

"Never mind. On second thought, maybe we shouldn't talk. Trying to be friends with you is like cuddling up to a firecracker." He looked like he was gulping down words he didn't need to let out. "You know, Elf, if you liked me less, you'd get over me faster if we had that two-week affair."

"You make about as much sense as Grandmother on one of her bad days. Don't talk to me, because I'm not listening. But be careful today." She helped him with putting his coat over the sling for his arm and then followed him back to the porch "Don't try to do too much. Take another nap if you need to. And, Hamilton, don't get shot again."

"Trying to run my life, Elf?"

"It's a full-time job." She smiled. "See you at home before dark."

"Before dark," he agreed. Then right in front of the whole town, if anyone happened to be looking, Blade Hamilton kissed her on the cheek.

She thought about threatening to kill him, but it's hard to threaten a man with murder when he's still dripping from two bullet holes.

twenty-eight

When Dan pulled up at the truck stop for gas, Blade went inside to buy the coffees. His only deputy was moving slower than usual, but a wounded special agent with the ATF was still worth more than a dozen volunteers.

He had Lauren and Tim answering phones and doing research. Dice Fuller had called to say he had a favor to do for a few friends, and then he'd be in to help.

Dan had little hope Tim and Lauren would discover anything by talking to folks and checking names on the internet. And he had a feeling Dice would be investigating Pearly by noon. She was batting her eyes at the old cowboy so often, Dan was starting to believe she might be having a stroke.

Lauren did tell Dan that there was no record of anyone except the Collins family owning the Bar W, so the story about the first Collins killing off the owners and stealing the land didn't hold water. She did say there was no record of what happened to D.R. Collins's older brother. He could be under a bridge somewhere, homeless, or who knows, his bones might be in the box canyon Lucas and Charley were talking about.

Dan made a mental note to ask Dice about the canyon. If any of the cowhands knew about such a place, it would be him.

Lucas said his father had mentioned the legend years ago. Lucas claimed his dad never saw any entrance to a small canyon, so whoever blocked it up must have done a great job.

Reid lived in the house where the map was drawn on the back of a painting. Surely he'd seen it. If so and he'd found it, what was he using it for? What new business would bring in more money than cattle?

Pieces, Dan thought, and none fit together.

As he pumped gas, he dialed his wife. If he didn't talk to her soon, she'd know something was wrong.

A mumbled hello whispered through the phone. That low sexy voice he'd fallen in love with the moment she'd said hello.

"Morning, Sleeping Beauty." He grinned, imagining what she looked like. "Sorry I woke you up so early, but I've got a full day and didn't know if I'd get a chance to call later."

"You didn't call last night," she said, still sounding more asleep than awake. "Songs were running in my head all night. All about loving you."

"I'm sorry I didn't call, but you can play them for me when you get back. I worked so late, I fell asleep at my desk." He didn't want to tell her all that was happening, but he couldn't lie to her. She was in Nashville working on her dream. She didn't need to worry about him.

"What's going on in the fast-moving metropolis of Cross-roads?"

"The usual. Death threats. Shootings behind the county of-fices. Dead bodies popping up every few days. A jail break. Oh, and Pearly's started dating Dice Fuller."

"What?" Brandi came full awake. "Pearly's dating someone!"

He smiled to himself. He'd told the truth, but the only part she'd believed was the gossip. "You've met the old guy. Dice Fuller cowboys for the Bar W. Last Christmas he drove the wagon that took us around town caroling. I should say he used to work for the Bar W. They've been shutting down cattle operations on the ranch. Fired all the cowhands. Having a mess of trouble out there."

"I don't care about some ranch." She giggled. "Tell me about Pearly. The last guy she dated had dementia and left the restaurant without her, and the one before that said he had trust issues on the first date and wanted her credit card number. Are you sure she's trying it again?"

Dan relaxed. Brandi wasn't going to ask about anything else. "Well, she showed up with makeup on a few days ago. Scared me so bad I almost dropped my coffee cup. She had thick eyebrows, said they were the 'in' thing, but I swear hers blackened half her forehead."

Brandi laughed. "She *is* dating. Did she paint her nails?"

Dan just smiled. "I didn't look. You know I only have eyes for you."

"I know, but look. If she left one painted black and all the others red, that means something, but I'm not sure what. Maybe it says, 'I'm ready for a midnight ride, cowboy.'"

"I miss you," Dan whispered. "I'd be totally unaware of what's going on in the world if it wasn't for you. By the way, what do your nails look like?"

"I miss you, too. I'll be home in a few days and I want to hear all about everything that's happened." She laughed. "Oh, by the way, I'm planning to have every other nail painted black."

"Go back to sleep, pretty lady. I have to get to work."

"I know you do but, Dan, I want you to know that whatever happens with this music career of mine, you are my happy-ever-after ending."

"Sounds like a song."

"It might just become one. Have a good day, honey."

He held the cell tightly for a few seconds. A part of him could never let go of her, even on the phone.

Hamilton walked up with two large take-out cups. "You know when you said we were going for coffee, I thought maybe a café or coffee shop."

"We don't have time for that. We've got back roads to cover. You up for the ride?"

"Sure. No pain."

twenty-nine

─────

Lauren pulled her long, straight hair out of the ponytail she'd tied up when working earlier at her pop's office. A curtain of sunshine danced over her shoulders.

She'd been waiting just off the county road leading to Indigo Lake for what seemed like hours. She didn't know this land very well. She could see the two houses that faced the lake. One was a low mission design with thick walls, the other a two-story. Behind the Davis home were barns and what looked like a small cottage with a sleeping garden on one side.

The two farms were separated by the water, but they didn't look like they belonged together. The lake had always been beautiful in a dark, brooding way. Neither house seemed to welcome visitors.

No one had lived at the Hamilton Acres farm for years. The land was too rolling and rocky to farm. One side bordered Ransom Canyon and another side bumped its rocky cliffs against the Collins land.

Blade Hamilton had come out to have a look at the place he'd inherited and Pop put him to work. Her father said this latest

Hamilton had no plans to stay and from the looks of the place, he didn't live there now. She'd expected to see a house-and-land-for-sale sign out, wired to the fence.

She relaxed back in her seat. It felt good just to be silent for a while. Working in the office with Tim was tense. When nothing was happening, he made up what-if scenarios. When Lucas called on her cell, Tim had been frustrated that she wouldn't tell him who called.

Then he'd been more frustrated when she'd said she had to run an errand. He'd even offered to go, but she'd rushed out, saying she'd be back soon.

In truth, she hadn't known how long it would take Lucas to get here. He'd just told her where to meet him. Strange place he'd picked, but Lucas seemed full of secrets lately. Wanting to be in jail. Telling her to keep a key safe because it was his future. Hiding out in Tim's house.

Maybe he was right. He wasn't the man she thought he was. She'd always put him on a pedestal, thinking he was more than a normal guy. He'd saved her life when she was fifteen. He'd set his goals and gone full-out to reach them. And now, he was a powerful lawyer fighting for justice.

Only, when she looked into his deep brown eyes, Lauren didn't see happiness or peace. She had a feeling Lucas still hadn't gotten what he wanted out of life and until he did, he wouldn't have time for her.

A tap sounded on the passenger window and she jumped. All she saw at first was his hat, and then, he turned and smiled at her. His worried eyes didn't match the slight smile on his lips.

She unlocked the door and he slid in quickly as if someone was chasing him. Her Lucas was in Western work clothes the color of the earth. She heard the tiny clink of his spurs, and his legs were wrapped in chaps.

He'd been riding. The smell of leather and horses and the wind seemed to surround him.

"Thanks for meeting me," he said as he put his hat on the dash. "I didn't know if you would come after the way we parted last night. I'll say I'm sorry as soon as I figure out what I did wrong."

Lauren didn't think a few words could fix what stood between them, but now wasn't the time to argue. "I assume that you want the key back. Since I'd promised not to tell anyone about it, I didn't have much choice but to come." She pulled the chain off and offered it to him. "Want to tell me what's going on? You owe me that."

He didn't take the chain or the key, and he didn't leave. He just leaned back as if he needed to draw one deep breath before he could speak. "I don't want the key back, Lauren, and I don't want you mixed up in what is about to happen."

She almost laughed. "You don't want me at all." For a moment in the silence of the car she was back in high school. The skinny girl with glasses. The only child of an overprotective father who just happened to be the sheriff. The girl no one asked out or invited to any party.

"That's not true," he said. "I want you so badly there's a permanent ache inside of me. You've got to believe that, Lauren. I just want it to be the right time for us. With you, I'd like it to be perfect."

It occurred to Lauren that he might not see the real her. Maybe they'd both been seeing each other through a tinted lens formed years ago.

"Lucas, if you want there to be anything between us, then start by telling me what's going on." She gripped the steering wheel. "Tell me the truth or walk away. There may never be the perfect time, but this could be the last time. Let me into your world or leave now."

He looped the chain with the key over her head. "Keep this. It's the future. We'll talk about it later. I've got to help your father with the mess at the Collins place first."

Lucas reached for her hand.

She pulled away. "The whole truth," she whispered.

Lauren thought he'd leave, but this time he didn't. His jaw was clenched so tightly she feared he'd break his teeth. They both knew they were one moment away from goodbye.

"Fine. I'll tell you everything I know but you have to swear you won't tell anyone. Not your pop or Tim O'Grady."

"I swear."

Lucas took a deep breath and seemed to relax. His voice came slow, matter-of-fact. Like he was testifying. "Charley Collins and I are riding onto the Bar W tonight. Your father told us not to even think about going in. He wants to wait for the warrant. In fact, he'll lock me up for real if he catches us, and Reid Collins will file trespassing charges on both me and his brother. Only, Charley is as set on this plan as I am. We're riding in tonight."

Lauren's logical mind didn't bother with the whys or wasting time telling him how dangerous it might be. She just waited, wanting to hear it all.

"Dice Fuller is riding with us. He told Charley a few hours ago that he knew of a place way back on the ranch where there is a boulder the size of a car. When the moon rises, the rock casts a shadow that looks just like a conquistador's helmet. That's the starting point on an old map that'll lead us to a box canyon that might have the answers to all the trouble happening at the ranch.

"Dice didn't know it, but he'd just given us the one clue we needed, the way that might lead us to answers. Your dad is getting a search warrant and plans to ask questions tomorrow, but in daylight, the helmet's shadow can't be seen. We have to go tonight. We'll get in and out fast, then in the morning the sheriff can go in all legal and he'll know exactly where to look for evidence. We believe they're doing something against the law. Smuggling maybe, or drugs. Maybe men have even been killed because they found out what it was."

She turned to him. "The ranch has posted no-trespassing

signs at all their gates. You'll be the ones breaking the law. You could be shot for being on another's land."

"We know. That's why you can't tell your dad. He'd never go along with this plan, but Charley and I have to figure out the truth. We find the spot tonight where they're hiding something, get the hell off the land before anyone notices us, and drive in tomorrow with the sheriff. It's a simple plan. None of Reid's hired thugs will even know we're there."

She took his hand as if needing to hold on to him. "Rumor in town is that Reid is being forced out. Some say he's losing the ranch because of gambling debts. Maybe everyone is trying to make something illegal out of just his poor judgment. The fires might have been set to hurry the sale along. After all, the two barns that burned were pretty well worthless. The burned man might have just been trapped."

"What about the second body, Coffer Coldman?" Lucas interrupted. "What about someone shooting Blade? This is far more than poor judgment. I might have believed Reid needed quick money, except for Coffer. He wasn't just killed, he was dumped in the ashes where the killers knew he'd be found. Blade may have been shot because he was mistaken for me."

"Why you?"

"My father's been feeding me information for months. Not just the ranch business, but the strange improvements on back roads no one uses and supplies shipped in that seem to disappear. I've done checks on the ranch manager who Reid had hired to act as the new ranch foreman. He's thought to be the strong arm for some pretty shady characters.

"Charley and I both agree that Reid is not in charge, but what we're dealing with is much bigger than gambling debts. The Bar W is like an island. No one will ever know what is there unless we go in." He covered her hand with his. "This isn't about Reid firing men, or the loss of control of the ranch, this is about more. Something far darker. A secret that has to be kept even if it means killing people."

Lauren nodded. "Pearly called and said my dad was looking for an entrance to the ranch that no one knew about, but he didn't find it. I don't think he knows what's wrong, but he's been sheriff so long he can smell trouble."

He laced his fingers through hers. "With luck we'll be in and out before anyone sees us. We all three know the trails inside. On horseback we can avoid any land where four-wheelers could follow, and the men with Reid don't ride horses. They won't be able to follow us into the trees or along the breaks at the border between the Bar W and part of both Kirkland's land and Hamilton Acres. There's not even a road out that far."

"You should let Pop know." Lauren didn't like this plan. It was too risky. Too many things could go wrong.

"No. It would mean his job if he were in any way involved in this ride tonight. You can't say a word, Lauren. Not to anyone. Our safety will depend on no one knowing about our midnight search. We'll be back before dawn."

"And if you're not?"

"Then call your dad and tell him we're being held against our will at the Bar W. If I'm guessing right, two men have already been killed for stumbling on the secret there."

Suddenly all the arguments didn't matter. Lauren leaned over and wrapped her arms around his neck.

For a moment she just held him as if she could keep him safe by never letting go.

"You remember what you said after I saved your life in the old Gypsy House a dozen years ago?" he whispered against her ear.

"Yes. I said I owed you a blood debt. I swore that someday I'd pay you back. I'd save your life."

He kissed her cheek. "Well, here is your chance. We need someone to stay out of sight but near enough to pick us up. We're not sure where we'll ride off the ranch, but when we do some-

one has got to be there. We'll help you hitch a trailer to that old
Ford Explorer of yours. Then you'll be ready to drive to where
we're heading and pick us up. I'll call you with the location.

"I didn't want to ask you, Lauren. I didn't want you involved,
but when it got right down to it, you're the only one I can trust
with my life. Reid's new crew at the ranch might think some
of my family was involved. I wouldn't be surprised if they're
watching the house where my parents were staying. But you,
the sheriff's daughter, could say you were just doing a friend a
favor and had no idea what we planned to do."

She rubbed her forehead against his shoulder, breathing him
in, fearing that she was collecting a memory.

"You'll find the horse trailer parked on Kirkland land where
we watched the stars. I'll call you when I know where we'll be
riding off the ranch. All you have to do is meet us if we switch
locations."

"Am I doing something illegal? It sounds a little like I'm driving the getaway car."

"No. The only thing we're guilty of is trespassing, and that
would be hard to prove since Charley is the owner's son and
I'm his lawyer."

"What about Dice?"

"Reid told him he could search for his friend if he wanted to
waste his time. I don't think it occurred to Reid that he'd be
doing it at night, but the old guy is the only one who has the
owner's permission to cross the fence tonight."

She knew this was going to be far more than a ride over land
they grew up on. She also knew it would be dangerous, very
dangerous, or they would have told Pop.

"I'll do it," she said.

"It's not going to be a big deal. If anyone stops you just say
you're picking up a friend who went horseback riding and must
have gotten lost."

"I'm worried," she whispered against his shoulder.

"We're just checking out a few things. We'll be careful, I promise." He slid his hand along her cheek and into her hair.

Then he kissed her full-out as if he truly loved her. This time there was no hesitation, no holding back.

"When this is over," he whispered against her ear, "we start over. I'll show you what that old key goes to. Until then, hang on to our future for me. Try to believe there might be an 'us' for just a bit longer."

Before she could answer, he was gone.

thirty

Blade sat in the passenger side of the sheriff's cruiser and studied the map while Dan Brigman covered every back road surrounding the Bar W. "Mind telling me what we're looking for? It's going to be dark soon and I'd like to know if we found it."

"A way into and out of the Bar W that is not on the map. This is my third time to circle the ranch."

"Oh." Blade closed the map. "Any reason we're looking for an invisible road?"

"If we could watch the back roads, we might find a shipment of something being delivered to the Collins place. I got a call from your headquarters saying they stopped two trucks heading north out of Crossroads yesterday. Both were loaded down with drugs. When they checked a truck matching the same description this morning about a hundred miles south of Crossroads, it was clean. The ATF can be tight-lipped, asking for help without giving much information, but I got the feeling they think there's a big drug operation around here."

Blade grumbled. "This is the first I've heard about it. They didn't call me?"

Dan smiled. "You're on vacation, remember. My guess is they don't even know where you are."

"They will as soon as I call in." Blade stared out the window. He hated the idea that drug dealers were anywhere near his land. "There are a dozen roads, not counting breaks in the barbed wire, where you could drive a truck through pasture. We'd need a dozen men to guard all this for just one night."

Trouble was too close to his land. The ATF didn't move in on a hunch. They had something, maybe not enough to make arrests, but they had something. *Too close*, Blade almost said aloud. Like it or not, his slice of Texas had claimed him.

Dan seemed determined. "We'll circle one more time and look for some evidence that one place has been used lately."

Blade thought it was a long shot, but he opened up the map and tried to help. "Funny how cracks in the earth break off this flat land. You can't even see most of them from the road, but from the air it looks like long ruts twisting through the plains."

"That's how several borders are marked between ranches." Dan slowed at a gate. No evidence of traffic on the road. He moved on.

"I know. One side of Hamilton Acres looks like a wiggly line ruining the farm being a perfect rectangle." Blade drew his finger along the map as if marking where his land started.

"I noticed that north side too. It's steep and rocky. Good divider. If it wasn't for that canyon running several miles, your land would touch the Bar W. It's a great natural border, too steep for even a horse or calf to cross."

Blade laughed. "Sheriff, you never cease to amaze me with your knowledge." He thought of asking, *What is it about you people? You talk of the land like it is a living, breathing thing.*

But Blade didn't say a word. Maybe to Dakota, the sheriff, even Grandmother, it was. He couldn't imagine loving any place that much. He was probably feeling a small part of it because he'd breathed in a few pounds of it in the past week.

He'd heard that people born near the sea long for the sound of waves every night when they sleep. Maybe it's that way with Texans. The open sky, the flat land, the sound of tall grass, is in their blood. If you take a Texan out of Texas, he's still a Texan.

Blade moved the conversation back to something he could understand. "Want to tell me where Lucas is?"

"He's staying with a friend tonight. To keep him safe, we need to keep him moving."

"Who is he with?" After seeing the steady stream of people visiting Lucas in jail, that narrowed it down to about half the town.

The sheriff glanced his direction. "You."

"Me? I don't even have a home, Sheriff. I'm staying with Dakota and her crazy grandmother who pops in hourly like some deformed cuckoo clock. I don't want him there. What if someone comes looking for him? I could protect him, but who'd protect the women?"

"Grandmother, probably. Dice told me the old woman can shoot dandruff off a bald head without even creasing the skin."

"Great. It'll be another shoot-out at Indigo Lake, and judging from the past, the most likely man killed will be a Hamilton, and I seem to be the only one breathing."

Dan laughed. "Lucas isn't staying with the women. He'll be with you. I talked to Jerry Cline at the construction site at your place. He said he'd have the upstairs ready for you tonight, but the one bathroom that was working two days ago has stopped working. You're both staying there in sleeping bags. And if you have to go pee, you're doing it outside and armed."

"This is crazy. Can't we go back to jail? I wouldn't want to stay at my falling-down place, and now I have a houseguest. It'll be like staying at the No Bed and No Breakfast from Hell."

"Only for a night or two. Until we know for sure those bullets you took weren't meant for Lucas, I plan to move him every few nights."

Blade shrugged. "What if they were really meant for me? Then am I going to have to hide out? It's not my style."

"Think about it, Hamilton. Who'd want to kill you? No one knows you well enough to want to shoot you. Give it time."

"After some study and soul-searching, Sheriff, I narrowed a list of possible shooters down to about half the women I've ever hooked up with," Blade answered. "I've discovered I don't know how to communicate."

"Some woman tell you that?" Dan asked.

"Yeah, how'd you know?"

"Lucky guess." The sheriff slowed once more. Another gate. No sign of traffic on the road.

Dan sped up and turned toward Crossroads. "How about we call it a day, Deputy? I need to go talk to a judge, and you can take off early."

Blade grinned. "But I haven't put in my eighteen hours yet."

"Maybe you need to get a life, Hamilton. You can't just hang around the office."

"That's a good idea. How long do I have?"

"About three hours. A few hours after dark Lucas will be delivered to your place. He'll be your problem for the night."

As soon as they were back in town, Blade called his home office with questions, asking that the answers be texted. Then he climbed into his truck and went in search of Dakota. It was late afternoon and he was hungry for a chocolate-dipped cone.

He found her in her office. For a moment he just stared at her as she worked behind her computer. She was too short, hair way too wild to ever be tamed, she had no idea how to dress, didn't wear makeup, and he still thought she was sexy.

It occurred to him that she might be working on toning her perfection down just to keep him from having a stroke, he was so attracted to her. He'd painted a mural on the back wall of his mind about what she'd look like in tight jeans and a cropped shirt, or in a thin silk nightgown, or in the Western clothes he'd bought her, low necked and short skirt. But, none of his mental paintings could match the memory of her trying to pull that T-shirt off.

Only one other theory made sense. If he wasn't going mad, he'd finally found a woman who would be hard to walk away from. Maybe even impossible.

She looked up with those big dark eyes and said, "May I help you, stranger?"

"You can. I'd like to take my girl out for an ice cream. Any chance she's available for a break?"

"Sure, but you're buying this time and I'm not your girl."

"Fair enough. You're driving." He pitched her his truck keys. If he only had one arm, he planned to use it for something besides holding the wheel.

By the time they ate their ice cream while parked in the back lot of the Dairy Queen, both had chocolate on their faces and clothes. They talked and laughed. He kissed her a few times, gentle chocolate ice cream kisses.

She seemed to enjoy their time. She was flirting with him, something he had a feeling she never allowed herself time to do.

They drove over to a new house that she'd be putting up for sale in a few weeks and he'd been surprised to learn that Dakota had worked on the floor plans with the builder. They walked through the home, holding hands, talking about all the little additions she'd made on the original designs.

Once, on the pull-down stairs to the attic, he'd trapped her on the steps and kissed her until she was out of breath. She giggled and ran up the stairs, then returned his kiss in the shadows of the attic.

Blade was surprised how much he liked just being with her. All the problems of the day slipped away.

She was having fun too. Teasing him one minute and cuddling close the next. They talked of nothing important. They laughed when she tried to teach him to talk with an accent. They looked at each other, really seeing inside.

She thought they were just having fun.

But he knew what was really happening. Foreplay.

It continued when they got back to her farm. In the tiny bathroom she'd checked the bandage at his side. No more blood. The healing had begun.

He leaned so close he could whisper in her ear as she worked. "Remember when you stormed in here wearing nothing but a body-hugging T-shirt?"

"I thought you were gone. I was in a hurry to get to work."

"You almost had that shirt off. I almost had a heart attack. You have beautiful breasts." He moved one hand along her side, barely brushing one of her breasts. "It was quite a sight."

"You noticed? I was hoping you hadn't."

"I could never forget seeing you through the foggy air. All wild and panicked and almost free of your clothes." He touched her again as his hand caressed her side. "I'll be dead in my coffin and still thinking about seeing you like that."

She giggled. "Laying it on a little thick, Hamilton."

He kissed her as she laughed. "You said you wanted to talk. I'm talking. I'm telling you what I'm thinking."

"I meant talking about something other than my chest…or any other body part." She finished taping on a clean bandage running an inch above his waist.

Just as she straightened and met his lips with what promised to be a deep kiss, a rap sounded at the door. "Any chance you two are finished doctoring?" Grandmother yelled loud enough for the ghost across Indigo Lake to hear. "Maria's started supper and I don't want to be late. I got to wash my hands, among other things."

Blade fought down a string of swear words while Dakota laughed.

"Later, we'll talk," she whispered as she pulled his shirt over the bandage.

Blade didn't trust himself to say a word. He knew in an hour or two the sheriff would call and he'd have to go over to his place and meet Lucas. It was safer to keep him there, but right now with Dakota was the only place he wanted to be. He opened the door and followed her out past Grandmother, who frowned at him until she finally disappeared into the bathroom.

"Ever think of building on another bathroom?" he asked as they walked into the kitchen.

"No," Dakota answered. "Never had a reason to need one until today."

Both the Davis girls insisted that he sit at the bar while they cooked supper. Maria talked on about the romance book she was listening to. "This couple were coworkers at a big company and secretly met for their own little private morning breaks. They didn't even know each other's names, but they had a mad passionate affair on the floor of the empty boardroom or in one of the storage closets. Once in an elevator. Once on an abandoned rooftop. He seemed to always have the key to any vacant room and she seemed to always forget to wear panties."

Blade frowned. "Couldn't have been too wild if it only lasted fifteen minutes. Maybe they should have met for lunch. And the storage room couldn't have been very comfortable."

Maria pointed a spoon in his direction. "You're just not romantic, Hamilton. Love grows romantic and hot even in the corporate world. Maybe fifteen minutes of passion is enough for some people."

Grandmother sat down at the other end of the long bar. "They must have been very thin people," she said as she stole pieces of the apple Dakota was slicing.

"Why?" Blade asked.

"They never ate the doughnuts that everyone in the big businesses always has on break."

"How do you know that?" all three asked.

"I see it on TV. Office workers are always having doughnuts or birthday cake."

Blade laughed, thinking he'd never had a more enjoyable conversation with three women in his life.

An hour later when he offered to help do the dishes, both girls told him to walk with Grandmother.

"Take your camera," Dakota suggested. "You might catch the last slice of the sunset."

Blade picked up his camera and followed Grandmother. She marched out as if she were going to battle and he was no more than the pup following along.

The sky was clear for a change and the night held a hint of spring. They walked to the water's edge and just looked at the water. Grandmother was silent.

"Did the Hamiltons and the Davises really fight?" he finally asked.

"You figure I'm so old I'd know?"

He grinned. "I figure you might be."

Grandmother was silent for a while and he decided she wasn't going to answer.

Finally, her words came low and serious. "I've made up many a tale, but this I tell you is fact. My grandmother told me a feud started when a Hamilton horse was found on Davis land. Rumor was it was put there on purpose to start the two families fighting, but no one knows if that was true.

"The Hamilton men accused the Davis men of stealing it. One thing led to another. The next morning a fight broke out between the families at the mercantile, where Crossroads is today. It left one Davis man dead and his son swore to even the score. A month later two Hamiltons were found dead after a snowstorm. Some say they were killed. Others say they just froze after wandering blind in the freezing weather.

"The Davis clan said they had nothing to do with the deaths, but a Bar W rider claimed he'd seen them out riding that wintry night as if they were hunting for something, or someone, to kill. The Bar W cowhand said they were leading extra horses, but he couldn't see who they belonged to because of the falling snow."

She walked close to the water, looking toward his land, and he followed. "The feud continued for years. A fight would break out between them now and then when they bumped into one another, but neither ever stepped foot on the other's land. If they had, both knew it was a killing offense. The Davis men blamed all accidents and bad luck on the Hamiltons. The Hamiltons did the same to the Davises. I don't know how many were true or how many years it went on.

"Finally, a Davis daughter was fishing in her little boat on Indigo Lake and decided to cross the water and try to make peace. She met a young Hamilton boy. They were both about fifteen, as the story was told. Every night when the moon was missing from the sky, she'd cross the water in her little boat and meet with him.

"Eventually, they were caught. He was told never to see her again. She was beaten because she wouldn't swear she would stop seeing him. She was stubborn like my people have always been, so her father beat her twice.

"The next night she was all bruised and weak. There were stormy waters on the lake, but she crossed, anyway. The boy fought to go to her, but he was locked up and she was turned away at the shoreline.

"She never made it back to Davis land. Maybe she was too weak or heartbroken. Maybe the storm fought her and won.

"When the Hamilton boy saw her boat float up to his shore, he knew she was dead. He just walked into the water until it covered him. Neither body was ever found, and the two families swore they'd never speak again. The feud ended, but the rules remained. Until you, no Hamilton has ever walked this side of the lake since."

"Is there a record of this?" Blade believed every word the old woman said, but he wanted proof. No matter how dark, he had a family history for the first time.

"At the cemetery on Davis land are the names of those killed. I've heard that high up in the rough ground of your land is another cemetery that has the same. It's in the back, where the breaks crack the earth, deep and rocky, between your land and the Collins ranch. It's told that the Hamilton dead stare out at the family who egged the feud on, hoping to absorb both Hamilton and Davis land into theirs."

Blade took the story in like hard whiskey on a cold night. It fired his body and left him a little sick.

"There!" Grandmother pointed across the water. "Do you see the ghost move?"

Blade studied where she pointed. He did see movement. But it wasn't a ghost. Someone was on his land.

The silhouette crossed in the darkness, melting into the shadows of the cottonwood trees and wild plum bushes.

Blade raised his camera and zoomed in. One man, tall and well built with what looked like a weapon strapped on his back. He stayed close to the rocks when he moved from the trees. Low. Fast. Obviously trained.

Then, almost lost in the wind, was the low sound of a car moving down the road. It didn't come onto his land, but parked just beyond. The silhouette swung over the fence and vanished into the car.

Blade snapped three quick shots, but knew he got nothing. Not even the make of the black car.

Feelings shot through his mind. Someone was on his land. *His* land.

Like a jolt from a live wire, Blade suddenly understood what these Texans felt. In one white-hot flash he knew. He didn't just own the land. He was a part of it. Legends, lies, curses and all.

He pulled out his cell and dialed the sheriff.

Before Dan could say more than hello, Blade said, "Don't bring Lucas out. Someone was on my land, moving like a shadow. I don't know if he is there looking for Lucas but I aim to find out."

Dan's laughter sounded tired. "You starting to believe in Granny's ghost?"

"I am." Blade didn't care if he sounded as crazy as the old lady. He knew what he saw.

"We've got another problem," Dan said. "Lucas seems to have slipped out of Tim's house and disappeared not long after I dropped him off there. He's not answering his phone but he left me a message that said, 'Don't worry about me. Will check in later.' Since he's not officially under arrest, there isn't much I can do but wait for him to come back. But it sounds like wherever he is, he's probably safer there than at your house."

"Maybe he's on a date?"

"Yeah, that has me worried too."

"I'll stay in touch, Sheriff. I'll be at my place if you need me." Blade hung up, realizing Grandmother had been listening to every word.

"What you going to do, Hamilton?" Grandmother asked.

"I'm going to go over there and be ready if our ghost comes back."

"He will," Grandmother whispered. "I've been watching him for weeks."

Blade walked back to Dakota's mission home and changed into layers, all black. He pulled off his sling and ignored the pain.

When he walked past the kitchen, he was fully armed. "I'll be back later."

Dakota raised an eyebrow, he winked at her. "Don't wait up for me, Elf."

"Oh, I won't, but I might dream of you across the lake dancing with a ghost."

Blade forced himself to move away when every cell in his body wanted to stay.

As he walked across the field and circled onto his land, his phone pinged. He got his answer from the home office. His vacation was over. It was time to go to work.

thirty-one

A midnight moon shone over the edge of Kirkland's land as Lauren watched three men saddle up. He might not know they were there, but Staten Kirkland was a friend. He'd stand with them if anything happened.

"You don't have to go, Charley," Lucas said. "You've got a wife about to have a baby. Just climb in your pickup and head home. Lauren's Ford will pull the trailer."

"Much as I hate to admit it, this is my family making this mess. I don't really care about the ranch or what's going on there, but I need to know my little brother is safe."

Dice walked between them. "Why don't you two pups stay here? I know the general direction I'm headed. Give me half an hour, and I'll find that hidden box canyon."

"We're all going," Charley said, obviously tired of discussing the matter.

Lauren knew the conversation was over. She moved close to Lucas and he folded her in his arms. "It's going to be fine," he whispered. "We'll be back before you know it. With luck we'll come out along the border here where I used to ride home every night after working for Mr. Kirkland. You won't have to go anywhere to pick us up."

She couldn't talk. She seemed to always be saying goodbye to this man. "If anything happens to you, I'm never speaking to you again, Lucas."

He laughed. "Then I might as well say something now. I love you. I think I always have. When I allow myself to think about the future, about forever, you're always there." He held her tight against himself and she felt laughter rise in his chest suddenly. "But I got to tell you, one thing is going to change when I get back. You are not sleeping with Tim O'Grady anymore."

He kissed her cheek.

"But Tim's my best friend."

"That's fine, but you're not sleeping with him. There won't be room in our bed."

Lauren knew there was no time, but she whispered, "What makes you think I'll sleep with you?"

"We'll talk about this when I get back, but married people do usually sleep together."

Before Lauren could answer, Charley shouted, "Kiss her, Lucas. I swear, the last time I rode with you I had to tell you the same thing. You may be a lawyer but you're downright slow at some things."

Lauren smiled. "No argument there." Then she kissed him fast and hard before stepping out of the way.

The three cowboys rode away, easy in the saddle, silent in the night.

Lauren climbed into her Explorer and cuddled under the blanket her father always insisted she carry along with a flashlight. She could barely make them out as they crossed the county road and rode onto the Bar W.

Lauren had no idea what they'd find tonight, but she had a feeling it would be trouble.

thirty-two

Blade walked the uneven ground around Indigo Lake. He could have crossed at the finished bridge, but he didn't want to make his presence known.

The big two-story house looked spooky in the night. A few windows were left open, probably because Jerry had been painting, and old rotting curtains from one upstairs window seemed to be waving at him.

Blade made it to the stand of trees near the house and decided this was a good place to watch from. About the time he'd settled in, a pickup pulled off the main road and headed over the new bridge.

Blade came to full alert.

He watched Jerry Cline climb out of the pickup and head toward the house. He wasn't exactly sneaking onto the land, with his headlights on bright and his flashlight at full power.

It didn't take long to figure out what the guy was doing. The one window upstairs was closed with a quick slam, followed by a few others.

Blade grabbed the rifle he'd borrowed from Grandmother and stepped out into the headlight's glare from the pickup.

Jerry was halfway down the steps before he noticed Blade. "You scared the devil out of me, Hamilton."

"Sorry. I'm just looking around the place. Didn't want you thinking I was hiding out."

"I forgot to close the windows so I came back." Jerry moved closer. "You come out here at night often?"

"No. Why?" Blade moved closer.

Jerry took the hint and lowered his voice. "Maybe I'm worrying about nothing, but a couple of mornings I'd swear someone walked across your land before dawn. One dawn, after it rained most of the night, I saw boot prints that looked like combat boots left in fresh mud. It's just a hunch. You know, when a cowboy spends a lot of time out by himself, you get a feeling when someone is riding the same trail."

"You should be a cop," Blade said. "That is exactly why I'm here tonight. I think I did see someone moving over my land." He didn't want to tell Jerry too much information but he wanted the man to know that he was alert.

They walked toward Jerry's truck. He said, "I thought I saw a black car parked in the trees about a mile back. If he's coming tonight, my guess is he'll come as soon as he knows I'm gone." Jerry laughed suddenly. "Sounds like we're in a spy novel or something. Nothing ever happens around here. Scariest thing I've seen out in this country is Grandmother walking after dark with a rifle on her shoulder."

"Do you come back out here every night?"

"Yeah. I don't live far. After supper I like to drive over and make sure everything was put up, closed up. If an animal got in with all that new paint, they could cost us a day's work." He grinned as he climbed into the cab of his truck. "Besides, if I stay around the house, the wife makes me help with the dishes."

Blade stepped a few feet back. "Keep your eyes open."

"Maybe they're stealing your wild plums. If they are, they're getting green ones."

Waving goodbye, Blade moved onto the dark porch. He didn't have to wait long.

The low sound of a car moving slowly whispered in the still air. He thought he heard a car door closing softly. Then he spotted a silhouette moving silently toward him.

The man was almost even with the house when Blade said softly, "Evening."

Before the stranger could reach for his weapon, Blade added, "Don't do anything foolish. I've already got you in my sights. You're on my land. I'm Special Agent Blade Hamilton and I'm looking for some answers."

The man straightened slightly and seemed to relax a bit.

"I'm not here to cause any trouble. I was told this place was abandoned, being fixed up to sell." The man stood perfectly still. "I've heard of you, Hamilton, but didn't connect you with this place. An honor to meet you."

Blade moved to the first step. "I got word there was an agent out on my land. Wanna tell me why you're here?"

"I'm watching for suspected illegal drug shipments. We're doing our best to clock every truck that comes off the Bar W tonight. From a point a mile back of your place I can see the whole west side of the Bar W."

Blade wasn't buying it. "How long you been here?"

"Three nights."

Blade shook his head. "The old lady who lives next door says she's seen movement for weeks."

The agent shrugged. "Not me. Must be a ghost. Look, I'm Agent Matthew McMillan. I've got my ID in my vest pocket."

Blade nodded once and held the rifle at ready as Matthew dug out his ID. It really wasn't necessary; Matthew had the look and the text had said that ATF had a man in the field but they'd both follow agency procedure.

Blade used his flashlight to study the badge, then handed it back. "So, we're on the same team. How can I help?"

Matthew looked up into the midnight sky. "I'll explain as we climb. Follow me. We haven't got much time."

The agent was jogging before Blade could decide what to do. He had a feeling his bandaged side was about to feel the burn of some serious exercise. So much for taking it easy for a few days.

thirty-three

Dan drove around for two hours, looking for Lucas. Not that he thought he'd find him, but he hoped.

Lucas knew most of the folks in town, so if he wanted to be somewhere besides Tim's place, he could be. Maybe he decided he'd be safer without the sheriff's help, or maybe O'Grady simply drove him nuts asking questions and talking about his latest book.

Dan was probably worried about nothing. Lucas could have decided to step away. Now he knew his parents were safely away, this really wasn't his worry. If so, he might have driven to Lubbock or even Dallas.

The one place he probably wouldn't have gone was out to talk to Reid, but he might have called D.R. Collins. After all, his firm in Houston had handled some of D.R.'s legal work.

Dan felt out of the loop, so for no particular reason he headed over to Tim's place. Maybe Lucas showed back up there. Or maybe his daughter would be there. He hadn't seen her all afternoon. It wasn't like her not to call just to see if he knew anything new for her website. Dan would be glad when she moved on to her next career. She wore writing like she was trying to walk in someone else's shoes.

When he passed his house on the way to Tim's place, Dan noticed Lauren's old Explorer wasn't parked there. It occurred to him that Crossroads was too small to have two missing persons.

Tim answered his door, wearing a swimsuit and his ski jacket. "Hi, Pop." Tim used Lauren's name for him. Dan hated that. "Come on in. I was just doing laundry."

Dan stepped inside. "Any chance you've seen Lucas?"

"Nope. I checked everywhere when I drove to town looking for Lauren. I'm nuts about your daughter, Sheriff. Sometimes I just like to know where she is."

Me too, Dan thought but aloud he said, "You're starting to sound like a stalker, O'Grady."

Dan almost added that Tim was nuts, period. Why was it some writers stopped making up characters and simply became one. If Tim got any more famous, he'd be the town eccentric. "I'm guessing you didn't find Lauren?"

"Nope. Dakota said she hadn't been at her office all afternoon." Tim shrugged. "It's not really my job to keep up with people, Sheriff. That's more in your line of work." He pointed to the kitchen. "Want some tuna pizza? I had a frozen cheese pizza and decided I needed more protein on it. All I had was a can of tuna."

"No, thanks. I ate yesterday. I've got another eighteen hours before starvation sets in."

Tim, as always, looked at the sheriff as if he didn't quite know if he was trying to be funny or simply telling the truth.

"Why were you looking for Lauren?" Dan asked.

"We had a date, I think. Looks like she stood me up again."

Dan frowned. "Maybe she's with Lucas." Even a lawyer was better than a writer for a son-in-law. Dan decided he should have a talk with his only offspring. She needed to be a little more considerate of him. After all, whomever she married, he'd have to put up with for years. He should get some percentage of the choice. Thirty percent maybe. Or better yet, veto power.

"She hates Lucas." Tim smiled.

"She does?"

"Sure. I thought everyone knew that."

Dan took one step backward and was out the door. "Nice talking with you, Tim. I think I'll call it a night."

As he walked out to the cruiser he dialed Brandi. Dan desperately needed to talk to someone his age.

Only, his wife didn't answer. She was probably out with the band, listening to music. If he didn't have a crime spree going on, he'd drive the night and wake her up in the morning.

A few minutes later he walked into his too-quiet house, reached for a beer in the fridge and decided to call it a night. He hadn't had eight hours in his own bed in half a dozen nights. As he walked to the bedroom, he glanced out the windows toward the lake and saw someone sitting on the deck.

For a moment he thought it was Lucas, but when he took a few steps closer he realized it was Reid Collins.

Dan swore, fearing he'd have to deal with a drunk tonight. Reid was too old to be pulling this kind of crap. When the kid had been wild after college, Dan had dragged him out of several bars when he was too drunk to walk, and a few cars when he was too deep into the bottle to remember what direction home was.

Dan opened the sliding door and Reid looked up.

"Evening, Sheriff." His words were slurred. Drunk, but not staggering.

"Evening, Collins," Dan answered. "You need something?"

"I don't want to go home, Sheriff. You mind if I just sit here awhile?"

"How'd you get here?"

"I walked over from the Two Step. I couldn't think of anywhere to go and I'm not going home. Lauren and I used to be kind of friends. I thought I'd stop by and say hello." He straightened the way drunks do, trying to act like they were sober. "We had a few dates at Tech and I'd like you to know I was a perfect gentleman."

"That's good to hear." Dan hated how drunks always thought they had to talk to prove they were still in control.

He didn't bother to tell Reid that Lauren had her own place, had for years. He doubted she'd want to talk to Reid, and Dan had no idea where she was. After she'd caught him checking up on her half a dozen times, she'd threatened to move back to Dallas if he didn't stop. She was right. She was twenty-seven and her own person. But when does a dad stop being a dad?

"You want to come in and have a cup of coffee? Maybe tell me what you know about the trouble on your ranch."

"I don't know what's going on." Reid stood and followed Dan in. "I got really wasted one night in Vegas. When I woke up some friends I'd met in Vegas said I owed them five hundred thousand dollars. We argued until my head hurt, then I agreed to help them out if they'd forget the debt. I thought I made a pretty good deal; all I had to do was let them use a forgotten slice of my land, but from then on something squirrely started going on."

The sheriff realized Reid probably had no idea what a mess he was in.

"My friends said they wanted to come out to my place and make improvements. I told Reyes to let them work but to stay out of their way. From what little I overheard, I thought they were building a road, but I didn't see any improvements when I came home."

Reid took a bottle from his coat pocket and drained it. "I didn't want to think about what my father would think when the friends suggested closing down the cattle operation on the ranch so I just drifted, thinking the guys would get tired and just go away. When they didn't leave, I wanted the ranch to go back like it was, cattle and all, but it was too late. All the hands were gone. Why does it have to be so complicated?" His words were coming out more slurred now.

Reid buried his head and almost sounded like he was crying. "I just want it over. My friends say they're helping me, but I don't think they are. The head guy is mad because it's taking so long. Then Coldman's body showed up and no one knows how." Reid leaned back on the couch, finally silent.

Dan stepped into the kitchen to make coffee, thinking of all the questions he wanted to ask Reid. If he could sober the guy up, maybe he'd get a few answers.

Only, when he got back to the den, Reid was sound asleep, and even shaking him didn't wake him up.

Dan was too tired to kick him out. He just covered him with an old quilt and went to bed. He'd deal with Reid in the morning.

To make sure the drunk didn't wander off before they had a talk, Dan handcuffed him to the couch, just for his own safety. Dan didn't want Reid falling off and hurting himself. If he woke up and yelled, Dan would let him free and begin asking questions.

thirty-four

Blade was in great shape. In his line of work it was important. Most weekends when he was home in Denver, he spent his time skiing in winter and running the mountain trails in summer. But tonight, following Agent McMillan up the rocky hill behind the house was hard work.

The agent must have had raccoon eyes because he had no trouble weaving between the rocks. Blade guessed that at one time, maybe a hundred years ago, there was a trail here wide enough to take a wagon through, but landslides and weather had eroded it completely.

Even in winter this back corner of his land was beautiful, and he couldn't help but wonder what it might be like in spring. As they climbed, the views were breathtaking. The land below seemed covered in shades of dark velvet, and the stars sparkled off Indigo Lake like black diamonds.

"I flew over this whole area a few times and found this point," Matthew said as he climbed. "Highest place for miles around. Took me two hours to find it on foot the first time I came out, but wait till you see the view."

Fifteen minutes later they turned into what looked like an abandoned cemetery. A few of the graves were as sunken in as dead eyes. Rotted wooden crosses were scattered about, reminding Blade of broken toys left out to decay. A few small headstone markers made out of rocks spotted the ground, and someone years ago must have circled the area with jagged rocks as black as flint.

Blade remembered Grandmother telling him about a Hamilton cemetery. At least that part of her story was true. What else had she said? Something about the dead overlooking the people who were believed to have added fire to the feud?

This was his ancestors' cemetery. He stepped to the edge of a cliff. Down below had to be the back part of the Bar W. The part Dice had said had no roads crossing the pasture. Was it possible that a hundred years ago the feud that killed several had been started by the first Collins?

Agent McMillan stepped up beside him. "I've been watching. I'm not sure what's going on down there, but I'd bet whatever they're doing, it's not legal. Why would people be moving around way out here after dark? I've seen trucks moving across the land like there was a secret road down there."

Blade studied the land below as the moon rose higher.

The agent continued, "Lately, when the moon is up, trucks drive in slow from a backcountry road. They turn off into a shallow stream just wide enough for them to move into the water. I can't get near the stream, but I'd bet the bottom has been fortified with something strong enough to hold the trucks' weight. Then, as soon as they come to the trees, they pull out and follow the line of dying elms until they hit flat pasture. From there they drive toward that canyon wall and just seem to vanish. One minute I can see them moving, and the next, nothing. It's like they vanish into the shadows of the cliffs."

Blade didn't say anything. He was figuring it out. Pieces of conversations were weaving together.

"How long has this been going on?"

"Less than a week ago we had an anonymous call to watch out for a couple of trucks heading north. We watched for them and followed for a hundred miles before we stopped them. The cattle trucks were empty but we found drugs hidden in false floors.

"We kept the watch up, but the rain came and no trucks crossed any of our checkpoints, north or south. Now it's dry enough for them to start the operation again. Last night I saw two trucks move in and disappear at the canyon wall. Tonight we're hoping they'll come out loaded and we'll have the whole operation."

Without a word, they moved to the edge of the cliff and lay down on their stomachs in the tall grass. The outcropping had to be hanging over Collins land. Only, they were forty feet up.

The night was so still Blade could almost hear himself think. This was a big operation. Someone had put in time and work figuring it out. There was no doubt in his mind what was happening. Transport of drugs. With the trucks, this had to be the distribution point. The center of the operation out here, so far from any town no one would accidently stumble on it.

Dice had commented that the ranch operation hadn't used the back pastures in years. Grass was spotty. Dirt so hard and rocky it wouldn't hold rainwater.

Suddenly, the silence of the night was broken by what sounded like rolling thunder. Out of the tree line came three men on horseback, riding fast, leaning low in the saddle as if all hell were chasing them.

Blade had ridden a few times, but nothing like these guys. They were one with their horses crossing like living lightning, hooves pounding the ground in a rumbling beat. At times the horses seemed to fly.

He pulled his camera up and started shooting. They were dressed Western, chaps slapping their legs, hats low on their foreheads, arms moving in time with the horses. For a moment he swore he was capturing a scene from a hundred years ago.

Matthew pulled his rifle forward and looked through his sight. "Too far to see who," he whispered. "But these boys were born to ride. Look at them go."

Then, the roar of engines blended with the thunder of hooves as three four-wheelers took chase. One man in each was standing, rifle resting on the roll bar, ready to fire.

Matthew whispered, as if they might hear him over the roar, "I don't know who those cowboys are, but the vehicles will catch them as soon as the horses hit flat land."

One shot rang out. Then another and another. The riders were taking fire.

Matthew laughed. "I don't know those guys, but I'm about to be their guardian angel."

His first shot hit the front tire of the first off-road vehicle. It rolled like a toy over tall buffalo grass. His second shot must have hit the engine, because it died so fast the men inside flew out like jelly beans exploding from a broken jar.

The third four-wheeler turned around and headed back toward the trees. The man with the rifle fired off several shots as he bumped along, but none looked like they hit the riders or horses.

The cowboys hadn't slowed. They were splashing across the stream and heading straight for what looked like a ravine winding its way along what must be the border between the ranches.

Blade rolled away from the edge and sat up. "I'm impressed, Matthew. How'd you learn to shoot like that?"

"Trained for the Olympics when I was in college. Dad said if I could shoot rabbits, I could shoot targets. I didn't make the final cut, so he made me go to college."

"How'd you know who the good guys were?"

"Didn't know for sure. I didn't want to kill anyone, just stop the fight. Didn't seem fair shooting at someone riding away."

They watched the men who'd been thrown from the ATVs walking back toward the trees. A few were limping, but all were standing. None looked in shape.

Blade also noticed none looked like they belonged on a ranch. "I can make a pretty good guess who two of those cowboys were. They were doing the same thing we were doing tonight— investigating the trouble on Bar W. And, you guessed right, they were the good guys."

Matthew strapped his rifle back onto his back. "We'd better get out of here. They'll come looking for us when they take the time to figure out none of the cowboys were firing back. And it won't be hard to guess where the shots were coming from."

"I agree."

The hike down wasn't nearly as hard. Once they were back at the house, Matthew and Blade sat on the porch and talked until a black car pulled up where his road turned off the main road.

"My ride's here." Matthew stood. "I've got enough to go on. You'll send me the pictures?"

"First thing in the morning."

Matthew offered his hand. "I won't be back. We'll be notifying the sheriff tomorrow before we go in. If those trucks I've been counting as they go in and out are full of what I think they are, we'll be making one of the biggest busts ever in West Texas." He stepped off the porch. "You be at the sheriff's office tomorrow."

Blade smiled. "I wouldn't miss it. I'll be in on the raid as both an ATF agent and a sheriff's deputy."

"I'd like to hear all about it over a beer when this is over."

"I'll buy." Blade realized every agent was his brother. He wasn't as alone as he'd thought he was on the job.

He watched the agent disappear and wondered if Grandmother was across the lake, thinking he'd hooked up with a ghost. It was long after midnight. Grandmother was probably asleep. There were no lights coming from the mission home across the lake, but he'd head that way, anyway. He liked the idea of waking up to breakfast cooking.

When he clicked on his phone, Blade hoped to see a message from Dakota, but there was only one message from Lucas Reyes.

I'm safe for the night. Don't worry about me. Tell the sheriff I'll be in to talk first thing in the morning. Tell him I said we found the box.

Blade had no idea what Lucas was talking about, except he obviously wasn't coming here for the night. Blade stood and walked over the bridge and headed toward Dakota.

Ten minutes later, he pulled his boots off on the porch and slipped through the unlocked door.

They must have expected him back. He smiled.

Halfway across the living area, he noticed Dakota curled up in an old stuffed rocker. She looked so tiny in the big chair, just as she had that first night.

Without thinking about it, he carefully lifted her, then sat in the chair with Dakota in his arms. Her legs hung over one fat arm of the chair and her hair covered the other.

She wiggled and settled her cheek against his chest. He drew her close as his foot tapped the floor to slowly rock them both.

"I told you not to wait up for me," he whispered into her wild hair.

She wiggled again and raised her head. "You're back. How'd you get in my chair?"

He laughed. "I'm on the bottom. You must be in *my* chair." He moved his hand along her leg, pulling her a bit closer. "We might be more comfortable in bed."

A snort came from the leather couch ten feet away. "You both might be. Then I could get some sleep." Grandmother's tone gave no hint of having been asleep. "You each got beds, go to them. And I plan to sleep with one eye open to make sure there is no sleepwalking in the hallway, all night long."

"Don't you have a house, Granny?" Blade grumbled as he lifted Dakota off his lap.

"Don't you, Hamilton?"

Good point, he thought. Maybe he shouldn't push his luck. "See you in the morning."

He followed Dakota down the hallway. She gave him a quick smile and disappeared into her bedroom. He walked on to the guest room, feeling his tired body ache to hold her. There was no doubt. He was addicted to her. After all his short affairs and one-night stands, this was the one woman he'd never turn away from.

He laughed. He'd fallen for the girl next door. It had taken him so long to find his home, he was very lucky she was still waiting.

Blade tried to go to sleep. Feeling lonely, really lonely, for the first time in his life. He wanted Dakota near. Even if she just talked to him. Even if she started telling him what to do with every day he had left on earth.

Deep into the night, he realized he couldn't sleep because he hurt inside. He felt the pain of her absence and he never felt pain. Only, this time he couldn't push it away. He couldn't ignore it. It was too deep.

thirty-five

———

Lucas, Charley, and Dice Fuller walked their horses the last mile up the draw to Kirkland's land. They moved over winter grass and found Lauren curled up asleep in her old Ford.

While Charley switched the trailer back to his truck, Lucas kissed her awake.

The moment she realized he was near, she hugged him so hard he could barely breathe.

"It is all right, *mi cielo*. I'm fine. I'm back without a scratch, see? It's all over. We found what we were looking for."

"I thought I heard gunfire far away. That wasn't you, was it?" Her blue eyes sparkled with tears.

"No. I heard it too. Probably someone just out hunting coyotes." He couldn't tell her about bullets flying over his head. He couldn't frighten her more than she already was.

Dice and Charley loaded the horses and with a wave they disappeared.

"Aren't you going to tell Pop?" she asked.

"In a few hours he'll be up and I plan to be sitting in his

kitchen, drinking coffee. We'll want to move fast, before they have time to load up and leave the ranch."

He didn't tell her the details. They made it in with no problem. Found the opening to the box canyon that was barely wide enough for the trucks to go in. Rode along the canyon wall and at one small ledge they could see down. Five trucks were parked, one had boxes being unloaded into a tent. A half-dozen guards were huddled around the opening. They'd almost made it down when a rabbit spooked Dice's mount.

The cowboy had stayed in the saddle, but the horse made enough noise to alert the guards. From then on it was a race to get out.

"Any chance your dad knew we were out there tonight?" he asked Lauren as he brushed her hair back.

"I don't think so. Why?"

"When we were riding out, I think we had a guardian angel. I'll tell you all about it later."

She cuddled close as if still half-asleep.

Lucas drove her Ford slowly back to Crossroads, thinking of all he'd seen. His father had told him of little things that were happening, but no one, including Reid or his father, probably had any idea what was going on in the far pasture.

When Lucas turned down the road that lead to Lauren's father's lake house, he had her tucked close under his arm. She'd always been a part of him and she felt so right, close like this.

"Drop me off here," he whispered. "Then go back to your apartment, and get some sleep. All hell is going to break loose in a few hours. I don't like leaving you, but I need to be here when your pop wakes up. We'll talk, make some calls, and get the whole thing rolling."

When he pulled up at her father's place he kissed her, loving how comfortable they'd become in each other's arms. It felt good. It felt right. "This is all going to be over tomorrow. Then we've got some talking to do. You're right. I have been pushing you away, but no more. I still may not be good enough for you, but I'm never walking away from you again. So go on home and get some sleep. I'll call you tomorrow."

She reached over and cut the car's engine. "This is my home. You may sit in the kitchen or take the couch to wait for Pop to wake up, but I still have my old room. You won't have to call me. I'm a light sleeper. I'll hear when you two start talking."

He nodded. "You're not one of those women who take orders, are you?"

"I never have been, Lucas."

He smiled. "I'm going to love that about you."

They walked to the door. His hand never stopped touching her. For once, Lucas couldn't get close enough. He'd always known it would be that way if he allowed her near. In the beginning, he'd feared she'd detour his goals, his dreams, but tonight he realized something. She *was* his dream. His future. Without Lauren, all the work would be for nothing.

She turned toward her bedroom and he turned toward the study. His quiet, shy Lauren didn't say a word, but he felt it in her touch. She didn't want to leave his side.

He stood, watching her walk away, and he knew there was only one place he belonged. With her. He'd always known that, but part of him had also feared he wasn't right for her. He came from a rowdy, noisy family and she seemed to live in a quiet world even in college. He loved excitement, be it fighting in court or riding full-out tonight. She'd chosen to live here, no big city.

But she was already in his heart. She always had been, and this time he wouldn't walk away.

Now he realized that she didn't want the powerful lawyer or the big-city life or the money. She wanted him. Just him, and she'd been trying to tell him that for years.

Lauren moved inside her room and pulled off her sweater. Her life was changing; she could feel it. Something had shifted inside her. Lucas had climbed back into her heart, or maybe he'd never left. Not as a hero, the boyfriend she wanted, or even the man she admired. It was more. They felt it in the few kisses they had shared tonight. A settling into place. In the way he touched her. In the calmness they both shared. Neither had said the words, but they both knew. They were together, not as friends or lovers, but forever as both.

Before she could find her pajamas, a tap sounded on her door. The house was so quiet, she almost thought she'd wished for the sound, but when it came again she pressed her hand against the wood.

If she answered, she just might be unlocking her heart for the first time.

It was time.

She opened the door with a smile, realizing that Lucas hadn't kissed her good-night, or good morning. Maybe he only wanted to touch her one more time.

She stood, waiting, and couldn't help but notice how he seemed nervous for the first time around her.

He didn't reach for her. He just leaned against the door frame. "I can't sleep on the couch. It's already occupied by Reid. In fact, he's handcuffed to the arm of it and I can smell liquor from a room away."

"Well," Lauren murmured, with a smile, "I guess you'll have to sleep with me."

A slow smile spread over Lucas's handsome face. "You think it's time we stopped hesitating?"

"I think it's long past."

She pulled him in and closed the door.

He circled her in his arms and whispered, "You ready to jump, Lauren?"

"I think so. I'd like to try."

He kissed her forehead as his hands moved over her. "Don't worry, *mi cielo*, we've got a lifetime to get it right."

She laughed softly against his shoulder. "Well, I guess we'd better start practicing."

thirty-six

Dan woke to his phone vibrating on the nightstand. "Five o'clock! Who calls at five o'clock?" He lifted his cell as he rolled back into bed. "This better be important."

"This is Agent Matthew McMillan with the ATF. We'll be at your office in less than an hour, Sheriff. We understand you have a search warrant and we're planning to assist in the raid of the Bar W. We have evidence of a drug operation in progress there."

"I'll be waiting for you and you'll have my full support." Dan could feel adrenaline popping through his veins. After all the work, the interviews, the worry, what he'd waited for was about to go down. ATF wouldn't have called if they didn't have evidence, and apparently they weren't wasting any time.

He dialed Blade and told him the news. Blade didn't seem surprised. All he said was, "McMillan doesn't mess around. I'll be there in one hour."

Dan pulled on his trousers before heading to the kitchen to make coffee. By the time he got dressed, the coffee would be ready. Today promised to be the Fourth of July and Christmas all mixed together.

When he flipped on the kitchen light he heard a low groan, like a dying animal was in his study.

Reid! He'd forgotten about the drunk.

"Wake up, Collins. You're coming with me. We've got a date at my office in fifty minutes."

Reid's only answer was another groan.

"I'll uncuff you after I get dressed and the coffee is ready. Don't worry about cleaning up. I have a feeling I'll just be moving you to a cell. It'll be best if you stay out of the way for a while. You can clean up there."

Ten minutes later, when he returned to the kitchen, Reid was sitting up with the lamp by the couch on. Not surprising, Tim O'Grady was sitting on the other end of the couch, and neither of them looked like they were speaking to the other.

"I got to get that sliding door fixed," was Dan's only comment as he got out three cups. "Tim, why are you here?"

"I saw the lights on and Lauren's car parked out front," Tim shouted as if Dan were probably hard of hearing by now. "I came over to talk to her." Tim frowned at Reid. "What's he doing here? Is he under arrest? Don't you have a jail you can put drunks in? This is way too much bringing your work home if you ask me, Sheriff."

"I didn't bring him home," Dan said in a low voice. Answering Tim's questions would be a waste of time; he'd only think of more.

Tim yelled a jumble of cusswords, then shouted, "I think he threw up on the coffee table."

"Four cups," Dan said as he reached for another coffee cup. "I'm sure you woke Lauren up, Tim."

"Five cups." Lucas stepped from Lauren's room. He had jeans on but no shirt. "I got to talk to you, Sheriff. You're not going to believe what we found last night on the Collinses' back pasture."

Dan slowly looked around the room. He didn't know whom to murder first. Part of him simply wanted to go back to bed.

The feds were moving in on the Bar W, Tim thought he lived here, Reid was still vomiting, and Lucas may have slept with his daughter.

Dan's phone rang. He answered in more a growl than a hello. Then hung up without saying a word.

"All of you have to be in my office in fifteen minutes. The highway patrol and the Texas Rangers are showing up at the party early and all hell is about to go knocking on the Bar W door." He hit 9-1-1. When Pearly answered he said, "Can you be at the office fast? We've got company coming in from all over the panhandle."

Dan didn't bother to say goodbye.

He looked back at the three men staring at him. Not one moved.

Dan straightened, becoming the general. "Lucas, get dressed and wake Lauren. She's about to get a big story for her online paper. Tim, uncuff Reid and help him clean up. All of you get to Lauren's car in five minutes and try to beat me to my office."

"Me?" Tim shouted. "Why do I have to clean up the drunk? Why do I have to go into the office before dawn? I worked all night on a new story, which by the way isn't near as strange as whatever's going on here. I haven't even been to bed. I'm too sleepy to take orders."

Before Dan could yell back at Tim, Lauren stepped to her door wearing what looked like Lucas's Western shirt, and all the snaps were not snapped.

"Morning, Pop," she said, just as she had every morning since she could talk.

Lucas had the sense to push her gently back into her bedroom. "We'll be ready in five, Sheriff," he said as he closed the door.

Maybe he thought Dan was about to say something he'd regret, but in truth, Dan couldn't think of a single word except maybe how he hated the way the lawyer felt it was his duty to help Lauren with her clothes.

Tim bumped his way around the sheriff as he dragged Reid to the kitchen sink and dunked his head under cold running water. Tim was yelling and Reid was screaming, but Dan simply put on his belt, pulled his service weapon from the safe and looked around for his hat. Maybe when he called Brandi tonight and told her what was going on, she'd make sense of it all.

Ten minutes later they all piled into Lauren's car and Dan followed them to the station. As they were getting out, Dan put his arm around his daughter and said what he'd said a thousand times over the years, "Are you all right, baby?"

"I'm fine, Pop. I love Lucas. I always have."

Dan looked at Tim cussing as he tried to unlock the office door and Reid leaning against a pole with his hair still dripping.

Dan whispered low to his only child, "I'm glad, honey. He seems to be the pick of the crop."

thirty-seven

Blade drove his rented truck as fast as he could from Indigo Lake, but he was the last to join the party. The sleepy little town's sheriff's office was busier than a New York precinct.

He moved through the crowd of Department of Public Safety agents in suits and Texas Highway Patrol officers in uniform. Mixed in were a few Texas Rangers in their white shirts and tan hats.

Pearly, who obviously hadn't bothered to comb her hair before she rushed to work, was standing on her chair yelling orders. No one listened to the lady who looked like she was dressed as an extra from the *Star Wars* cantina scene.

Dice tapped his way down the stairs in his cowboy boots. His wide smile sent wrinkles all the way to his ears as he twirled the cell keys on one long, thin finger.

Blade decided to talk to him first. "What are you doing here, Dice? Up a little early, aren't you?"

"I didn't want to miss this day. It's been heading toward us on a slow train for months. I was with Pearly when she got the sheriff's call and I knew he'd need extra deputies, so I deputized myself and came on in."

Blade nodded and asked, very officially, "What's your assignment?"

"Don't know. Had to make one up for myself. I just finished locking Reid Collins up for being stinking drunk. Put Tim in the cell with him for no reason at all. Thought Tim might talk him to death. Save the state a trial if Collins turns out to be mixed up in this mess."

Blade wasn't sure, but he thought Dice had just committed at least a half-dozen illegal acts. "You riding with the posse to round up the bad guys?"

Dice shook his head. "Someone's got to stay here and hold down the fort, protect the womenfolk, answer the phones, eat the doughnuts."

"I'll keep you informed," Blade said. "I think I'd like to be part of this roundup. Have any idea what we're facing?"

Dice never let the fact he didn't know anything keep him from talking. "I heard one of the highway patrolmen say they stopped a Bar W cattle truck just over the line into New Mexico a few hours ago. Truck had a false floor. When they pried up a few boards they discovered the whole bottom of the trailer layered in five inches of drugs. Everything from crack cocaine to heroin, packed in neat and tight." The old cowboy smiled. "Heard they got a tip. Anonymous person, of course."

Brigman's voice suddenly carried over the crowd. "Hamilton. I need you in my office."

Blade wove through the uniforms and stepped into an office almost as crowded as the lobby. He nodded once to the sheriff.

Dan introduced him to Sheriff Fifth Weathers from one county over and a rancher named Staten Kirkland. Both men were well over six feet. They shook hands with Blade as Dan rolled out a map. "We're each taking a side of the ranch. Kirkland, you take the side that borders your land and part of Hamilton Acres. Fifth, you take the side closest to town. I'm going in on the west side with plenty of men to handle any trouble, so, Blade, you'll guard the east road."

All three men nodded, but Blade was the only one who looked at the map.

Dan continued, "We've got some miles to cover but you'll each have three highway partrol cars. One rule: anyone leaving the Bar W is to be stopped and detained. I don't care if he's driving a truck or riding a horse or walking out. No one leaves."

Blade had driven the east border of the ranch with Dan yesterday. He remembered seeing three gates and a few other places where a man could drive out across pasture. The east side would not be hard to watch.

Jerry Cline sliced his way in between Blade and the sheriff. "I've rounded up several men who used to work at the Bar W. We're hauling horses that are already saddled. We'll go in with you and be ready to ride whenever you say the word, Sheriff."

Dan nodded. "When this is over, I want to talk to you, Jerry. You're a good man and I figure it's about time you started wearing a badge."

Jerry smiled. "I'll think about it."

Jerry disappeared back into the crowd, and Blade decided the sheriff was right—Cline could handle the job.

As the others started rounding up their men, Blade asked, "What about Lucas? He knows that ranch better than anyone here, except maybe Dice."

"He and Charley Collins are riding with me. The paperwork came in a few hours ago. Lucas's office is sending it over. D.R. Collins filed all the legal papers we need to have his full cooperation. But he didn't give Lucas the power of attorney he asked for. He gave it to his oldest son, Charley." Dan nodded to a young rancher standing next to Lucas. "Charley didn't want it, but he agreed to stay with us until we get this mess cleaned up. He'll give us permission to search wherever we need to and with the help of the cowboys I don't plan to miss a spot on the ranch."

Suddenly, like a stirred up ant bed, everyone was moving at once. Picking up orders, climbing into cars, heading out as the rest of the town still slept.

To Blade's surprise, one more person climbed into the sheriff's car. Dan Brigman's daughter.

The press. She had a camera around her neck and looked very official.

By the time the town came awake, Blade had a feeling news reports would be coming in and the raid would be over.

Two Texas Rangers signaled that they'd be following Blade. Another climbed in the passenger seat as though Blade had invited him. Like race cars lining up, four convoys headed out. When they reached the county road, Blade veered off to the east with several cars following him.

He saw the lights of one of the other lines of cars, moving silently to the north. Climbing up to the breaks where the land was rough. Kirkland's caravan. They'd be close to Hamilton Acres.

His land, Blade thought.

If he'd expected it to be exciting, Blade would have been disappointed. Not one shot was fired. All they did was stand around watching, talking low, waiting.

One of the officers in Dan's party was texting facts, keeping everyone informed. The Texas Ranger read each report aloud with a raspy voice that sounded like he should have been announcing rodeo events.

Sheriff Dan Brigman and his team met the men left at the Bar W at the headquarters' door. Most weren't even dressed for work, and only one had taken the time to strap on a weapon. When he saw twenty lawmen looking at him, he quickly raised his hands.

While the sheriff and his crew arrested them and read them

their rights, Lucas was in one of the cars, heading to the far pasture along with several cowboys on horseback.

Surprisingly, the men on guard at the box canyon hadn't tried to block the entrance. It stood wide-open and the two men assigned to guard the trucks inside were asleep.

When they were tapped awake with the barrel of a rifle, they complained that they'd worked all night trying to fix the trucks so they could all roll out at dawn.

Lucas called his information in and all the lawmen listened as he rattled off the facts. Two more trucks with fake floors were loaded and ready to leave the ranch.

Dan and Lucas also texted back and forth as Blade waited on the east side with nothing to report. The highway patrolmen and Texas Rangers had spread out along the east side. Too far apart to see each other in the dark, but each knew a blink of headlights would signal if they needed help.

The Texas Ranger who'd ridden shotgun in Blade's truck finally stepped out to watch the sunrise. He was a man in his late fifties who looked solid as a rock. He'd be called an old-timer in the ATF, but not here.

"You know what we're doing, Hamilton?"

"Guarding the road?" Blade guessed.

"We're standing the gap. You probably wish you were with Brigman, riding in like the posse, but in the overall picture what we're doing is just as important."

"I'm happy here. I got enough holes in me, sir."

The Ranger laughed. "You must be the deputy who was shot a few nights ago. You in any pain?"

"No," Blade answered honestly. "But it bothers me that I have no idea who shot me."

"I have a feeling we'll know that by noon. As soon as we round up all the drug dealers, and drivers, and lowlifes who cook the meth up, they'll start talking, telling on each other like first-grade boys on the playground."

Blade smiled. "You think so?"

"I do. I've seen it before. They all watch too many cop shows and think if they talk they'll get a deal, but we're not in the habit of playing that game."

An hour passed before the sheriff's last text came in.

All men accounted for. All teams report to the headquarters for further assignments.

Blade was fascinated at how smoothly it had worked as he pulled up to the headquarters. A dozen men were in handcuffs. One by one the highway patrol picked them up to be transported to Lubbock. Since the truck the ATF found last night had crossed the state line, the feds were moving in to handle the questioning.

Blade felt like an outsider among all the officers and agents. These weren't the lawmen he usually worked with. He finally wandered into the huge house and found Lucas and Charley at a long table going over stacks of paperwork.

"This place is really something," Blade whispered. "Swimming pool and tennis courts. A regular country club."

Charley looked up. "I always hated living here. Still hate even walking in the door. If D.R. gets back, this will be his problem. I'm going home to Lone Heart Pass."

Blade smiled. "You know, I understand completely. It's something, all right, but it doesn't feel like home. Why do you think your dad named you to take over?"

Charley shrugged. "I guess he ran out of sons he could disown. But I'm not interested in running a spread like this. If he doesn't come back, I'm hiring Lucas's father back to run the place. He has been for years."

The cleanup lasted all day. Blade had no idea it would take so long. Without Lucas's midnight ride, they might not have found the operation's headquarters, or it would have seemed like a small operation. But thanks to the tents in the box canyon, and records found at the house, the men in this operation were going away for a long time. The friends Reid had met that night in Las Vegas turned out to have several drug operations across half a dozen states. The feds said this break was helping with several other investigations.

It was almost sunset when Blade drove Lucas back to the office. For a while both were silent, trying to take it all in.

Lucas finally said, "I should say I'm sorry about you being shot. It was my fault."

"How do you figure that?"

"I knew too much. I guess they'd assumed my dad was passing information. I wanted him safe and then I thought if I stayed in jail, they'd think I knew more than I did and they'd make a move. They'd come after me, but I'd be just out of reach. I had to give my parents time to disappear. I never thought they'd try to kill me. I thought I might be offered a bribe, or at worst, threatened."

Blade grinned. "No one ever kills the lawyer, right?"

"Right, but I was talking up how I was going to get in touch with D.R. and get him to come home to find out what was going on at the family ranch. I guess they must have panicked and just decided to get rid of me."

"You think Reid was mixed up in this?"

"Yeah, but he was also being blackmailed and used. I'll do my best to get him off."

"You're going to represent him?"

Lucas nodded. "I know it doesn't make sense, but he needs a good lawyer, and I did grow up with him."

"I saw his face when the sheriff found the first body," Blade said. "He was shocked, sick at the sight. I'd bet a month's pay he didn't know about it."

Lucas nodded. "I heard he almost passed out when he heard about Coffer Coldman. All I can figure out is that Coffer must have left the ranch by a back gate and just happened to run into one of the trucks. Some of those thugs know who killed him. They'll rat on each other fast enough."

They pulled up to the county office and found Dice sitting on the steps, his head low, his cowboy hat on the ground. All else was quiet. All the excitement was over and in a few hours it would be nothing but yesterday's news.

Both men jumped out of the truck and hurried to the old man.

"You all right, Dice?" Blade asked.

The old guy shook his head. "I'm pretty low, fellows. I got some bad news. That body in the barn fire wasn't my friend LeRoy. The report came in while all of ya'll were out rounding up bad guys."

Dice scrubbed his chin. "It was just a drifter who must have snuck in looking for a place out of the rain and got caught between the fire and a locked door. One of the cowboys told the sheriff that Collins told him to put a lock on the barn by the road to keep the drifters out."

Lucas patted Dice's bony shoulder. "That's good news. LeRoy may still be alive somewhere."

"Oh, he is. He's in the lobby cuddled up by Pearly's desk. He'd caught a ride to Abilene to visit his sister. Said he was so down, it was either that or spend all his money drinking. When he heard on the news that all the trouble at the ranch was over, he hitchhiked back to pick up his truck and trailer before the ranch gates were locked. Didn't even occur to the old fool that I might be looking for him."

"That is good news he's alive though, right?" Blade said.

"I guess, but it turns out he was dating Pearly now and then before he left. They were having a fling and neither one of them mentioned it to me. She thought he was gone and took up with me, but now he's back, she can't make up her mind which one of us she wants to fling with."

Blade thought, of all the problems of the day, this was a minor one, but it seemed the end of the world to Dice. He tried getting the old guy's mind off Pearly. "Is Reid still in jail?"

Dice didn't raise his head, but he answered, "Nope, the feds came and got him a few hours ago. I tried to get them to take O'Grady too, but they didn't want him."

Pearly and an old cowboy who had to be LeRoy walked out onto the porch. LeRoy had the same hangdog look as Dice.

Blade decided to step back and watch. Lucas did the same. Standing five feet away they tried to act like they weren't listening.

"I've been thinking," Pearly said. "Since both of you men have slowed down some over the years there is only one thing I can do."

They both waited for the bad news.

She straightened. "I don't want to come between your friendship. That's something worth keeping. So, I've decided to keep seeing you both if you two agree to one rule."

"What might that be?" Dice didn't look like he was buying into this group-dating thing.

"You two don't talk to each other about me. LeRoy, you get the odd day of the weekend and Dice, you get the even. And I expect a real date. Going out to dinner or something, not just dropping over. I don't want you both showing up at the same time, either. My house isn't big enough to handle a waiting line. During the week I work and I got my shows to watch every night, so don't bother calling me. I don't want to talk."

Blade had to step inside because he was losing his ability to keep from laughing. Lucas was right behind him.

"You think they'll work it out?" Blade asked.

"I think Pearly already has."

Lucas offered his hand. "It was nice spending time in jail with you."

"Same here. I'll miss our chess games."

Lucas looked him straight in the eye as he always had. "You

wouldn't happen to have been on that high ridge at the back of your land last night. Someone covered us as we rode out from the box canyon."

Blade smiled. "I didn't fire a shot."

Lucas looked like he didn't believe him, but he didn't argue. "Well, tell whoever it was that I'm grateful."

Blade shook his hand. "I'll do that. See you around, Lucas."

"See you around," Lucas echoed as if the two men lived in town.

Blade walked past the three senior citizens arguing on the porch and headed for his pickup. The day was over. It was time to go home.

thirty-eight

Lucas found Lauren in her office finishing up articles for the *Fort Worth Star-Telegram* and the *Dallas Morning News*.

"I want to talk to you," he said without any other words like *hello*.

"Wait a minute. I just got news that one of the thugs confessed to setting the fires in the barns. He was smoking in one, while he looked for something to steal. When it caught fire, he moved to the next and set it thinking he'd blame it on the cowboys who were mad and leaving."

Lucas leaned against the file cabinet and watched her work. He'd always thought that she was hiding out here in Crossroads, but she was happy here. She loved being part of the community and writing. Everyone he ran into in Houston from back home read her *Crossroads News*.

"You love writing, don't you?"

She didn't look up. "Almost finished."

"I'll wait." He couldn't resist moving a strand of her sunshine hair away from her face. "I'll wait forever," he whispered.

"What did you say?"

"Nothing."

Her fingers flew across her laptop, then suddenly, she shouted, "Finished! This story is going to get me into papers across the country."

Her big eyes blinked at him. "Of course, I wish it hadn't happened, but I did cover it completely, step by step. And I'll keep it up, the investigations, the interviews, the trials and, of course, the wrap-up of how it all affected our town."

Lucas just smiled.

"What?"

"I don't want to talk about the Bar W. I want to show you something."

"Sure." She stood up and leaned into him as if she'd done so all her life.

He moved his hands along her body. "Last night was the best night of my life. I felt like… I felt like…"

"I know," she said as she kissed him. "I felt the same. I didn't know I could feel that way."

"What way?" he teased. "Like you were exploding with pure joy. Like you'd died and gone to heaven. Like you'd never feel that good again."

She nodded.

"Don't worry. That's never going to happen. I'm here. I'll take you to heaven any night you want to go as long as I can go with you."

She buried her face against his chest and he couldn't tell if she was laughing or crying.

"I said I loved you last night, and I'm never taking that back, Lauren. Never. Now we have to go. I want to show you something before the sun sets."

She began gathering her things.

He took her hand. "You don't need anything. Just walk with me."

"All right."

They left her office and walked along the sidewalk to Dakota's tiny little real estate office. Her door was locked up for the night.

When they reached the third office, Lucas stopped and stared down at her, smiling.

"That office has never been rented," Lauren said. "It's twice as big and has a real apartment upstairs. Dakota saw it once and said it has a big window on the side that looks out over the whole town. All I've got is a living room/kitchen in front and a bedroom with a tiny bath in back."

"You want to see this one?"

"The owner lives out of town. No one has the key."

"You do." Lucas smiled. "It's around your neck."

She looked at him as if he were playing some kind of trick on her. Slowly, she pulled off the chain and tried the key. It worked.

"But?"

"I rented it the last time I came home and saw where your office was. I wanted to know that if I ever moved home, you'd be close."

"You're moving in here?"

"No, *mi cielo*, we're moving in here. I'll have my practice downstairs and we'll live upstairs."

"But."

"No *but*." He laughed. "Your pop told me we were getting married. None of this living together until we know each other better. We've known each other all our lives."

"I won't be rushed." She straightened.

"I know. I feel the same. How does tomorrow sound?"

"I'll think about it." She laughed as she walked into the huge space.

A few minutes later they were standing in the open living room that spread into a kitchen. Dakota was right, a huge window faced the town.

"Every evening we can stand right here and watch the sun set over our town. How would you like that?"

"I think I'd like that very much, but I'm keeping my office and my job."

"Good, then we won't starve." He hugged her. "You want to go tell Pop?"

She shook her head. "I'd like to try out the bedroom first."

"But there's no furniture. No bed."

She pulled him along. "Trust me, Lucas. You won't even notice."

thirty-nine

Blade pulled up to Dakota's place just as the last of the sunset faded. He was almost up the steps when he saw her sitting in one of the wicker chairs.

"You made it home before dark," she whispered as she stood.

He circled her waist with his arm and lifted her up to kiss her. "I have to leave tomorrow, but I'll be back as soon as I can. It seems my vacation has ended."

She held on tight. "I don't want you to go."

"I know, but there are things I have to do, Elf." He smiled, loving her tears. Loved knowing she cared enough to cry.

Without a word, they moved inside and joined Grandmother at the kitchen counter while Maria cooked. Blade told them all about what had happened at the Bar W and Grandmother swore the whole feud between the two families had been started by old man Collins because he was always wanting more land.

After supper, Blade kissed each of the women good-night. Maria stood still and let him kiss her cheek. Grandmother rubbed her kiss off, but grinned for once. Dakota walked him to the guestroom and kissed him twice.

"Don't go," she whispered.

"I have to, but I swear I'll be back. Believe me." He kissed her one last time, but she didn't answer him.

Once in his room, he felt the pain again. Deep in his chest. Pain he couldn't ignore. Pain he couldn't stop.

He tried to sleep. He walked the floor. He even made a list of all he had to do, but the pain wouldn't go away.

She didn't believe him. Dakota didn't think he'd be back.

Blade thought of waking her up just to tell her one more time that he was coming back. But if she still didn't believe him, the pain in his chest might crack his ribs.

He was staring out the window, looking at the lake, remembering the sad story Grandmother had told him, when the bedroom door opened slowly.

When he turned, just for a moment, he thought he was staring at a vision. It couldn't be real. Dakota was standing there with her white T-shirt pulled halfway off.

"I've come to sleep with you, Hamilton."

"I'm coming back." He said the one thing he had to say again.

"I know. I wouldn't have come if I didn't believe that. This isn't a one-night stand, you need to understand. This is the beginning of forever."

He crossed the room, helped her with her T-shirt and picked her up. As he carried her to bed, he realized the pain in his chest had stopped.

"I think I'm in love with you," he whispered as he began kissing every part of her. "I think home isn't a place, but a person, and you're mine."

She put her small hands on either side of his face and met him eye to eye. "Hamilton, stop talking and make love to me."

He grinned. "You running my life, Elf?"

"Looks like I've found my calling."

They both laughed and began their one-night stand that might just last every night of their lives.

The next morning she cried as he left at dawn. "I'll be back," he kept saying but she didn't stop crying. He couldn't tell her when—a day, a week. His job was unpredictable.

"I'll call," he whispered as he kissed her one more time.

"No. I don't want to talk to you until you're here."

He turned and walked away. Feeling sick inside. He was doing just what he said he would do. He was leaving her. Duty called and deep down he wasn't sure she'd be waiting for him when he came back.

A few days later Maria called to tell him Lauren and Lucas were getting married, but he said he couldn't make it home by Friday. They were in the middle of a big investigation and they had to work fast.

Jerry called later to tell him the repairs on his house were coming along. It was ready to move in soon.

No word from Dakota.

On March 15, he pulled up to the Davis house and ran to the door. For the first time the old adobe house was locked up. He tried Grandmother's house. Locked up. Not a light on at either place.

He drove over to his land and turned on all the lights. Then he parked the new Dodge Ram he'd bought in the middle of the road. Dakota would have to pass his place to get home, and he planned to sleep in the bed of the truck to catch her.

Finally, he heard her old pickup rattling down the road. He walked out in the center of the road.

Dakota braked hard and jumped out of her truck. "Get out of the road, Hamilton. I almost ran you down."

"Come home with me, Dakota. The house is almost finished. I want you to see it."

"No. I can't step foot on your land."

"You don't believe that old curse, do you?"

"I believe Grandmother. She says I can't live on Hamilton land."

Grandmother climbed out of the truck and Maria did the same. He was going to have to face all the Davis women—and to tell the truth, he loved them all. They were his family.

"I'm not giving you up, Dakota. I'm staying right here. Not moving until we work this out. I want to live the rest of my life with you, so you'd better tell me what you want because I'm not going anywhere."

Grandmother circled him slowly as if he were a tree that sprang up in the road.

Dakota turned to her grandmother. "What do I do? He's crazy as any Hamilton ever born, but I love him."

Grandmother poked him in the stomach with her walking stick. "Load him in the truck and we'll take him home. You don't know him well enough to marry yet, so we'll just keep him for a while."

Blade smiled. "I'll follow you in. If it takes a year, I'll talk you into marrying me."

Dakota kissed his cheek. "What if I don't say yes in a year?"

Blade winked. "Then I'll marry your *shichu*. If I can't be your husband, I might as well be your grandfather."

All three women laughed.

Without another word, he gathered up his family and went to the Davis house. He'd meant what he said. Home wasn't a place; it was a woman, and he'd be happy as long as he was with Dakota.

forty

Dan was finally alone in his office. Everyone had gone home. Since the excitement at the Bar W, everything seemed quiet now that all was back to normal. It was a little early to call Brandi, but he needed to hear her voice.

She'd been gone much longer than they'd planned. It seemed every time they talked, she pushed the day she'd be home back. Her songs were taking off and everyone needed her in Nashville. Her two-week trip had stretched into over a month.

Only, he needed her, too.

He punched her number.

She picked up on the second ring. "Evening, Sheriff," she said in her low voice. "How was your day?"

He didn't want to talk about the day. "I miss you. What I wouldn't give to hold you right now. If you're not coming home soon, I'm flying out there."

"How much would you do for me if I was there? Cuddle up and make love to me all night and then get up and make breakfast for me?"

Dan laughed. "I'd do that."

"Would you run away with me for the weekend and stay with me in an expensive hotel that had room service?"

"I would." He loved this game. She was giving him ideas about what she wanted.

"Would you walk to the county offices' front porch and yell as loud as you could that you loved your wife?"

"I would," he answered.

"Well, then, do it right now and I might just hear you."

Dan didn't walk, he ran. When he swung open the door, Brandi was standing right there at the top step of the county offices.

He picked her up and swung her around and whispered, "I love my wife."

She smiled. "I know."

"I love my wife," he said louder.

She laughed. "I know, Dan."

"I love my wife!" he yelled.

Cap Fuller's raspy voice came from one of the retirement homes across the street. "We know, Sheriff. The whole darn town can hear you."

★ ★ ★ ★ ★

Can't get enough Texas romance?
Keep reading for WINTER'S CAMP,
a special RANSOM CANYON *bonus story*
from New York Times *bestselling author*
Jodi Thomas!

WINTER'S CAMP

one

———

Ransom Canyon, Texas
1872

James Randall Kirkland took one last look at the sun's blinding light before heading into the canyon's narrow entrance. Shadows danced along the jagged walls as if holding secrets and danger below. The beauty of the rocks ribboned in the colors of the earth almost calmed his fears. Almost.

The only way to get to Ransom Canyon from the south was along one path barely five feet wide and far too steep for a wagon. Midday seemed to pass into early evening in a flash as the walls grew higher above him and the temperature dropped. Winter already whispered through the fall air, warning him of how little time he had left to prepare.

The trades he'd make today would restore his staples even if the trip down into the canyon might be dangerous. James had lived with risk all his life and bore the scars to prove it.

Anyone in Ransom Canyon who didn't want him showing up today would have a clear shot from above. But even among outlaws and Comancheros, there was a code. For a few weeks every year when nature turned from green to brown, any man could ride this trail and trade for what he wanted or needed. With the nearest trading post more than two hundred miles away, supplies were hard to come by in this part of Texas. Winter was coming on early; James knew he'd need blankets, food supplies and at least two more horses.

He had crossed the plains of this northernmost part of Texas before. Once in 1866, when the need to roam open country to clear the blood of war from his mind had grown too strong. It hadn't worked. Dreams of drowning in blood still haunted him. He had ridden over the Llano Estacado again in 1869 as a scout for the army. Settlers were moving into Texas fast and the army knew the fort line would have to be extended to where Comanche and buffalo roamed.

James might not live to see his thirtieth birthday. A wanderer's life was the only one he had known since running away from a mission in San Antonio at the age of twelve. All was adventure and freedom then. Now he longed for what he'd never had: roots. Deep roots so generations of Kirklands would live out their lives on the same land.

A priest had once told James he came from noble English blood. But all James knew was that his family blood must have been thin, for his father had been gunned down a few months after they'd arrived in Texas and his mother and little sister had been dead before their first winter in Texas had passed.

Now, as he and his companion, a buffalo-hunter-turned-guide, rode into Ransom Canyon, James kept his rifle over one arm and his Colt ready to slide from its holster at the slightest sound. He didn't trust the men they were about to meet or the buckskin-clad man who rode beside him. It had taken a war and several gunfights to make James realize he couldn't afford trust.

"I know you don't like this, Kirkland." Two Fingers broke the silence that had lasted all morning. "But you need horses and supplies to last the winter on the plains." The old ex-slave, who'd lost his middle two fingers on a bet down in Fort Worth, scratched his neck with his thumb. "I can speak enough of any language we come up against in this place, but like I told you before, you'd be better off to ride south with me and not stay on this land. We could winter near a fort and both still have our scalps come spring."

"I want to be alone out here for a while. I plan to scout this land and find the best spot for a ranch. Then, come spring, I'll stake my claim." James did not add that he had saved enough to buy a hundred head of cattle. The money, along with a small inheritance from his father that he had never touched, was waiting for him in a bank.

"If these traders know you're squattin' near here, they'll come calling and think nothing of killing you and taking back their goods. You might have been the great Captain Kirkland in the war, but out here alone you'll be nothing but dead if they find you."

James nodded. It had been seven years since the war and he still couldn't shake his past. Even Two Fingers, who hadn't known him long, had picked up on how some of the men had treated him in Fort Worth. Halfway into the War Between the States, he'd gone mad and ignored danger. He had been lucky to have survived but in the years since, his legend had seemed to grow, not fade, as he wished it would.

When he'd hired Two Fingers, James's plan had simply been to scout the land, but once he'd seen the beauty he'd known he would have to stay a while if this was the place he planned to live out the rest of his life. With his hunting skills and more supplies, he could survive the winter alone.

Now that Two Fingers had started talking, he couldn't seem to stop. "A man without a horse in this country might as well whittle his own headstone."

When James didn't answer, Two Fingers continued. "Most of the men we'll run across today are just traders. A few might even be rangers looking for captives taken in raids." He shook his head. "Lots were kidnapped during the war years without menfolk around. The children and the women go wild or crazy after a while. Lawmen do them no good by taking them back."

James had heard the stories. "I'm not interested in captives or the slave trade. I'm only here for horses." The war against slavery might be over, but no one had told the outlaws and Comanche. Ransom for captives could pay well.

As they moved into the crossover shadows, James made out a dozen men camped at the bottom of the canyon along the riverbank. Goods were laid out on blankets and stacked in wagon beds. Movement in the cedars told him more traders with mule teams were in the shade. He noticed Comanche traders and what looked like outlaws from both sides of the Rio Grande. They were hard, weathered men who wore their supply of bullets crossed over their chests.

He spotted a makeshift corral with thirty or more horses. Most looked like half-wild mustangs, but they'd do. He needed horses or mules to pack supplies in and hides out come spring. If the hunting was good over the cold months, he would make enough to stock the new place for a year, maybe more.

As they walked their horses closer only a few people in the clearing seemed to notice them. A small group of Apache camped by the water, the women mostly doing the work while the men traded. The chief stood tall in the center of the camp even though he had to be over fifty. They were a ragged group, the leftovers of a tribe whose young braves had been killed in battle. The few ponies they had looked too young to break to saddle. One sported an army brand.

James was about to turn away when he caught sight of a woman standing at the edge of the Apache camp. She was wrapped in a dirty blanket as mud-covered as her face and hands. She simply stood staring at the ground; not moving, not interested in his passing.

One of the older women in the tribe walked near and struck her with a stick. The muddy woman, with hair so matted it might never comb out, finally looked up.

For a moment James could only stare. Her huge eyes, framed in dark circles, looked wild and mindless, but they were the crystal blue of a mountain lake.

"Best move along, Kirkland," Two Fingers ordered.

They moved on toward the main camp. "Did you see the color of her eyes?" James whispered. "She has to be a captive."

Two Fingers shook his head. "When I was a boy, I ran away thinking I'd be free, not a slave like my ma, but Apache found me. I was lucky. I was taken in by the tribe, treated as good as if I were a real son. I learned the language and had a grand time living the life, but now and then I'd see a woman who'd been traded from tribe to tribe as though she was nothing but a horse. No—a woman like that is lower than a horse. If they were lucky, if you want to call it that, they were taken in as a third or fourth wife. They'd do all the work the other wives didn't want to do and only eat when there was plenty. The number-one wife usually had the right to beat the last wife and did regularly."

Two Fingers swore in Spanish. "If they weren't so lucky, they fought for scraps with the dogs. Once they started looking and acting like that woman we passed, there was no hope. If they didn't kill themselves or get beaten to death, they were left to die. Her mind's gone, Kirkland. Don't look at her. Some say if you do, she'll steal your soul and take it down to hell with her."

James thought he was beyond caring about anyone but himself; that his heart and soul had hardened to rock. He'd lost every friend he'd had in the war. He had lived so long without a family he'd decided he never wanted one. Never wanted anyone to die on him. Never wanted someone grieving when he died. It didn't matter that he felt sorry for the woman covered in mud. He could not save her or heal her.

"She's mad," Two Fingers said again as they climbed off the

horses. "Forget her. I knew an Irish trapper once who bought a woman crazy like her. She stabbed him in his heart the first time he fell asleep. In some tribes when a woman covers up in mud like that the tribe calls her 'no one.' She's nothing to anyone. She's no more than part of the dirt."

"Why don't they just kill her?" The leather creaked when James leaned his long frame forward in the saddle.

Two Fingers shrugged. "You don't kill *nothing*, Kirkland."

They moved into the group of traders. James forced himself not to look back for a while. But when he did, the woman was just standing as before, wrapped in her ragged blanket, her eyes glazed over. The rest of the tribe moved around her as if she wasn't there.

James traded for the supplies he'd need and paid five times what he would have at a fort, but he didn't have the time to make the long trip back to a settlement or town.

As he packed the supplies on the two mustangs he'd bought, Two Fingers moved up to his side. "We'd better be getting out of the canyon. If we have to camp here tonight, one of us might wake up dead." He pointed a thumb at James.

"What makes you think it would be me?"

"Same reason rattlers don't usually strike each other." He glared at James. "I'm one of *them*. I may have been born a slave, but I consider myself Apache. The reason you're still alive, Captain Kirkland, is that I figure I might need you one day. Times are changing in this part of the country. Maybe not this year or the next, but they're changing. I can feel it in my bones. When they do, men like me won't be tolerated. Men like you will run this country. I do this for you, Kirkland, and you'll return the favor one day."

"What makes you so sure?" James asked.

"'Cause you're an honorable man. The only one in this canyon, I'm guessing. So whatever else you need, I'll help with the bargaining. When we leave, we part ways, but you remember me and one day I'll ask for that favor."

"All right, Two Fingers, but I have a small request before we go. I want you to bargain for one more thing."

"What's that, Kirkland?"

"The woman." James glanced toward the mud woman. All day, she had barely moved. Twice he'd seen the old woman hit her with a stick to move her farther from the campfire. Both times the blow had almost knocked her down. Now, she was so far away from the fire, she could not have felt the heat, assuming she could feel anything at all.

Two Fingers shook his head. "You don't want her. She's mostly dead already."

"You don't understand. I don't want her. I want to help her."

Two Fingers waved his hands in the air with the two remaining fingers on his left hand pointing to the sky as he swore. Finally he turned to James, still cussing. "I knew I shouldn't have gotten mixed up with an honorable man. If I even suggest trading for her, the old chief will think we're both crazy."

"Make whatever deal you can," James ordered in a tone he hadn't used in years. Pulling an old pocket watch from his pack, he added, "See if they'll take this. I've nothing left to offer."

Two Fingers looked at the watch. "Does it work?"

"No."

Two Fingers grinned. "Then we might have a chance. Trading something worthless for something worthless might just work. They'll see it as a joke. The Apache love a good joke."

James watched as the old buffalo hunter walked over to talk to the Apache chief. He pointed at the woman, then pointed at James, and the whole tribe laughed.

Finally, Two Fingers pulled out the watch James had carried with him since the day his father had been killed.

He remembered the ranger who had stepped in after the gunfight that had caught James's father unprepared. The lawman

had collected his father's belongings and made sure he and his
mother were on the next stage to Houston. As the ranger had
said farewell, he'd told James's mother to put her money in a
bank the minute she reached Houston and then he'd handed
James the watch.

Two Fingers walked toward him carrying the stick the old
woman had used to hit the mud woman. "Well, if I weren't the
best trader in the south, this wouldn't have happened. They took
the watch for her and threw in this stick. Apparently the only
way to get her to move is to hit her."

James took the branch and stared at the woman still looking
with dead eyes at the dirt.

"We'd better ride," Two Fingers said. "Trust me, you don't
want to be here much longer."

Handing Two Fingers the reins to one of the packhorses,
James approached the woman with his horse and the other mustang he'd bought.

She didn't look up, not even when he stood two feet in front
of her.

For the first time he noticed how small she was, barely over
five feet. With the mud and the blanket she'd looked rounded,
but up close he saw her hands and arms were so thin they were
almost birdlike.

He lifted the stick.

She raised her head and waited for the blow.

He took the branch in both hands and broke it across his
knee. For an instant he thought he saw a hint of surprise flash
in her eyes.

"If you'll come with me, I swear I'll never raise a weapon or
my hand against you. It seems you've been lost for a long time.
I'll do my best to get you back to your people. I'm not looking
for a slave or a wife. I want to help you."

She showed no sign of understanding a word he'd said.

He reached down and took her hand. For a moment all he

did was brush off the dried mud. Even with the dusting of dirt over her skin he could see the bruises. "It's time to go," he said as he turned, tugging her hand gently.

To his surprise, she followed.

When he lifted her up onto the mustang, she pulled her hand from his and dug her fingers into the horse's mane. He knew without asking that she wouldn't fall off during the ride.

"You're going to be all right, Little Dove," he said, knowing she probably wouldn't understand.

The gash on her wrist he had noticed earlier was still bleeding. He pulled off his bandanna and wrapped it around the wound wondering how many others were on her body.

When Two Fingers joined them, James whispered, "We ride out with her between us."

"Why? You think she'll bolt?"

"No," James answered. "Because she's the most precious cargo we carry."

two

────

Millie watched the man carefully. He was tall and lean with a strength about him. His words sounded familiar, as if she had once understood them a lifetime ago.

Of late she paid little attention to what was going on around her but she knew all the people came to the canyon to trade, and she seemed to be one of the things traded. It did not matter. She had been traded before. Only, no one had ever put her on a horse.

She had been twelve when the Comanche had taken her from her home. She'd been too much of a woman to be adopted into the tribe and too much of a child for any brave to claim her. Three summers later they'd traded her to an Apache tribe and given her to the chief's blind mother. The old woman had kept her tied to her camp by a long rope. When she'd needed her, she tugged on the rope. The old woman had been neither cruel nor kind. Millie had quickly learned that she was nothing.

When the old woman had died the next winter, she'd been traded again. These past two winters with the woman and the stick had been the worst. Millie knew she wouldn't have lasted much longer. Stick Woman had grown tired of having her around and begun to hit harder every day.

Now, at eighteen, Millie faced another change. In her life change meant things usually got worse, never better. This man of the canyon looked strong enough to kill her with one blow.

Not that it mattered. Nothing mattered anymore. Days passed, seasons passed. That whole first year she'd thought her father would come for her, but he hadn't. She remembered seeing her mother dead, facedown in the mud the day the Comanche rode onto their farm. Mother was dead and Father never found her. How could he? She moved from tribe to tribe like something worthless shuffled off. After a few years, she'd given up hope and tried to forget about her life before. It was too painful to remember.

The dark-skinned man with only two fingers on one of his hands frowned at her as they rode out of the clearing. The other man with hair the color of the yellow walls of the canyon, talked as if trying to tell her something. She did not care where they were going. Away could be no worse.

Her new owner smiled at her now and then when he said something, but she didn't know how to answer. For as long as she could remember, any sound she'd made had caused some-one in the tribe to hit her.

Slowly, the canyon man's words settled her. He never yelled. He was not young. The sun had wrinkled the corners of his eyes. But he was not old, either, because he had all his teeth and rode with the skill of one who had been born to ride.

They were long onto the plain flatland when they stopped to camp. The tall man lifted her down from the horse carefully as if he thought he might hurt her. He looked worried, as though he feared she might try to bolt. He could not know that run-ning had been beaten out of her years ago.

She stood still and silent in the dark as he built a fire. When he moved her close to the fire, he tried to pull off her blanket, but she held tight. To her surprise, he laughed and gently pushed her to the ground closer to the fire.

The men talked a language she had not heard in years. Words drifted around her, reminding her of another life. The canyon man gave her food. She watched him eat his and followed suit.

"Spoon," he said, holding up the tool he ate with. "Cup."

The dark-skinned man in buckskins shook his head at the canyon man, but he watched her as though considering roasting her on the fire. She did not like the way the man breathed through his mouth as he glared at her.

"Cup," Canyon Man said again as he caught her attention.

She didn't answer, but she stored the knowledge away.

"James," he said as he patted his chest. "I'm James."

She looked away. Inside her mind she'd remembered her other name before the Apache and Comanche called her names. Sometimes all that kept her sane was whispering *Millie* in her mind.

Millie, she thought as she patted her chest. *I'm Millie.* But she didn't trust this man enough to say her secret word aloud.

The dark-skinned man never spoke to her. He curled up in the shadows to sleep, but James stayed by the fire, his hand resting on his weapon.

Millie watched him until he fell asleep, then she moved closer so that her blanket almost touched his. She didn't sleep for a long while, waiting to be beaten and made to move away from the fire.

Finally he rolled over and looked at her, saying words she didn't understand. His hand reached across the dried grass and patted her mud-covered fingers.

Millie closed her eyes. She would not be hurt tonight.

Maybe tomorrow, but not tonight.

three

———

James wasn't surprised to find Two Fingers gone at dawn. He *was* surprised to find the woman still curled by the fire.

When she looked at him, he patted his chest and said, "James." Maybe she'd get the hint and give him her name.

No answer. Just those huge blue eyes staring up at him. Fear sparked in her gaze this morning. James wasn't sure it was an improvement over the dull, dead eyes he'd seen yesterday.

As he began to make coffee, she stood and moved silently toward the stream. Since the horses were in the other direction, he doubted she planned to run. If she did, he'd have no trouble catching up to her. In this part of Texas, he could see for miles in every direction.

He watched her by the water. She wasn't washing. She was applying a new layer of mud. She disappeared from sight for a while, but he decided he'd give her some room. Even a mud woman needed her privacy.

It was full dawn when she came back. If possible she looked dirtier than when she'd left. Her muddy hands were cupped, carrying something.

She offered him a half dozen eggs.

He'd seen the prairie chickens last night, but had no idea where their nests might be.

"Breakfast." He smiled and took the eggs. "Thank you."

She moved away without looking at him. James almost asked how she'd like them cooked, but he knew she wouldn't answer. He scrambled the eggs while the coffee boiled, then handed half to her on his one plate while he tackled his half from the skillet.

He talked while they ate, wondering if anything he said was getting through to her. As he loaded up the horses, he realized she was watching him, not simply glaring at nothing. Once he was ready, he walked over to her and took her hand. "We'd best be heading out. I've got a campsite picked out about twenty miles from here." He brushed the dirt off her hand as he talked, then he tugged her to the horse and set her up bareback.

When he turned loose of her hand, he patted his chest one more time and said, "James."

Shyly, in a whisper he barely heard, she said, "Millie."

"Millie." He laughed. "Nice to meet you, Millie." She had gone back into her shell and was not even looking his direction.

They rode hard all day, stopping at noon to let her rest and drink from a canteen he'd insisted she keep and a few times to water the horses. He found a good place to camp before sunset. Taking his time, James studied the land, thinking about where he'd someday build his home. He liked the idea of using the can-yon cutting across the land for miles and miles as a natural bor-der. He'd also need a creek or stream for water. Land was almost free, but without a good water supply it would be worthless.

When he lifted her down from the mustang, she didn't look at him, but she helped build the campfire this second night they shared.

As before, when he handed her dinner, she watched him be-fore she ate. James tried to talk, but it wasn't easy carrying all the conversation. He finally took her hand and led her down to the water. He washed the dishes and his hands and face, hoping she'd understand what he was trying to teach her.

She watched, looking as though she feared for her life.

He didn't want to frighten her more, so he simply walked back to the fire. She stayed by the water for a long while. When she returned, she curled on the grass close to where he sat and closed her eyes.

James didn't move. He studied the muddy woman beside him. "Millie," he finally whispered, thinking that he was making no progress. Trading for her had seemed a good idea. He'd wanted to help her. Only now, out here a hundred miles from civilization, how could he help her? At least she wouldn't be beaten, he reasoned. He'd take care of her. Maybe this calm land would allow her to heal. Come spring, he'd get her to people who could help her.

The rise in the ground where they'd camped made a natural wall that hung over them almost like a rocky roof. By building the fire beneath the overhang, the smoke drifted over the roof through tiny openings and disappeared into the night. No one would see their fire or the smoke from it. The rock behind them also offered a break from the wind that constantly blew.

James made his bed on the other side of the fire, facing out into the shadows. He loved the sounds of the night. That's why he'd come back to this land. Here, he would start fresh.

He drifted to sleep listening to the bubbling sound of the stream, the swish of the tall grass and the rustling of the dead leaves still clinging to the cottonwoods near the water. He relaxed thinking that someday every man for miles around would know this was Kirkland land. His land.

At dawn he woke to a cold fire and blue eyes watching him. Sometime in the night, she'd moved beside him. It crossed his mind that if she'd walked the distance without waking him that she could have easily killed him in his sleep. His hunting knife lay beside the fire where he'd left it.

"Morning, Millie," he said.

Blue eyes stared at him with less fear than yesterday. They were making progress.

He showed her how to make the coffee, frowning when the coffee beans went into her dirty palm. They ate from the supplies he'd bought at the trading day. He'd bought enough for one. Now, with her to feed, they'd not last the winter. He'd have to take time to hunt more. He'd also have to find more firewood and close off at least one more side of his camp. He didn't mind waking up to frost covering him, but he didn't like the thought that Millie'd wake up frozen. She didn't have enough meat on her bones to keep her from freezing.

Plus, he was getting real tired of the filthy old blanket around her shoulders. Maybe if he could keep the half-cave warm, she'd take the blanket off at least long enough to wash it.

He spent the morning building a corral for his horses, then decided to go exploring. If he went a different direction every day, he'd know the land before long.

It was almost dark when he returned.

She'd started a fire and had made a soup out of a potato and jerky the way he'd showed her the night before.

James took care of his horse and sat across the fire from her. She didn't look at him when he praised her but he noticed her hands were clean. Maybe the coffee wouldn't taste like mud tonight. A dozen eggs sat next to the supplies. She'd done her share of the hunting for food it seemed.

She wasn't mad as Two Fingers thought her to be. She wanted to stay alive, but she didn't want to communicate with him.

He talked to her as they ate, telling her all about what he'd seen that day. She fell asleep without giving any hint that she was listening to him. James leaned back on his saddle and relaxed. Just before he dozed off, he watched her move near him and curl deep into her old blanket. Maybe she wanted to be near him, he thought, or more likely she was simply afraid of the dark.

Smiling, he decided Millie might not like him, but she felt safer close to him.

The next morning when he washed his hands and face, she did the same. The sight of her face, clean of mud, angered him. Deep bruises ran along one jaw and under her left eye. Along her throat were signs of rope burns.

For the first time he was thankful for the blanket because James knew it covered more bruises and scars. If he could have, he would have gone back to Ransom Canyon and made every one of the Apache pay. Only, deep down he knew wrongs were done on both sides, just as they had been committed during the War Between the States. Maybe Millie was more like him than James had thought. She might just want to get away from people for a while.

He reached to touch her, but she jerked away.

Give her time, he thought. Let her have control over herself. He had a feeling it had been a long time, if ever, that she'd felt she had any say in her own life.

Keeping his voice low, he began to show her how to fish. While he waited for her to accept him, he'd teach her to survive.

The day was warm by the time they'd caught enough for supper. While she watched, he pulled off his shirt and boots, then waded into the water to wash his shirt and body.

He knew she'd have to remove the blanket to wash even though that one filthy, ragged blanket was her armor. As long as she held it around her, she had a buffer against the world.

That night, in the light of the campfire, he shaved with his hunting knife, then combed his hair. He offered her the comb.

She tried, but her hair was too matted.

"I guess you'll just have to cut it off." He laughed, thinking that her hair looked like a tumbleweed packed with mud.

She gave up after several tries and handed back the comb.

That night, when she moved to his side, he reached across

the foot of grass separating them and took her thin hand in his. "Good night, Millie," he whispered.

"Good night, James," she answered in a voice that sounded as though she hadn't used it in years.

"Your mind's not gone." He smiled. "Whatever you had to go through didn't drive you insane. When you come out of this dark place you're in, I'll be waiting to help. Just remember, they didn't break you. You're not mad."

The next afternoon when James returned to camp, he changed his mind.

Millie sat by the fire, his hunting knife in her hand, her scalp bleeding from a dozen tiny nicks. Almost all of her muddy hair was piled in front of her.

Looking up with those huge eyes, he saw her sorrow. She'd done what he'd suggested. She'd cut off her hair. He wasn't sure if she thought his words were an order. If she did, this mess was all his fault.

Kneeling beside her, he took the knife from her fist, then walked to the creek and wet his two clean bandannas.

Still sitting by the fire, she didn't look up when he came near her. She'd gone back to that place inside herself where she must have gone every time she'd been hurt. That safe place where nothing registered, nothing mattered.

"Millie," he started, "I'm not going to hurt you. I'm going to clean the cuts so they don't get infected."

She didn't move as he carefully cleaned the blood and dirt away from her head. Then, as if he were shaving, he scraped the last few tufts of hair from her scalp.

When he walked to the creek for water to fill the coffeepot, he thought he heard her crying, but he couldn't be sure. The whole night seemed to whisper sorrow from the lone coyote's call to the wind whining through the trees.

Without making any effort to talk, he untied the rabbits he'd killed for supper. As he skinned them and roasted them, he was surprised to see her begin to work with the furs, stretching them out on stick frames.

He ate alone, watching her, wondering where she'd gone in her mind as her hands worked.

An hour later she moved toward the roasted rabbit he'd left on their one plate and began to eat like an animal who feared some-one would snatch the food away at any moment. The thought occurred to him that maybe, in the tribe, she'd never been al-lowed to eat until the work was done.

Before he turned in for the night, he built the fire a bit higher, worried that she'd be cold. But, as she had every night, she waited until she thought he was asleep and curled up beside him. She may only be six inches away, he thought, but it might as well be an ocean between them.

He thought of reaching out to touch her hand, but guessed she'd pull away. Silently, he promised he'd keep her safe. Maybe she had family? Maybe one of the missions would take her in.

Silently, James swore he'd not leave her until the fear in her huge eyes was gone.

four

Every night Millie watched the canyon man who called himself James. He never yelled at her or hit her. And he never stopped talking no matter how hard she tried to show him that she wasn't listening. Days passed, the last of the cottonwood leaves fell, the wind howled of winter at night and still he talked.

She couldn't stop observing his every move. He took the time to show her things. He taught her each detail as if one day he'd leave her alone and she'd have to know how to survive on her own. Fishing, cooking, washing. All the while, he talked and each day she understood more of what he said.

Three nights after she'd cut her hair, he presented her with a hat made of rabbit skins. A week later he tried to make her moccasins out of more hides. As soon as he left camp the next day, she finished the job with much more skill. For the first time since she'd outgrown her boots, she had new shoes. Fur-lined. Warm. A perfect fit. Over the years she'd made many, but they'd always been taken away.

Canyon Man was a good provider. Millie hadn't gone hungry since he'd traded for her, but hunting wasn't the reason he was going out each morning. James was looking for something.

As the days passed she took on more of the cooking, finding that she liked being alone all day and didn't mind his company at night. She wasn't sure what she was to him. If a Comanche had traded for her, she might have been a slave for his wife or mother, but James had no wife or mother, and he never treated her like a slave. She thought that maybe she was his wife, but he never touched her. Besides, a man like him could find a better wife than her.

The moon made its second cycle over the big, empty sky and Millie felt her mind calm. Her favorite time was at night when he'd lie on his back and point out the stars. He'd sometimes say that his father had known many of their names and that someday he'd know them all.

Each week she watched James wash in the creek but she never joined him. The habit seemed strange, but she remembered years ago being clean. She'd washed in a house with a fire, warming the air even in winter. Slowly the memory of her mother, her father, her little brother, drifted into her mind and for the first time in years, she let them settle there for a while. Another time. Another world. Her world once.

One warm morning, after James had left, she took his soap and went to the water. Slowly she removed her blanket and stepped out of the bloodstained shift she'd worn for years. She remembered she'd had a dress once, until it had fallen off, piece by piece. Then she'd had a petticoat and shift. Now she only had a shift.

As she walked into the cold water, she almost ran back to the shore, but a bath was long overdue. There was no reason for the mud anymore. No one would try to touch her now.

Slowly, one limb at a time, she washed. Her body was so thin. A girl's body, she thought, not a woman's. She'd started her bleeding three maybe four years ago. The mark of a woman.

Two months later the flow did not come back. That winter had been hard. Food was short and she was always the last one in the tribe to eat. The bleeding that made her a woman had never returned.

As she scrubbed off the dirt, she realized she was no longer the last to eat. James always ate with her, and he cut each portion in two as if they were equal.

Cleaning her inch-long hair with the terrible-smelling soap, she decided she could not put on the shift again, so she walked back to the campsite nude and cut a hole in a blanket James had tried to cover her with several times. Poking her head through the hole, she tied her waist with a rope and pulled on her moccasins.

When he returned, she would have a stew of meat and a potato cooking.

Whirling, Millie felt grand. She was clean and dressed in clothes no one else had tossed away. She couldn't wait for James to see her. Her name was no longer Mud Woman.

An hour later she watched James climb off his horse downstream from her. He studied her, shaded his eyes as if to make sure what he saw, then yelled, "Millie, is that you?"

She looked down. "I washed."

As he walked toward her he continued to talk. "You look great, Millie. I almost thought someone else was in our camp when I rode up. Without the mud and that old blanket, you seem half as wide." His hand lightly brushed over her clean hair. "Your hair is chestnut brown, not mud color. I'm telling you, Millie, in that clean blanket you are quite stunning."

She moved away from his touch, but didn't jerk in fear as she had before. Over the weeks together, she'd learned not to be afraid of him. If he had planned to hit her, he would have done so when she'd spilled coffee on him one morning or when she'd forgotten to start the fire one afternoon, or when she wouldn't answer him no matter how many times he said her name. But he never hit her. James just kept talking as he smiled and shrugged off his frustration. Her canyon man was a good man.

While he staked his horse, she finished cooking supper.

They ate in silence, then both watched the fire. The air was still for a change, whispering around them. Now and then the wind moved in the dead leaves, sounding almost like someone walking.

Finally, when it was long past the time he usually turned in, he looked at her and said, "Talk to me, Millie. It's so lonely out here with me doing all the talking. I know you understand most of what I say. Just talk to me. I know you can, you spoke today when I rode in."

"James," she whispered.

He laughed. "That and 'good night' are all I've ever heard you say."

Millie thought about what she should try to say to him. Finally one thing came to mind. "Sleep beside me."

Standing, he grabbed the extra blanket and spread it out full on the ground beside the fire, then reached for his bedroll blanket and floated it on top. Pulling his boots off, he lay between the two blankets and lifted the top one. "I'd say come to bed, Millie, but I haven't seen a real bed in so long I've forgotten what they feel like."

She curled in beside him, pressing her back against his chest. The nights were getting colder and his warmth along her back felt so good.

To her surprise, he wrapped his arm over her and tugged her closer. "I'm going to have to fatten you up if we're going to cuddle through winter."

She fell asleep on his arm feeling something akin to happiness.

By the time the moon turned from full to a slice she'd grown used to him sleeping beside her at night. She liked the way his low snoring tickled her ear and how he often covered her shoulders with the blanket in the night. Now frost would be on the top of their blanket at dawn, but she always felt warm.

On clear nights he'd point out falling stars, laughing as he counted them as if each one was putting on a show just for him.

One cloudy night he asked her to talk to him again, though she thought she was managing several words a day. Her body had filled out a bit and her hair was now almost as long as her little finger. It seemed to curl around her face and she didn't mind when he brushed his fingers through it.

"Talk to me," he said against her ear.

Millie shook her head. She didn't know the words to say.

"Tell me what would make you happy, Millie." He rested his hand on her waist. "I don't have much out here but if I could make you smile, I'd count myself a lucky man."

She had no words. How could she tell him about all the things she was grateful he never did? He didn't yell at her. He didn't beat her. He never made her go to sleep hungry. He hadn't been angry when she'd cut up one of his blankets or forgotten how to do the things he'd showed her.

James sounded frustrated. "What can I do, Millie? Except when I feel you next to me at night, I'd swear I'm invisible to you most of the time. There must be something that you want."

She'd had enough talk. "Sleep with me," she whispered.

"I am. I keep you warm, don't I?"

She covered her hand over his resting at her waist and moved his fingers up to her breast. "Sleep with me," she repeated.

He rose to his elbow and looked down at her. "Are you asking what I think you're asking? Do you want me to…to mate with you?"

She nodded, thinking maybe "mating" was the word she had been looking for. She'd seen the old chief mate with each one of his three wives in the shadows of the tepee. They did not seem to mind at all. Once he tried to climb on her, but his first wife had pushed him off. She'd screamed at him that night and the next morning she had beat Millie so badly she could barely walk for days.

After that she'd put more layers of mud over her and slept outside unless the ground froze.

Maybe she was not James's wife, maybe she would never be anyone's wife. But, she wanted this. It had been so many years since she had been close to anyone, or cared if anyone around her lived or died. She wanted to feel a kind touch. It might wash away a few of the shoves and hits and slaps.

Deep inside she knew her need was more. Millie couldn't explain why, but she *wanted* James's touch. He mattered to her and for some reason she seemed to matter to him. She might not understand much of what happened between a man and a woman, but Millie knew she wanted to press her heart against his and know she was alive.

Without a word she rose and pulled off the blanket she had made into clothing. Then she huddled back under the cover and waited. Whatever this mating was, she wanted it to happen with someone she cared for. James had made her want to live again.

It took him a while to make up his mind, but slowly he began to touch her and, as he had done with a hundred other things this season, he taught her how to mate.

At first she was not sure she liked it. It hurt a little and he'd whispered that he was sorry and promised it wouldn't hurt next time. She had lain awake wondering why the first wife had wanted it or why the other wives never cried out as the old chief had moved from one to the other's blankets. The coupling felt strange, awkward. She liked when he touched her lips with his and she felt warm when he moved over her, but it brought her little pleasure.

He held her when they were finished and fell asleep. She stared into the night sky and tried to make sense of what had happened.

Deep into the night, she shook him awake, asking him to do it again.

This time he did not hesitate so long. He seemed better the second time, more comfortable in touching her. Millie decided all he needed was practice and all she needed was to learn how to do what he liked. Next time she would touch him.

At dawn she awoke to the sound of him whistling as he worked on a shelter for the horses. When she sat up and smiled at him he came to her and knelt down beside her. His hand moved beneath the blanket and brushed along her body as he kissed her lips.

When he backed away, he looked worried. "Are you all right, Millie?"

She nodded once thinking again how kind this strong canyon man was. His heart rested over hers in the night. She knew its rhythm.

"Again, James," she whispered.

He laughed. "Tonight. The weather promises a storm. I'd like to get the road from the east marked off. When or if I return to this land I want to have everything planned and staked out." He cupped her face in his hands. "I'll be back soon."

While they ate he talked of how he'd mapped the land making sure there was water every mile and where he'd put barns someday.

They didn't talk about what had happened in the night. Not that morning or the next or the next. Millie silently understood. What happened in the night was not mentioned in daylight.

Someday was not a word either of them knew how to use.

So, as winter raged, she woke him at least twice a night so they could practice until one morning, just before dawn, she decided they got it just right. Finally, she understood why James did not talk about their mating. There were no words.

Leaning back, she let her breath slow as his hands slid along her damp body. She liked this part as much as the mating. He always took his time touching her after they mated, as if she were something very special, and she drifted into sleep knowing she was safe.

five

————

James rode the boundary of what would be his land come spring. His thoughts should be on cattle and building his herd, but his mind kept drifting to Millie. He felt as if he knew her body, but he didn't know her. They'd never talked of love, or even caring for one another. Most nights he felt as though they were simply two strangers surviving the winter together. Soon she'd be stepping into a world she hadn't known in years and he'd be back on this land building. Strange, he thought, he'd miss her even though they didn't talk. He'd miss her more than he'd ever missed anyone.

It had to be February. Another month and they'd be packing up and heading to Fort Worth. He'd file papers and buy his land. He'd pick out stock and hire a few hands to help him haul all he needed to build a house and proper corrals.

He might even buy furniture and hire real carpenters to help him. The money his father had left him had been sitting in the bank for years. Half his salary since the war had added to his account. He wanted everything ready and right once he found the land. Everything seemed to be falling into place, except for one thing.

Where did Millie fit into all this? She still never said a word to him except when she had to. Most days he wasn't sure she even liked his company. When she got tired of listening, she seemed to slip someplace in her mind that he'd never be able to reach.

Plus, just because he had paid her ransom with a broken watch didn't give him a right to sleep with her. There was something childlike about her and he was taking advantage of that, no matter that she had asked him to mate with her. She couldn't be more than eighteen or nineteen. That would make him almost ten years older. Old enough to know better. He hadn't said a word about love. Hell, he didn't even believe in love. And he didn't know if she understood what marriage meant so there was no point talking to her about it.

Only, he loved the way she made love. There was something wild and untamed about it. As if she'd never been told to hold back, to be a lady or not to act as though she enjoyed it just as much as he did.

He smiled. When they slept together she never made him feel as though he was taking a thing from her. If anything, she took from him. She might go along with everything he said all day, but in the darkness of their cave of a home, she demanded his attention. James grinned. If he didn't take the time to satisfy her, he knew she'd be poking him in a few hours. He'd roll over and ask what she wanted and she'd whisper "you" in that low, sexy voice that he could never refuse.

Not that he was complaining. He'd give her what she wanted no matter how many times a night she asked.

What would he do about Millie once they stepped back into civilization? What they shared here was like a dream. Come spring, they'd have to live in reality.

When they got to a town, he'd have to notify the rangers. What if she had a family searching for her? She'd never answered a single question he'd asked about when she was captured. Every time he'd asked, her eyes would glaze over and she'd go to that place out of his reach.

James had never found a woman he wanted to do more than spend a little time with. As soon as his troops moved on, or the cattle drive started, he was usually more than ready to leave any woman's bed. In his daydreams of the future, he'd considered the possibility of marriage a few times over the years. If he got the ranch started, and things calmed down in this part of Texas, he might ride into some settlement and pick out a wife. Someone who'd be a good cook and look after the children. He wouldn't even care if she was pretty as long as she gave him sons.

James shook his head. He'd heard men talk about their wives and not much of it sounded good. Seemed as though they always complained about being nagged and none ever mentioned being awakened at night to mate.

Maybe he should just keep Millie. He might get used to her silence, and he could find someone to teach her to cook. The mating thing, she had down pat. If folks came by the ranch he'd just say they were married. As little as she talked, no one would ever hear otherwise from her.

Only, keeping her didn't seem right. What if one day his son or daughter asked them about their courtship? James would have nothing to say except, "Oh, I traded a broken watch for her and she asked me to mate with her so I kept her."

His offspring would probably haul him down to Austin to the insane asylum, and Millie would just wave goodbye from the porch without saying a word.

James swore. He'd never been a man to worry. Maybe if he didn't think about it things might just keep going on as they were.

He'd stay here, studying his land, mapping out the spot he'd build his headquarters and roads. Then, as soon as he trusted the weather, he'd ride to town and make the dream he'd had all his life come true.

Three weeks later when most of the supplies had begun to run out and the weather turned milder, James packed up. It was time to travel to Fort Worth. This part of his life would have to become a memory. By next winter he'd have a cattle ranch that spread for miles.

He could tell Millie didn't want to leave the campsite. The next morning she unpacked about as fast as he packed. When he growled at her, she walked away.

A few hours later, when she returned, she refused to look at him.

He sat in the camp cutting down a pair of trousers to fit her. When she walked past, he said without any greeting, "Put these on."

She did as he'd told her, but never spoke.

"I want you wearing them in the morning," he said as he turned away to hand her the last meal they'd cook at the winter camp.

She didn't talk to him that night. He was surprised she cuddled next to him after dark. Without a word, he made love to her, wishing he could read her mind. He knew every curve of her body, but he knew nothing of her hopes and dreams.

The next morning she wore the trousers and her blanket, but she refused to look at him or to speak. As he broke down the camp, he snapped, "We have to go, Millie, and that is all there is to it. So stop acting like I'm not taking you with me and climb up on the horse."

She looked at him, her blue eyes swimming in tears. "I go, too?"

He saw it then. The fear, the hurt she must have felt when she'd thought he was leaving her. He dropped his last bag and walked to her. "Of course you're coming with me."

She hugged him so tightly he knew he could never let her go. A part of her would always be cuddled into his heart.

When he finally pulled her arms from his neck, he tried to get control of feelings he'd thought were long-ago dead. "Now get on the horse, Millie. We need to make twenty miles before nightfall."

She did as he asked.

They rode southeast, eating up the distance faster than he'd thought they would. She was healthy now and rode as well as he did. The trip seemed easier with two people working to make camp every night. He'd often hunt while she built a fire and took care of the extra horses now loaded down with pelts.

At night he'd hold her as they watched the sky. He thought of her as his falling star. There was no telling where she'd land.

Spring warmed the days as they rode closer to Fort Worth. He knew he could have gone into several settlements along the way, but James wanted time with her. This winter had been the most peaceful of his life.

Logically, he told himself that his bank was in Fort Worth so it made sense to go there. Cattle would be easier to buy at the stockyards. Men trained for what he needed would be there.

But he knew the real reason was that he couldn't let go of Millie. Whatever happened once they reached civilization, things would change. As they rode closer and closer to Fort Worth, her blue eyes grew wider. She'd point, wanting to know about everything she saw. Farms, barns, trains.

As they crossed through the streets of the town, she stopped again and again, looking into windows or staring at people. She'd grab his hand and hang on as if she feared all the population might sweep her away. His grip was solid but he could feel her slipping away.

A block from the ranger station he stopped in a café and they drank coffee and talked. He tried to prepare her for what was going to happen, but he wasn't sure he knew. She spoke slowly, answering questions he'd never asked. She must have felt change coming, also. Two hours later he knew her story. Looking at her now, her warm brown hair curling around her face and her big blue eyes holding his attention, he marveled that such a delicate creature could have survived.

Finally, armed with her name and the few facts she remembered, James walked into the ranger station in Fort Worth.

"I've found a captive woman," he said simply to the first ranger he saw, a broad-shouldered fellow of not more than twenty. The circle star on his shirt marked him as a ranger, but James guessed he was yet to see any battles.

The young ranger at the desk nodded as if he'd heard the story before. "Is she alive or did you find a body? Does she know her name or where she was kidnapped from? Where'd you find her?"

James felt as if he'd fired off a few rounds in the small office. It had been so long since anyone had talked to him using so many words, he had to fight to keep from backing up.

He stepped outside and lifted Millie down from her horse. She didn't want to go, but he held on tight to her hand as he walked back into the station.

The young man with a badge stood as she entered the ranger office.

"Go slow, mister, or you'll frighten her," James ordered. "She's been through enough. We're not going to make this any harder on her than we have to."

The ranger nodded and offered her a chair. "My name's Drew, miss. Ranger Drew Price. I'm here to do the best I can to help you. If you've got family, we'll see you get home safe."

James stood at her side, guessing she wouldn't say a word to this stranger. "Her name is Millie O'Grady. She was kidnapped from a farm near Jefferson, Texas. She thinks she's eighteen or nineteen. She was twelve when kidnapped. She says her mother is dead but her father may be alive. She said she did not see his body. A little brother—she called him Andy—was also kidnapped. They were separated after the first night. She doesn't know if he's alive or dead but she remembered his hair was red like her father's."

The ranger glared at James. "Can the lady talk for herself?"

James grinned when Millie shook her head.

The young lawman knelt in front of her. "Are you injured, miss? Do I need to call a doctor?"

She looked up at James and he knew she'd lost a few of Ranger Price's words.

He smiled down at her. "She had many cuts and bruises when I found her. But she's fine now. I don't think there is need for a doctor."

While Ranger Price wrote up the report, James studied Millie. She was afraid but not terrified. He'd promised her no one would hurt her in Fort Worth.

When the ranger left to send a few telegraph messages to places that kept up with missing people, James pulled a chair near Millie's and talked to her in a low, calm voice. Slowly, she relaxed.

Another ranger came in; older and battle-scarred from the war, James guessed. The minute he met the ranger's eyes, James knew the man recognized him. The ranger straightened as if coming to attention. "Wilson, sir," he said. "How can I be of service, Captain Kirkland?"

James repeated all the facts he'd just given the young ranger. Neither he nor Wilson mentioned the war. They may have fought together once, but those days were long buried.

Wilson offered them coffee and was very polite when he spoke to Millie. He seemed to understand what she'd been through.

"We get several parents dropping in every year, hoping for news of their children. The odds aren't good, but now and then we get lucky and find one."

When Millie looked away as if not listening, the ranger continued to speak quietly to James. "Women have it the worst, I figure, Captain Kirkland. The tribes seem to like children, even adopt them as their own. The men are usually killed, not kept as captives, but the women, they go through hell. This one must have been too old to be adopted into the tribe and too young to be taken as a wife."

James didn't want to talk about what she'd been through. He'd already guessed that covering herself in mud may have saved her life.

A few hours passed and James insisted on walking Millie down the street to a café for dinner. He invited the ranger to join them, but Wilson said he was on duty.

"You will be coming back, Captain?" Wilson asked when they reached the office door.

"We will. If there is news, you can find us at the first café." James relaxed his shoulders. "And, it's just James Kirkland now. I'm no longer a captain."

"Yes, sir." Wilson nodded once. "Mr. Kirkland. If no news comes tonight, we've got a sweet widow a few blocks over who'll take Miss O'Grady in for a few nights. Her man was a ranger."

James wanted to insist that he'd take care of Millie, but she wasn't his. She never had been. He'd meant to save her, to get her to safety, to turn her over to her family. *She wasn't his.*

They took their time eating at the café. She did what she always did; she watched how he acted and mimicked his every move. But this time Millie merely picked at her food, obviously troubled.

He could think of nothing to say. He had no idea how to comfort her. Part of him wanted to simply hold her as he had all winter, but he couldn't do that now. People were all around.

So, he just looked at her. The bruises were gone and her cheeks were no longer hollow. Her chestnut-colored hair curled softly around her face. Even in her blanket of a dress and his old trousers, she was beautiful. All the months together, he'd never really noticed.

He'd caught people staring all morning and thought it was because of the clothes or her unfashionably short hair. Suddenly, he realized, they were admiring her. Somehow this beautiful creature had survived, wrapped in a filthy blanket with mud covering her body.

After they'd finished their meal, he ordered dessert. First one, then two, then every one on the menu board. Millie loved them all. She took tiny bites of each, closed her eyes and drank in the sweetness like fine wine.

Smiling, he thought of all the good things she was about to experience and realized he wanted to be the one to show her, to teach her.

About dusk, the young ranger they'd first met rushed into the café, his fist full of papers. "I have news, finally," Ranger Price said, taking the chair opposite James. "It took me longer than I thought it would. I had to telegraph Austin twice and Dallas several times to make sure my facts were right."

James leaned forward. Millie moved her chair closer to him.

The ranger smiled up at Millie, but she looked away. He addressed his news to her, anyway. "We've found a record of your father's death, miss. You have my condolences. Your father passed away three years ago in Jefferson. After you were taken, he stayed on the farm, hoping somehow you'd find your way back."

Both men watched her, but no emotion showed. If she understood, she didn't seem to care.

James cupped her face and turned her head toward him. "Millie, your father is no longer alive. Do you understand?"

She didn't try to speak, but one tear bubbled over and trickled down her cheek.

He brushed it away with his thumb. "I'm sorry, Little Dove."

Price shuffled his papers. "That's not all. I have some good news and some bad, I'm afraid. A boy, who might be her brother,

was located. He's about the right age—twelve. He has red hair.
He was caught stealing horses a few months ago down near
Austin. The sheriff tried to hold the boy, but he escaped. He
was recaptured two weeks ago and, according to the sergeant
who telegraphed me back, he's been raising hell down near Fort
Richardson ever since. Claims he's Apache. Won't speak a word
of English."

James raised an eyebrow. "Is that the good news or the bad?"

"The bad news is he shot a guard. Almost killed him. They're
hanging the kid as an adult at dawn four days from today."

A tiny cry came from Millie. She leaned closer to James and
pressed her face into the hollow between his shoulder and throat.
"No," she whispered. "No."

James looked at the ranger. "Can I get there in time? If I don't
bring him back, we'll never know if it was her brother or not."

"It would be a hard ride, but you could make it."

"Telegraph the fort and tell them to hold off the hanging
until I get there. Tell them family is riding in to see the boy."

Price looked at James. "You family, Captain?"

James wasn't surprised Wilson had passed on a few war
stories about him to the younger ranger.

"Joe told me who you were," the young ranger admitted.
"Said you were the bravest man who ever fought for the South.
They say most bluecoats thought you were the devil come to
fight."

"I'm just a rancher now, Drew. The war has been over for
a long time." James thought about how it seemed more like a
lifetime than seven years. "I think this boy might be the only
one who can heal Miss O'Grady. The kid's all the family she's
got left. It's worth a try to bring him here."

"You want me or Wilson to go along?"

"I doubt I'll need help with a kid, but I'd appreciate it if one
of you would check in on this lady. Talk to her, tell her what's

happening. She might not talk back, but she'll understand. I'll wire when I can."

Price looked at James. "I'll do what I can to delay the hanging, Captain. If there's a ranger at the fort, I'll send orders to burn the gallows if he has to." He turned to Millie. "I'd be happy to visit her every day. Widow Harris feeds every ranger that drops by."

James stood and shook hands with Drew as he added, "Show me the widow's house." He swung Millie up into his arms. "This little lady has had about all she can take tonight. I'll see her safe and then I'll ride."

The ranger followed James out. "Before you leave, stop by the office. Wilson said you should be sworn in before you go after the kid. We'll give you a list of places that will trade out horses with rangers. If it doesn't rain, you'll make it."

six

Millie tried to understand what was going on. James had left his other horses at the ranger station, and they rode away from the main street through dark roads hemmed in by cold, windowless buildings. The brick walls formed a canyon without beauty. James held her tightly in front of him as the ranger trailed behind. He talked but she did not listen. All that he'd told her in the café whirled around in her mind. Her father was dead. Her little brother might be alive, but it meant James was leaving her. Sorrow, joy and fear were at war in her mind.

"I swear I'll be back," James whispered against her ear. "I'll leave you somewhere safe, I promise. If this boy at Fort Richardson is your brother, I'll bring him back."

Pressing her cheek against his chest, she fought tears. He had never lied to her.

His hand brushed over her shoulder. "You'll have family again, Millie. You'll have Andy back."

She nodded slightly. That world she had been ripped from long ago seemed more a dream than real. Her life was with James now, even if he did not see it or speak of any future.

All too soon they reached the edge of town where a cottage sat in a forest of fruit trees. A round little woman with sunshine in her smile greeted them. Millie liked her right away. The kind woman spoke slowly and waited for Millie to answer or nod before she moved on.

Millie understood she had to stay at this place, but when James stood to leave, she could not seem to turn loose of his hand. "Take me, James. Take me with you."

Mrs. Harris was a kind old woman, but Millie wanted to go with him. She had to stay with him. Nowhere else in the world was safe.

He knelt beside her chair in a house filled with so many things she could not look at them all. "Millie, listen to me. I'm coming back."

She shook her head. In her experience people never came back.

"I want you to rest here. Do what Mrs. Harris tells you. The rangers will check on you. If I can, I'll let them know what I find at the fort." Slowly, he pulled his hand from hers. "I'll let you know when I'm on my way back with Andrew."

Turning his back to Millie, James handed Mrs. Harris a pouch. "Take what you need from this for her keep. Buy her clothes and anything else she needs."

Millie closed her eyes. James was not trading her away. He was paying someone to take care of her. He'd told her many times at the camp that all he wanted was to start a ranch. His dreams were in the money pouch, he'd said. Now he was giving part of what he had saved away to pay for her care.

"Millie, listen to me." He surprised her when she opened her eyes and found him close. "I'll be back in a few days and when I do I expect you to have learned to make an apple pie as good as the one we just ate. Mrs. Harris will teach you."

She tried not to listen, but he was too close to ignore.

James smiled at her. "If you could make a pie like that, you'd be just about perfect, Millie."

She remembered all the nights he had wished for a dessert. She had not remembered desserts, but James would rhyme off all the things he loved. Apple pie was always the first on his list.

Moving closer, Mrs. Harris smiled at Millie but spoke to James. "I'll be happy to teach her, Mr. Kirkland. She can sleep and eat all she wants, but if she wants me to teach her to cook, I'd be tickled."

Millie followed him to the door as he said goodbye to the others. On the porch, he pulled her against him and kissed her. "I'm coming back for you, Millie. I swear. No matter how long it takes, a few days or a month, I'm coming back."

Nodding, she straightened. This man had never lied to her. She would believe him now.

He smiled down at her and said, "Stay here. Learn what you can." For once the words seem to come hard for him. "You hold my heart, Millie O'Grady."

Then, as if he had said too much, he was gone.

Millie stood staring into the night, wishing she could see one more glimpse of him, but the brick-and-wood canyon of the town gobbled him up. She fought to keep from trembling. He had said she would be safe. He had to go find Andrew. She had no choice but to stay and wait.

The porch door creaked and Mrs. Harris stepped outside. "This is a place of peace, child. You'll like it here."

Millie turned to the little, round woman. "Thank you." For the first time since the day she'd seen her mother die, she trusted someone quickly. James would be back. Until then, she had Mrs. Harris.

"I want to learn everything." Millie straightened her back.

"Then we'll have long days," Mrs. Harris said. "And some fun talking."

Millie kept to her promise. She learned all she could each day, but during the nights, she cried for her canyon man.

seven

Dawn feathered along the eastern sky as James rode into Fort Richardson. The sight of so many men in blue uniforms bothered him. Memories and nightmares danced in his thoughts, but he pushed them aside as soon as the gallows came into view. Three nooses hung empty, waiting above the ten-foot-high stage. James couldn't change the past, but if he was lucky, he might be able to change one boy's future.

Walking up to the guard on duty, James announced, "I'm here to see Sergeant Gunther." James straightened, trying to not look as tired as he felt. "I'm..." He hesitated, almost saying Captain Kirkland for the first time in years. "I'm James Kirkland from Fort Worth."

"Yes, sir." The private stared at the badge James wore. The circle star marked James as a ranger. "This way, Ranger Kirkland. We've been expecting you."

James thought they'd take him right to the stockade, but the private marched him into post headquarters.

"The sergeant is at breakfast but will be in as soon as he's finished with muster. Our captain and the lieutenant are in Austin, so Gunther is in charge." The private nodded toward two chairs in front of a massive desk. "Please, Ranger Kirkland, make yourself comfortable."

The room was still cast in morning shadows, but a freshly lit fire warmed the frosty air. James was asleep in one of the chairs almost before the door closed.

He dreamed of cold nights at his winter camp. Millie was curled in at his side, sleeping so soundly she did not wake when he ran his fingers into her soft curls and kissed her forehead.

James woke when footsteps sounded just outside the door. He had no idea if it had been five minutes or five hours. A moment before the door popped open, James noticed full daylight filled the window.

A sergeant whom he assumed was Gunther—wide as the door—stormed into his office, followed by two men dragging five feet of chained trouble between them. The prisoner was dressed in traditional Apache clothing. From the looks of his leather and beaded vest he, or his adopted father, was of high rank in the tribe. Braids hung over his thin shoulders. Red braids, the same shade of the Red River mud.

James stood and stared. Every inch of skin showing on the kid seemed to be covered with bruises or cuts or dried blood. One of his eyes was swollen closed and the other glared straight at James with pure hatred.

Blue eyes, James noticed. The same color as Millie's.

The sergeant took command. "I'm assuming you are the Kirkland the rangers have been telling me is coming."

"I am."

"Well, here's the boy you wanted to see. Claims he's Apache. Won't speak a word of English, assuming he knows any. I don't like the idea of hanging him like a man. Anyone can see he ain't full grown, but no one will claim him. In coloring and age he matches an O'Grady child who disappeared several years ago.

I've no place to send him, and if I let him go, he'll keep stealing and trying to kill anyone who gets in his way."

The kid jerked and jabbed his elbow into the ribs of one of the guards holding him. When the soldier folded over in pain, he slammed his bound hands against the man's face, drawing blood where the chains connected with his jaw. The other guard responded, almost knocking the prisoner down with one swing.

The boy slumped, too hurt to fight back.

James studied what might be Millie's brother; her only living relative as far as he knew. "Your men put all these bruises on him?" James stared directly at the man in charge.

"For every one he's got, I've got a guard who's got two." Gunther swore. "I've seen tornadoes cause less damage to the fort."

"He's just a boy," James said, guessing the kid wouldn't stop fighting until someone hit him too hard and he died. He must be scared and angry and alone...and deadly.

Sergeant Gunther stood almost nose to nose with James. "Ranger Wilson said to grant you with full authority of the rangers behind you. If you want him, Kirkland, he's all yours, but if you find out he's not the boy you are looking for, you're not to bring him back here. Do I make myself clear?"

James knew if he *was* wrong, he'd be in real trouble. He walked over to the kid, who raised his head until one blue eye glared up at him.

"You're coming with me, Andy. Your sister Millie is waiting for you."

The flash sparked in the boy's eye so fast James would have missed it if he hadn't been staring. But it was there. His name, or maybe his sister's, had brought back a memory.

Turning to the sergeant, James said, "I'll need a wagon and all the rope you can spare. I'm taking him back to his family."

"You want chains?" Gunther grinned, happy to see one of his problems leaving.

"No. I'll tie him up so he doesn't run. I don't consider him a prisoner." James raised his voice. "If he cooperates, there will be no need for chains."

The sergeant looked at one of the men. "Loan him a wagon and all the rope you can find. Pull down the third noose and toss that in, too." The big man glared at James. "You're taking quite a risk, Kirkland. What's the kid to you, anyway?"

James shrugged. "I think he's about to be my brother-in-law."

The sergeant's laughter shook the building. When he finally calmed down, he ordered everyone to help tie the kid in the wagon. As they walked outside he added, "I married a woman once without meeting her mother. When she came to live with us, I swore she was the devil's sister, but, Kirkland, she was nothing compared to this kid. If I were you I'd give up sleep permanently."

Six men saddled up to escort James far enough away to be out of the fort's territory. After that, they would be on their own. For a moment James feared he might not be up to the task. They had many miles to cover, and he couldn't stay awake all the way back even with a bloodthirsty wild kid waiting for his chance to kill him.

While two men stood guard the first night, James tried to catch up on sleep, but the boy worried him. First, he feared Andy might kill one of the guards trying to get away, or if he tried and failed, the guards might gang up on him and murder Andy while James slept. All six seemed like good men. They also all had bruises, and none treated Andy as though he was anything more than an animal.

Traveling by wagon was slow. They would be lucky to make half the distance he'd made on horseback. With the wagon, they had to follow roads and couldn't cut across country.

By the third day James was tired of listening to the prisoner kick and struggle with the ropes, so he started talking.

He wasn't sure if his talking bothered Andy, but it sure bothered the guards. They said their quick farewell as soon as James woke the fourth morning on the trail. All at once he was alone with a tied-up kid.

Unlike Millie, Andrew O'Grady, if that was his name, didn't silently ignore him. James might not know the language, but he had no doubt that he and all his ancestors were being cussed out. Every time James said something, Andy shot back with what had to be an insult.

Judging from the fire in his eyes, Andrew would happily murder James if he got the chance.

After two sleepless nights James was happy to see a town. He talked the sheriff into locking the boy up, his hands and feet still tied. While Andy gulped down a meal, James went to sleep a few cells away.

The kid must have been just as tired because the sheriff said they both slept the clock around.

The next day as they started off, James didn't secure Andrew with as many ropes as usual. Dark clouds promised rain and the boy looked as though he planned to sleep the day away. Some of the fight must have gone out of him, or maybe Andy had realized James meant him no harm. Though James still talked about the ranch he would build someday, Andy stopped yelling back. He might not be listening, but at least he was quiet. James saw that as progress.

That night, both were soaking wet by the time they made camp inside a rough lean-to built for travelers. James let the kid sit by the fire and eat his supper. He wasn't friendly. For the most part he simply ignored James—until Andy took a few swings at him. James tied him to the wagon wheel but left enough lead so that Andy could curl up under the wagon to sleep.

The next morning when James woke, the boy was gone. After he cussed himself for a few minutes he realized two things. Andy hadn't taken any of the horses and he hadn't tried to kill him in his sleep.

Both facts pointed to one thing: the boy was in a big hurry. Must've been almost first light when he'd worked himself free.

Using skills he'd learned in the war, James began to track the kid. The rain had stopped, but the mud made tracking easy. Five hours later he found him asleep in a pile of leaves at the base of a tree. He must have run as far as he could and then collapsed in exhaustion. The boy was dirty, cold, bone-thin and still rough as they come. If he lived to be a man, he just might be worth the knowing.

Funny, the tough kid didn't look near as mean curled up in sleep. He looked more like a frightened child.

James stood above him, really seeing him for the first time. Despite all his fire and anger, he was still just a boy.

Slipping a rope gently over Andy's wrists, James circled a loop around the tree behind Andy and secured it. He tugged hard and sat on the boy's chest.

Andy woke with a start, but couldn't move. His hands were pulled above him and James's weight held him down.

"Now, I'm only going to say this once, Andy." James hoped the kid understood. He pointed south. "I'm taking you to Millie. If you keep fighting and running, we're never going to get there… She told me your mother called you Andrew Jackson O'Grady when she was angry. So, Andrew, listen up. We're going back to your sister one way or the other. You're all the family she has and Millie remembers you whether or not you remember her. Now, will you go along without a fight or should I just sit awhile right here?"

The boy simply stared for a long moment. Then, to his surprise, Andy nodded once.

James had gotten through to the kid. He could see it in the boy's eyes. Andy might still hate him, but he remembered his sister's name and if he had to, he'd put up with James to get to her.

Slowly, holding the rope tight, James stood. If they didn't

reach some kind of a peace he doubted either of them would make it back to Fort Worth.

Andy waited for him to remove the rope from the tree, then the kid followed James, his hands still bound.

"Millie," James said as he waited for the boy to climb into the wagon.

To his surprise, Andy nodded once and rolled into the wagon bed.

It might not be peace, but at least it wasn't all-out war. James could live with that, he decided as he looped the ropes over Andy's hands and feet. "I'll get you back to Millie. I promise."

James secured to the kid to the wagon during the day, but Andy no longer fought or yelled. He seemed to be waiting to see what would happen next. As the days passed, James gave up trying to talk to the kid but he never let his guard down.

He thought about Millie and what he'd say to her when he finally made it back. There was so much he'd never said. At night he dreamed of holding her. Each day he pushed the horses as hard as he could, but the trip seemed endless.

Deep inside he knew Millie was waiting, missing him just as dearly.

When they reached Fort Worth, James stopped by the ranger office for Drew Price. If the ranger thought it strange that James had a boy tied in the back of the wagon, he made no comment.

"I dropped by Mrs. Harris's house every morning, Captain," Drew said as if reporting in. "Your Millie is doing well. I've always heard that the widow could do wonders, but I'd never seen it before. Two days after you left she had Millie wearing proper clothes. Yesterday, the two of them were talking so much, laughing about their cooking lessons, that I could hardly get a word in."

"Millie was talking?" James had seen her smile a few times, but never laugh.

"Sure. She talks. Goes slow sometimes, like she's tasting a word before she spits it out, but she's talking." Drew hesitated. "Is she your woman, Captain, or are you just helping her out?"

James didn't want to answer the question. The hundred times he'd sworn he'd never marry sat in his mind. He ached to hold her, but if he were being honest he'd have to admit she didn't belong to him. "She's not mine."

When he glanced over at Drew, James frowned. The young ranger was smiling.

Telling himself he needed to check on her, James wouldn't admit that he couldn't wait to see her. He slapped the reins. A few minutes later they were climbing out of the wagon and hauling Andy into Mrs. Harris's house with them.

The fight was back in the boy. He struggled to get loose, but it wasn't full-out war. Maybe he was finally afraid of something… facing a world he'd once known.

When James stumbled into the parlor the two women turned from their sewing. Mrs. Harris looked surprised, but Millie jumped up and ran to him. She was dressed in calico and lace; a proper young lady now with combs in her hair and an apron around her waist.

She was almost in his arms when she spotted Drew Price in the doorway, holding the boy.

She went pale, and for a moment James thought she might faint. She moved slowly to the door and stared at the boy. They were almost the same height. Even through the layers of dirt and bruises on Andrew there was no doubt that the two were related.

Reaching out, she gently touched the bruises that marked his arms, then glanced back at James.

"He was in worse shape when I picked him up," he said. "Fought everyone who came near. Not one bruise is my doing, Millie. You have my word."

She nodded and turned back to the boy. "Andy," she whispered. "My brother."

The boy watched her, not as accepting or trusting as she was. Finally he spoke to her in Apache. Only a few words, but Millie seemed to understand.

She nodded then translated his words for James. "He asked if I am from his tribe long ago."

James let out a breath that he felt he'd been holding for almost two weeks. He'd found her brother.

He watched as Millie untied Andy's hands and pulled him to the table. Drew, James and Mrs. Harris watched quietly as brother and sister talked, mixing Apache with English.

An hour later Mrs. Harris served them pie, which Andy ate with his hands. As soon as he finished his slice, he pulled the pan over and began to finish off the entire pie.

Without comment, Millie moved to the seating area off the kitchen so she could talk to the others and still watch Andy. "He says he will not run unless I go with him." She smiled at James. "I told him I wish to stay with you. I'd like to go back to the winter camp and help build your ranch. You've done so much for me, it is the least I can do."

James smiled. "How did Andrew like that idea?"

"He says if you raise a hand to me, he wants to be close enough to kill you." She hesitated a minute, then added, "He said if I raise my hand to you, he'll hold you for me."

"The open spaces might be a better place to settle the O'Grady clan. I can't see your Andy walking the streets of Fort Worth dressed as he is."

"Then we travel northwest with you, James." She put her hand on his shoulder and leaned her hip against his side.

"It's time I said good-night," Drew announced, disappointment in his gaze as he stared at Millie's hand resting on James's shirt. "Thanks for the pie, Mrs. Harris, but I hate to see a family fight, especially this one. I have a feeling there are going to be a few before they even get the horses loaded up."

James laughed. "I was thinking I'd better tie the kid up tonight or, better yet, use one of your jail cells."

Millie shook her head and James knew that would no longer be an option.

An hour later when he finally pulled Millie into his arms in
the hallway, he whispered, "I missed you, Little Dove. Let's go
to bed." He kissed her soundly, loving the smell of her clean
skin and starched clothes.

She pulled away. "No."

"No?"

"Mrs. Harris said not to lie with a man until marriage."

"What?" Up to now he'd liked Mrs. Harris. "But, I know
you missed me as much as I missed you." His hand moved over
her body, but so many layers of material seemed to block the
feel of her.

"If you force me, I will tell my brother." She stood her ground.
"Before there were no rules, but you brought me here and I
learned, just as you told me."

James frowned. He had never forced her into anything and he
never would, yet all at once she had this guardian devil watching over her. The kid still looked like he'd gladly run a blade
through his chest. Which meant no sleeping together.

The chances of him getting a good night's sleep were looking slim.

He reluctantly put some space between them. James frowned.
He needed to think. All he'd worked for since the war was
about to come to fruition. He'd have his ranch and a starter
herd. To make a go of it, he'd need every bit of his energy for
a year, maybe more. He didn't have time to take on a wife and
her wild little brother. And he wouldn't be hurried into marriage by what Mrs. Harris said.

A man had a right to make up his own mind about what was
right for him and when was the right time. Only, he couldn't

head back without Millie. Any terms she set were fine as long as she came with him.

He stared into her beautiful blue eyes and promised, "I'll never hurt you, Millie. I broke the beating stick, remember? I'll never force you into anything and no one, including Mrs. Harris, will force me into marriage. It's something a man has to step into willingly, not be forced into, if he's going to settle down and be content."

The urge to sweep Millie up and ride back to their winter camp was powerful. He wanted the peace of the days on what would be his land and the wild, wonderful nights with this woman in his arms. He wanted what they'd had, but layers far heavier than cotton were keeping them apart.

Big tears welled up in Millie's blue eyes as she nodded and turned away. Silently she walked down the hallway and disappeared. To James, it was as though she took a piece of his heart with her. She had no idea how much she was asking. He'd been alone, totally alone, almost all his life. He'd survived the war for five long years by never getting close to anyone, not the men he fought with, not the women he'd met along the way.

Marriage was something far in the future, if at all.

Yet somehow this quiet woman and her wild brother had become his family whether he wanted it to happen or not.

He went back into the kitchen where he found Andy bedded down on the floor by the low fire and Millie asleep on the sofa a room away.

Walking toward the little room off the back porch where Mrs. Harris had told him to sleep, James decided he hated himself because no matter what happened he'd regret this decision in a year. If he married Millie, she'd be unhappy. Millie was beautiful, even Ranger Price had noticed. She wouldn't want to be stuck on a ranch with him. And if he didn't marry her, he knew he'd miss her and worry about her every day left of his life.

He lay in his bed wishing he could see the stars instead of the ceiling. Sleep didn't seem to be an option, so he just waited for dawn. In his brain he began list after list of all he'd need to buy and collect to make the trip. He'd have his ranch before fall. Only, he'd be alone.

An hour, maybe more, passed.

Then, as gentle as a breeze, Millie climbed into his bed.

James thought of fighting, or arguing, or demanding they talk, but instead he did something Captain James Kirkland had never done in his life.

He surrendered.

eight

Spring warmed the air in Fort Worth as Millie waited for James to return from his business dealings as she did every night. Now that her brother was always with her, her canyon man didn't talk to her as much.

He was busy making all the dreams he had told her about when they were at the winter camp come true. He had land to buy and cattle to choose for breeding his herd. Even when James was near her, there always seemed to be something between them. She missed his rambling about one subject or another. Their nights under the endless sky when they watched for shooting stars were over. She longed to feel him next to her, holding her safe and warm as he slept.

Millie missed the James she'd known. Now everyone called him Captain or Mr. Kirkland. Mrs. Harris whispered once that there was no doubt he would be a very important man one day. The men he hired to work for him were all cut from the same cloth as James. Most weren't far into their thirties, but they'd been hardened by war and seasoned from cattle drives. All wore chaps and spurs and guns strapped to their legs.

Millie felt as if he'd stepped up as a leader in a world she couldn't enter. Every night men circled the table poring over maps and numbers. Every morning James was gone before dawn.

Mrs. Harris continued to teach her to cook and sew, and Millie worked with Andrew every day. Her brother wasn't as hungry to learn as she had been. He gave in to bathing, but he still insisted on wearing his Apache clothes. He spent his mornings beside her, but disappeared into the wooded area every chance he got. In the afternoons he wandered the garden, picking tree branches to fashion into bows.

Late one afternoon, as she watched Andy in the yard, James appeared at her side. "What's the kid doing?" he asked.

Millie folded her arms, frustrated at her brother. "He's building an arsenal."

"I figured that." James put his arm lightly around her waist. "He sees himself as a warrior. He's preparing for battle."

"Who is he going to fight, James?" She fought tears, afraid of the truth.

"Me, I'm thinking."

For a moment she leaned into James. For years she hadn't cared about anyone and now the two men she loved seemed destined to be on different sides. James didn't trust Andy and her brother had told her once in Apache that James had cold eyes, the eyes of a killer. She knew he'd been in the war. She'd heard Ranger Price talk of it. Millie didn't know that side of James Kirkland. She only knew the one who was gentle, the one who touched her heart.

When James pulled her closer, his voice stayed calm in case Mrs. Harris was within hearing distance. "What do you and Andy talk about, Millie? Does he ever mention his home or your parents?"

"He wants to talk to me only in Apache, telling me of the great adventures he's had. After a few days, I realized my years as a captive were a lower kind of hell, but for Andrew, those years were heaven. He never went hungry. He learned to hunt and fight, but was never beaten. He said he was adopted as the son of the chief and has three brothers. Over and over he tells me he would go back if he could, only he will not leave me. I'm his blood. He said when we were first separated, he cried every night for me until the chief told him it was time for him to be a man."

"He's twelve, Millie. Even if he'd argue the point, he's still more boy than man. Give him time. He'll come around."

She nodded, but didn't believe. Sometimes she wondered if the little boy in Andy remembered her and her mother as one. When she looked in the mirror now, at her hair pulled back with combs, she thought she looked exactly like her mother.

"You'll always be kind to him, James."

"I will."

She pulled away. "And if we leave your ranch one day, you will let us go."

He closed his eyes and nodded before whispering, "I will." Slowly he smiled and added, "The woman I traded for a broken watch is gone. You've a mind of your own, Millie, and I'll respect that no matter how much I want you near."

"I'm here now," she admitted, "but I have to belong to me before I can belong to anyone else ever again."

For a long while he just held her, both feeling the world changing.

Finally he shifted and switched into a casual stance. "Did I mention that your brother slipped into my room a few nights ago? He stole my hunting knife."

"I know. I saw him with it. He's also taken a few of Mrs. Harris's kitchen knives. I tried to make him give them back, but he refused."

"Let him keep my knife." James shrugged. "After all, if he planned to murder me in my sleep, he's already had the opportunity. Once we're on the road, he might need them to hunt."

"Is there a chance of trouble on the road?"

James nodded. "Apache might attack. Or outlaws robbing travelers. I think I could count on Andy's help with outlaws, but if it's Apache, he's liable to fight for the other side."

She laughed. "Maybe you should work on building a friendship?"

"Not much chance of that. He still won't speak to me."

James took her hand and they walked in to dinner. As they climbed the steps, his fingers moved over her back; a tender caress no one saw but that warmed her insides.

Andy retuned to the house after dark and ate alone, then curled into his blanket by the fire. In her world, his behavior had become the norm. Tonight, as she sat helping Mrs. Harris quilt, Millie didn't worry about her brother. Her thoughts were on James as he talked with his men a room away. She could still feel his touch.

The next evening Millie waited for James on the porch, hoping for another moment alone with him.

Only, the sun set and he did not come. The thought crossed her mind that maybe he'd left without her. Rain rumbled in but she couldn't seem to budge from her chair on the porch. She needed to see him.

Finally, slicing through the rain, he stepped onto the porch. For a moment she saw the worry and exhaustion in his face before he spotted her and smiled.

"Millie," he whispered, and she was in his arms. "Millie," he said again as he held her so tight she couldn't breathe.

Then, like a man starved, he kissed her. His hands moved over her with need. When he broke the kiss, he laughed low against her ear. "You're filling out, my little dove. I've missed holding you something fierce. I know we agreed to sleep apart, but that doesn't stop the need I have for you."

She smiled, loving knowing he still felt about her as she did about him even if he wouldn't say the words she longed to hear.

She told herself it was enough that he thought of her and she could be near him, if just for a few minutes every evening.

Mrs. Harris opened the door and they moved apart. She was a kind woman but she didn't approve of a man who didn't offer marriage touching a girl. If she'd known that Millie had slept with him that first night he'd returned with Andy, Mrs. Harris would have been outraged.

Millie didn't really think of it as right or wrong. It just was. Part of her felt as though she belonged to James. Part of her wanted always to be with him. She didn't want to be treated like a third or fourth wife. Even though no other women stood between them, Millie still felt as if she was down the line in importance. She'd rather be alone in her bed than matter little to a man.

"I hired a few more men today." James broke into her thoughts as he held the door for her to step into the house.

She wished he would say he missed her, but talk of the ranch always came first. As they ate, she listened while Mrs. Harris asked questions. James was in his world of planning.

He was still talking of supplies when they moved into the parlor with their coffee. A box of Andy's clothes sat between them. Or what was left of them. He'd used James's knife to cut every pair of trousers and all the shirts into long strips.

James picked up what had once been a jacket. He hadn't said a word to Millie about the clothes or the cost. "Your brother will kill me one day. I see the hate in his eyes."

"He will not." She said the words strongly as if she could make them true but she knew her gaze mirrored the worry in James's eyes.

"He's not ready to live among people. If we take him to the ranch with us he's just as likely to go wild as to settle down."

Looking up at him, she picked her words carefully. "Are you sure you want me to go with you? Maybe everyone would be happier if I stayed here. I'll not leave Andy."

"I'd like you to come along, Millie, and your brother would be safer on the ranch."

She nodded, knowing he was right.

James hurried on as if worried that she'd ask questions he wasn't ready to answer. "Once we get to the ranch, I won't have time to watch him. I'm having lumber delivered for the house. The men will stay to help me get the house framed out. If Andy runs, I can't chase after him, Millie. I lost enough days this spring going to fetch him. We have to work hard to get ready for winter. I'll have cattle to brand and fences to build, not to mention the barn and a house." He stopped and looked at her. "For as long as you stay, the house will be yours. I'll not step foot in it unless I'm invited. If you'll come back with me, you come on your own terms. The way you want it to be. As far as I'm concerned your brother does the same."

She wanted him to want her with him, not just to invite her because of her brother. "We will be trouble for you. Are you sure you want us to come?"

"Yes." He leaned forward, almost close enough to touch her. "We got along in the winter camp, didn't we? It'll be much better with a house and supplies. If you like, I'll get you one of those new sewing machines. Both you and Andy will have a place to call home for as long as you like."

Millie spoke her mind before she lost her courage. "I'll not sleep with you again, James. Not until the time is right." How could she tell him it was more than just marriage she wanted? She wanted to be important to him. No. More than that. She wanted to be vital in his life.

"I dreamed you were in my bed the other night." He smiled.

Millie shook her head. "The dream will not follow us to your ranch. Mrs. Harris said you do not own me even if you traded for me."

James watched her so closely she was afraid to move. "Mrs.

Harris is right. I do not own you. You can leave me if you want to, Millie."

She knew he was setting the rules. Giving her the choice to go with him. Only, he didn't want to tie her to him in marriage. If she went without being his wife she would be nothing again. But if she did not go, her heart would break.

"I will go, James," she said simply. "You are right about Andy. He is not ready to stay among people yet. But I may not stay with you for long." He had to know. He had to understand that she was free.

For a blink she saw anger and hurt in his gaze, then it was gone. For the first time she wondered if this man who had always been kind might not let her go so easily.

A tiny idea had settled into the corners of her mind. She'd seen the money James collected for hides and furs. If she and Andy were on their own, they could hunt and survive. Ranger Drew had told her that her father's small farm was east of Dallas, still waiting for her. Maybe she and Andy could live there? Once they got settled she'd buy chickens and a milk cow and raise pigs. Mrs. Harris had taught her how to make butter and bake. She remembered plums and cherries growing wild on their farm. They wouldn't need much.

Andy wouldn't fit in now, but he would one day. He was still a boy. He needed to learn a few things first about ranching and how to use a rifle. James could teach him that. Once her brother knew more, they would make their choice to go or stay. Until then, she would go and help James set up his dream. She'd learn and grow, but she would not be his *nothing woman* no matter how much she longed to be near him.

Two weeks later they moved out of Fort Worth like a small wagon train with a hundred head of cattle, thirty horses, two wagons of supplies, pigs, chickens, four wagons of building materials and another wagon carrying all they'd need to set up a windmill on the land. Millie drove one of the small covered wagons with all the household items. Two hired men had brought their own wagons covered in wood as if they were houses on wheels. Their wives, dressed with colorful scarves around their heads and waists, drove the wagons. James had told her the men were farriers with blacksmithing skills. As Gypsies, the men had a hard time getting work in Fort Worth, but with their knowledge of horses they'd be invaluable on the ranch. James had let Andy pick out his own horse. She thought maybe James wouldn't care if the boy ran away, but she knew Andy wouldn't run without her by his side. She felt his commitment to her. If only James could feel the same.

When they stopped for the night, Millie would work with Andy on the words he'd lost over the six years he'd been with the Apache. She soon noticed the Gypsy women moved closer to them and listened in. Slowly, she included them and felt as though she was teaching a class in a language she was still learning herself.

She slept in the household supply wagon each night with all her things around her: a trunk of clothes and dishes Mrs. Harris had insisted she take. A new sewing machine. Quilts and blankets. Four chairs for a table not yet built. If all this were truly hers she would be a rich woman indeed, but only the clothes and one quilt were hers. Everything else belonged to James.

Andrew slept beneath her wagon, his horse staked out a few feet away. He seemed happier now they were in the open air. The cowhands James had hired mostly avoided him, but one boy not more than two years older than Andy showed him how to use a rope. By watching him, her brother learned how to work the cattle.

Along the trail they sometimes passed small settlements. James or one of the men always went in for supplies. James had hired an older man and his wife to cook on the trail, so Millie didn't have to cook when they camped each night, which was fine with her. The jerking and bucking of the wagon left her exhausted and sick at her stomach most nights.

The older couple talked to her now and then, but, as with everyone, they didn't quite know what Millie was there for. She wasn't James's wife, or even his woman. James seemed to pay no more attention to her than he did to anyone else. So she held her thoughts and her sickness to herself.

Andy was the only one who noticed. One evening he disappeared for a while and brought back a root that he told her to chew on. She did and her stomach calmed.

"You are sick?" he whispered in English.

He might never speak to anyone but her, but he listened to everyone. She answered him in English. "I'm not sick. I just don't like riding in the wagon."

"You ready to leave?" he asked in Apache. "We could travel faster alone and not scar the earth like these men do."

She shook her head. "No. We've much to learn. If we decide to go back to our father's land, we must be ready. There may be no one to help us then."

"I know enough, but I will not leave until you are ready," he said in English. "When you leave, I will go with you. You do not need to be afraid."

Looking at him, she noticed he was now a half inch taller than she was. He wouldn't be a boy much longer. How could she explain that it would break her heart to leave James, but that she couldn't stay with him if she didn't matter to him?

The morning dawned cold and rainy. Millie felt no better, but she climbed onto the wagon bench and watched the land go slowly by. They'd been on the road three weeks now. James always spoke to her at supper, and now and then he'd ride alongside her to see how she was. When the traveling was easy, she drove the wagon, but on rainy days or on uneven ground, one of his men would tie his horse to the back of the wagon and drive the team.

Millie always lied when James asked how she was doing. All those years of traveling with the tribes, she had learned that sick people might be left behind. Especially if they were no one to the others in the tribe.

This morning he rode close and smiled. "We're almost there, Millie. Another week at the most if this rain doesn't slow us down."

She nodded and tried her best to look excited.

"How're you doing?" he asked and leaned closer.

She didn't answer. She was cold and sick at her stomach and lonely and afraid. If she started telling him, she might never stop.

Tying his reins around the saddle horn, he lifted his arms to her. "Come on, Little Dove, ride with me a while."

She slipped from the bench into his arms. He opened his coat and wrapped it around her and she felt warm for the first time in days. As he walked his horse at the pace of the wagons, she cried softly against his chest. Her warm tears mixed with the rain.

She wanted to share his joy. James seemed happy, excited. For the first time in his life, he'd have a home, a real home. But all she could feel was change turning her world upside down again.

"Don't cry, Millie," he whispered. "Everything is going to be all right. We'll have the house built by winter."

When she didn't answer, he asked, "You want me to sing you a song?"

She sniffed. "You can't sing."

"The cows don't seem to mind." He kissed her forehead. "You've been listening to me sing the cattle to sleep for a month and now you tell me I can't sing."

Directing his horse away from the others, he whispered, "I love the feel of you next to me. I've missed you." All the wagons and cattle disappeared in the fog, but she could still hear the harnesses clanging and the rumbling sound of a hundred cattle slowly thumping the ground.

She liked the way the rain closed in around them, almost making her believe they were alone once again.

This was the first time he'd made an effort to hold her on the journey. There was no privacy on the trail. He must have missed her, too, for he whispered, "I've thought of coming to your canvas door at night, but that brother of yours is always right outside. I swear, one night he smiled as I came near, as if he was itching to slice off one of my ears if I came too close."

Giggling, Millie didn't argue.

"I thought about it, anyway. After all, I got another ear and I was missing holding you something terrible."

She shook her head. "If you only had one ear, your hat would fall off."

"You got a point." They rode for a while before he spoke again. "When we get to the land, we'll settle in and get this worked out between us. I've never thought of myself as a marrying man, but I don't like the idea of living here without you. All I've ever wanted and worked for was to own my own spread. I feel like if I think about anything else right now it might just slip through my hands. I can't let that happen. Will you wait for me awhile, Millie?"

James was asking her to wait while he followed his dream. Well, he might be able to push back his life, but she knew she could not push back hers. Disappointment clouded her heart. She leaned against him, knowing that from this point on she needed to store up memories to take with her.

She was leaving her canyon man. Not today, or next week, or maybe even next month, but she was leaving. She might never be the most important thing to anyone, but she couldn't stay with James and be less than that to him.

That night, when she was alone with her brother, she told him to be ready.

Andy nodded. Silently he reached and placed his hand on her stomach. The boy saw what the man hadn't noticed.

nine

James thought he might explode with pure pride as he crossed the canyon and rode onto his land. This was the place he had looked for half his life. There might be trouble with the Indian Wars to the north and cattle sickness to the south, but here on his land there would be peace.

The wagons were a day behind him, but he couldn't wait. He had to see what was his. As the cattle and wagons circled miles north so they did not have to cross the deep part of the canyon, he set up camp on the spot where he would build his house.

James Randall Kirkland could see it all in his mind. His headquarters, spread out like a small town. The main house. The barns. A bunkhouse. A smoke shack. Millie would probably want a hen cage, too, and a big garden just like Mrs. Harris had back in Fort Worth. Packed away with her few belongings were bags of seeds that would do well in the fall. Potatoes, pumpkins and beans.

The dream that got him through the dark nights during the war and the lonely years of drifting was finally happening. He'd never touched his small inheritance or any of the money he'd deposited after cattle drives, anticipating the day he found the perfect land so he would have money for a real start. Here he'd watch the sun rise and set every day for the rest of his life.

The memory of an arrow landing inches from his boot one night on the trail flashed through his thoughts. James decided he might want to build a little place for Andy, maybe over in the cottonwoods. The idea of sleeping in the same house with the wild boy bothered him. They had been traveling together for a month, and the boy had not said a word to him but he carried his bow and full quiver strapped to his saddle.

Andy usually glared at him with that wish-I-could-kill-you look in his eyes. The arrow that night had simply been a reminder that one day he'd finish the job.

James pushed dark thoughts from his mind. He focused instead on the wide porch he would build on the house, and someday he might buy Millie and him rocking chairs to use in their old age. If she would have him… He had asked her to wait. Surely she knew that as soon as he had the ranch up and running he planned to ask her to marry him. The idea had settled in slowly, and he would not say more before he had a real home to offer her.

At twilight a lone figure rode up from the canyon and waved.

James laughed. "I figured you'd hear us coming, Two Fingers."

The hardened ex-slave slid off his horse and walked toward the campfire. "I knew you'd be back, Kirkland. I was camped down in the canyon near where we traded for that mud woman when I got word. Took me two days to ride here. Passed that wagon train of supplies you got coming in." He looked around. "See you got rid of the crazy woman."

"Yeah, she's gone." James grinned to himself.

Two Fingers smiled. "Run off, did she? You're lucky she didn't kill you first. I tried to tell you, once they go mad they never come back."

James didn't want to talk about Millie. "How'd you know I was near?"

"Trappers stopped by and said you were heading toward where the canyon snakes north." Two Fingers rocked on his boots for a few seconds as if debating with himself. "Word is, raiders are planning to hit you as soon as you settle."

"Apache or white?" James figured he would have to fight off one attack, maybe more, before he convinced outlaws he wasn't worth bothering. Every cowhand he'd hired knew how to fight.

Two Fingers shrugged. "They're a new gang that's been roaming this area for a few months. Got a little of everything in their mix. Mexicans who've been cattle rustling over in the Badlands, Apache too bloodthirsty to live with any tribe, a few rebels still mad about the war and a couple of outlaws willing to kill for a dime. They're like a pack of wild dogs, so mean they'll eventually turn on each other."

James watched the horizon. "How long before they hit?"

Two Fingers's grin was missing even more teeth than last time James had seen him. "A month, maybe two," he said. "They might let you settle in, then come after the cattle. If they're smart, they'll leave you alone and just take the stock. Then, they could come back in a year or six months and hit your place again."

"Are they smart?"

Two Fingers shook his head. "My guess is they'll take everything they can sell and kill the rest. This land is settling all around. Their kind will die off soon. If Mackenzie ever stops Quanah in the Palo Duro Canyon north of here, this part of Texas might calm down. When that happens, I'm moving on."

James had worked most of the day marking off where each wagon coming in would unload. Now all he wanted to do was to sleep, but the ex-slave's words would keep him awake. Quanah was said to be a great Comanche chief and Colonel Mackenzie never backed down. The Palo Duro would run red with blood before the battle was over.

"You're welcome to share my meal. I got beans and biscuits."

"I'll do that." Two Fingers pulled off his saddle. "I'll share your fire, too, if you've no objection. The canyon's not a safe place to be after dark."

"I'll be glad for the company," James lied. In truth the old scout smelled so bad he would need to be a mile away before the air cleared.

They drank the coffeepot dry and talked about the past before Two Fingers drifted off to sleep midsentence.

At dawn the next morning James stood waiting for his life to begin. All the years of having nothing slipped from his shoulders. He was a rancher now. He would carve his place right here. He'd build something to be proud to pass down. Something that would last for generations.

Finally the wagons appeared on the horizon.

Two Fingers crawled from under the buffalo hide he'd slept in all night and stood beside James. "Holly hell, Kirkland. You've hauled the whole damn town up here."

James laughed. "Tell the raiders, when you see them, that we'll be waiting. If they ride onto my land, they won't be riding off."

Two Fingers watched as wagon after wagon came into view. "This is too many people. I think I'll be moving on."

"You're welcome at my table anytime," James said as the old trapper loaded up.

"A man so settled he's got a table is too settled for me, but I might ride by and check on you now and again, Kirkland. See if you still got that pretty lady driving one of the wagons in." He shaded his eyes for a better look. "I'll bet it cost you plenty to talk her into coming out here."

"A small fortune," James admitted. "One broken pocket watch."

Two Fingers shook his head. "No. Impossible. That's the Mud Woman?"

"Afraid so. I told you she was of great value." James glanced to the east. "Too beautiful for the likes of me."

"True," Two Fingers said. "Maybe I should go over and introduce myself. I was told a few years back that I'd be quite a catch."

"You can try, but the lady drives a hard bargain. It's marriage or nothing, I'm afraid."

Laughing, the old tracker saddled up. "Too high a price. But if she's heading this way, she's already won, my friend. You're just too mule-headed to know it."

James slapped the tracker's horse and waved as he galloped off.

The work began. Most days James was up and dressed an hour before dawn and worked until long after dark. He saw Andy sometimes riding with the other cowhands but he rarely saw Millie.

One night he felt a longing just to say her name. He knew the ranch needed far more work before he talked to her, but he wanted to know she was all right. As he stood around the campfire eating a hearty chili with hunks of sweet corn bread crumbled in it, James asked one of the carpenters named Patty if he'd seen Millie.

"You mean, Miss Millie? She's right fine, she is." Patty blushed to the top of his bald head as if he had said too much.

"Go on," James encouraged. "How is she getting on out here all alone?"

"Oh, she ain't alone, Captain. The two women in those wagons work with her most days. She's teaching them to quilt and they've been helping her with the garden. Mrs. Sands drops over to her place, too. I think they have tea together. Funny, out here in this wild country women work hard, but they still do their visiting."

"She's working?" James asked. He'd never told her to do anything but fix the house up the way she wanted it.

Patty nodded. "She helped us frame up the house the first week. Swung a hammer as well as most men I've seen."

When James stood silent, waiting, the carpenter continued. "When Old Man Sands had to quit cooking 'cause his wife got down in her back for a few days, Miss Millie did a far better job than the old couple together ever did. You ask me, Sands should go back to preaching. His wife helps when she can but Miss Millie told Sands to help build the barn and she'd cook. You'll not find a carpenter or a cowhand complaining."

"I've never noticed her by the chuck wagon." James always rode in dead-tired, but surely he would have seen Millie if she moved among the campfires.

"Oh, you won't. After she gets the meal ready, Sands takes over serving and cleans up. He claims she's too fine a lady to hear the rough talk around the campfires."

James nodded. "Good point." When he glanced toward the house where Millie stayed, the carpenter vanished into the shadows. James didn't care. He had learned what he'd needed to know. Millie was all right.

Slowly, one change a day, the headquarters took shape. By the time the carpenters left a month later with their wagons empty, James felt as though his dream was materializing.

He slept around the campfire most nights, knowing that if he stepped inside the house, he'd want Millie. He needed her so badly in the stillness of night he couldn't sleep. When he finally saw her a few evenings later, she looked tired and sad. The work was wearing on her, he thought. He'd told her to slow down, but he could see she wasn't listening.

For some reason she was turning away, going to that place where he couldn't reach her. Even the old woman said that the pretty lady rarely spoke. Maybe this life wasn't right for Millie. Maybe it was too hard for her out here. She used to laugh when she'd lived with Mrs. Harris; he had not heard her laughter since they'd left Fort Worth. The last time he'd held her, she'd cried in his arms.

At night James walked toward the house and watched her moving in the kitchen. What would he do if she wanted to leave? Was he strong enough to hold her? Could he be strong enough to let her go?

Finally, when the first hint of fall whispered in the air, the memory of the day he'd traded for her at Ransom Canyon wouldn't leave his thoughts. That evening he walked to the house wanting to thank her for all she'd done to help. His men were well fed thanks to her cooking, and the garden she had put in when they'd arrived looked as though it would feed them well all winter.

"Millie," he called as he neared the porch he had finished off while she'd cooked one morning. "Millie?"

She stepped out onto the porch but didn't say a word. Her hair was down, brushing her shoulders, and her big blue eyes warmed his heart. "Missing her" was not powerful enough to express how he felt.

"I think it's about time we had a talk." He made it two more steps before one of his men rode between him and the house.

"Captain Kirkland, we got trouble in the north pasture. Looks like someone shot one of our cows." The cowhand added, "Rustlers moon tonight."

James turned away from Millie and started yelling orders to his men. He'd seen a few signs of someone camped just beyond the border of his land. He knew Two Fingers was right: a raid would come one day.

As he swung onto his horse, James glanced back at the house. Millie wasn't there. She must have gone inside. Like a shot firing through his heart, he realized how afraid she must be. She had been in a raid. She'd seen her mother die. She knew the terror of being captured.

He wanted to comfort her. To pull her into his arms and tell her everything was going to be fine; that he wouldn't let anything hurt her. He had prepared for this. But there was no time to hold her. He had to ride. He had to protect the ranch. He had to protect her.

His men knew their jobs. Some would go with him; a few would take lookout posts in the loft of the barn and around the perimeter where they wouldn't be easily spotted. They would protect the headquarters while he and his best hands would make sure outlaws never came near.

As he circled the men riding, he spotted Andy among them. He carried a long bow and arrows filled the quiver strapped to his back. The kid had grown a few inches since James had reunited him with Millie. He was more of a man now, but not enough to join this fight. James would not insult Andy tonight. Not in front of the men he fought so hard to ride equal with.

James shouted as he rode near, doubting the kid would listen to any order. "Stay at the headquarters, Andy!" James yelled over the thunder of hooves. "I trust you to protect your sister. Do whatever you have to, but keep her safe."

The kid didn't look happy, but he nodded and dropped back.

If James had a minute, he would have told Andy that Millie would never speak to him again if he got her brother hurt...

Andy hated him, but now wasn't the time to worry about it.

James and his men rode hard toward the north pasture. Cattle were on that section, not enough to risk a life to steal, but maybe enough to draw men to a fight. As he cut across his land, he planned. No matter how many years had passed, part of him would always be a soldier.

By the time they reached the north pasture, the last light of the sun allowed him to see across his land. One calf lay dead. Two wolves were twisted and bleeding beside it.

One man, walking his horse, moved toward James. The horse had no saddle.

James raised his rifle. "I'd stop right there, stranger, if you want to live."

The man raised his hands. "No trouble, mister."

The trespasser's voice was laced with a thick German accent. James nudged his horse closer but didn't lower his rifle. "Want to tell me why you're on my land?"

The stranger didn't look armed and even in the shadows James could see that he wasn't dressed like a cowboy. His was big, though. Well over six feet with a broad chest and big, beefy hands.

"I come for work. Heard a big outfit come to this place. Do I talk now to Mr. Kirkland?"

"You are," James said as he stopped his mount five feet away. "Who are you? And what do you know about that dead calf?"

"Name is Wagner." He pronounced it *Vahgner*. "I carpenter by trade. The wolves kill calf. I kill them with ax, then think I have to come tell you even if it means no job."

"You alone?" James didn't trust a man who waited until dark to show up.

"*Nein*. I have wife and children with me. We travel from Fredericksburg to Fort Worth. Ranger named Drew Price told us to find you. He said if I say his name you give me job."

James lowered his rifle and dismounted. "Why didn't you ride into headquarters?"

"I plan to tomorrow. *Die* wife, she want to wash clothes first. Tonight I walk to the peak and try to see your camp."

James waved the other men in. Any man who could kill two wolves with an ax would be good to have around.

He offered his hand to Wagner. "Welcome to the ranch, Wagner. We'll talk about your job in the morning, but if Drew Price sent you I'm guessing I'll be lucky to have you."

James called out to the cowhands as they neared, "Help Mr. Wagner and his family get back to headquarters. Make sure they have supper and get bedded down in the barn."

The big man smiled. "I try to shoot wolves before they kill cow, but I not a good shot so I run to them with my ax."

"Can you make rocking chairs?" James thought of the man's first project.

Wagner's chest swelled even bigger. "Best in state."

"How many children you got?" James liked the idea of children running around.

"Seven," Wagner whispered. "All girls, maybe boy for next time."

A few of the men laughed and then stepped forward to shake hands.

James climbed back on his horse and nodded once at Wagner before he turned back to find Millie.

He wanted to be the first to tell her that everything was all right. Tonight he would try to put into words how much she meant to him.

She filled his thoughts as he rode home, but when he got to the house, not a single lamp burned. He searched the campsite thinking she might have thought she'd be safer somewhere else like the barn where men stood guard, or the smokehouse buried halfway in the ground.

When he didn't find her there, James checked the barn.

The boy was gone, too. When he asked about her, no one, not even the men who'd been on guard, had seen Millie or her brother.

Storming through the house, he searched every room. All was neat, every towel folded, every dish clean. It was as if no one lived there. As if the house had been readied but not lived in.

Slowly he circled one last time. Fear set in as the thought that someone might have taken her settled over his panic.

Finally he remembered what wasn't in the house that should have been. Her trunk that she'd used to pack her few dresses and the seeds for her garden. The rolltop box with a sewing machine inside. The quilt she and Mrs. Harris had made those last few days they were in Fort Worth.

Anger and heartache ripped through his chest. She'd left him.

He had said he would let her go, but he couldn't. He couldn't live without her. She was his. He had paid her ransom. She was his. And he loved her.

James stood on the porch where he imagined they would grow old together and realized one fact. She wasn't his.

He was hers.

ten

James circled the headquarters looking for any sign of Millie or her brother. Nothing made sense. How could they have disappeared?

As the men settled in around the campfire, James grabbed a lantern and continued to search. The Wagner family were all tucked in the hayloft. As he walked through the barn, he heard Wagner's wife singing the baby to sleep and two of the girls giggling.

James forced himself to concentrate. He passed the two Gypsy wagons. There, he heard the soft sounds of couples whispering and the memory of how he'd held Millie at the winter camp drifted in his mind. They had cuddled beneath their blanket and watched for shooting stars.

He glanced up thinking that if she had truly left him, he'd never study the night sky again. How could she have become such a big part of his life and him not know it? When he thought a raid was coming, all that mattered was Millie. Not the ranch or the cows, just Millie.

He walked around to the back of the corral where extra mounts shifted in the shadows.

The lantern swung at his knee. For the hundredth time he glared down at the dirt, but this time he saw something that made no sense. Horse tracks scarred the ground leading away from the fence. It looked as if three of the extra mounts had simply walked through the fence where no gate had been cut.

Setting the lantern down, he knelt. It took him a minute, but he solved the puzzle. The three fence boards had been shaved where they went into the posts. No nails held the fence railing up at this spot, just notches cut into the cedar pillars. Someone had taken the time to make it where they could slide the slats, let the horses out and then replace them without a sound. He, or she, wouldn't leave a trail unless one of the men walked around the back of the corral, and no cowhand was likely to do that. This far point almost bordered a jagged cliff where an arm of the canyon dropped down.

James circled back to the barn and saddled the nearest horse as he pieced it all together. Andy had made the invisible gate just in case he ever needed it. He had taken Millie. The third mount must be carrying the trunk, the sewing machine and probably enough supplies to last them a few weeks. They both knew the way to Fort Worth, though he doubted that was their destination.

Part of him wanted to believe that Andy had taken Millie against her will, but he knew that wasn't true.

Maybe they'd thought he wouldn't let them go. That would explain why they'd picked a time to slip away when no one would be watching.

James fought the urge to yell for all his men. They could spread out and find a kid and a woman within an hour, but this was something he had to do by himself. The men might hurt the kid when he protected his sister or Andy might hurt one of them.

He rode to the edge of the canyon. The land was flat until

the sudden drop. It looked as if a man could see the curve of the earth in all directions, but the canyon ran for more than a hundred miles, wide as a mile in places, almost small enough to jump across in others. The canyon branched out like fingers of a huge root, barely scarring the ground in places and dropping a thousand feet in others.

He looked down at the shadows below where rocky ground left no tracks. They had picked their way before dark. Now, if he started into the canyon at night, he'd be risking his life. Dark rocks and holes looked the same and shadows hid any path.

Without hesitation he started into the canyon.

He might never find them. Not tonight or after a month of searching. They could turn left or right a dozen times and if he missed one turn they would be miles away before he could backtrack.

James felt his world shattering. He would give up everything he owned, all he had saved and planned for all his life, to have Millie back at the winter camp where they had one blanket to share.

Only, he had lost her. In all the talking he had done since they met he'd forgotten to tell her how much she mattered to him.

A shooting star flashed across the sky as if reminding him of a wasted future without Millie.

James swore. He should have told her how he felt. He should have married her when she'd wanted him to. He should have stormed the house and slept with her so she wouldn't have looked so lonely.

Another star arced across the sky, adding a flash of light for him to see the path. The light dimmed as it peaked and fell, winking out before it hit the ground.

James looked up at the night. Shooting stars don't arc.

Another tiny light shot up out of the canyon.

James turned toward the light. It took two more flashes before

James realized what he was seeing. Arrows. Flaming in the almost moonless night sky. Flaming arrows showing him the way.

Ten minutes and a dozen arrows later, he saw Millie and Andy on the canyon floor. Andy stood still holding his bow in front of a tiny fire. The strips of a shirt James had bought him lay scattered by the fire. Millie was wrapped in her beautiful quilt.

James dropped the reins of his horse and ran toward them. When he was ten feet away, he saw that Millie wasn't moving. Her eyes were closed, as though she were sleeping.

"What happened?" he demanded as he knelt beside Millie and brushed her beautiful hair away from her face.

"She fell. I should have moved slower." Andy stared at the fire, not meeting his eyes. "I knew you would come. I only had to show you the way."

James glanced at Andy, who looked terrified. "It wasn't your fault, Andy. It was an accident. Your arrows may save her."

As gently as he could, James moved his hands over her, trying to find where she was hurt. He felt blood in her hair and found a knot and a small cut near her forehead.

"Why'd you bring her out here?" James didn't bother to look at Andy as he worked. He found no cuts or broken bones on her arms or shoulders. She was warm, still breathing, but he wouldn't move her until he knew where she was injured.

"She said we had to go." Andy's words were cold, full of hate.

"Why?" James asked as his hands moved down her sides.

Andy pulled the last arrow from his quiver. "Because a man who does not want a woman will not want the child she carries."

The boy's words struck James just as his hand spread over her rounded middle.

If Andy had pulled his bow and shot an arrow through James's chest it could not have hurt more. She was carrying his child and she feared him. Afraid he didn't want her.

"We have to get her back," James said, his hands shaking as

he tied his bandanna around her head wound. Looking up, he saw Andy standing there, arrow at the ready.

There was no time to tell the boy how wrong he and Millie had been. All that mattered was trying to save her and the child. "I'm taking her home, Andy." James gently lifted her. "She's my life, whether you believe it or not. If she dies, let that arrow fly and bury me beside her."

Andy glared at him. "I will do that," he said calmly, as if it were a promise.

They didn't say another word. James held her close as he rode and Andy led them out of the canyon.

The kid pulled open the corral, then followed James to the shadows of the barn where he raised his arms to lift Millie down.

James lowered Millie off the horse, then climbed down and took her gently from Andy. "If you'll close the corral, I'll get her to the house."

Nodding, Andy stepped back. "I will go back for the other horses when I know she is safe."

"Good." James knew the kid would not leave her now.

The night guard spotted them as he walked out of the barn carrying Millie. By the time James reached the porch, people were coming from every direction.

Mrs. Sands ran toward him as fast as her legs would carry her. In her white nightgown and nightcap she looked more ghost than woman.

"My wife is hurt," he said. "I'll need your help. She's had a bad fall."

The chubby woman starting giving orders like she was second in command. "I'll need water and bandages and one of the Gypsy wives to help."

He didn't know the names of the farrier's or blacksmith's wives, but he saw both of them hurrying toward the house.

When he laid Millie on the bed, Mrs. Sands told him and Andy to get out.

"I'm not leaving her." James stood his ground.

"I will not go," Andy echoed.

James had a feeling that if Millie died, he'd feel the arrow through his chest before one tear could fall.

"Then stay out of my way, the both of you," Mrs. Sands announced.

Wagner, a little girl on each arm, poked his head in to say his wife wanted to help. "No English, but she know about babies."

Mrs. Sands nodded once. "Tell her to come in, then you stand outside the door and yell back in English anything she says. It's not time for the baby to come, but the fall may have hurt her."

The newly hired carpenter disappeared and his wife waddled into the room obviously near time to deliver that boy Wagner had been waiting for.

Mrs. Sands held the quilt while the German lady examined Millie. James turned his head fearing Mrs. Wagner's hand would appear covered in blood.

The exam took several minutes before she said something in German. Her husband yelled back the translation. "*Das* baby to be all right. No blood. Three more months to carry."

A cheer went up from the other side of the bedroom door and James let out a breath he'd been holding. He looked at Andy. The kid finally set aside the bow he'd had in his hand.

"Does everyone on the ranch know Millie is with child?"

"Yep," Mrs. Sands said as she cleaned the blood out of Millie's hair. "We just didn't know you two were married. Neither one of you said anything about it, but a blind person could tell you loved each other. She listened for you each night and you watched the house."

"We've never said the words but—"

Mrs. Sands shook her head. "Ain't no buts. You either are or you're not. If you haven't said the words, you're not."

"I'd say the vows right now if we had a preacher." James didn't want there to be any doubt that he loved Millie.

"Wait till she comes to, Captain. A woman usually likes to be conscious at her own wedding."

He sat by the bed until Millie finally opened her eyes, then they talked softly late into the night. He never touched more than her hand, but the knowledge of how near he came to losing her rocked him to his core.

The next morning James put on his only clean shirt and waited on the porch for Millie to appear. She'd agreed to marry him, but Mrs. Sands suggested Millie sleep on it first. Her exact words were, "A man too dumb to admit his love is probably too dumb to come in out of the rain."

James had glared at her, but the old lady had just smiled, letting James know she planned to pester him until one of them died.

Andy swung over the railing and stood at the door as if still on guard. He frowned at James with death-threat eyes as usual.

"I see you found a shirt and trousers. You giving up being an Apache?" James didn't add that he'd done the worst job of cutting his hair that James had ever seen except for when Millie had cut hers.

"No. I must stay. I be uncle soon. I should look like the rest of the cowboys if I stay." Andy glared at him.

"You giving up hating me, kid?"

"No. Your blood will mix with mine when the child is born. I will not kill the husband of my sister unless he deserves it."

"Fair enough. Nice to have you in the family, Andy." Darn if the kid wasn't growing on him. "If you stay and work this land, I'll cut you off a piece of it when you're eighteen."

Andy shook his head. "You pay me for work and I buy my land." He pointed across the canyon.

Grinning, James realized Andy's land would be out of arrow range.

Millie, her bandaged head wrapped in a beautiful scarf, came out of the house on the arm of Mr. Sands.

The old guy might not be much of a cook and no better as a carpenter, but by the time the wedding was over James had no doubt that he was fully married and the old man could preach.

That night when they held each other tightly in bed, James told Millie just how much he loved her. When he was out of words, he looked over and noticed she'd fallen asleep while he'd talked.

He lay awake thinking he was the happiest man alive. He had a wife, a baby on the way, land to pass down to the next generation and a brother-in-law who'd gladly kill him if he didn't get it right.

An hour later Millie poked him.

"What do you want, wife?" he asked as if he'd been asleep.

"You," she answered.

James Kirkland did what he knew he'd always do.

He surrendered.

epilogue

The Indian wars on the plains of West Texas ended a year later in 1874.

Colonel Mackenzie won the war with the last great Comanche Chief Quanah in a battle in the Palo Duro Canyon. Mackenzie died a few years later of wounds suffered in battle. Quanah Parker took the last name of his mother, a captive, and lived out his days as a rancher, a judge and a lobbyist in Congress.

Andy O'Grady bought a farm twenty miles away and married one of Wagner's daughters. He was buried in moccasins and reportedly carried a bow and arrows to every family dinner at the Kirkland Ranch.

James and Millie Kirkland lived long enough to use the rocking chairs as they watched their grandchildren play. They never talked of how James had bought her from an Apache tribe in Ransom Canyon, but Millie gave him a watch every anniversary.

He owned fifty-three when he died.

★ ★ ★ ★ ★

Don't miss HOME BY TWILIGHT,
the big, exciting new novel
from Jodi Thomas,
coming in April 2018!